T0354542

IN TOO DEEP

JESSICA BADRICK

Order this book online at www.trafford.com
or email orders@trafford.com

Most Trafford titles are also available at major online book retailers.

Printed in the United States of America.

ISBN: 978-1-4669-3891-5 (sc)
ISBN: 978-1-4669-3890-8 (e)

Trafford rev. 06/14/2012

 www.trafford.com

North America & international
toll-free: 1 888 232 4444 (USA & Canada)
phone: 250 383 6864 • fax: 812 355 4082

It's been four years, you would think they would lay off I can feel them all staring at me waiting for me to slip up. Every scrap, every bruise, every bite it's worried looks and third degrees. No one ever believes a cutter when they say "I stopped".

CHAPTER 1
ANTHONY

DAVE RAPPED ON THE DOOR, I nod and he came in. "You ok?"

"Thanksgiving is tomorrow" I sighed.

Dave is much older than I am and is in charge of the hall I work in. He has salt and pepper hair and deep sorry eyes, with an ever growing waste band "Do you need to talk to someone?"

"I *need* it not to be the holidays; I *need* to find the something other than Ana and this job that makes me happy you know the thing that feels like it's missing . . ."

"Your name is on the . . ."

"I know, one less day as Buddy's punching bag is what I *need*" I laughed, rolling my shoulders "He hits hard"

"You think?" Dave laughed giving me a hand off the floor "That's why the jobs not for the weak."

"Then why do I work here?"

"You're not weak, I'll rephrase it for you this job's not for the *physically* weak."

"Thanks now you're saying I'm not mentally strong enough for the job."

He swatted me "Don't you start that I have your Mama on speed dial." He chuckled and handed me a razor we had confiscated earlier "Go ahead."

"No!" I pushed his hand away shuttering at the scar on my wrist, the razor offer was a common test if Dave was worried about me. Thankfully he worried the least.

"Good answer" He put the capped razor back his pocket "Anything else you may *need* or wish to speak about?"

"He's 8 Dave, he is only 8!" I shook my head. The newest member to our hall was a very small shy boy whom had been there almost three months and would not talk to anyone or go near anyone but me.

"You, Alex of all people should know this addiction has no criteria for its victims."

"No addiction does, Dave, but this one . . . sta andando concludersi sui morti (it's going to end in death)." I looked at my scar. It was barely visible on my ivory toned skin, it was not horizontal it was long and vertical that hurt to see. "And like you said *dovrei sapere* (I should know)."

"I didn't mean that way" He made a face at me "Stick to English or Italian not both it gets confusing . . ."

"Sorry."

"And you don't know if he will end up dead, your Mama is still alive and so are you."

"I know it just bothers me he's just so little, keep an extra eye on him for me?"

"You got it kiddo extra special care."

"Thanks Dave, well I have to go; Ana's waiting in the car and Mama wants me to grab some cranberry sauce for tomorrow, Uncle Chris forgot it. Have a good Thanksgiving."

"You too and tell your Mama D-hall Dave says happy Thanksgiving."

I laughed "Mama doesn't call you that any more, I don't think."

"No she doesn't but it reminds her how to behave to hear me called that, and you tell those brutes in the C-hall they wake my boys tonight, old D-hall Dave is going to call their mommies."

I laughed again putting on my coat "Ok, I will just tell Bruno to duct tape their mouths for you."

"That would be grand, take care of yourself, kiddo."

"I will" I shook my head and pushed open the heavy door that led from the time out room to the D-hall, Ana would be worried if I didn't come out soon. I looked into Anthony's room he was sitting on his bed rocking back and forth and shaking. I shook my head he was only eight years old. He looked at me, his eyes pleading with me to let him cut just one more time just to take the edge off. I had to look away; I knew that feeling all too well. I was lucky I never had to be placed in a center; both of my mothers understood what was going on and allowed me to work through it on my own watching me carefully and teaching me to meditate. Cutting is an addiction normally caused by stress and abuses and sometimes for attention. I like my mama had cut to reduce stress and panic attacks. I was in no hurry to find out Anthony reason.

"Long day" Mama said hugging me.

"Yeah" I said.

"Want to talk about it?" She smiled.

"No, I'm good, Dave says to have a good holiday."

"That old coot, is he still there around the clock? I should pay him a visit some time I haven't seen him in a while."

"He is not an old coot, JJ, he is the reason I am alive" My godfather leered at Mama as he headed out to tell everyone it was almost dinner time.

"Remind me to thank him for that" She laughed swatting him.

Mama's name was Jessica but every one called her JJ, she was warm and welcoming. She greeted ever one with open arms and a loving trusting heart. Mom was loving too but she was more reserved, she was also shy. I did not love one more than the other I love them equally. Mama handed me a stack of plates.

Mom was heavy set with long thick brown curls and hazel eyes; they were green when she was happy and near to black when she was mad. Her name was Christina and every one called her Tina for short. Mama was shorter than Mom with long thin blonde hair and stunning crystal blue eyes.

My eyes were chocolate brown and my hair was almost black, thin and nearly to my waist. Mama said I looked like my daddy. My father had died before I was born; he died in a fire or something like that. It was fine with me I was happy with my mothers. Mom and Mama both told me his name and everything and said they were sorry I couldn't meet him, and once or twice a month I tried to make sure I visit his grave.

Kenny entered the room and sat next to Mom, holding the phone at his side, he was two years younger than me. Kenny looked like Mama with the stunning blue eyes and thin blonde hair. "Mom" He said, I knew what he was going to say. He had become rather predictable since he started dating Juliet. "Can she come for dinner please?"

She looked up at Mama and shook her head "Non som (I don't know), Kenny."

"Please, please, please" He instantly started to beg.

My mothers held their secret eye conversation, then Mama said "How about Friday, Sweetie, tonight it's kind of crowded and it is Colt's birthday."

"Ok" He pouted back out of the kitchen and back up to our room.

"L'OH li ringrazia, grazie, grazie (Oh thank-you, thank-you, thank-you)" I said hugging Mama "I can't handle another night of *the love bug.*"

"Be nice you" Mama swatted at me, laughing "Tina holler at il vostro figlio (your son)."

Mom laughed "Tell me he's not right."

Mama made a *work with me* face "Do you remember us at his age?"

"Ok, ok, Alex don't tease your brother" Mom tried to stifle her laughter.

I sat down and laid my head down for a second before everyone started to pile in to the kitchen, I had been working weekends with my uncle Marc ever since Ana and I's fight where I decided that the pool hall, karate, and other hang outs weren't fun. First my Godfather came back in with his children Tyler, Jaydeh, and Tavi. Tavi was short for Octavio, and Mama said my Godfather should have let her name him and maybe he would have a better name. Then came my uncle Mike and aunt Amy, Mom and Mama told me once when I was little they wished they could get Uncle Mike a new wife for his birthday, I have yet to see them try they always get him this awful smelling cologne. Next my uncle Christian and Uncle Chris came in they both kissed Mom and Mama's cheeks. My brothers all but Kenny came filing in last. The twins Christopher Michael and Christian James were four years younger than me. They were identical beasts with shaggy thin bright red hair, freckles and Mama's stunning blue eyes. Nick was seven years younger than me; he had Mom's hazel eyes and thick dark curly hair and glasses. Colt was the youngest; he was named after my father. He was ten years younger than me and looked just like me. Mom said it was just her genes showing through in us but neither one of us looked like Nick; besides I looked like my father. Uncle Christian told her it was unbecoming of a lady to lie, every time she said it.

Jaydeh evil eyed Colt as he took his seat near me. Colt pulled on my sleeve, so I bent down for him. "Ho messo una vite senza fine falsa in capelli del Jaydeh (I put a worm in Jaydeh's hair)."

I tried not to laugh she was a bit snobbish "That wasn't very nice, nor should you be torturing Uncle Chris's fishing stuff with her hair."

"But it was funny."

"I know" I tickled him until he couldn't breathe.

"Un (one) . . . due (two) . . ." Uncle Chris started to count stifling a laugh.

"KENNETH JOSEPH, ORA (now)!" Mama bellowed up the stairs to the bedroom him and I shared.

"Coming" He yelled back.

She stomped back to the table "I may have given birth to him, Tina, but that child is all yours."

Mom laughed "Let me guess he is on the phone to *Il suo dolce cuore* (his sweet heart)?"

Mama sighed and hollered up the stairs again "Un (one) . . . due (two) . . . due e un mezzo (two and a half) . . ."

"Bye, love you, got to go" Kenny came flying down the stairs tossed the phone on to the base and slide in to his seat near Mom.

We sat down and ate, it wasn't fancy just apple pancakes but they were Colt's favorite. I looked up from my plate Chris and Christian had a fork full of pancake aimed at Nick's head, Uncle Christian just stuck out his arm and caught it; discouraged the twins went back to eating.

Mama was talking with my Godfather's children "So, my Angel baby" She addressed Tyler "Any one special in your life?"

"Yes Auntie" He blushed "My girlfriend is still up at school. She chose only to come home for Christmas this year she is focusing extra hard on her grades as she wishes to be valedictorian." Tyler was six years older than me and was in his final year of college. I am also pretty sure that at twenty-seven he no longer wished Mama to call him her angel baby.

"Jaydeh, how is school going for you?" Mama smiled at her.

"Good" She said politely, she was going to school to be a special needs teacher. She was only three years older than me.

Tavi was two years older than me, he was going to school for animation. Currently he was sitting next to my Godfather with head phones on shaking and rocking back in forth.

"He ok A.J.?" Mama asked concerned.

"Yeah, he's fine I knew one of them would get my bad genes" My Godfather answered.

"Bella" Uncle Christian pointed at a welt on Nick's left arm and gave her a questioning look.

Mom shrugged and mouthed "Twins?"

"Nick how was your day?" I asked.

"Ok" He mumbled

"What did you do?"

"Went to school" He hesitated and gave me a 'please don't do this Alex' look "It was pretty boring."

"Let Mom see your arm."

"Non sono voi Alex."

"Fine, if you're so not me just show Mom your arm."

He rolled his eyes and stuck his arm out "*See.*" The welt looked like it was from a rubber band. "Are you happy now?" He sneered at me refolding his arms.

Uncle Christian glared at the Christian "Elastici ora (rubber bands now)" His voice was soft and icy "You may carry my name young man but you have a lot of growing up to do before you have earned it."

Christian made a mocking face and handed over his rubber bands. "You'll get it for this, Nicky" He growled under his breath.

I stood and clearing my plate and several others. "Nella vostra stanza?" I asked Mama in reference to the location of Colt's birthday presents.

She nodded "Yes, you can bring them out."

I went into Mom and Mama's bedroom; it was dark even with the lights on. The walls, carpet, bedding, and curtains were all black along with ninety percent of Mama's clothes. One side of the room had a desk with neatly placed books, notebooks, pens and a computer printer scanner copier set up. The other side had a desk full of scattered pencils, markers, and papers. I grabbed the stack of presents in one arm and the bike by the handle with my other hand. Careful not to trip over Uncle Chris and Uncle Christian's cots; It looked like Uncle Chris had made them instead of the perfectly neat way Uncle Christian made them.

Uncle Chris was a few inches taller than Mama with the same bright blue eyes and thin blonde hair, Mama called him C.J. Mama and he tried to swear they were not twins but Uncle Christian would tell them it was unbecoming of them too lie so I believed they were, also Nana said they were. Uncle Christian was six foot nine with long thin brown hair to his waist and eyes similar to Mom's but more brown, more like mine. When Mom and Mama were my age Uncle Chris and Uncle Christian had been their body guards.

A camera would have been a great thing to have when Colt saw his bike. He came running over to me and then back to Mom and Mama, hugging every one. "Mommy, Mommy, is it really mine?" He squealed in delight, he was way too hyper off the cake and ice cream.

Mama laughed "I don't know that came home from work with your Uncle Chris."

Colt crawled up in to Uncle Chris' arms and made a pleading face.

"Ok, Ok" Uncle Chris laughed "Yes, it's yours. It's from Nikki and I, Nikki can't be here tonight though she's working."

Colt wrapped his arms around Uncle Chris "I love you, I love you."

Mama laughed "Colt what do you say?"

"Grazie Uncle Chris" Colt ran back and forth between the bike and Uncle Chris.

I laid the rest of the packages on the table and handed Mama a notebook and Pen. She wrote C.J. bike, Alex movie. Colt sat on his Bike making motor noises.

"This one's from Uncle Mike" I said handing him a small package.

He unwrapped it; it was a new video game for his hand held. It did not take him long to open his gifts. Uncle Christian got him a helmet to go with his bike. My Godfather gave him a 3-d puzzle to add to his collection. Mom and Mama gave him several board games and a new jacket that matched mine. Kenny gave him some cologne and the beasts gave him a sling shot and paint balls. Uncle Marc who was still on vacation in Europe sent him money; Uncle Troy who lived two towns over and had to work gave him a new sled. Uncle Fred had sent him a gift card, Uncle Danny mailed him an I owe you and Uncle Jesse and Uncle Tim had mailed him money. He would get his gifts from both our grandparents and Mom's brothers tomorrow and his party for his friends had been last Saturday.

"Look Alex, I'm Uncle Christian" He smiled he had on Uncle Christian's helmet and my leather jacket.

I laughed It looked like Uncle Chris had painted Colt's bike to look like Uncle Christian's Harley.

"Jess, are you really going to let him go to work with Alex?" Aunt Amy tried to pick a fight with Mama.

"Of course we are, Colt has fun with Alex now stop trying to instigate or leave my house" Uncle Christian stopped her, he may worry just as much as Mom or Mama but he didn't let anyone try to bring it up unnecessarily.

After every one left Christopher and Christian sat drawing which was never good if Nick was in the same room, they were perfectionist with Mama's icy temper, especially Christopher. Nick was curled up in between the two couches on the floor reading. Kenny was up in our room with the phone doing homework and talking to Juliet. My parents and uncles were all watching some old detective show. Colt was sitting in my lap talking a mile a minute about girls and school and his new bike.

"She's super beautiful, Alex, like Mommy."

I laughed when Colt was little he said he was going to marry Mama when he grew up. "What does she look like, Colt?"

"She has blonde curls and green eyes, her name is Danni."

"Yeah?"

"Uh-huh, Alex how come you don't like girls?"

"I do" I choked "What do you call Ana a boy?"

"You don't like her like her do you?"

"I do she just might not like me like that anymore."

Mom made a yeah right noise and Mama frowned.

"Danni is super pretty. I want to hold her hand and carry her books" Colt continued to ramble about Danni.

At ten I put Colt up on my shoulders and stood up "Mama I'm going to go tuck Colt in."

"Ok I was going to" Uncle Christian looked at me like I was growing horns "You're awful pale, you know."

"I feel fine, you can tuck him in" I handed Colt to Uncle Christian and took his spot near mom.

"Sì(yes)?" She looked at me "You alright?"

I looked at my wrist.

"Alex?" Mama looked at me concerned.

"I'm fine; just work coming back to me."

"Voi pronti a comunicare con me?"

"No Mama I don't want to talk about it I'm fine."

"Alexander, don't lie to me!" Mama said sternly startling Nick and Kenny, whom had come down stairs to use the computer. "I know four boys whom have better things to be doing than sitting in this living room."

"Um we need . . ." Christopher started.

". . . Different supplies." Christian finished as they ran towards the stairs.

"I should go . . . sorry Al I can't think of a good excuse enjoy your talk with our parents" Kenny grabbed the phone and headed up the stairs behind the twins.

"Mom with you and Alex's permission may I please stay down here until Uncle Christian is done tucking Colt in."

"I don't care if Nick stays" I sighed, agitated I didn't want anyone knowing something was wrong it would just be more accusations of me going back to cutting.

"Ok" Mom said looking at the stairs knowing he didn't want to go near the twins if they were unsupervised at least until Christian was over having his rubber bands taken.

"You going to tell us what happened at work?" Mama gave me a 'you better' look.

I sighed again "Yeah, the little eight year old we brought in three months ago, I'm just worried about him. I am still the only person he will talk to and he keeps clawing open his old cuts." I had started to shake "If it's ok tomorrow after dinner may I go check on him?"

My mothers held one of their eye conversations, looking at me with very worried expressions.

"Ouch" I heard the twins yell in unison.

Uncle Christian dragged them into the room by their ears. "Extra ears, Bella" He smiled at Mom.

"Is Alex ok, Mom?" Christopher asked

"If not can we have his car?" Christian added.

Uncle Christian swatted them "Last this world needs is you two with a car." Uncle Christian shook his head "Mio Piccolo again you hath named them wrong that one over there should be Christian."

Mama laughed "This one is my Alex and he is fine, but it is bed for you two and Nick as well we have an early day tomorrow."

"But . . ."

". . . Mama . . ." The twins objected.

"Now!" Mama growled.

"Ok" They bounded up the stairs behind Nick probably pushing him down every few steps.

"What did I miss?" Uncle Christian asked holding my shoulders back and my hands apart.

"I'm fine" I said shakily.

"Both of your mothers use to tell me that." He smiled "And like I told them I'm just making sure your fine in the morning as well."

"C.J. is going to watch those five if you'll join us; we're going to take Alex to check on one of suo piccolo (his little ones) down at the center" Mama looked up at Uncle Christian hopefully.

Uncle Christian nodded; he never went far from Mama I suspected even after twenty one years he still didn't believe she wouldn't go back to cutting herself.

"Chris you make sure Nicky is tucked in and double trouble stay in their room and away from him. Also tell the love sick puppy dog off the phone by midnight" Mom added.

Mama sat in the back with me holding my hands apart despite the fact that I had told her several times it was unnecessary. Mom drove and Uncle Christian sat in the front passenger seat.

"Those twins are beasts, JJ" Mom shook her head.

"Yeah, I know they have a streak" Mama laughed "I told you they would. Ok Alex, we are here."

I shot out of the car at top speed, Mama, close behind me.

"Dave" Mama greeted Dave.

"Miss Jessi" Dave smiled "Pleasant surprise; you here to liberate one of my boys, again?"

Mama laughed "No sir, A.J. is no longer here."

"Dove è (where is) Anthony?" I spat shaking almost in tears.

"Whoa" Dave's eyes got wide. "English, Alex, please?"

"Yeah, this is why we are here tonight" Mama smiled.

Dave nodded "Mmm I knew I should have called your Mama when you left here earlier, Alex, come here let me pat you down."

"He's has nothing, Dave, Christian cleared out his pockets at the house, when he started to shake" Mama shook her head.

"And you" He said sticking out his hand.

Mama rolled her eyes and handed over three dollars and forty-three cents and her house keys.

"Egli è così (He is this way)" I said dragging Mama towards Anthony's room.

"Alex" Dave tossed me the keys "And English Alex please, English."

Anthony was asleep; I knelt by his side his white T-shirt had blood stains from where he picked his scabs. "Dave può io avere un panno insaponato caldo della lavata, prego?"

"I don't know what you said because like I said English, Alex not Italian" Dave sighed, knowing very well I asked him to hand me a warm wash cloth.

I gently shook Anthony "Hey little guy can you wake up for me?" I sat on the edge of his bed.

His eyes flickered "Is it morning?"

"No, just about midnight" I answered.

"Mr. Alex?" He crawled in to my arms.

"Just Alex, here take your shirt off I'll get you a clean one." He looked at his feet. "What? Don't worry I'm not mad, I'm just going to clean the dried blood off your chest and stomach. Then you can tell me what happened."

He spotted Mama and clung to me "W-whos's that?" He whispered.

"That's my Mama."

"Oh" He said taking off his shirt. "I've been bad you won't punish me?"

"No, just clean you up and put you back to bed." I smiled taking the warm wash cloth and clean shirt from Dave."

"Alex, miele desiderate rimanere qui la notte?" Mama asked.

I looked at Dave.

"I didn't say it but I don't care if you sleep in the time out room, to keep an eye on Anthony" Dave smiled at me.

I nodded "Please? Sorry Mama."

"It's ok with me, that's why I asked, I'll pick you up in the morning."

Dave walked Mama to the door. "He does this a lot, not just the little ones the older ones too; some like Anthony will only talk to him."

"I'm glad he has found something he like's other than Ana, he told us he was put on the willing to adopt list, has he said anymore to you about it?"

"Not really, how is A.J. doing?"

"He's A.J.; they were over earlier for Colt's birthday."

"How are you doing Miss Jessi?"

"I'm fine; Dave, since Alex was born and I don't plan on doing it anytime soon."

"Glad to hear it."

"You take good care of my Alex he's his Mama's true love."

"I will, you go home and take care of your other boys; I hear those twins are something else."

"They'd make Jake proud" Mama laughed.

Dave winced "He was awful, sweet boy, smart, kind, sweet, loving but oh he was an evil child."

"Have a good Thanksgiving."

"You as well Miss Jessi and tell Miss Tina and your body guard I say to have a good holiday."

"I will."

I sat rocking Anthony in the time out room; he was rather small for an eight year old. He had shaggy thin light brown hair and bright green eyes. He kept wincing away from me every time I tried to rub his back due to huge almost fully healed scars suggesting someone had hit him hard in the back repetitively with a belt or something similar.

Dave came in right as Anthony had fallen back to sleep, he had brought two pillows and two blankets with him. "Are you ok?"

". . . Suo(he) . . ." I stammered pointing at Anthony's back.

"I know about his back, but you need to speak English, please Alex, I only speak English, ok fine that look was uncalled for. I speak English and scattered Italian and only cause you can't remember to speak English."

"But . . ."

"Don't worry Alex, he isn't going back to his parents he's a ward of the state now, he'll complete the program here then go in to the system."

I looked down at him; he was so tiny and so gentle. I shook my head, there was a chance he'd never stop cutting he'd be in and out of treatment centers like my Godfather has been or he would end up cutting to deep in the wrong place and not make it.

"I know what you're thinking" Dave frowned at me "It is written all over your face. You know as well as I do there is no definite yes or no in this place, only maybes. So, we can't say for sure yes he will make it or no he won't."

"I know" I sighed "It's just . . ."

"Just what Alex? Last Saturday I put a boy in here for hitting someone I came back to check on him he was trying to strangle himself with his shirt, a day before he was suppose to leave. And just yesterday a boy came back to tell me how great he is doing. Alex, there is no straight yes or no only maybes."

I sighed again I knew Dave was right, and it was pointless to argue with him. Self mutilation was a serious addiction and very hard to stop it took a lot of time you had to retrain your body how to handle your emotions. It had been compared more than once to heroin. Most people thought it was a phase they'd out grow or that it wasn't bad because they were only hurting themselves and it wasn't like it was a drug. Many of the adults I had met thought it was a suicide attempt, when it was not.

The best thing about this room was my legs fit without being folded or diagonal and it was soft, it was all mattresses except where the door window was they had cut that mattress specifically for the door. I had laid Anthony down on his pillow and covered him with his blankets and then laid down a few feet over with the pillow and blanket Dave had brought for me. I woke to crying and turned to see Anthony balled up rocking trying to pick a scab. "What's wrong?" I whispered, the light coming from the hall suggested it was not morning yet.

"Bad dream" He shivered clinging to me.

"It's ok, want to tell me what it was about?"

He shook his head no trying to dig at a scar.

"No, little guy, doing that's not a good idea. It's ok, you can tell me when you're ready to. Your eight, right?

"No I'm six Mommy said I was older so I could go to school."

I felt my heart catch in my throat, no wonder he seemed so small "Uh stay here I need to get Dave."

"Why?"

"So he can fix your files, so you don't have to act older than you actually are."

"Can I come with you? That thing over there is scary in the dark."

I laughed "The straight jacket won't hurt you but if it makes you feel better you can come; I'm glad you do want to be in it." I picked him up and pounded on the door till Dave came out of his office looking like he had been a sleep as well and let us out in to the hall. "È sei!(he's six)"

"What who?"

"Anthony, è sei non otto!"

"Whoa, Alex slow down, I don't understand you speak English."

"Anthony" I lifted Anthony eye level with Dave "Is six, *sei*, not eight, *otto*."

"Don't get smart with me you know you are supposed to stick to English and Anthony's records . . ."

"Anthony, tell Dave what you told me." I adjusted him so I didn't drop him.

Anthony took a deep breath "Mommy told the teachers I was older than I am so I could go to school. Told me I was smart and it was ok to tell the teachers I was five even though I was only three and that, that one little lie wouldn't hurt, she was tired of me under her feet."

"So you are six" Dave nodded. "Well I will fix that as soon as I can. What grade are you in?"

"Third but it's really hard." Anthony buried his face in my shoulder.

"Dovrebbe essere dentro primo! (He should be in first)" I growled startling Anthony.

Dave gave me a look that said I need to calm down "I can put you in the right grade here by Sunday, Anthony."

Anthony adjusted in my arms "Can we go back to sleep?"

"Yeah were going as soon as I put band-aids on your cuts so you can't scratch them."

Three boxes of band-aids, a lengthy discussion and twenty three questions latter Anthony was finally back to sleep. I laid back down pondering my discussion with Dave much earlier about what I wanted and wondered what Ana would think about having a child and if we were still actually dating. It was hard to tell; we had been but then she made it clear I was upsetting her, then her mom died and we graduated, then her brother's car accident and I just didn't no anymore after that last big argument. I mean she told me every day she loved me and she still hugged me, but I didn't know. Even if she was or wasn't still my girlfriend would they let us adopt. We had both taken the state mandatory back ground check, and parenting course associated with being able to put our name on the willing to adopt list at work and we had both put our names on it. Even after that would my mothers care that there would be an extra person in our house? I drifted in to a thought filled restless sleep.

CHAPTER 2
THANKSGIVING

M<small>AMA SHOOK ME AROUND SEVEN</small>. I was disoriented and had to look around, Anthony was asleep with his head on my chest in a pile of his own drool. I wondered when he moved and curled up on me.

"Don't you look comfy?" Mama smiled.

"Hush" I hissed "Abbiamo avuti una notte lunga."(We had a long night)

"Dave told me, but we have to be at your grandma's in two hours. Sometimes I swear that women can't do . . ."

"Mama" I hissed again carrying Anthony back to his room and tucking him in. "Vostro andare svegliarlo." (You're going to wake him up)

"Alex" Dave caught me outside Anthony's room "I better not see you a second before seven am tomorrow morning. You can't pamper him; you have to let him run the program like everyone else. We have had this talk before, Alex, look at me. Go home have a good thanksgiving get a good night rest and I will see you tomorrow at seven."

"I know" I sighed, "Happy thanksgiving Dave."

"You too, Alex, and as for you Miss Jessi, hold your tongue at your mother in-laws, and you won't have a repeat of last year and be patient with your own mother, please try and see it from her eyes."

Mama opened her mouth like she was going to object then closed it and instead said "I know, I know, happy thanksgiving you old coot." And she waved him off and head down the hall to the main doors. I just started laughing following Mama to the door. It was a well know fact that Mama did not like Mom's mother and that it started with my grandmother not liking her. She also didn't get along well with her own mother. I don't know why we even go because Mom doesn't get along with Nana at all; I don't even know why Nana and Mama didn't get along. I suppose we go to Mom's mom out of manners and we go to Mama's mom to see Mama and Uncle Chris' little brothers. They don't seem very close though, Mama's older brothers never go only Uncle Jesse whom Mama calls J.C. and Uncle Tim. Uncle Tim is only five years older than I am so we get along ok but he's kind of moody. Uncle Jesse is seven and a half years younger than Mama and seems really laid back. He is an architect and really in to playing drums.

"You're late, Jessica" Grandma said as we walked through the door. I had made Mama stop and let me shower.

Mama winced at her full name "I had to pick Alex up from work, Ma." Mama said adding a few choice words under her breath following Grandma to the kitchen. I wondered when Mama had lost her respect for her mother; if I had even thought of reacting to either of my mothers that way my uncles or my mothers would knock me unconscious.

Colt came flying in with a remote control motor cycle "Alex, look what Grandma gave me for my birthday."

"Cool little man" I hugged him and headed to sit with Mom on the couch.

"Feel better?" Mom asked.

I nodded "Voglio adottare un bambino."

She looked at me stunned and shell shocked "Ok" She nodded "Uh how about we talk about this after we get home tonight?"

"Ok, sounds good." I listened to a few cabinet doors slam with expert force. "Mom, I think Mama may need you out there."

"Oh she's fine, dear, your uncles are out there with her" A few more cabinet doors slammed and Mom gave me a worried look. "Maybe you are right, Sweetie" She said and left to join Mama in the kitchen.

I leaned my head back and closed my eyes I was exhausted and had not slept well at all. I opened my eyes when I felt something or should I say some things staring at me.

The twins stood over me with evil grins on their faces "Hi . . ."

". . . Brother."

"What do" I looked at Christopher "You want?" I glared at Christian.

"We were wondering . . ."

". . . If what Colt overheard was true?" They beamed.

I groaned "Depends on what he overheard."

"That we are . . ."

". . . To be uncles" They beamed with extreme excitement.

I laughed "You'll find out after dinner." I got up and joined my parents in the kitchen.

"Hi Uncle Christian" I hugged him tight "Thanks."

"You're welcome, are you feeling better?"

"Yes, much despite being cornered by creep and crud."

"Creep and crud huh?" He chuckled "Let me guess Christian is creep?"

"Mmhmm."

"I don't see why your Mothers didn't name you Christian you look and act more like me anyway."

"Ugh" Mama laughed hugging him "You big dumb rock, because he is my Alex. And as for your brothers" She looked at me "Take it up with your Uncle Chris teaching them evil stuff when they were babies."

"Did no such thing" Uncle Chris grinned at me an evil cheesy grin the kind Christian made when he was up to no good.

"Christopher James, don't lie" Grandma laughed "You have been a terror since the day you were born."

Nick looked up from his book oblivious to the current conversation and sudden tension "Grandma may I please barrow a pen."

"Of course" Grandma handed him a pen. "Jessica Where is Kenny?"

Again Mama winced at her full name and then made a face that said 'I don't know and currently don't care' "Mom I wasn't here you'd have to ask Tina."

"Probabilmente avvitando la sua ragazza." I muttered under my breath.

Uncle Christian looked over at me and chuckled softly ignoring my crud statement "He is outside playing soccer with Tim and Jesse."

Mama opened the back door and called out to Uncle Jesse "Hey old man, aren't you too old to be running around like that?"

"Sissy" Both Uncle Tim and Uncle Jesse came running to hug Mama.

Later that night once we were home again Christopher and Christian sat drawing, Kenny had glued himself to the phone and was laying on his stomach on the floor in the middle of the living room, Nick had found a book and a corner and I hadn't seen him since, Colt was hanging off of me doing pull ups off my arm and my parents were in the kitchen talking.

"Alex" Mama called to me "Please come out here."

"Coming" I called back lifting Colt and setting him on Kenny's back "Have a present lover boy." I laughed as the weight of Colt immobilized Kenny.

Mom frowned "That wasn't nice, Alex, If Kenny stops breathing your taking him to the ER."

"Ok, ok" I choked back my laughter.

"I hear you wish to adopt a child." Mama smiled at me. "Am I correct to believe it is the little boy you were so worried about last night?"

"Yes, ma'am, Anthony, he's six and it wouldn't be for a while."

"I see" Mama smiled "This is your decision and we will support you no matter what you decide but I would like you to think about it, a child is a large responsibility they take large amounts of time and money. Have you spoken to Ana about this?"

"Not yet I was going to but she's at her uncle Ken's today so I'm going to try tomorrow and I know he will be harder to care for because of the back ground he comes from."

"Alex no one is saying you can't take care of a child we just want you to think about it" Mom frowned at me "I think you need some sleep you have been awfully mean today."

"Fine, I will think about it but I am near to positive this is what I want, good night." I hugged my uncles and hugged and kissed my mothers good night.

"I may have given birth to him" Mom sighed "But that one is *your son.*"

Mama laughed kissing Mom and hugging her tight "And you love me anyway" Mama laid her head on Mom's shoulder "Do I get points I did not loudly express my opinions of neither your mother nor mine."

Mom laughed "Yes sweetie" Mom lifted Mama's head and kissed her again.

"Whoa, maybe you two should take that to the bedroom" Uncle Chris teased.

My mothers ignored him staring into each others' eyes "I love you Jessi" Mom said.

"I love you too, Tina." Mama smiled dreamily into Mom's eyes like there was no one there but them.

I laid on my bed doing exactly what they told me to thinking; it didn't matter that I had thought all last night. I looked over at Kenny's side of the room it had blue walls with black blinds over his windows. He had posters of girls and cars, cds were scattered everywhere. His desk was so cluttered I was sure you had to dig about four inches down to find the true surface of his desk. His computer and science books lay wherever they landed and how ever they landed. The clean and dirty clothes mixed in huge scattered heaps all over his floor. Pictures of Juliet sat on his night stand desk and dresser. I got up and shut the divider, laid back down and looked at my own side of our room. I had black walls and bedding. My carpet was a dark grey and my windows were covered with heavy blood red black out curtains. My side was meticulously clean, clean clothes in the closet or in the proper dresser draw, dirty clothes in the hamper. My posters were of dragons, wizards and some really old rock bands from like when Mom and Mama were kids. My full size bed took up a large portion of my room; I visualized it with another bed. It would be severely cramped but not impossible. Kenny came in and slipped through the divider I fell asleep listening to him talk to Juliet.

CHAPTER 3

ANA

FRIDAY WAS FAMILY DAY AT the center; it made every one crazy including staff. The center was crawling with social workers it was enough to make my skin crawl. Colt was half asleep and rode through the metal detectors and security check on my shoulders. We were running late so I hadn't gotten a chance to speak with Ana at all on the way to work, which wouldn't bode well for me. I sat Colt down putting any and all of our extra things in my locker. I went in to the office and grabbed my work folder to see where I belonged, normally on Friday's Dave had me with the level fours just making sure they get off to a good start to the weekend with their families and then spending the rest of the afternoon with Genevieve until Ana got out but today that was not the case. I was getting the feeling I should have stayed in bed. If Colt's fight to get up and going was any indication on how he felt and was going to behave, I should have just crawl back in bed and hid.

"Morning" Dave greeted us with his normal Friday 'I just swallowed half a bottle of Mylanta and Pepto-Bismol' face.

"Morning do you hate me, you gave me Kevin."

"You will be fine if you hadn't noticed you also have Anthony it is his first visitation I think you should talk to his social worker I saw that look on your face last night."

"Why Kevin, why?"

"Alexander quit whining he is not poisonous, you have never spent the day with him he may like you, here I'll take Colt down to the family room While you get everyone Kevin's in the time out room. I know you are ready for more than just watching the older kids leave for the weekend; besides Trenton quit this morning I need someone that can think like this group and still be tough enough to deal with Quentin."

"It wasn't a question of if he liked me Dave; I'm the only one he hasn't bitten. I'm just not sure I can take care of . . ."

"Alex, shut up and go to work" Dave gave me a 'please Alex' face and took Colt off towards the family room.

Kevin was in the straightjacket lying on his side kicking anything and everything he could reach. "It is only quarter to eight in the morning; you have only been awake for forty-five minutes. You best have a good reason for being in here or you are staying in the straightjacket through your visitation."

He looked up at me "Hi Alex."

"I asked you something Kevin." I sighed Kevin may have been bad but deep down I was happy I did not have to spend the day with his brother, Buddy, or Kyle's roommate, Curtis.

"Buddy, I bit Buddy, he tasted *so* good" Kevin rolled his eyes.

"Your sarcasm, Kevin, is highly unappreciated and will not help you any. Up you go" I said picking him up "How about we go get Kyle and the others."

"What about that little boy?" Kevin inclined his chin towards Anthony's door; Anthony had his nose pressed to the window.

"Yes, we have to grab Anthony as well."

"He likes you; he was talking to Cory at dinner yesterday, told Cory he didn't see why he couldn't just live with you because you care about him."

"I care about all of you, Kevin."

"Even me?"

"Yes, Kevin I care about you, I even care about Buddy and Curtis." I sighed unlocking Anthony's door.

"Alex" Anthony shot in to my arms "Your back, your back"

"Yep, little man told you I would be" I shifted him to my shoulders.

I finally got everyone into the family room. Kevin's mom did not look pleased to see her son in a straightjacket and his father looked like he needed to be in a straightjacket. Kyle's sister had come with his parents and she greeted him with the biggest hug a five year old can give. Corey and Serena's parents also greeted them with open arms. Anthony just kind of stared at Colt like he was about to cry.

"Who's he?" Colt asked, even half asleep his jealousy of Anthony in my arms was clear.

"This is Anthony" I smiled Rocking Anthony who had started to cry, "Anthony is six."

"Where is his Mommy?" Colt asked, innocence would be my enemy today, and with that question a whole new set of tears started to pour from Anthony's eyes.

"He doesn't live with his Mom anymore Colt; his social worker will be here soon." And just as I said that a little boy toddled up to me and pulled on Anthony's leg.

"My Anony!" He proclaimed loudly.

I smiled "Your, Anthony, huh?"

"My Anony, My miss My Anony." The little boy said making a face like he was trying to be tough and stand his ground, I laughed.

Anthony turned around in my arms and tried to pick the younger boy up. The little boy was half his size and more than likely half his age.

"Anony, it my Birtday yeserday can I take you home yet?" The little boy looked hopefully into Anthony's eyes.

"No Paul" Anthony sobbed giving way to a fresh set of tears and clung to me. I bent down and lifted the toddler.

"Anony has to stay" He started to cry as well.

"Hey shh its ok" I hugged both boys "Anthony, want to tell me who your friend is?"

"Paul" He cried; the look on my own brother's very jealous face said it all "He's my brother."

A tall woman walked in she had short mousey brown curls that were starting to grey, a tight fitting business suit and sharp looking high heels. "Paul, come here" She said sounding tired "You can't keep running off like that, dear, I really am getting too old to play tag."

"Found my Anony" Paul slid off my lap he was barely up to my knee with toe-head blonde hair and stormy blue eyes that looked like marbles.

I stood up and set Anthony down next to Paul "Hi I'm Alex Williams" I smiled extending my hand.

"Julian Myers" She said shaking my hand "The boys' . . ."

"Social worker, I know, Dave said you were coming."

"I see; how is his progress?"

"Well ma'am he has only been here three months and will only talk to me, but he is doing remarkably well for his age and circumstances, but if you wish I can arrange for you to speak with his consoler, he would know more than I do."

"No thank-you I'm just going to speak with the boys." She looked at Anthony with a big fake smile and I thought I was going to have to cover Colt's mouth. "Hi Anthony" She said "Do you remember me?"

I truly should have acted on my notion to cover Colt's mouth "He is not a baby he's just scared and relocated" Colt growled, I wanted to die of embarrassment.

"Colt" I said sternly "Apologize now! E se non si riesce a mantenere le vostre opinioni a te si può andare seduto in ufficio con Ana"

He gave me a 'please Alex look' and muttered sorry.

"Louder" I growled.

"Sorry" He said and sat down in a chair to watch the T.V.; ignoring that I told him to go sit with Ana in the office, if he couldn't behave.

"Sorry Ma'am" I repeated. "He is too much like our mother for his own good."

"Its fine" She smiled and went back to talking to Anthony and Paul.

I checked on every one and sent a message to the office with Colt telling Ana I need to speak to her. I was just about to ask Ms. Myers about adopting Anthony and Paul, when Kevin started to attack his father. I grabbed my walkie-talkie "Dave, Kevin, run."

"On my way" His response sounded scratchy and aggravated through the walkie-talkie.

I grabbed Kevin and pinned him the best I could being kicked was not my idea of a good time. Dave and Bruno came quickly and took him back to his room or to the time out room to cool down.

"You alright, kiddo?" Dave asked me.

"Indennità appena, benissimo" I growled.

"English!"

"I'm fine, I'm just fine."

"Mmhmm, see me after work you look sick."

"Benissimo."(fine)

He shook his head at me. "Ms. Myers, Nice to see you I heard you were assigned to Anthony. Well I have to go make sure Bruno is ok Kevin can be tough" With that Dave left.

"I am very sorry ma'am visiting day can be hard on everyone" I smiled recomposing myself.

"It is fine, what were you going to ask me?" She smiled standing back up from where she had been talking to Anthony. "You have seemed to have made quite an impression; he was unhappy at the thought of foster care and wanted to know why he couldn't just live with you or Dave."

I smiled to myself "Well see, that is what I wanted to ask you about, adopting them, is 'Anony' Paul's only brother?" I laughed as Paul kept rambling to Anthony.

"Yes he is," She chuckled, "Paul is three but it looked like his mother was trying to pass him off as five."

I nodded "Anthony told me she did that to him, he is actually six."

"Yes, we found both of their original birth certificates and are straightening everything out." She handed me a business card "This is Mr. Thompson's office number you will want to call him in regards to adopting Paul and Anthony."

I looked over the business card "Thank-you ma'am."

"You're welcome." She smiled at me and turned to Paul. "Come on Paul, time to go."

"No" Paul cried "Me stay wit me Anony."

"You can see Anthony next week, right now I need to take you back to Mrs. Grear, I have other children to visit today" She smiled at Paul.

"Anony come too?"

"No Paul I told you Anthony is sick, when he gets better he can come with you, now please Paul we are on a short time schedule" She pleaded with him.

"No," Paul clung to my leg, "I stay, me live here with me Anony and him Alets."

I stifled a laugh lifting him in to my arms. "Hi buddy," He clung to me "I will make a deal with you, you go with Ms. Myers now and next Friday I will have a surprise for you." Dave had taught me positive bribery.

He wiped his face on my shoulder and looked at me "Colts?" He asked hopeful.

I laughed "No little man, Colt will be in school next Friday; but I promise you will like it."

"Ok Alets" He choked back more tears wiping at his eyes and hugged me tight again just as Dave walked in.

"Visiting time over" Dave said. Turning to Ms. Myers he said "Julian this is the boy I was telling you about, the one who wanted Anthony . . ."

"And Paul" I quickly added, watching Anthony and Colt play checkers.

"Yes, he was inquiring about that." She smiled "I suppose you want me to put a good word in and have proof of your good word."

"Of course I do, I have known his parents since they were about thirteen and so has Cleveland . . ."

"Ok, ok" She laughed "I get it; I will put in a good word."

"Thank-you, see you next week, Jules" Dave smiled triumphantly.

"Yes, see you next Friday; come on Paul time to go." She said taking Paul from me and left.

"That woman is hideous" Colt scowled.

"And you are too much like Mama for your own good" I glared at him. "Go sit with Ana!"

"He's right she talks to me and Paul like we are stupid" Anthony objected.

"It is Paul and I; and she is still your elder and you will show her respect" I said firmly.

Dave laughed "Colt is just like your mama."

"Funny" I sighed "Mom says I am."

"Well there is nothing wrong with that. Your mama is a strong outspoken woman and a well respected member of the community. You take Kyle and Anthony back to their rooms and meet me in my office" He took Corey and Serena and left.

Colt walked off towards the office muttering about stuck up snobs. I just smiled at Kyle's Mom and step dad. "Sorry I woke him early today."

Kyle's step dad laughed "She was a bit on the snobbish side, Alex; you will make a great dad."

"Thank-you" I blushed "Ok Kyle you ready to go to consoling, I bet Danny is waiting for you." Kyle took my hand in a death grip he looked like the world was ending "It's ok, bud" I smiled down at him.

"Oh, Alex," Kyle's mom said catching my arm "How is he doing?"

"Good actually, he just made level three and you should be hearing soon about taking him home on weekends."

They said their good-byes. I walked Kyle to his consoler's and Anthony back to his room. Anthony chattered about Paul the whole walk

"Alex who wants to adopt Paul?" He looked up at me slightly frowning.

"Who said it was just Paul?" I smiled at him.

"No one would want me, I am a bad boy."

"No you aren't, you are a good little boy who has been through a lot, and the person wanting to adopt Paul also wants to adopt you." I hugged him wondering how he knew someone wanted to adopt them I was sure I asked out of ear shot.

His face lit up "Really?"

"Yes, really"

"Do you know her?"

"I have known *him* all my life, and he is more than happy to adopt both you and Paul."

He smiled and sat at the desk in his room "I still have homework from yesterday."

I sat on the edge of his bed "Do you need any help?"

"No they moved me back down to first grade, it is really easy."

"That's good" I smiled "Well I will see you Sunday, if you need anything have Dave call me and don't forget you have consoling at three."

"Ok, Alex" He hugged me good bye."

I looked through the window to the padded room; Kevin was lying on his side kicking the wall.

"Thorezine would fix that boy" Dave came up behind me.

I laughed "You said it not me."

"I was your age when I started this here; doing the same thing you're doing now. I have seen many kids and many state regulation changes, but none wild as Kevin have ever made it as far as Kevin has to going home."

"I don't think he wants to, I can't blame him either have you met his father?"

"More than once, but if this is what you want you call Cleveland, right this second. Julian Myers is one of the top social workers in the state, if she said she'd put a good word in for you she probably already has."

I nodded pulling out the business card, took the phone and dialed.

"Hello Thompson here, how may I help you?" He picked up.

"Um . . ." I froze.

Dave took the phone from me "Cleveland, Dave here, I got some one here interested in adopting the Kingston boys, Jules said she was going to put in a good word for him."

"Ah yes, a Mr. Alex Williams age twenty-one. Lives with his mothers, works there with you, completed the state required courses already. I already did a file check and left a message with his mother for Tuesday."

"Thank-you Cleveland, are you still coming for poker after work?"

"Your welcome, Dave, you know it."

Dave hung up "Looks like you're going to be a father, Alex."

I smiled "I hope so; well I better get to Colt before he says something to Ana that will embarrass me for life."

"That's his job, Alex; you two have fun at the movies."

"Thanks, Dave, see you Sunday."

"Colt says we are going to a movie." Ana greeted me.

"His I er . . ."

"Birthday I know, I hear we are adopting?" She raised an eyebrow at me.

I gulped "I . . . no . . . we . . . I um meant . . ."

"We can talk after."

"Hey Alex, you're a bit red; kind of like Kenny when Uncle Christian catches him and Juliet making out on the porch."

"I am not" I gulped turning a deep scarlet.

Ana laughed "He's right dear you are a little flush" She punched us out and grabbed our checks. She wrapped her arm around me and my heart caught in my throat, it felt good to hear her call me dear it meant we were dating again.

I would have preferred my first real boyfriend/girlfriend time with Ana since our fight minus Colt and a more mature movie, but this was fine. We sat in the back and I focused hard on the movie to avoid panicking, Ana cuddled as closes as she could to me it felt great to have her back in my arms.

"You ok, Alex."

"I'm um" I nodded I was fine; I was more than fine I was great.

"Ok" She smiled at me and whispered "I never left you, you pulled away from me never ever do that again."

"Uh I um" I choked, I pulled away! I pulled away! Her mom died her, brother got in a hideous crash and I straightened myself out, we got busy with collage and work and then there was that huge fight, but she was the one with work and school and hiding in the house on her days off.

"Sshh"

"But . . ."

"Hush" She wrapped my arms tighter around her.

I had invited Anna back to the house but she declined, said she had to go but it was me who pulled away right. I walked her to the door and then went the rest of the way up the drive only stopping to grab Uncle Marc's mail. Colt bound up the stairs ahead of me, at home; I walked slowly thinking about the kiss she gave me at her door. When I got into the hall I could hear someone arguing with Uncle Christian but I couldn't tell who it was. Entering the kitchen I saw Uncle Jesse arguing with him something about Mama.

Uncle Christian rolled his eyes "Here is the door, see you at Easter." He opened the back door practically shoving Uncle Jesse out.

"Er" I sat down "Is Mama working?"

"Yes, both of your mothers are or should be working." He answered stirring the macaroni and cheese "Hear you might be a father?"

"If I am approved."

"That's good, how are you?"

"Great!" I smiled ear to ear.

"Glad to hear, come è Ana?"(How is Ana)

"Colt" I sighed "She's my girlfriend again."

"Never knew you were apart just thought you were being stupido."

I sighed what was with every one blaming me "No, but I better go talk to Mom and Mama before Colt does, may I be excused."

"You are excused, but I feel you are too late to beat your brother."

Mom was lying on her bed and Mama was at her desk. "Good afternoon Mom, Good after noon Mama" I gulped.

"Sit down, Hun." Mama pointed to Mom's desk chair. "How was work?"

"Pretty good, Kevin had a fit and nearly kicked me to death, but I am ok" I sighed.

Uncle Chris whom was sitting on the foot of Mama's bed raised an eyebrow at me "And you call that a good day?" He gave me another questioning look.

"Hush you" Mama frowned at him. "We got a call earlier from Mr. Thompson; you have a 10:15 appointment this coming Tuesday."

"I know Dave had me call him from work right before I left."

"So, I am going to be a Grandma?" Mom asked.

"I hope so, and if not by me by Kenny; him and Juliet are up in our room and asked for privacy." I forced myself not start laughing.

Mama made a disapproving face.

Mom made an equally disapproving face and sighed "Oh that boy, I swear, how was Colt?"

"He was Colt" I gritted my teeth.

"That bad?" Mama raised an eyebrow like Uncle Chris did; I don't care what they say I knew they were twins, besides Uncle Christian tells her it is unbecoming of her to lie when she say they are not twins.

"No, not bad, he is never bad he was just his outspoken little self. He showed his true feelings of Anthony's social worker with no concern of my embarrassment level."

Mom laughed "That's my boy."

I sighed "He told her she was speaking to Anthony wrong just not in those words and not exactly friendly either; also after she left both Colt and Anthony proclaimed they did not care for her."

Mama sighed and shook her head "She was speaking to Anthony as if he was an unintelligent infant I assume?"

"Sì."

"Yeah, that would send Colt over the edge" For a moment I wondered if Mama meant my father or my brother then she said "How did he do sharing you?"

"Jealous as always, I swear he would be jealous of a dust flake if it had my attention."

"I think your uncle would die if he saw a dust flake in here he has become quite the house wife over the years" Uncle Chris laughed and Mama stifled a laugh as well. Mom on the other hand smacked the back of Uncle Chris' head causing Mama and I both to stifle more laughter.

"I hear you kissed a *girl?*" Mom changed the subject as Mama sobered herself from her laughing fit with a coughing moment and her inhaler.

"COLT" I growled then started laughing again; I leaned back in the chair and spun "Ana."

"Henry's daughter, Ana?" Uncle Chris pried.

"Uh-huh only Ana I know" I sighed happily. "I have a girlfriend."

"Always have" Mom mutter under her breath.

"Does she know you wish to ad . . ."

"Yes" I beamed thinking about Ana, her gorgeous eyes, soft lips, and gentle touch.

"Alex" Mama startled me from my thoughts "Dinner, come on let's eat."

Christian and Christopher sat flicking things at Nick. I walked up behind them, smashed their heads together and growled "Knock it off or you will know why your scummy little friends are afraid of me."

Uncle Christian looked at me "Va tutto bene Alex?"(Is everything alright)

"Benissimo(just fine), as soon as these two leave Nick alone."

Uncle Christian spun around from serving dinner and grabbed them by their ears dragging them towards Mama; her, Mom and Uncle Chris were making their way through the living room to the kitchen. "*Your* sons are relentlessly torturing Nikolas."

She turned and looked at them "What did you two do?"

"We were just . . ." Christopher gulped.

". . . Messing with him a little" Christian tensed.

"I better not here you were *messing* with him again tonight or I'm going to *mess* with you. For now you are going to bed early and no phone."

"Yes ma'am" They both scowled.

It was one thing for Uncle Christian to Growl at you and take things a way for being anything less than a well educated proper young man; but to have him drag you to Mom or Mama for punishment was bad. Colt, Nick and I took a depth breath and stayed very still and very quiet as the room got very icy. It was at moments like this I truly wished for something more concrete than a four person breakfast bar and a sofa to separated the kitchen from the living room.

Kenny came down the stairs stopping dead in his tracks. "Mama" He braved. "May Juliet stay for dinner tonight?"

"Yes, go help you brothers finish setting the table." Mom said saving Kenny from Mama's temper.

"Twins cause the ice zone?" He breathed to me, joining us near the table.

"You know it" I answered.

"Picking on Nicky?

"Always"

"They will never learn."

"They will if I have to teach them myself." I gave Nick an extra hug and ran my hand through his curls. Kenny shuttered; I had taught Kenny not to tattle *my way*. He still had a few scars from it. He had been the one to tell Mama that I cut, we made our peace a long time ago but he had not tattled about anything since and he still winced every time I lost my temper near him. Nick and Colt took their seats; Kenny set a place for Juliet whom had just joined us down stairs and I finished serving so our parents could speak with the twins.

They returned to the table looking very miserable "You will . . ."

". . . Pay for this" They hissed.

Uncle Chris laughed and Uncle Christian made a disapproving face.

"So Alex" Juliet smiled at me "Kenny tells me you're adopting a son?"

"Ana and I are adopting two boys, Anthony is six and Paul is three."

"Kenny and I are waiting until we are married to have kids."

I saw Mom, Mama, Uncle Christian, and Uncle Chris' faces relax in relief not enough to say they fully believed her but enough to say they were glad she was thinking. It wasn't that we didn't like Juliet, she was nice and had good grades, nice to Colt and Nick even to the beasts, and she was even polite to Ana and I. Juliet had decent manners and was not rude or money hungry; but Christopher and Christian said it best as they sang "*If I only had a brain*" only loud enough for Nick and I to hear every time she said something. Colt sat on my other side just outside of ear shot of the twins with a face that said he was thinking the same thing. Juliet did not hear them or notice them on the far side of the table and continued to speak.

Colt looked at me then at her and very bluntly said "Do you ever shut up?"

I thought Kenny was going to kill him as nearly the whole table had to stifle laughs including Uncle Christian who seemed to have the best control and commanded Colt to apologize instantly as he and I cleared the table.

"*Sono spiacente*" Colt muttered.

"In English" Kenny demanded "She can't speak Italian."

"Only speaks airhead" I heard Nick mumble.

"*I'm sorry*" Colt repeated in English this time loud in slow to suggest Juliet spoke a foreign langue.

Kenny looked ready to kill again "You better be you evil mutant" Kenny growled chasing him half way through the living room and back.

"Whatever" was all Colt felt was needed of a response.

After Juliet left we sat in the living room; the twins were drawing, Nick was packing his things to go to a friend's house, Kenny was on the computer talking with Juliet, Colt sat on my knees as we watched television, my parents and uncles were talking.

"So you are going to make me a grandmother?" Mama asked again.

"That's the goal" I smiled at her.

"Awesome we are . . ."

". . . Going to be uncles" Christopher and Christian beamed.

". . . We can teach him . . ."

". . . How to be cool" They smiled at me.

"You two aren't allowed near them unless Uncle Christian is breathing down your necks."

"We thought you were . . ."

". . . Only getting one."

"Well he has a brother and I don't believe in splitting them" I sighed.

"What are their names?" Nick inquired.

"Are you kidding me? Anthony and Paul" I was starting to get annoyed.

"How old are they?" Uncle Chris looked up from his word search.

"What was everyone out to lunch at dinner I mean I realize Juliet is an air head but I already answered these questions, ugh" I took a pillow to the stomach from Kenny and continued "Anthony is six and Paul is three."

Uncle Christian gave me a 'mind yourself" look but ignored my snapping at Uncle Chris, he probably would have joined me if it was a proper thing to do.

Colt turned around on a commercial break "I'm not sharing my room I already share it with Nick."

"Si ha potuto dirvi lo stesso"(one could say the same) Nick mutter from inside his overnight bag.

"We will be converting one of the guest rooms in to a bedroom for Anthony and Paul if Alex is able to adopt them." Mama said making it clear that Nick and Colt had no need to argue over territories.

"Everyone will have to adapt to the changes" Mom added to prevent further whining.

"We are . . ."

". . . More than excited" The twins smiled. "We will . . .

". . . Be uncles."

"That means you can bug someone other than me for a change" Nick hissed at them on the way to the door.

"Don't count on it . . ."

". . . We love tormenting you . . ."

". . . You are our favorite . . ."

". . . Target."

Kenny rolled his eyes at them "Al is the younger one potty trained?" He asked me.

"To the best of my knowledge" I sighed, I was trying to watch the Steelers game and everyone was interrupting I was waiting for Colt to scream shut up or something just as off balance and rude.

"Good, diaper prices are outrageous." Kenny worked at Baby World part time to help with his schooling. "Oh, and there is this toddler bed on sale for the next month race cars and fire trucks if you want I can put one aside."

I nodded and changed the channel the Steelers we were losing anyway "Ok Colt bed." I threw him back on to my shoulders and carried him up to his room and tucked him in. "Night" I said.

"Ok" He yawned.

I looked around his half of the room it was trains and trucks, but mainly it was Harley Davidson motor cycles. Nick's half was under water sea life and astronomy. Nick seemed to have been the one to get all the intelligence not that the rest of us weren't smart but something in Nick screamed for miles geek or nerd. I wondered what Paul and Anthony would like on their walls. On the way down stairs I stopped and looked in the twins' room they had not split their room in two at all; the divider was tied back as far as they could tie it. They had turned their beds in to a bunk bed and pushed their dressers together to make it look like one dresser not that they used it their dark clothes laid all over the floor blending in with the black carpet, bedding, walls and curtains. They had identical telescopes, back packs and everything else cluttering the floor with a small path to their beds. Down stairs I pulled out my banking stuff, I handed mom my rent and looked at the left over balance; fifty-five thousand three hundred and forty-five dollars and ninety-five cents. One day the bank would outlaw ninety-five cents being a balance total and I'd be happy because no matter what I did it was always there. The three hundred forty-five was mine from working and the $55000.95 was what my dad left me. I guess he had been a really great guy he is the only friend my parents spoke of other than Ana's family.

"Kenny, want to go shopping with me tomorrow?" I asked, not wanting to go alone and end up having a panic attack.

Psycho, Mama's black lab, came flying in dragging a stick. Mama laughed "Psycho" She frowned at him; he dropped the stick and settled on Mom's feet.

"Er, why?" He looked up from the computer.

"The boys will need things" I said making a list.

"Ok, but I have . . ." The phone cut him off "It's for me" He jumped and dashed for the phone. "Oh hi Ana, yeah he is right here" He handed me the phone.

"Williams" I said taking it ignoring his faces and kissing noises.

"Alex, you busy?"

"Not really, why? What's wrong?"

"Nothing, we need to go to the center Dave has been trying to reach you for three hours."

"Oh sorry my cell was off. I'm on my way."

"I am driving."

"Fine."

I worried all the way down to the car I knew Dave held an employee and DCS card game every Friday after the boys fell asleep and I occasionally attended but for him to call Ana to reach me . . . This was no card game thing. Ana was at the car when I got to it, she greeted me with a deep kiss. "So I wasn't dreaming."

"Nope," She smiled "We are done fighting, I got tired of waiting for you to realize we were done when the fight it's self ended."

"No, not that," I blushed, "How good you kiss."

"Ok *Mr. Smooth*," She laughed, "Let's get going; it isn't bad actually I think you are going to laugh."

"Ok."

When we got there Tim, the night guard, told us to go straight to the family room. I rushed putting her purse and our coats into the office and ran the four corridors to the family room.

Half way through the door something little grabbed my leg I looked down "Alets" Paul giggled.

I smiled lifting him, "What are you doing here?"

"I miss Anony!"

"I bet Anthony is sleeping and you should be too."

"Yes he is" Dave said "Doing quite well, actually."

"You must be Alex" A tall man with balding gray hair and glasses stuck his hand out, "I'm Cleveland Thompson."

I adjusted Paul and shook his hand "Alex Williams, nice to meet you. This is my girlfriend Ana."

"His foster care provider called me said he was rather distraught screaming and yelling for Anthony and you."

"Me?" I looked at him.

"You have Anony" He giggled.

"Oh I do, do I? I think Dave does let's see. Dave can I have the keys to Anthony's room?"

"Sure" He tossed me his keys.

"See Dave has Anthony." I showed him the keys.

"That is D-hall Dave to the little man" Dave said.

"E-all Ave?"

"Close enough" I laughed hugging him tight he was wearing batman Pajamas "Let's leave these guys to their cards and go see Anthony." I tickled him as I carried him in to the hall.

"Deal me in boys, I came to play" Anna laughed sitting down.

In the hall Paul toddled down the hall next to me running his hand down the wall. "So I you like Batman?" I asked.

"No, these are arrowed leepies."

"Oh, Ok so what do you like?"

"Taz!" He spun around making slobbering noises, "And the inedible hulk" He struck a pose.

I laughed "What is your favorite color?

"Geen"

I smiled "Hey how would you like to live with me?"

"Anony?"

"Yes, Anthony, too."

"Otay." I unlocked the door and he peered in. "Is he cold?"

I walked in Anthony was balls up on his bed rocking, I sat on the edge of the bed "Come here, what is wrong? Bad dream?"

He crawled in to my arms next to Paul. "I dreamed we got new parents and they were meaner than Mommy."

"It's ok; are you worried about the person who wishes to adopt you?"

"Yes, what if they separate me and Paul? What if they don't like us?"

"It is Paul and I not me and Paul, and like I said I know this person he was originally going to adopt just you but then found out you had a brother and wishes to adopt both of you. And Anthony he doesn't just like you he loves you." I squished both boys in a tight hug.

"Anony we live with Alets"

Anthony frowned "I wish Paul."

I smiled "Anthony, listen to Paul he knows who wishes to adopt you."

"No Anony *we live with* Alets." Paul said with as much force as his little three year old body could muster.

Anthony looked up at me "You?"

"Yes" I smiled choking as he hugged my neck extremely tight.

"Will we have a mom?" He asked.

"Er, you will have grammas and uncles and great uncles and . . ." before I could say Ana a commotion broke out in the hall. "Stay here."

"Otay Alets" Paul yawned.

Anthony nodded his little face showed he was deep in thought.

———— ⬥ ————

"Kevin! Kevin clam down!" Bruno was dragging Kevin to the time out room.

"Kevin!" I said forcefully "Stop kicking."

We got him into the room and straight jacket with the door shut and locked. We sunk to the floor outside the door. Bruno had brown hair and brown eyes, he was a thin short wiry man about 36 or 35 "Thanks Alex, why you . . ."

"My hope to be sons and Dave's card game."

"Sons?"

"Anthony and his brother."

"Ah yes, Dave said something about that."

"Well I will let you recuperate from wild man and go tell Anthony and Paul everything is ok."

Paul was asleep on the bed and Anthony was writing in his guidance log he handed me a sheet of paper with a list of questions "I am proud of you, may I ask you a question?"

"Yes."

"How long have you been cutting?"

He winced "Four months, may we talk about those now?"

"Yes, we can, you are very smart."

"Thank you."

I looked down at the questions the biggest fear I had was he didn't want to live with me. I read the first question aloud "Will I go to school?" I looked at him "Of course, you will go to the same private school I went to."

"What grade will I be in?" He asked.

"First, first it is your appropriate grade."

"Oh"

The next question made me laugh "I don't know if you will have your own room. There is a good chance you will have to share a room with Paul."

"He snores" Anthony wrinkled his nose.

"I noticed" I wrinkled my nose back at him making him giggle. The next question made me want to cry "I do not know kiddo; I hope they find no reason why I can't have you. There are a lot of people helping me with this my moms, my uncles, my brothers . . ."

"Colt too?"

"Yes Colt too, Ana, and Dave."

"Who is Ana?"

"My girlfriend, you know her, she works in the office . . ."

"Oh her" He smiled "She is really nice she plays connect four with me."

"Yeah" I blushed slightly "But as for you having to stay here, unfortunately I think you may have to successfully complete the program. I hope not, not that there is anything wrong with the program just my family and I have different views and could care for you just as well."

He nodded like his world had just imploded "Do I have any aunts?" He asked as if it had just sunk in that I didn't mention any.

I laughed "Well you will have great aunts, I have no sisters.

"Oh your mommy had all boys?"

"Yeah my mommies must have lost it six boys."

"I'll have six uncles?"

"No, five I make six. It goes oldest to youngest me, Kenny, Christopher, Christian, Nick, and Colt."

"Oh you're the biggest."

"Yep I'm the oldest by two years."

"Oh" He yawned

I looked down and read aloud "Will I have a mommy? Well as I was trying to say before you will have an Ana, and she's more than happy to have you."

"Oh ok."

"Can I ask you a few things?"

"Yes"

"How many Band-Aids?"

"Three less than you put on me, two healed and one fell off in the tub" He pointed at his arm.

"Good, is Paul potty trained?"

"Yes, but he still has accidents sometimes; and if he isn't careful the potty eats him when he sits on it."

"Good to know" I laughed.

"Are you happy it is me?" I held my breath.

"Yes! I have never had a daddy before I think you would make a great daddy."

"I hope Mr. Thompson feels the same way, but it is bed time nine-thirty is awful late for you to be up."

I picked up Paul and tucked Anthony in. Paul was dead weight in his sleep, it felt like I was carrying a bolder but I snuggled him close getting a tighter grip. When we got back to the family room I laid down on the couch with him on my chest while they finished their card game.

"How is Anthony doing?" Dave asked.

"Good he is sleeping now; he had questions when I got down there. We would have been back sooner but I stopped to help Bruno get Kevin in to the time out room." Why I was telling Dave what I knew he already knew was beyond me.

"Oh that boy" Mr. Thompson said "I work with his father let's just say the apple doesn't fall far from the tree."

"I was telling Alex just earlier some thorozine would fix Kevin" Dave laughed.

Mr. Thompson laughed "His father too."

I shook my head "Hai detto che non me" (You said it not me).

"Alex" Dave frowned at me "English"

"Oh let the boy be Dave speaking two languages fluently is a great skill he could share with the boys."

I watched Paul sleep. He had perfect baby features; I ran my hand through his hair and down his back.

"Penny for your thoughts, dear?" Ana asked me.

"Race car or fire truck bed?" I smiled.

She chuckled "Fire truck, when I saw him this morning he was running down the hall going 'whooo whooo I a ire uck I save Anony' so defiantly fire truck."

I laughed "He loves his 'Anony'; I will have Kenny put that fire truck bed on hold for me."

Dave smiled at me "Confident are we?"

"Wistful thinking, they are perfect look at him he is such a sweetheart."

Mr. Thompson smiled "You really want this don't you?"

"Oh yes sir, I am sure I want to adopt them, this is the most sure I have ever been in my life."

"Well it is getting late I better get him back to his foster care provider, I will see you Tuesday" He lifted Paul out of my arms it felt like he ripped my heart out, but I stood up and shook his hand anyway. "As for you, you old coot" He said to Dave "I will see you next Friday for a rematch."

"Old coot? Look who's talking you old fool and I'll stomp you next Friday too." Dave laughed.

"Good night Mr. Thompson; nice seeing you tonight" Ana smiled; as she moved over next to me.

"So" Dave said.

"They bo . . ."

"I know and you know I know. Walkie-talkies are magnificent inventions."

I rolled my eyes laughing "Mama and Mr. Thompson are right you are and old coot."

"So I have been told. Your mama has been calling me old coot since she was seventeen. When I told her, that her and Ana's uncle Kyle were going to give me grey hair."

I shook my head "Well I think I need to go join Kevin for a minute if Ana doesn't mind."

"Come here honey," She pulled me in close kissing me passionately.

"Hi" I smiled "I think I'm I think . . ."

"I think Anthony and Paul want siblings" Dave laughed at me.

Ana laughed "Feel better?"

I tried to nod "I take it you want to drive?"

"You know it, see you Monday Dave."

"Night love, you take care of that one he is mine." Dave walked us to the door.

"Oh I will I am bringing him to his mommy" She laughed.

"Mommies" I corrected.

"Yes dear, I know, but Mama is probably in the shower."

I nodded Mama showered every chance she got "There is a good chance you're turning me over to my Uncles."

"Your Uncle Christian takes good care of you."

When we got back it was about 10:15, Ana had a lead foot. I invited her in. As predicted Mama was in the shower, Mom was playing a video game with Uncle Chris and Uncle Christian was at the kitchen table organizing things.

"Ciao come era il vostro gioco? (Hello, how was your game)" Uncle Christian asked.

"Good, I guess, I didn't play; Mr. Thompson was there with Paul so I took Paul down to see Anthony."

Uncle Christian nodded looking up from the cable bill "Well Miss Ana has been a long time since you graced us with your presence."

"Hello sir" She smiled hugging Uncle Christian "I have been very busy since Al and I's fight."

"He or Colt may have mentioned that" He winked at me.

I blushed "Mom, Ana, is here."

"I know who she is Alex, I was there when she was born. Your mama is her Godmother."

I blushed hard "We um we're dating."

"Know that too, known since you were 10 and Kenny told me he didn't see you kissing her in the back yard so he didn't know where you were."

I turned scarlet and sat next to Ana on the couch.

"I told you he saw us back then" Ana laughed.

"Hello Ana" Mama came out of the bathroom. "How are you?"

"Good, how are you?" She got up and hugged her.

"Clean, Kenny spilt my India inks I cleaned it up, I was covered in ink myself."

"More like you would have done anything for a fourth shower, JJ" Uncle Chris laughed at her.

Ana laughed "Did Alex tell you we are done fighting?"

"He might have" Mama smiled "Get tired of waiting for him?"

"Sì, si è rifiutato di prendere i miei consigli . . ." (Yes, he refused to take my hints.)

I blushed again "Suggerimenti (hints)? What hints?"

She laughed "Don't worry dear." She kissed me taking my breath away again.

"So how was your card game?" Mama asked

"I didn't play I went with Paul down to see Anthony."

"What was Paul doing there?"

"He freaked out on his foster parents crying for Anthony and Alex" Ana answered.

"Really wow." Mama sat in front of Uncle Christian for him to comb her hair. Her hair had never been cut other than dead ends and was now down to her knees "So what have you been up to lately, Ana?"

"Work, school and helping Daddy" She answered.

"How are they doing?"

"Good, some days are better than others but most are good. Davie gets mean and angry when he is frustrated and that worries Dad."

"That is good to hear, not his temper but the other."

"Tomorrow we go up to Mum's grave, oh Alex I meant to ask you if you would come with me."

I stared blankly at Mama. I would feel really out of place, and Ana's dad gave me the creeps. I would make a complete fool of myself, but she was my girlfriend and asking for my support. "Mama, do we have plans tomorrow?"

"Um, in the afternoon but you . . ."

"We go in the morning, dear" Ana chimed in.

"You may go Alex and then Ana can come back and go with us to the winter carnival" Mama said.

"OK" I looked at Mom then at Mama, my parents nor I did large crowds well "Is Uncle Christian coming?"

"Alexander Joseph, when was the last time you saw your uncle let me or your mother out of his sight?"

"Mai."(never)

"Then what kind of question is that?"

"I don't know Mama; I think I am just getting old."

Uncle Christian laughed "Maybe you should have been on bed restriction."

Ana looked at me "Everyone on bed restriction?"

"Colt was mouthing off to a teacher, Nick is at a friend's for the night, those beasts" Mom shuttered "Were torturing Nick, and Kenny is out with Juliet."

Ana pulled my arm around her.

"Er, oh, yeah" I blushed "Mama I am going to walk Ana home that is if she is ready."

"Honey you know might be easier if you slept at my house."

"I am, I'll be right back" I ran up stairs and quickly packed and kissed my mothers good night.

I made my pallet on Ana's bedroom floor. She laughed at me "Honey we are not ten anymore you can sleep in my bed."

I looked at her little twin bed and tried not to laugh "Sì, come hai detto tu non siamo più dieci (Yes, like you said we are no longer ten), I won't fit."

"Then I shall sleep on the floor with you" She said undoing my pallet redoing it and adding her blankets to it. She striped down to her bra and panties, I turned around. "Alex you have seen me in a bikini same type of thing."

"Uh yeah" I gulped; I started to pull off my shirt then stopped.

"Dear" She said pulling my shirt off "How do you sleep at home?"

I blushed "In my boxers." She unbuttoned and pulled off my pants "Hello!"

"Hi" She giggled

"My draws."

"Yep" She laughed.

"Uh ok then." I lay down on my back and started to think next thing I knew it was morning and Ana was asleep on my chest; thankfully unlike Anthony she didn't drool; although, she had an immobilizing death grip on me. I ran my hand through her long hair. She made it look easy as if we hadn't been fighting. She was my best friend, in school we were named class couple, and her dad was always asking me when the wedding was. I just didn't know it seemed too easy to me.

"Honey" She yawned "Don't think so hard your body tenses."

"Yeah well you hug like a boa constrictor" I laughed and gently hit her with her pillow. She laughed and stood up and pulled off her panties. I buried my face in my pillow "What are you doing?"

"Undressing, showering and starting my day; I have a shower off my room remember."

"Uh-huh yeah"

"Honey, do not give me that look I know you need a shower to start you day."

"Uh-huh yeah."

"Alex, pull your head out of your pillow and go get your shower."

"Are you decent yet?"

"Looking yes, am I dressed no, most people don't shower with their clothes on."

"I . . ."

"I am showering with you."

"I uh . . ."

"Alex stand up!"

"Ok" I stood up and covered my eyes."

She pulled my arms down "Open your eyes."

"You're naked."

"And your about to be, please Alex, we use to bath together when your parents baby sat me."

"We were five!"

"That's it Alex this is ridiculous" She pulled my boxers down, I instantly covered myself "Oh please I have already seen that or do you not remember the prom."

I blushed deep scarlet at our senior prom my friend Wilson Needlemyere pants me in front of everyone. "Oh please my brother use to walk around in his tighty-whiteys. So either you get in that shower or you sit there sucking your thumb and I call your mom to come get you."

"I am not sucking my thumb; so much as I was taught to respect ladies" I objected stomping to the shower.

"Siete piuttosto immaturi (You are being rather immature). Please you need to relax. Ti amo (I love you), we are dating, I want to marry you."

"Sorry" I mumbled feeling slightly embarrassed.

After our shower I repacked all my things about seven times to make sure they were packed just so and waited for Ana to finish.

When she came out she wrapped her arms around me and whispered into my chest "I love you."

I choked, I wanted to say it back; I had loved her since I met her at five years old when we came back from Italy. I opened my mouth to speak then closed it and held her as tight as I could, rocking her a little.

"Honey, are you ok?"

I nodded "Yeah sorry day dream" I kissed the top of her head "Let's go down to breakfast I thought I smelt bacon."

"I bet you did" She smiled belting down the stairs ahead of me.

CHAPTER 4
WHY ME, WHY ME?

"Morning Daddy, Morning Davie" Ana greeted her family.

"Good morning Sir, good morning David" I managed to choke unevenly.

"Sit down, Alex, eat up" Her dad said.

I nodded he handed me a plate with pancakes and bacon "Th-thank you, sir."

"Your welcome, Ana tells me you two are adopting two boys."

"Yes sir," I gulped "A three year old and a six year old."

"So when is the wedding?"

I dropped my fork and I spilled orange juice all over my hand, cup and the table. "I er . . ."

"Daddy, stop it." Ana protested in my defense "You're scaring him." She handed me the paper towels.

"S-s-sorry" I managed.

"Don't be baby, it is ok, Daddy, is just a goon" She gave him a look.

At the grave yard Ana and her dad cleaned off the grave and I stood with David near the van feeling ultimately stupid and useless. Ana came over and buried her face in my chest and wrapped my arms around her. I felt like a total jerk I didn't know what to say or do and unable to stop her from being in pain. "You ok?" I said without thinking. Well duh stupid she is not ok she is crying.

"I am fine, Alex, it just still hurts sometimes."

"What hurts baby doll?" I spoke again without thinking. Stupido! Stupido! Stupido! I was making a complete fool of myself.

"My mom's death" She looked up at me. "Honey, are you still on our planet in there."

"Yeah sorry, I knew that, I spaced. Sono spiacente (I'm sorry)." I was sorry and I hoped she knew that I was, and I wanted to slam my head really hard in to the van door repeatedly.

"Let's help Daddy get Davie in to the van or he will never go and then we can see what your mama wanted to do with us."

"Er yeah" I nodded "Mama."

"Alex, dear you're shaking?"

"Cold" I shivered.

She laughed "I told you, you would need a coat it's nearly December."

I hugged my uncle Christian as tight as I could "I think you forgot something here." He said hugging back.

"My brain? My common sense? My confidence?"

"Your inhaler."

I laughed "Yeah that too, curse genetics"

"Curse what you will, but you are going to stay breathing." He stared off at something over my shoulder. "Go motivate those twins, your mother came to her senses we are going to see a play on broad way and out to eat."

"Awesome, much better than the winter carnival" Ana smiled.

"I guess" Kenny groaned "Juliet can't go she has to baby sit."

"Sorry bud" I tried not to laugh or show my excitement of no Juliet.

"Hey how did it go?" Mama asked coming out of the shower.

I nodded "Benissimo(fine)."

"Panic attack?"

"No, well almost" I gulped.

"Mama" Ana smiled "You worry too much he was fine."

Fine? What planet was she on? I made a complete fool of myself. My thoughts must have shown to at least Uncle Christian because he gave me a look.

"Alex, how about we go clean out the van so there is enough room for everyone." Uncle Christian pushed me slightly toward the door.

"Yes, sir" I gulp "Permission to be excused Mama?"

"Of course dear" She laughed "I have to rattle your brothers, and I wouldn't win against Christian trying to force you to clean the van."

"Ho rovinato tutto!(I blew it!) Ho rovinato tutto! Ho rovinato tutto!" I beat my head against the back of my seat waiting for Uncle Christian to come back with the vacuum. He could be quiet a neat freak.

"Blew what?" Nick said climbing in next to me.

"Nothing bud, the beasts leaving you alone?"

"Yeah for now; how was your date with Ana?"

"I think you know the answer to that."

"Blew it, blew it, and blew it?"

"Yep, made myself out to be a complete asino."

"Ouch, I am sorry but I think Ana feels differently."

"Why do you say that?"

"She is up stairs telling Mama how great you are."

"She is being polite"

Uncle Christian caught me by my pendants "I would prefer I not have to choke you, quit falling out of motor vehicles."

"Yes sir" I pulled myself together a little and shot Nick a look for laughing.

"Nikolas andare ad aiutare la mamma a trovare la sua borsa, la cosa è stata mal riposta. (Nikolas go help your mother find her purse, the thing has been misplaced)" He looked at me "sedere(sit)" The command was sharp and icy, I obeyed immediately. "I am glad to see you wearing those", He was referring to my pendants.

"Sharp edges" I sighed.

"I know there is. Your father would be very proud of you today if he were here to see you."

"Thank you sir, but I am pretty sure he is rolling in his grave at my failure this morning."

Uncle Christian frowned at me the way he did at Mama when she was displeasing him. "You feel you have failed but Ana does not. Why do you feel you have failed? Because you didn't know what to say? Didn't have all the answers? Couldn't heal the pain?"

"Yes sir and I got yelled at for being a gentleman."

He raised an eye brow "Sometimes it's ok to see her indecent, especially when she is inviting you to."

I blushed.

"As for the other what do I do when I can't fix things?"

"You hold Mama until she pushes you away."

"Sì, sometimes is all that is needed is assurance that someone outside of the issue cares."

"Uncle Chris doesn't take Mama crying as well as you do."

"They have been through a lot together, that severally strained their friendship; but what does he do when your mom cries?"

"He holds her until the tears stop, unless Mama can hold her."

"Seeing a pattern?"

"Yes sir."

"Still think you failed?"

"Not so much, thank you sir."

"Il vostro benvenuto (you're welcome)." He wrapped his arms around me until I pushed him away. "Come on we are going to be late and I wish good seats last time we went *the lady with the over sized hat* sat in front of me."

After the play we went to dinner at a fancy restaurant at which point I wished I was an only child or my parents had gotten rid of the twins. All Mama said was it was their job to embarrass me and that I need to relax a little. She was probably right about me relaxing a bit as every time I grabbed my glass to get a drink the ice would clank from my shaking. To the point Mom had to grab my hand to steady it. Ana acted as if nothing was wrong and on the way home she noticed my pendants.

"What is this?" She asked holding up my pentagram.

"My pentagram."

"Oh so that is what one looks like," She lifted my dragon and wolf pendants "I have not seen these in a long time."

"Uh yeah, Mom gave me the pentagram last year for my birthday and well you know these were my dad's."

She smiled "He would be very proud of you."

"Grazie(thanks)" I choked "I keep hearing that today."

"Then don't doubt yourself" She kissed me.

"Ooo . . ."

". . . You got a kiss" The beasts teased.

"Ooo grow a life" Ana said pushing them back in their seats kissing me deeper.

I sighed.

"Easy killer at least get back to our room before you do that." Kenny laughed at me.

"Kenneth do not be crude" Uncle Christian said trying to stifle a laugh.

"Thanks, thanks a lot Kenny; at least no one thinks Ana is an airhead."

He turn red opened his mouth like he was going to object then shut it fast thinking better than to aggravate me.

We dropped Ana off at her house and I walked her to her door and kissed her good night. When we got in Christopher, Christian, and Colt went straight to bed. Mom, Mama, Uncle Christian and Uncle Chris joined Nick in front of the television watching some cartoon on the Disney channel. I sat in front of my uncle facing him.

I took a deep breath "Permission to speak freely in your presence, sir."

"Of course; you can always." He looked at me as if I had told him I was going to cut my hair and become a non liberal politician.

"She told me she loves me today and I could not respond."

"Why?"

"I do not know I mean I wanted to of course, it was as if my brain locked."

"I see" He said thinking.

I leaned over and patted Psycho. Why my mama named her dog Psycho was beyond me. I remembered Mom's dog Bear he was an awesome dog. Sometimes I felt bad for my mothers they were completely surrounded by guys, but they looked happy. I looked up and saw them cuddling, they made it look so easy.

"Are you ok Alex?" Kenny asked me, setting the phone back on the base and sitting down next to Nick.

"Yeah I'm fine, just thinking."

"Your ghost white and shivering I don't think that is considered fine."

"So I am a little cold" I shrugged.

Uncle Chris popped the thermometer in my mouth "Do not talk and stop giving your brother dirty looks if he hadn't noticed someone else would have." The thermometer beeped and he showed Uncle Christian.

"Come on you" Uncle Christian cleared off the longer of the two couches. "Kenny get his bedding . . ."

"Ancora nel mio zaino (still in my backpack)" I pointed at my backpack.

"Good you are sleeping on the . . ."

"Yes, yes I know on the couch." I sighed grabbing my pillow and blanket; I did not want Kenny going through my pack he would make it an awful mess.

"You wrap tight in that blanket."

"Yes, Uncle Christian." I would have rolled my eyes if I could have gotten away with it.

I woke up sweating to death around three am. I shook off my dreams and rolled in ward so I was facing the back of the couch and tried to go back to sleep. Someone started rubbing my back.

"Zio Christian (uncle Christian)?" I muttered half a sleep.

"No dear." Mom said "But if you need me to I can get him."

I blinked and shook my head. "No, no. Don't wake him Mom I'm fine I just thought you were him. I am glad it is you. I love you, Mom, night." I closed my eyes and let her rubbing my back to put me to sleep.

The next time I woke it was morning and my cell phone was ringing out of control and I didn't have a music ringer or even one of those sweet soothing chime like ones, no it was loud and annoying it had to be, I had an on call twenty four hour job.

"Williams" I said groggily slurring my words.

"Honey, you ok?" Ana sounded really worried.

"Morning dear, what time is it?"

"Just about six you have to be to work soon."

I muttered several choice words and phrases none too nice. "Ok sorry thanks baby doll I got a high fever last night and was made to sleep on the couch."

"It is ok; can I still ride in with you though?"

"Yeah" I said shaking myself awake more "Oh yeah it's Sunday."

"Ok baby I will be over in a few minutes"

Ana's voice made me feel like I was floating or maybe it was the fever. I felt my forehead and said a few choice phrases in its honor as it had not gone away. I quickly and quietly put away my bedding, grabbed clean clothes, put the past two days of dirty clothes in the hamper and was standing in my boxers in between the front door and the bathroom door head for the shower when Ana walked in. I forgot she had a spare key.

"Morning" I kissed her "Showering be right out breakfast is on the table if you need it."

She pushed open the bathroom door "I am going to keep you company."

"Are you feeling well?"

"I think it is I whom should be asking you that."

CHAPTER 5

KEVIN

AFTER MY SHOWER WE BUCKLED into my car "You know it is Sunday right?"

"Yes, but Louise called out so I said I would fill in for her." She smiled at me and I nearly ran a red light.

"Honey?"

"Yes dear?"

"Are you ever going to cut your hair?"

I reached around and felt my pony tail it wasn't as long as Uncle Christian's but it would be there soon. "Do you want me to?"

"Oh no, I love you're your hair long."

I sighed in relief trying to find a way around the rush hour mess we were stuck in. "This is why I can't over sleep." I muttered gesturing towards the traffic.

"It is ok baby" She kissed my cheek, "Wow, Alex you are burning up."

"Yeah I know it is this bloody fever."

She frowned at me "No need to cuss."

"Sorry, I had it all night."

"And you didn't call out because . . . ? Look at you Al your pasty pale and shivering and where is your coat?"

"Home didn't have time to grab it. I have to be there I promised Anthony I would be there today."

"I think he'd . . ."

"I promised him." I snapped a bit too harshly.

She gave me a worried look "Alright honey."

"Kevin!" I said in disbelief as I put my stuff in my locker "Kevin! What am I being punished for now?" I muttered and cursed all the way down the hall. "Keys" I said to Dave.

"Are you . . . ?"

"KEVIN!" I said to him as if he didn't know who he had assigned me to today.

"He is not in there, he is at breakfast today. He remembered it was a good Idea not to pick a fight before breakfast."

"Sono per me non lui . . ."

"Alex English please, I get that you are upset but you need to speak to me in English its early and my Italian is far from decent."

"They are for me not him." I repeated this time in English.

"Alex, Ms. Meyers is stopping by to see you, to observe how well you inter act with the children."

"Is that why I have KEVIN!"

"Alex relax please, Bruno just needed a day off you will be fine Kevin may like you. Try to relax just be yourself, Jules is coming in on her day off to move this along for you."

I rolled my eyes "Mi piace di lui bene, ma Ho ancora bisogno di queste chiavi dopo il lavoro (I like him, but I still need these keys after work!)!"

"Alex it will be fine you can go think after work for now please just go find Kevin" Dave laughed, "But remember Kevin doesn't know Italian so either get happy or remember to speak English."

"Yeah, Yeah" I waved him off.

"Morning Kevin" I greeted him with a smile.

"Alex" He hugged me.

I looked at him, I was shocked and hugged him back "Ok what do you want?"

"Don't make me go to visitation."

"Kevin, it's only Sunday."

"Please" He begged.

"I will make a deal with you, you behave all week and I will do my best to keep you from having to attend visitation."

He nodded in agreement "I hear you and Ana are getting real *serious*." He waggled his little 12 year old eye brows at me.

"Yes," I laughed "We are back together, Kevin." I wanted to know where he was getting his information from.

"I saw her she's doing intake in the B-hall today."

"I know, we car pool."

"So you are really with me today I don't have to be with Quentin at all?"

"Yes."

"Only me?"

"Yes."

"Sweet!"

Kevin sat in his desk in a school room with seven other children all in the seventh grade including his brother, Buddy. Buddy was normally his favorite target to attack so I made sure they were nowhere near each other. I watched Kevin, he paid exceptionally well attention to his lesson and he was very smart. He sat and did some of his homework while we ate lunch.

"Pre algebra already?" I asked him.

"Yes I love math" He smiled.

"Yeah he is a little geek" Buddy said as he passed us. Buddy should not talk he was almost fifteen and only in seventh grade I am not saying he didn't have any learning disabilities but he was hardly ever in class; he had logged the most time in the time out room of every one there. "Needs a pacifier and a book."

I watched Kevin trying to control his temper "Alex may we sit the rest of lunch in the family room?"

"Sure," I smiled when we got to the family room I hugged him "I am proud of you, but I assume his teasing you is why you attack him the most?"

He looked at his feet "Buddy is just like dad he pushes and pushes until I snap for fun. Only peace I get is in that dumb time out room. The little boy the new one with the little brother and the state lady that . . ."

"You mean Anthony?"

"Yeah, him, he swears you're going to be his new dad, tell him he is lucky he has his own room. They were bringing me back to my room the other night, old D-hall and Bruno, and he was looking really lonely."

"He misses his brother."

"Well I will gladly trade he can have Buddy, his little brother looked cute and nice."

I smiled "Have I told you about my brothers?"

"No, only Colt and that is only because I have seen him."

"Well you'd be allowed to speak to him if every time I brought him you weren't losing control; he is only a year younger than you. After school I will tell you about them right now it's time for class."

I walked him back to his class room; Buddy was being restrained and carried out of the room.

We stepped aside for them to remove him "Why do they called him Buddy?" I whispered.

"It is a nick name because he is named after dad." He whispered.

"Ok"

"I think that is why he is so like dad, he even looks like dad."

Kevin was right Buddy looked like their dad, but Buddy wasn't allowed visitations after he nearly knocked his mom unconscious. Kevin enjoyed the rest of his class time. They were not allowed pens or pencils until level four and then only under supervision; they were allowed crayons for their homework. He did his home work and had me check it he was very determined to get good grades.

"Are you going to tell me about your brothers?" He asked when he was done.

"Oh yeah, thanks for reminding me, I am the oldest of six boys from oldest to youngest there is me, Kenny, Christian, Christopher, Nick, and Colt. We don't really see Kenny anymore . . ."

"Why?"

"He is busy, he works and is in college and has a girlfriend, but when we were younger he was the one to tell my mothers that I cut."

His eyes got wide "I bet you were mad."

"Mad was an understatement, I *taught* him not to tattle no matter what. Looking back I wish I had not hurt him so badly. I mean the broken bones and bruises healed but it put a large dent in our relationship. We have made up and everything but he still flinches when I raise my voice or lose my temper weather it is with him or not."

"Did you get in trouble?"

"Of course I did, I was grounded for a full year, but what was worse was Kenny and I share a room and I had to see him hurting from the pain I caused every day until he healed. I have never hit anyone to that extent again. Friday when I got home I saw my twin brothers . . ."

"Which ones are . . ."

"Oh sorry, Christian and Christopher, they were teasing Nick, they are always teasing Nick. They tease him because he is like our mom he is quiet, shy and reads a lot. I brought this to my parents attention and they are now defiantly in trouble, although it has not stopped them. I have not seen it as much since I told my parents but I can still see the wall they are creating by teasing him. I asked them once why they tease him they said it was because they love him. Have you ever asked your brother why he teases you?"

"Yeah he said he wasn't teasing me he was teaching me not to be stupid, that was dad's excuse also."

"I'm sorry Buddy probably feels he is doing something good because he learned it from your father; and your father may have learned it from one of his parents. See we learn to be parents from watching our parents if our parents treat us badly sometimes we will treat our children badly unless we break the cycle. I'm not saying it's right or should go uncorrected it just explains one plausible cause of the action. Does that make sense?"

He nodded and sighed "May I change my request for visitation?"

"To?"

"May I just see my mom?"

"I will try my best, if you keep up your end of the deal."

They brought Buddy in he sat at his desk he did his homework and left Kevin alone.

"Can you please pass me my log book?" Kevin asked me.

"You know they are thinking of making you a level four?" I handed him his log book.

"Yeah me, I'll get a real writing utensil and still have only a spoon to eat with."

I frowned at him "Kevin that's a good thing."

"I guess."

"Don't you want to go home?"

"I don't know."

I sighed and looked to make sure Buddy was still doing his homework. They had school Sunday through Thursday leaving Friday and Saturday for visitation, group, long consoling sessions, and down time. Kevin pulled out some paper from his log and began to draw dragons and wizards. "Want to go down to the family room? I bet some of the others are done, maybe Kyle is done."

"I can go down there?" His face lit up.

"Yeah, why couldn't you?"

"I don't know I just figured I wasn't allowed. Can we watch TV?"

"Sure" I smiled "Come on."

I was right several others were done including Kyle and Anthony. Kyle had his eye bandaged.

"Anyone want to play yatzee?" I asked trying to include the other kids thinking Kevin would be happier if he could make friends with more than just Kyle. Two girls from the B-hall and Anthony said they would but Kyle looked away.

"Kyle what's wrong, you like yatzee, come play with us." I asked.

Kyle looked out the window.

"Kyle what happened to your eye?" I tried again.

Kyle looked at his feet.

"It was an accident, Alex, I promise," Anthony looked at me pleadingly "I was sound asleep . . ."

"It's my fault Alex I was up to use the bathroom and he was screaming so I asked Dave if I could go with him to see if Anthony was ok, and Dave said yes and I shook him gently but he still swung in his sleep and his elbow met my eye."

"Ouch" Kevin said "That had to feel great."

"Want to see?" Kyle smiled.

"Sure . . ."

"No, leave the bandage on" I laughed "Kyle are you going to play?"

"No sorry I have to go talk to Danny" He smiled and left.

We played two rounds of yatzee before someone came and told the girls they were being looked for, Steve came for Anthony around 3:30 and I helped Kevin find some cartoons. Ana came in around four and snuggled up next to me.

"Hi" Kevin smiled at her "I get to see TV today."

Ana smiled back at him and whispered in my ear "I am out how, did it go today?"

I whispered back "lui(him)? Benissimo(fine), that woman just starting at me like that from the side lines hideous."

At five I took Kevin back to the dining hall and went down to Dave's office in the D-hall to get the keys for the time out room and decompress. Ana stayed in the lunch room to talk to and get to know Anthony better.

"How was your day?" Dave asked me as I grabbed the keys.

"Vinco" I said.

"Pardon? That is one you never taught me?"

"I win; Kevin doesn't want to go home. He is smart, sweet, polite, and he doesn't want to go home because his brother and father push him to snapping point."

"So vinco is I win?"

"Yep"

"I learned something new today" Dave laughed heartily "I think you did too."

"Yes sir."

"Here" he handed me the keys "Have a good meditation before you go talk to Anthony."

"What did she say?"

"Nothing kiddo, don't think on it, she was headed to talk to your parents."

"Oh boy" I gulped. I quickly unlocked the door, gave Dave the keys back and laid myself on the soft mattress to lose myself in my thoughts.

I don't know how long I was there but it was a long time for Ana was outside the door pacing when I came back out "Oh baby Sono così spiacente(I'm so sorry)" I kissed her.

"No don't be sorry, Honey you needed it, are you ok?" She held me tight.

"Yes I was just meditating and thinking."

"Alright" She loosened her grip on me "Go kiss him good night he is already tucked in bed."

I unlocked his door and handed Dave the keys back and went in "Alex" He squealed jumping in to my arms "I was afraid you were mad at me and not going to come."

I pulled him in to my arms tight and not letting go "I promised I would be here that means I will be here angry or not although I am not angry with you it was an accident and his eye will heal he is twelve black eyes are cool to him I doubt he is upset about it.

"Here" He said handing me a new set of questions as I sat him down.

"Why do you sit in the time out room after you get out of work?" I read aloud "To meditate and think, it was how I was taught to decompress and relieve some of my stress, it lessens my panic attacks if it didn't I would be a grump" I screwed up my face "Like this" I said tickling him.

He giggled "Can you teach me?"

"I can't while you are here I am sorry, I wish I could but they would not allow it not so much Dave but the state."

He kind of pouted.

I read the next question "Um no Ana does not live with me yet, but she lives next to me, we grew up together, My mama is her Godmother if her parents had followed how they were raised It is possible I would have been betrothed to her," I stopped because he looked lost, "Promised to her at birth um, a prearranged marriage does that make more sense?"

He nodded still looking slightly lost "I like her she is nice."

"Good I am glad" I let out a breath I didn't know I was holding. "Your room or more likely your half of you and Paul's room will be how ever you wish it to look as will Paul's."

"Cool" His little face was full of deep thought.

I sighed too tired to think "My mothers are self employed artists and authors, my uncle Chris works construction with my other uncles, my uncle Christian is unemployed, my brother Kenny works at Baby World, and my double trouble twin brothers work weekends at the mall. My mothers believe idle, er, still hands are not healthy for your soul."

"Did your uncle use to work?"

"Um I believe so now he just cleans the house and takes care of every one in it." I chocked on the next question. "Um I know my brothers will be busy and my uncle Chris has to go to work, but my mothers may be free."

"Really?"

"Yes and of course I will be here and Paul is coming." His next question ripped my heart out, I pulled him tight in to my arms. "What makes you think I would ever stop loving you? My love for you has nothing do with the state's decision." I tucked him in and kissed his forehead "No matter what they say you and Paul will always be my boys; don't worry, worrying is my job yours is to be a six year old little boy." I tucked the blanket tight around him like Uncle Christian use to tuck me so I didn't fall out during a nightmare. I locked his door behind me hugging Ana as tight as I could, still clutching his question list.

She pulled it out of my hand as I buried my face in her neck. "I see" She said "Deep thoughts for a six year old."

I nodded still buried in her neck "Sono così molto nervosa(I am so very nervous)."

"Alex" Dave said "You will be just fine with the state but if you don't call your parents I think I will be missing my best employee."

"Sure" I nodded finally seeing the clock instantly hugging Ana tighter "Sono caro così spiacente Non ho fatto(I'm so sorry dear I did not . . .) . . ."

"Shh" she pushed her finger to my lips "Stop worrying."

"Thank you honey how about you get our stuff and start the car while I call Mama."

"Sounds good, I love you Alex."

My heart caught in my throat and I choked again doing the only thing I could think of; I kissed her and told her I would see her in the car. "Ho rovinato tutto, Ho rovinato tutto, Ho rovinato tutto." I muttered as she sighed at me and walked away.

"No you did not blow it you are just shy and you turn eight shades of red every time she says that to you." Dave laughed handing me the phone.

I dialed home and listened to the rings "Hel . . ."

". . . Lo" The twins answered.

"Give me Mama" I groaned.

"Ok . . ."

"Alex"

I rolled my eyes. "Mama?"

"Are you ok?" She sounded panicked.

"Yeah sorry, long day, I am heading home now. Why are the twins still up?"

"They were finishing their homework and your uncle's nerves. We will talk when you get in drive safely I love you."

"Love you to Mama" I hung up and handed the phone to Dave. "Night Dave see you tomorrow" I started to jog to the exit.

"Hang in there kiddo" He called after me.

"Right Dave." I called back over my shoulder "More like hang myself."

Dave shook his head laughing as he settled in to his office.

"Let's talk" Ana said the second I got in to the car.

I swallowed hard "ok."

"I love you, Alex."

I nodded starting to choke opening my mouth to try and say it back.

"Ti amo, Alex."

I nodded this time starting to choke.

"Alex" She turned her x-ray vision stare on me and I shuttered "Do you love me back, Alex?"

I nodded so vigorously that I made myself dizzy. "I am trying to say it honest it is just . . ."

"Shh it is ok, I understand." She kissed me. "Our little boy is sweet, Alex. I asked him about his band-aids, he says you told him he had to wear them on his cuts."

"Oh no don't you go there that was all Dave he wouldn't stop picking the scabs." I objected.

"I asked him how many he had; he told me he would have twenty-one more band-aids to lose to make you proud."

"I am proud of him every day."

"I know you are. He asked me if he got rid of all his band-aids would they let us have him Paul. I told him he had no effect on their decision and not to worry so much. That is when he got paper and crayon and wrote those questions for you."

I smiled "He asks a lot of question and he is very smart."

It was quarter to eleven when I finally got in. Mom handed me my diner and her, Mama, Uncle Christian and I sat in the kitchen to discuss their visit with Ms. Meyers and how things looked to be in my favor. After I ate I excused myself to go straight to bed still tortured by the relentless fever that was making me feel like a slug. My brothers were already sound asleep. I set my alarm and fell right to sleep myself.

CHAPTER 6

LONGEST DAY IN MY LIFE

"BEEP, BEEP, BEEP" I SLAMMED off my alarm so hard the batteries fell out. 5:00 AM came early; my eyes burned as if acid had been poured in to them. By the time I had showered, ate and got to the car Ana was waiting for me.

"Are you ok, dear, you look awful?" She greeted me.

"Meraviglioso e voi(wonderful and you)?" I muttered.

She frowned at me "You wake up like this?"

"Nope went to bed like this."

She frowned again "I am driving you have a lead foot when you're in this mood."

"Benissimo, non mi preoccupo(Very well I do not care)."

"Where are your head phones?"

"The beasts broke them."

"Where is your CD?"

"In the CD drive."

She smiled and hit play, twenty something year old thought drowning heavy metal blasted out of the speakers. I closed my eyes and started to relax.

"Oggi medio ritenente, vita che non va il mio senso . . ." I sang with the CD. The CD was by a group named Korn and had been my mother's when she was younger. She said that it made her feel better and she gave it to me in hope that it would do the same for me and it was. "Ritenere abbastanza frustrated e proprio odiato . . . . ORA . . ." I screamed along with it. Ana was trying hard not to laugh Italian gave the song an interesting sound and so did my off key half asleep singing.

"Talk to me" Ana said.

"I am nervous" I sighed.

"Don't be everything is going to be fine."

"They check our health records today; I don't find that fine in anyway."

She looked hard at the highway avoiding my frustration and nerves. The wind and rain seemed to be as stormy as my temperament today and we were head in to rush hour traffic. Although today was my short day I was not looking forward to it.

"It will be fine" She finally said, patting my leg. I could feel the warmth of her hand through my thin work pants.

I stormed through security and stomped in through the office to the lockers. I had two hours before I had to be to work, so I head down to Kevin's consolers office. I didn't really know him, but his office and his attire seemed to give a stereotypical impression of a psychiatrist and it gave me the creeps.

"Can I help you?" He smiled standing up to greet me.

"I hope so; you are Kevin Roberts' consoler correct?"

"Yes, Yes, please sit down um Alex" He read my employee badge.

I sat in a chair in front of his desk "He wishes to know if there is anyway just his mother could visit him and not his father."

He nodded "Kevin has asked me that many times."

"Well I told him if he behaved this week I would see what I could do."

"I have spoken to his mother multiple times about leaving his father at home seeing how negatively it affects Kevin, but she says she is unlicensed and he is her only way here."

"There has to be someone . . ."

"I have told her we could send someone for her. She said she would think about it. I think I will give her another ring this afternoon."

"Thank you."

"You're welcome, nice to finally meet you, Alex; many of the children speak very favorably of you."

"I am glad to hear that, nice to meet you too." We stood and shook hands and I left headed to the D-hall to tell Dave to pull me out before my speech but he meet me in the C-hall and told me to go straight to the office I had a phone call.

"Alex" Ana smiled "This is Mrs. Grear and you know . . ."

"ALETS!" Paul squealed jumping in to my arms.

I got a steady grip on Paul and stuck my hand out to shake "Nice to meet you Ma'am."

Mrs. Grear was an elderly women with a warm welcoming smile "You too, Anthony and you are all Paul talks about."

I kissed Paul's little cheek "Did you go wild again, mister?"

"No" He giggled

"No, actually Mr. Thompson said to meet him here with Paul" Mrs. Grear smiled at me.

"Oh Alex, I almost forgot" Ana blushed "You have a phone call."

I tried to shake my head clear but it didn't work "Ok here bud meet the most beautiful girl in the world" I handed him to Ana.

"ANA" He squealed running a crossed her desk jumping in to her arms as I took the phone.

"Line two, dear" She laughed playing with Paul.

I hit the flashing button "Williams" I said trying to sound more coherent than I felt.

"Alex" Mr. Thompson greeted me "Mrs. Grear and Paul should be there?"

I cleared my throat "Yes sir, they are. Paul is telling Ana all about fire trucks."

"Ok good Ms. Meyers will be there shortly to talk to you" He hung up.

"I hate cell phones, poor reception" I put the phone back in its cradle and picked Paul up off the paper work Ana had him on.

"Excuse you, Alex, we were talking" Ana laughed.

"Well I am sure Ralph wants the level reports wrinkle and Paul free" I pointed to her desk.

"You are a hot potato today, Paul" Mrs. Grear said to him.

"I a hot tato?" He crinkled up his nose.

We all laughed.

"Mrs. Grear how is he doing?" I asked.

"Call me Cindy, please. He is doing well, he asks for Anthony a lot but that is expected. He tells me daddy Alex has Anthony."

I smiled trying not to show that it boosted my ego "He is three correct?"

"Yes he just turned three last Thursday."

"Oh wow he is little and he is very smart." I tickled Paul.

Ms. Meyers basically explained that I was the only one wishing to adopt Anthony and Paul, that it looked good for me she just needed to talk to Mr. Thompson, and that she would see Paul Friday. I hugged Paul and left to get to the group room early I was not feeling well and hoping Dave would excuse me for the rest of the afternoon once I spoke to the new children.

I looked in; there were three girls in our section between twelve and sixteen. Dave was in the back of the room collecting forms, the parents were starting to file out. Some looked angry and others were crying the girls looked the same way. I opened the door letting the last couple out and walked in. Dave shot me a "You're in trouble" look. I gulp I wasn't late but I was still in trouble for something. Then I noticed my arm was bleeding from where Curtis had bit me when I stopped to help Bruno get Curtis in to the time out room.

Dave pulled me aside "I will give you the benefit of the doubt but you better have a good reason for that cut."

"Cut no, it is a bite" I wiped some of the blood revealing the teeth prints.

"Kevin?"

"No Curtis."

Dave bandaged my arm checking my shoulders as if he didn't fully believe I hadn't cut. "Think you can go the next five minutes without getting bit or dislocating a shoulder?"

"I hope so." I took my seat next to Carrie and Carol. Carol was Mama's age and had no personality and Carrie was my age with less than no personality. Dave welcomed everyone and did his speech about rules and schedules, then introduced me.

"Hi, good morning, I am Alex, how are you ladies today?" I felt my fever taking over turning the air surrounding me to a balmy five hundred degrees.

"Lousy" One said.

"Ok I guess" Another said, that one had cut recently I could tell because she wasn't affected by things, that would affect someone who hadn't cut.

"How could you ever know or understand how we feel" The gothic looking one said.

"Well I see you and I are both having a *good* day." I smiled this would defiantly be one of the children I got to spend time with after introductions.

"My day is nowhere as good as yours"

I nod "Right, because I don't cut my day is good? Wrong everyone has a bad day here and there, some more than others but everyone." I pulled up my sleeve "I been on that side of the podium I know exactly how you feel. So, let's try this again. Hi I am Alex and today I feel in over my head. How are you today?"

"Hi Alex, I'm Sarah and today I feel like my mom gave up on me." The first one said.

"Much better" I said, she would do very well here.

"I'm Chrissie and today I feel like I'm watching the world pass me by."

"Good, that happens to everyone from time to time too." I looked at my gothic princess and held my breath; she was going to give everyone a run for their money? I wonder if my mothers had been this way or more placid like the other two.

"I am Tiffany" She glared at me as if x-raying me with her eyes.

I was a bit taken back Tiffany did not fit this young lady's looks "And . . ." I prompted.

"And I don't feel like playing your little game."

I bit my tongue; it was good enough for an entry statement for her files "Nice to meet you all. You're all here because you have an addiction your parents feel they cannot help you with. Weather you got caught, someone told them, or you got brave and are ready to change things and told them yourself; you are now here to 'get better'. Well I don't like the term 'get better' it makes it sound like you are sick and need to be pampered so your cold will leave. I prefer find a better out let for your negative energy or get clean."

"Like that" Tiffany pointed at my bandage.

"No this is a bite I got early from an upset person on his way to the time out room."

"Ouch" Chrissie winced.

"Prime rib today" Tiffany laughed.

"Actually I did not feel it until Dave pointed it out to me, but back on topic I won't lie to you I use to cut I am twenty one and I have been clean four years. I won't tell you cutting didn't feel good it did it felt great to be able to be void of all emotion and feeling to escape what I could not control or handle."

"Then why stop?" Tiffany sneered.

"Because, like most addictions it is unhealthy for you. I hit rock bottom the scar I showed you was an accident someone startled me while I was cutting. I nearly cut to deep, it scared me and I got some help and cleaned up. I hope this program helps you ladies do the same. Feel free to ask me any questions now or anytime."

"How tall are you?" Sarah asked.

I chuckled I expected that question. "I am seven feet even, my mom is pretty tall and I guess my dad was too."

"You guess?" Tiffany raised and eye brow at me.

"My father died before I was born."

"Is that why you cut?" Chrissie asked.

"No my cutting was a stress relief and a control for my panic attacks."

"Panic attacks suck" Tiffany said bluntly.

I nodded "I have learned to control them without cutting."

"How?" Sarah asked.

"Many years and lots of practice."

"How long is your hair?" Chrissie asked.

"Not as long as I'd like it to be but it's getting there" I turned around and took down my hair for them.

"How long do you want it?" asked Sarah.

"My waist." Out of the corner of my eye I saw I had bled through the bandage and had a flash mental image of my arms covered in blood and cuts. I held the podium feeling really dizzy.

Dave gave me a look "All right, Alex?"

"Yeah, appena ho ottenuto una punta vertiginosa, io penso che stia ottenendo un freddo capo."

"What was that?" Tiffany glared at me.

"Alex speaks Italian and English; he said he just got a little dizzy and thinks he is getting a head cold." Dave said giving me another look but joining me at the podium to brace me. "Anymore questions for Alex, ladies?"

"Was it hard to stop?"

"Of course it was all habits or addictions are hard to give up, I relapsed many times and my mama fears I still will relapse. There are no guaranties like all addiction it's all in how bad you want to give it up, and it isn't picky with its victims age, size, shape, color, sexual orientation, ethnic background, social class, money, hair color, eye color it does not care."

"Well you can all ask Alex a hundred thousand things later on but right now Carrie and Carol are going to help you settle in to your new rooms and show you to your class rooms." Dave said getting a better grip on me. Once they had left Dave set me in a chair. "Do I need to call your uncle?"

"No! I mean I am fine I just have a huge fever that won't go away and I got a bit dizzy."

"Well I can't have you dizzy and working punch out and meet me in my office."

I did as I was told. Dave's office was cramped. Lots of papers everywhere, walkie-talkies, walkie-talkie batteries, battery chargers, his desk, a computer, I little fridge sat on top of a dresser, and he had a bed in there as well.

"Sit" He pointed at the bed shoving a thermometer in my mouth.

I obeyed, his bed looked comfy and I was tired.

The thermometer beeped he looked at it "101.6."

"It's gone down it was 102.8 yesterday."

"How has your asthma been?"

"Fine it is stress induced it wasn't so fine yesterday but it is ok now."

"Good, you just lay down and take a nap Ana will wake you when she is out."

I obeyed that happily, I was exhausted.

Ana woke me hours later "Honey she shook me. Alex, Alex wake up; you have a phone call."

"Huh I?" I took the phone not opening my eyes "Williams" I said barely awake.

"Alex, Cleveland Thompson here everything looks good health records, stable home, and a good job."

Stable home, I thought, what the . . . I shook my head waking up more sitting up still not ready to open my eyes as my brain switched on "Grazie, signore. I mean thank you, sir."

"Did I catch you at a bad time?"

"No sir, sorry, I was just resting my eyes waiting for Ana.

"Dave's room?" he laughed.

"Yes, sir" I laughed "I thought my mama was kidding about it when she said he lived here."

"I know" He laughed "Anyway if possible I would like to meet with you in the family room in a few minutes."

"Yes, of course."

"Good meet me with Ana and your sons in the family room I'm like three minutes from the center."

I must have dropped the phone because the next thing I knew Ana had said good bye and was hugging me. I finally opened my eyes. Paul was on the foot of the bed watching cartoons.

"How long . . ."

"About an hour after you he passed out on my desk." Ana brushed lose hair out of my eyes.

"Paul" I called to him.

"Daddy Alets" He jumped into my arms.

"How long has everyone else known?" I smiled hugging my son.

"The call came in right after you feel asleep" Dave said "I told Cleveland you were helping a child. When you and Paul get home tonight you thank your mothers for never sending you to a psychiatrist or a place like this the state has no record of you cutting and my records are not on paper."

I hugged him tight "Di ringraziamento(thank-you), di ringraziamento."

"Yeah, yeah don't do anything to make me regret it and speak English."

"Paul say thank you to Dave" Ana said as she took his hand.

"Thank-you E all Dave" Paul smiled and hugged his leg.

I laughed "Tomorrow, Paul, you and I are going to check in to pre k and speech programs. Thank you so very much again, Dave."

"Anything for you kiddo, but you better get going."

"Keys I need get my other son" I was ecstatic.

"I am going with you now walk before I give you a room here." Dave unlocked Anthony's door.

I ran in and scooped him up out of his desk chair "Guess what?"

"I'm five feet in the air" He looked at me "And you're late."

"Sorry I feel asleep in Dave's office please forgive me I have two things that will make it better."

"What?" He spotted Paul "Paul is here?"

"Yes apparently he has been here all day?"

"And no one told me?"

"No one told me either. Did you have a bad day?"

"No it was just boring."

"Did you go to consoling?"

"Yes, I went and look one less band-aide."

"Good I am very proud of you *my son*" I hugged him tight.

His eyes got wide "You mean I'm . . . they said . . . you're my . . ."

Paul answered for me "Daddy Alets" he hugged my leg.

I picked up Paul and hugged them tight as I could. "My boys, also my uncle and Paul will be here to see you Friday."

Dave pulled me out of Anthony's room "Let's go."

"Go where?" Anthony asked as I sat him down taking his hand.

"The family room" Ana smiled at him taking his other hand.

Mr. Thompson was already in the family room when we got there.

"Sorry" Dave said "We had a few mushy moments slowing us down."

"That is good I am glad." Mr. Thompson laughed "Well Alex they are yours, you can fill out all the paper work and stuff like that tomorrow. Dave pushed me all weekend to move things along. And everywhere I turned I heard only good things about you."

"That is good, so I can take Paul home today?"

"Absolutely."

"Anony?" Paul crawled down me hugging Anthony.

"I am sorry Paul; Anthony has to stay here until he gets better." Mr. Thompson smiled down at Paul.

I tensed and Anthony's grip tightened on my hand the look on Ana's face said he had done the same to hers "Don't worry Paul, Anthony will be home soon and you can still see him every Friday. Boys say thank-you to Mr. Thompson and Dave they worked very hard so we could be a family. Paul and I must leave to get Ana home in time for school."

"Thank-you Mr. Thompson, thank-you D hall Dave" Anthony said and Paul attempted to say.

I glared at Dave "I do not want you teaching my sons that nonsense" I laughed.

Dave chuckled "All my children call me that, even your mama called me that at one point."

"Yeah" Mr. Thompson laughed "Every time she broke his Godfather out."

"You know my mother?" I looked at him with intrigue.

"Of course I do that old coot and I use to work side by side I started right where you are now." He lifted his sleeve so only I could see there was a very old scar over his fore arm "Only back then they labeled you suicidal."

Dave winked at me "So, daddy how's it feel?"

"Great!" I smiled.

"Good you take your baby home, Miss Jessi is probably waiting to hug and cuddle him."

"Mama knows?"

"Not yet but she isn't stupid, boy; return my patient and get your girlfriend home before she is late for school."

"Yes sir," I said to Dave.

"And kiddo" Dave added "Take care of yourself I better not see you a minute before seven am Wednesday morning."

"Unless my son needs me" I laughed.

Paul came with just the clothes he was in, a car seat and a coat. I strapped the car seat and Paul in to the back seat, and then climbed in my seat.

Ana shot me a look.

"Yes dear?" I acknowledged the death glaring she gave me.

"You left our son with Kevin."

"Kevin won't hurt *our* son and *our* son will give Kevin's brother a whole new thought,"

"Mmhmm, spero così(I hope so)." She frowned at me "Ti amo(I love you), Alex."

I choked "I . . . I . . . L . . . Ti amo anche." I sighed in relief. I said it back even if it wasn't in English.

"Thank you, you are getting better." She looked back at Paul "Ready to go home?"

"Home?" He tilted his head.

"Daddy's home your new home" She smiled at him.

I got Ana home just in time for her to change and go to school. I unbuckled Paul as Kenny and Juliet pulled in to the drive way. "Hey Ken" I called to him "Come meet your nephew."

He ran over to me as I pulled Paul out of his seat and into my arms "Witch one?"

"This is Paul we need to go shopping later."

"Paul huh, he's so small."

"Of course he is small he just turn three last week, besides most things are small compared to me." I looked down at Kenny who barely came up to my shoulders. "Get everyone in the living room and I will wake him."

"Ok Al" He walked off in to the kitchen.

"Uncle Christian" I whispered, so only he heard me.

"Yes . . . awe."

"Shhhhh" I hissed, "Please stand in the door and block every ones view?"

"Assomiglio ad una parete a voi(I look like a wall to you)?" He raised his Eye brows standing in the door way for me.

"Do you really wish I answer if you look like a wall, sir?"

"No, you best not."

"Grazie" I set Paul on the floor and took off his coat placing it on my coat hook and his shoes placing them in the shoe rack, and shook him gently "Paul wake up we are home."

He blinked himself awake "Home."

"Yes, home, ready to meet everyone?"

"Every ones?" He stood up and looked around spotting Uncle Christian and clung to my leg.

I picked him up "Uncle Christian turn around" I whispered.

Uncle Christian turned "Hi Paul" He smiled.

Paul hid his face in my chest.

I heard Mom yelling at the beasts "Do I . . ."

"Hanno portato a casa un ratto guasto(They brought home a dead rat)" Uncle Christian laughed.

I shook my head and laughed "Then they can eat their dead rat for dinner." I called in to the living room "Is everyone ready?"

"Yes!" Everyone screamed back, Paul's eyes widened.

I brought him in to the living room. "Everyone this is il mio figlio(my son), Paul."

There was a blast of yeah, yippee, and go Alex; Paul clung to my leg.

"SILENZIO! (silence)" Uncle Christian growled "Paul has just woken up."

The room got deadly quiet "As I was saying this is my son Paul. Paul this giant you saw first is your great uncle Christian." Paul looked lost "He is my uncle."

Paul nodded and looked at him "You and daddy Alets is big."

Uncle Christian laughed "Yes, we are, his dad was *big* too."

I sat Paul down and he crawled over to Colt "Colts, Colts."

Colt laughed "Hi Paul miss me much?"

"Yes, miss Colts" Paul hugged him.

"Wow, he's small" Nick said

Paul jumped and I picked him back up "Paul that is your uncle Nick."

"N-Nick" Paul repeated. Paul spotted the beasts and looked back and forth between them and clung tighter to me.

"Gees" Colt laughed "You do that to all small children?" Mom shot him a look.

"Shush . . ."

". . . Colt . . ."

". . . We . . ."

". . . Didn't do . . ."

". . . Anything . . ."

". . . . He looked . . ."

". . . At us . . ." The beasts objected.

Paul looked at me like they were crazy. "I know Paul, I know but Mom still won't let me sell them." I hugged him "That is your uncle Christopher and your uncle Christian." He looked back at Uncle Christian. "It will get easier" I pointed at Christian "Christian is named after him" I pointed back at Uncle Christian.

He nodded slowly as if contemplating if the beasts were safe then looked at Mom "Grandma?" He asked.

"Yes Paul but you are a very special boy you have a grandma and a nana." I answered him.

"Ana?" He looked at me questioningly.

"Well yes you have an Ana but I said nana."

"Nana" He pointed at Mama.

"Yes, Paul, I am Nana" Mama smiled ear to ear "Can I have a hug?"

I sat Paul down and he ran over to Mom and crawled up her legs and hugged her "My grandma." Then he crawled over Uncle Chris to get to Mama and she hugged and kissed him.

I laughed "Mom, Ana told him all about you and Mama in the car until he fell asleep."

"Hey Paul what am I chopped liver" Uncle Chris laughed.

"C.J." Uncle Christian frowned laughing "Your looks will terrify the boy."

"Destra, gigante verde allegro(Right, jolly green giant)." Uncle Chris laughed at him.

Paul looked back and forth and then at Uncle Chris "Chop sliver?"

Christopher laughed "How old is he?"

"He barely speaks" Christian added.

"I three" Paul said defiantly.

Mama lifted him in to the air and he giggle "That fool that told you he was chopped liver is your great uncle Chris."

Paul looked lost again and came back to me.

"He just turned three last Thursday" I answered the beasts.

Paul pulled on my pant leg and pointed at Kenny "My uncle?"

"Yes that is your uncle Kenny and his girlfriend Juliet."

"Ooliet?" He crinkled his nose.

"Hey look he is smart too" Colt laugh, Mama shot him another look.

"Awe he is so cute" Juliet cooed.

Mama got this look that said she could look but not touch and so did Mom. Paul solved their problem all on his own "potty" He said holding himself dancing around.

"Of course right this way" Uncle Christian escorted him to the bathroom.

Mama stood up and hugged me "How was your day? Dave called and said you got sick?"

"Yeah I just got a bit dizzy during my speech, I blame the bite." I showed her my arm.

She shook her head "Kevin?"

"No, Curtis."

"I thought you were getting two?" Asked Kenny.

I rolled my eyes "They aren't cattle Ken and I did adopt both of them Anthony just has to stay at the center until he runs the program through."

Mama started to mutter than said "It is dinner are you hungry, Alex?"

"Yes, I am."

"Daddy" Paul asked "What's super?"

"Steak, peas, carrots, mashed potatoes and gravy" Uncle Christian answered him, setting his plate in front of him.

"Thank you, Uncle Christian but I could have done that" I said.

"I prepare dinner almost every night, do I not?"

"Yes, sir you make dinner every night" I gulped.

"And do I not serve it every night?"

"Yes sir, you do."

"Then I shall serve him as well, is that clear?"

"Yes sir, crystal clear" I looked down at my plate my meat was cut as well, I looked up at him.

"I love you kiddo, we can talk later."

I smiled he knew he didn't make a large fuss or announce it to the world but he made sure I knew, he understood.

After dinner I put Paul in a pair of Colt's old pajamas they were too big so I took them off and hemmed them, then put them and his coat back on.

"Where we go? We go home?" He asked.

"Ciò è casa, This is home" I repeated it in English after dinner it occurred to me that Paul was going to have to learn Italian or I was finally going to have to make my English stronger after all these years of fighting so hard not to. "We are going to get you a bed and some clothes, books, and a few toys."

"Shopping" Paul squealed.

"Yeah, shopping" I lifted him up he started flipping my pony tail. "That's my hair bud."

"I know it long" He giggled.

Out side I sat him down Uncle Chris and Uncle Christian had moved one of the twin beds to the porch to move into storage until he was old enough for it and Uncle Chris was now building a book shelf.

"Chop sliver" Paul smiled.

I laughed "I think he likes you, Uncle Chris."

"I hope so, he is smart. Here" He handed me two hundred dollars "Get him some books and don't tell your mothers I did that and don't you dare argue with me."

"Yes sir, Thank-you. Paul say thank you."

"Thank you Chop sliver"

I laughed "We will work on that" I buckled him in to his car seat

"I am coming with you" Uncle Christian said sliding in the back next to Paul.

"Er ok, does Mama know?"

"Yes I would not leave without telling her, she told me to have fun and besides that your mothers are perfectly capable of taking care of your brothers and themselves" He answered making a face at Paul's car seat. "I don't like it I will fix it."

I shook my head "They are going to spoil you, Paul." Kenny climbed in the passenger seat "In the back Romeo, Ana is sitting there."

"Ana" Paul squealed.

"Wow he is . . ."

". . . Excitable" The beasts showed up behind me.

"You two wish to go?" I acknowledged there evil existence.

"Oh no, he needs Crayons and Paints, Crayola only" Christopher handed me a ten.

"An easel brushes and paper as well." Christian added handing me a twenty.

"Er, thanks guys but you really . . ."

"Shut up Alex . . ."

". . . He's our nephew." They laughed at me running off to their bikes.

I shrugged "Ok Paul lets go get Ana."

"Ana!" he squealed.

With what I needed at Baby World I was glad for Kenny's discount and that the book store and Wal-Mart were close by. Kenny and I headed straight for beds. While Ana and Uncle Christian took Paul to car seats; despite the fact that I had argued that the car seat he came with was perfectly fine. To prove his point Uncle Christian had removed the seat and placed it in the Salvation Army box.

"Fire truck right?" Kenny asked finally finding one.

"Sì" I grunted helping him lift it off the top shelf and in to the cart.

"Siete buoni? Siete bianco del fantasma(are you good you are ghost white)."

"I am not ghost white!" I objected trying to deny being pale "And I am fine I just can't shake this fever.

"I am sorry."

We met Uncle Christian back at the car. Paul had a brand new car seat with dinosaurs on it and was holing a stuffed puppy. I shook my head.

"Hush, boy, I spoil whom I choose."

"Yes sir" I sighed arguing with him about whom he should and shouldn't spoil was a head ache waiting to happen. I put the bed in the trunk. Uncle Christian strapped in the new car seat. I shook my head again.

"He originally wanted the fire truck one but it had the same issue as that other one poor locking device I don't like it, not safe" Uncle Christian muttered.

I sighed "Come on Paul lets go to the book store, they close soon."

"Books, books" His eyes lit up.

"What's your friend's name?" I asked in reference to his puppy.

"Teddy" he hugged it.

Uncle Christian stifled a laugh and mouthed to me that he would explain it to me later.

In the book store I stood in front of shelf of books. So far I had selected him the complete sets of Mercer Meyer's Little Critter, Marc Brown's Arthur, The Bernstein bears and the Froggy books. I was down to twenty dollars and having selection trouble. I chose <u>Where the wild things are</u> and a few Leo Leoni books. As I was headed for the check out Ana dropped another stack of books on to the cart. I gave her a look.

"Shut up Alex, as far as I am concerned that is my son too" She clucked her tongue at me.

"Pengin, pengin" Paul pointed at the top book.

I looked down at the book "<u>Tacky the Penguin</u>" I read the title to him.

We paid for everything it came to two hundred and sixty dollars with the sales and Mama's discount.

"Who is your friend?" Ana's uncle Ken asked me of Paul.

"This is my . . ."

"Our" Ana gave me a look "Son Paul the adoption is final tomorrow."

"Ah yes JJ did say something about that" He laughed "You have fun, Alex, and tell your uncle Christian deep breaths and lots of chess games."

"Yes sir." I smiled "Good night."

"Good night you two and Kiddo take care of yourself." He stopped me as Ana and Paul left and handed me sixty back "On the house."

I shook my head and handed Ana her money back. Paul was more than happy with his new books. He sat in his new car seat playing with his puppy listing to Kenny read his penguin book.

"Wal-Mart bound" I sighed.

"Pengin, pengin" Paul bounced in his seat.

I smiled "Oh, Uncle Christian, Mr. Wittson says to tell you deep breaths and lots of chess games."

"Oh how I despise that game" He laughed.

We started in clothes with four packs of underwear. One Thomas the tank, two incredible hulk, and one Looney Toons. We got four pack of socks destined to be lost in the sock buck like every other sock in the house. I got him two dress suites and an entire winter wardrobe including ski pants, hat, scarf and gloves. From there we went to bedding to get sheets and blankets. He chose an incredible hulk set. The incredible hulk had become popular again due to a recent release of the remake. After bedding we went to toys. First I picked up his easel, a handful of coloring books, a big box of Crayola crayons, a thing of Crayola poster paints, a painting apron, brushes and a large pad of paper. Adding it up my brothers new there prices. Then Paul picked a bunch of cars, trucks and dinosaurs. I added some board games age appropriate for a three year old. Then we went to hygiene for a tooth brush, bubble bath, kids soap and shampoo. After a fifteen minute argument with Uncle Christian over proper tooth brushes we back tracked to shoes for sneakers, dress shoes, and snow boots; when he got older I would get him work boots.

We got home around nine, Paul had fallen asleep in the car I carried him in. His bookshelf was finished and in his room. I turned on his light and laid him in the twin bed that would be Anthony's. Then I went back down and grabbed his books and the Wal-Mart bags. Kenny and Uncle Christian were already assembling his new bed. Anna helped me carry some of the bags which we set on the kitchen table to dig out the bedding. I brought the bedding into put it on the bed. I put the sheets on and Kenny moved Paul. I tucked him in, kissed him good night and shut out his light. Kenny retired to the living room and I to the kitchen. Uncle Chris had fallen asleep on the couch with his guitar again; Uncle Christian was now trying to move the guitar and or Uncle Chris and there was a note from Mom and Mama saying they had gone to my Godfather's and would be home by ten. I unpacked Paul's toys first taking off all the tags and wrapping, they had all been Uncle Christian approved, I stacked them neatly in one pile. Next I did his books separating them by their set, author, and alphabetical order neatly writing in the top inside front cover corner this book belongs to Paul Williams. Then his clothes pulling the tags off and folding and separating them in to neat stacks. I placed his shoes back in there box and into the shoe rack. His ski pants and coat now laced with his hat and new mittens went into the hall closet, his toys went into his room neatly as Uncle Christian was not done building his toy box, his clothes into their respective draw or closet hanger. The easel and art supplies I left in the kitchen with a note saying "This is your area, double trouble, have fun with your nephew—love Alex." Then went back in to his room and took off his ratty sneakers and old coat. I threw the coat out it was stained and ripped so I couldn't even put it in the salvation army box, the shoes I gave to Psycho, Mama's dog was as weird as his name and nothing like the dog we had when I was little. I looked at Kenny's iguana Andrieos; it rolled its eyes at me.

"Want to stop moving, Honey?" Ana said rubbing my back as I redid my bank book. Then I noticed his dog he called teddy; and went and put it in his room, on the foot of his bed and made sure he was still breathing.

"Alex" Mama said as I sat back down "Come è andato(How was it)?"

I jumped sky high relaxing again when I saw it was only Mama "Benissimo(fine)."

"Good I am going to hug Paul" Mom said headed down to his room.

"Don't wake him" I called after her.

"We won't" Mama kissed my head following her.

I went back to my "to do" list for tomorrow, enjoying my back rub. Mom went upstairs to check the boys then woke Uncle Chris and told him to go to bed. Then she sat next to me. "How was your day?" She asked.

"LONG," I laughed, "And yours?"

"Ok I played phone tag with my editor and publisher; I watched your Mama draw like it was the easiest thing in the world."

I smiled "I am glad you had a good day Mom."

Mama came out of Paul's room glaring at Uncle Chris who had just stood up. "Christopher James" She growled at him "I told you not to leave those nasty work boots out of the shoe holder I just nearly fell."

He let out a long audible sigh of relief "Sorry JJ" He winced "Oh hey kiddo, Paul in his room?"

"Sì, è addormentato sano(yes, sleep is healthy)" I said.

"Ok well I am going to bed, too" He headed towards the stairs half asleep.

Mama laughed "Wrong way old man you don't sleep up there any longer."

"Huh" Uncle Chris looked up "Oh yeah sorry" He yawned heading towards their room.

Mama shook her head and Mom rolled her eyes at him.

Uncle Christian laughed sitting down to comb Mamas hair. "Deep breaths and chess games."

Mama looked at him "Did you see Kork today?"

"Yes he says to tell you hi. Respirazioni profonde e giochi di scacchi(deep breaths and chess games)." He laughed repeating himself. He finished Mama's hair and went to bed.

"Oh I am sorry here let me wa . . ."

Ana cut me off "I am staying here tonight remember?"

"Oh yeah" I yawned.

"I think we should head to bed though, its nearing midnight."

"Ok few minutes baby doll" I went back over my bank book "Mama how's my Godfather?"

"Fine dear, Taylor needed help with Tavi, A.J wasn't even home"
She said.

"Ok, Mama di buona note(good night), mamma di buona notte"
I hugged and kissed my mothers good night and showed Ana up to
the room I shared with Kenny. I shut the divider striped to my boxers,
climbed in bed, set my alarm clock and wrapped Ana in my arms.

CHAPTER 7

PAINT, WALL PAPER AND PAPER WORK

WHEN I SMASHED THE ALARM off and woke myself the next morning I found the note Ana had left me. 'Morning honey, don't worry I didn't over sleep. I will see you after work. Good luck today. Love you—Ana'. I could hear Kenny moving around his side of the room "Good morning" I called over to him.

"Morning" He called back.

I grabbed my pajama pants and threw them on, then grabbed my dress suit and headed down stairs.

"Woo woo" Paul was sitting on the kitchen floor playing with his fire trucks.

I grabbed the rest of the Wal-Mart bags removing the soap, shampoo, bubble bath, boats and tooth brush. "Morning Mom" I kissed her cheek, she was stirring her coffee and looked like she had just woken up as well. "Mama in the shower?"

"Where else would she be, Sweetie?" She laughed.

I nodded in agreement "How long has he been up?"

"None of your business" Uncle Christian said handing me a plate of waffles.

"Has he eaten?"

"Yes he had waffles with me. Now stop your worrying and eat your food." Uncle Christian scooped up the bath stuff and Paul, "Bath time goober."

I shook my head "I see they are having quality time."

"All morning" Mama laughed coming out of the bathroom off her and Mom's bedroom.

I stood to greet her "Morning Mama" I hugged her and kissed her cheek. "You should have woken me."

"Your uncle did the same with you boys. It will not kill him to spend time with la mia roccia(my rock), do you feel deprived because your uncle . . ."

"No, Mama, I just don't want anyone thinking I can't take care of him on my own."

"We know you can, Honey" Mom said "Relax, eat your breakfast and get ready for your appointment with Mr. Thompson."

When I got out of the shower Uncle Christian had already gotten him into his dress suit. He looked so cute in his suit, little dress shoes and clip on tie witch he was stretching up to his nose and making silly faces into. He was sitting with Mama in her rocker and she was reading a Clifford book to him.

"Daddy" Paul ran and hugged my legs and ran back to Mama before I could pick him up and hug him back. I slipped my dress shoes on and grabbed my coat and his new coat.

"Come on Paul, time to go" I called to him.

"Go?" He made a face like he might cry, but crinkled his nose instead.

"Yes go, andare" I said it in Italian for him. "We have to go see Mr. Thompson this morning, then we are surprising Ana for lunch and we need paint and or wall paper for your room."

There was a deep look of thought on his face "Ok" He smiled and ran over to me.

I put his jacket on then mine. "Ok Mom we are leaving, Mama, do you need me to pick up anything?"

"The list will be with your aunt Amy when you get to the hard ware store" Mama smiled "You boys have a good day."

The stack of paper work on Mr. Thompson's desk was intimidating at the very least.

I gulped "Morning sir."

"Good morning Alex, Good morning Paul." Mr. Thompson smiled "Aren't you looking sharp today, Paul."

"Good morning" Paul smiled "Daddy shopped."

"Say thank-you Paul, Mr. Thompson gave you a compliment."

"Thank you" Paul beamed.

I smiled "He liked shopping my uncle Christian has been spoiling him." I picked Paul up and set him in the chair next to mine.

"Well Ana has already signed everything she needed to sign this morning. I was out there picking fun at Bruno because it's his birthday you know and I figured I would just have her sign it then instead of after she got out of work. Bruno definitely has his hands full with that Buddy."

"Yes, definitely" I agreed slightly lost then I caught on Ana insisted in signing the mother slot, I thought she was kidding but she wasn't.

"Ok let's try and make this quick and painless" Mr. Thompson smiled "Before you start are you sure this is what you want this isn't temporary Alex, I didn't want to say it in front of Anthony" I quickly covered Paul's ears if it wasn't meant for Anthony it defiantly wasn't meant for Paul. "But their mother signed her rights over willingly last Wednesday."

I nodded he didn't know how much that relaxed me "I am positive where do I sign."

He smiled "Everywhere there is an 'X' just sign or fill out the area and don't look so scared most of that stack is doctor and school records."

I looked at the stack one of the file folders said Paul Michael Kingston it was thick and looked like the kind you saw at a doctor's office I didn't know if it being thick was good or bad. There were a lot of "X's". About half way through the stack of papers Paul started to get antsy so I gave him my key chain to play with, there was about as many keys as there was "X's" so I hoped that they would hold his attention.

"When I had finally finished all the paper work and everything was final. I fixed the names on their file folders to read Williams and put their adoption papers and their birth certificates in the glove box. "Ready to go see Ana?"

"ANA" He crinkled his nose "Yep."

I laughed swinging into McDonalds drive through "Two number Threes and a chicken nugget kid's meal" I said to the speaker.

"Two trees and a chicken . . ."

"No" I yelled "TWO NUMBER THREES AND A CHICKEN NUGGET KID'S MEAL."

"Oh, sorry what would you like to drink with those?"

"Chocolate milk for the kid's meal, a vanilla shake and a coke."

"Sorry, just pull up to the window please."

"Fine" I sighed.

The kid in the window I knew, he had been my best friend in high school but I couldn't remember who he was because I had not kept in contact with anyone except Ana for about three years and he had gone in to boot camp the second we graduated. "Sorry about that Alex they are supposed to be fixing that. What was the order again?"

"Yeah, it's ok, no problem. Two number threes one with a vanilla shake one with coke and a chicken nugget happy meal with chocolate milk."

"Got it all this time, $14.68."

I handed him a twenty "Thanks" I said as he handed me the fries and kid's meal, trying to put a name with the face.

"Burgers are coming. So how is Ana? You two still together?"

I shook my head "Yeah we are still together that's our son in the back adoption was final this morning."

"Sweet what's his name?"

"Paul, he's three."

"Cool" He nodded "Debbie and I are still together."

"That's good." I tried to remember who he was I knew the voice.

"You don't remember me do you?"

"Sorry" I blushed "I mean I know who you are just can't remember what to call you today no sleep and yeah . . ."

"It's ok no one has recognized me since I got back. Wilson Needlemeyre."

"Wilson!" I looked at him shocked "Wow."

"Yeah I suppose you wouldn't recognize me."

"Well hell man, you grew about a two feet lost your face metal and wow you're a blonde?"

He laughed "Army will do that to you. Well, here is your meals give me a call some time now that I am back, especially if you find Sam."

"Again?" I shook my head "I will look for him."

"I whipped into my parking spot at the center. I pulled Paul out and grabbed the food.

"Sorry Alex, I can't let you in" Harry smiled "Dave's orders, you need to stay home today."

"I have Ana's lunch."

"Alright Alex, but Dave's not going to be happy, Ana is down in the D-hall, if Dave . . ."

I growled "Harry come non è Dave sta per accorgersi di me(how is Dave not going to notice me)."

"Fine, fine" He said looking terrified at what I might have said as Paul and I pushed past him.

"Ana, Ana, Ana" Paul toddled down the hall driving his happy meal car down the wall.

"Alex!" Dave jumped as I entered his office "Harry was . . ."

"Ed ho detto Harry che eravamo qui per avere pranzo con Ana(I told harry we were here to have lunch with Ana)."

"ANA!" Paul squealed.

"I see you went shopping" Dave smiled inspecting Paul in his new suit and dress shoes. "And more like bullied Harry I already spoke to him." He shook a walkie-talkie at me "Don't bully people with a second language" He frowned at me.

"I had to if I didn't my parents would have. Well I will see you tomorrow we better eat before the fries get any colder. And telling him there was no way you wouldn't notice us is not bullying."

"No growling is" He shook his head at me.

Paul toddled back down the hall talking a mile a minute to Ana and driving his car over the floor and wall.

"Next time wake me, Honey." I hugged her and kissed the top of her head.

"Ana" Kevin said peeking around the side of the couch.

"Huh, Kevin, what are you doing here?" She looked at him startled.

"Has classes stared back up?"

"No, why aren't you in the cafeteria?"

"I'm sorry I know this isn't behaving but Buddy was harassing me so I came in here to avoid him."

"No it is ok I would rather you do this than the other" I said offering him some fries "We will walk you back to class when we are done eating."

"Thanks Alex," He said pulling books off the book shelf.

Ana and I talked while we ate. Paul ran back and forth between his food and Kevin; highly fascinated by Kevin's ability to build with blocks. When I was done I cleared the garbage and took Kevin back to his class. He was a bit early but it was better than putting him back in the cafeteria with Buddy. On the way back to the family room I filed room change papers for Kevin to be in with Anthony.

"Daddy, Ana home soon" Paul greeted me.

I smiled and looked at the clock "Yep two hours, she will get home in time to help with your room, but we have to go to the hardware store and get the paint and Uncle Chris wanted me to get some stain for your bookshelf and toy boxes."

"Chop sliver" He crinkled his nose.

"Yes, Paul *chopped liver*" I laughed.

We hugged Ana good bye and he drove his car back along the wall and out to the car. The hardware store was on the other side of town.

"Hi Alex it's all right here, your mom called and had me get it ready because they changed a few things."

"Thanks Aunt Amy; how much?" I looked at the sixty mom had given me.

"Fifty four, She says to go over to the carpet place and pick up the order under Williams and she will pay you back when you get home."

I paid "Thanks Auntie, see you later."

I put the paints and stains in the car and we walked over to the carpet place to run out some of Paul's excess energy. Mom had me picking up a car mat rug like I had when I was little.

I took off my coat and shoes putting them where they went then lifted Paul so he could put his coat on the hook that had been added just for his coat. I went to his room and grabbed one of his new out fits and changed him out of his dress suit, then changed myself in to jeans and a t-shirt and threw the dirty clothes in the hamper. When you grow up in New England wearing a t-shirt in November and December is normal, or so my mothers said I just thinks it means I run hot.

"NANA, NANA" Paul rushed around the kitchen and living room looking for Mama.

"Paul" She called to him from his room.

Uncle Christian was taping plastic over his bed, toys, and everything we could that we didn't want to get paint on. Uncle Chris had helped Uncle Christian finish Paul's toy box it had dinosaur frames and it was cute. Paul spotted it and went ballistic digging through it like something was missing.

"What are you looking for, Hun?" Mom asked him.

"My uck, the big camion" He looked completely undone but he sounded so adorable.

"Over here, Paul" Uncle Christian said "All the fire trucks are over here in their garage."

I looked where Paul ran too; Uncle Chris had made a fire station for his fire trucks. I smiled at the site of him playing.

"Paint?" Mama said.

"Oh yeah, sorry I left it in the kitchen I'll go get it" I ran back to the kitchen as someone knocked on the door. "Oh, hi honey" I hugged and kissed Ana letting her in.

"Mm, dear miss me much?" She teased.

"Maybe, come see Paul's room."

"Hey Mama" Ana hugged her "Looks good."

"Oh, don't get her going Sweetie, she will give you a list of mistakes" Mom laughed.

I lifted Paul's toy chest to move it in to the hall so we could lay the new rug. Paul automatically went crazy pushing my legs back and crying "Noooo, noooo my good boy those is me toys."

I just looked at him shocked "Yes you are a very good boy we are just moving your toys to put down your new rug." I gave Uncle Christian his toy box and picked him up, I held him close until he calmed down, then I wiped his tears and his nose. I showed him where his toy box would be until we were done with his room.

Around three Nick, Colt, thing one and thing two came in and sat at the breakfast bar to do their homework.

Paul went straight over to Nick practically cramming the truck up Nick's nose. "Play uck!" Paul demanded.

"After my homework little man" Nick smiled at him.

Paul pouted.

At four Kenny came in, Mom and Mama were half way done with Paul's room. Ken plopped his ball cap down on Paul. "Hi little guy what's up?"

"Ire uck, broom, broom. Whoo, whoo." Paul drove his truck in circles on the kitchen floor."

"Cool" Kenny smiled at him. "Mom I'm home, I'm taking a shower."

"Ok, hon." Mom called from Paul's room.

Ana laughed as she helped me carry the dresser back in to Paul's room.

"Shower two" I said.

"Three" Uncle Christian stifled a laugh "He was home at noon."

"Well I can't complain that he isn't clean" I said.

"Honey you only shower once, twice a day tops and you aren't stinky or dirty" Ana looked at me.

"I know he is just a bit odd."

By dinner the room was almost done Mom and Mama had just a few more things to paint. Dinner was pasta. Uncle Chris came in and set his tool box by the back door.

"Chop sliver" Paul ran and jumped in to his arms.

"Hi little guy, I told you I'd be back. How are those fire trucks?"

Paul climbed down and dragged Uncle Chris to his room to show him the trucks. "Play ucks!"

"We can play after dinner, bug."

"Ok" Paul climbed up in to his chair with his new booster seat Kenny got him after he nearly fell out of the chair at breakfast. "SIPPY" He squealed when he saw his new plate, cup, bowl and silver wear set Mom had gotten him.

"Wow talk . . ."

". . . About excitable."

"Does he . . ."

". . . always squeal?" The twins held their ears.

"Sorry guys" I said "He seems to like certain things a lot more than others starting with Uncle Chris and fire trucks."

Ana laughed "Well I . . ."

"Sit" Mama said "It's dinner time and don't try saying you have classes today I already spoke to your father."

"Yes Mama" She blushed.

After dinner we had Uncle Chris' and Mama's birthday cake; no one really talked about or celebrated Mama's birthday. The only reason there was cake is because Uncle Christian instead on it. Uncle Christian also said it was safer just to let her pretend her birthday wasn't important or not there at all he said it caused her a lot of bad memories; so we just enjoyed cake and gave her, her gifts and Uncle Chris his.

She hugged Paul tight in a bear hug "I have the best present anyone could ever ask for" She smiled "My family I don't need anything else."

At seven-thirty I scooped Paul up his room finally done I said "Bed time lets go read some books."

"Ucks, ucks." He started to cry.

"You can play with your trucks tomorrow you and Uncle Christian can play all day while Ana and I work."

"Anony come home?"

"Not yet but soon. I know you miss him" I sighed. I laid him on his bed, tucked him in, and grabbed four random books. He fell asleep in the middle of the third book; I put all the books back in there right space. I checked to make sure he was breathing that his pajamas weren't too tight, and that he was covered good.

"Worry wart" Uncle Christian said as I sat back down at the kitchen table.

"Me? Yes" I laid my head on the table.

"No your Mom but that fits you as well. She thinks your Mama is getting sick again."

"No Mama isn't getting sick, she doesn't sound like a space man yet" I laughed.

"That's what I said" Uncle Chris laughed.

"Is my nephew sleeping?" Kenny asked.

"Yes" I sighed "He has more energy than Colt did."

"Colt was nothing compared to Kenny or even worse the twins." Uncle Christian laughed "Kenny may look like and shower as much as your mama, but those twins are your mama straight through to their evil little grins JJ was not an angel."

"Mama was mean" Ana asked?

"Mean nothing she was evil, constantly up to no good right along with your mother, Ana."

"My foot you just couldn't keep up with me" Mama laughed.

"Potrei (I could)" Uncle Chris smiled evilly.

"Well yeah" Mama laughed "You were helping me."

Just then someone knocked on the back door. Mama answered it "Henry what a pleasant surprise, how are you?"

"Hi JJ, I am good and you?" He said.

"I am fine just listing to Christian tell Alex how evil I was as a kid."

"Not worse than Mike and I" He laughed. "May we come in?" He asked, helping David up the last step.

"Of course" Mama stepped back letting them in.

"Sorry Daddy" Ana said "I . . ."

"It is ok Ana I knew where you were." He turned towards Mom "He looks more and more like his daddy every day, Tina."

"We know Henry, some days it hurts" Mom smiled slightly.

"How are you, Chris?" He asked.

"Alright mate and you Hen?" He answered.

"I'm good I will be better once the season passes you know, but other than that I am good. Keep asking Alex when the wedding is, but he won't tell me. Yet I hear I have two grandsons?"

"Well Sir," I gulped "They are my boys . . ."

"Ours" Ana insisted "The adoption was finally today, Daddy"

"Well then where are my grandsons?" He smiled; I noticed Ana had her dad's smile.

"Anthony can't leave the center, Sir, and Paul in his room asleep, Sir" I gulped.

"May I peak at him?"

"Of course. He's such a doll." Mama said showing him down the hall.

I sighed "Sorry, honey your dad scares me."

"It's ok dear, my uncle Kyle scares me" She smiled at me.

Uncle Christian sighed laughing to himself "Respirazioni profonde e giochi di scacchi(deep breaths and chess games)." He sighed again "Ana your uncle Kyle is harmless and Alex, Henry was one of the first people to hold you when you were born he would never hurt you. He took a deep breath "Christian fancy a chess game?"

"Sure Uncle Christian" He beamed.

"Hey you fool that's my pencil" Christopher growled at him.

"Oops" Christian switched pencils with him.

I don't know how they could tell everything those two owned was identical and over half of their actions too. I sat down to watch some TV with Ana while our parents talked about things that made no sense to me. Colt was playing a video game, Nick was curled up on the floor reading a book, Kenny was on the phone and Christopher was drawing. There was already a pile of crumpled up paper balls near Nick's back but not like they were being thrown at him more like he was placing them there by himself. A paper ball launched towards the wall, Nick stuck his arm up and caught it placing it in the pile. I shook my head and picked up a paper ball, he was drawing Nick. I hugged Ana and headed down stairs to play my keyboard and drums.

"Mama" Ana said "If Daddy says ok may I stay the night with Alex, again I am worried about him."

"Of course dear, you are always welcome here," Mama said "But I promise you Al is fine. He is just down there with his key board or my drums."

Daddy?" Ana pouted.

"Ana you are almost twenty-two years old you don't need my permission but I appreciate you telling me where you will be."

"Thanks Daddy I'm going to run and get some more clean clothes."

I had the amp on as high as I could and was playing with my eyes closed, so I didn't hear Ana come in. The down stairs was nearly an apartment unto its own it was just missing a kitchen. My parents used it as a studio, entry hall, laundry room, and storage.

"Ehm" Ana got my attention "You realize its ten dear."

"Sorry, baby here I'll walk you . . ."

"I'm staying the night again. If you wish?"

"Of course I do" I stood and wrapped her tight in my arms breathing in the sweet scent of her shampoo. I suppose in this case my height was a good thing.

"What were you playing? I was gorgeous."

"Una canzone di amore che il vostro padre mi ha insegnato quando eravamo piccolo(a love song your father taught me when we were little)."

"It is gorgeous."

"Well I was thinking of you while I was playing. Let's go up to Mama, she'll be worried.

"She has beautiful hair" Mama looked at Ana as I combed her hair. "I just wonder where the brown came from, Henry."

"Oh, don't start that" Mr. Wittson laughed. "Marc is in Germany and I do not think Christian can chase Chris if he freaks out."

Everyone out in the kitchen laughed

"Please Hen" Uncle Chris laughed "I won't freak out."

"No we honestly don't know why her hair was brown. Well, dad's always was and so was Robert's, Nalanie's dad, you remember him Jess don't you? But . . ."

Mama nodded.

"Mine, Mom's, Nalanie's, was blonde even granddad had blonde hair."

"I'm telling you it is all that dye you two put in your hair especially you" Mama laughed at him.

Ana's dad laughed "Now it is barely there, well we had better get going Davie and I have an early day tomorrow" He stood and hugged and kissed the top of Mama's head. "You take good care of her Christian" He laughed and flipped Uncle Christian a quarter.

"I told you I don't work for money" Uncle Christian laughed flipping the quarter back.

"Your nutso, man."

"I may be "nutso" but at least *my* hair was never two toned."

Ana's dad laughed "Good times" He sighed "Good times" For a second he looked like he was going to cry. Then he said come on Dave lets go home."

"No, go without me I will get up later." David said, he was on the floor flipping through the video game rack.

"David James I said we are going home." Ana's dad helped him up from the floor.

"Bye Henry" Mama said "If you hear from Ky tell him we send our love."

"He is still overseas still, I am hoping they send him home soon and not in a body bag."

Mama laughed "He'll be fine, Hen."

"Happy birthday C.J., happy birthday Jess and J.J. you can be angry all you want" With that he left.

I was lost Mom and Mama never talked about their pasts or whom they were friends with. All I knew was this had been Mama and Uncle Chris' house since they were eleven.

Mama stood up and smiled "I guess it was a pretty happy birthday" She hugged Mom.

"Mamma notte(night), Mama notte, zio (uncle)Chris, zio Christian notte, notte" I yawned.

"Night Alex" They all said.

I wrapped my arms tight around Ana "Penny for your thoughts Alexander?" She leaned up and kissed me.

"Infanzie delle mie madri(my mothers' childhoods)."

Ana laughed "Good night sweetie. Set your alarm and tomorrow talk to Dave or my dad about your mothers' childhoods."

I sat up right "What do you know that I don't?"

"Non molto, solo che avrebbero, buona note(nothing much, just that they would know, good night)."

I set my alarm. I was getting use to the whole sleeping with and sharing bathroom space with Ana. I held her close to me and drifted right to sleep.

CHAPTER 8
UNEXPECTED VISIT

As if Monday had not been enough Wednesday started by helping Bruno get Buddy into the time out room.

"They don't pay me enough" I said holding my eye.

"Kid you are a glutton for punishment working these halls" Bruno laughed.

"Nope" I said "Just doing my job."

He shook his head "What is your rotation for today?"

"I don't know only thing in my folder was a 'see me note' from Dave."

"Joy oh joy, you better get going then."

I knocked on Dave's office door and walked in "Dave you wanted to see me?"

"I was wondering if you would like a few more hours and a permanent group of kids?" He asked not looking up from his paper.

"Most definitely" I said "For the first time in my life my bank account is less than $55,000.95"

"Awe poor baby" He laughed handing me my rounds.

I walked into the hall reading my rounds 7:30 to 12:30 with Kevin, 12:30 to 4:30 with Kyle and 4:30 to 7:30 with Tiffany. Wow, definitely hour increase and it didn't affect Ana's hours either which was very good.

"I found Kevin in class sitting happily with Kyle. "Hi Kev" I smiled.

"Alex!" They greeted me and hugged me; their class had not started yet.

I hugged them back "How are you guys today?"

"Good" Kyle smiled.

"Ok" Kevin sighed "Who are you with today?"

"Well" I sighed "I'm with you until 12:30, then I'm with Kyle until 4:30 and then I'm with one of the new young ladies until I go home."

I got another set of hugs then they sat back down for class. Kevin sat paying close attention to his lessons. They were having their math lesson first, today. I sat and watched. Kyle kept checking to make sure I was still there. Halfway through the class one of the boys from the B-hall vomited on his desk, it wasn't self induced but, it was nasty and disrupted the class. Kevin looked at me.

"What is wrong?" I asked stopping him from leaving his seat.

"I told him Alex, I told him not to eat the eggs. I need fresh air before I'm . . ."

"Ok I got you; my Ana is the same way." I told the teacher and took Kevin out into the hallway.

"Thanks" He said "I told Hans not to eat the eggs today, they were looking kind of green themselves."

I smiled "And what did you eat?"

"Cheerios, I always have cheerios, I trust the cheerios."

I laughed; Hans came out holding his stomach, "Alright Hans?"

"Mrs. Peer wishes to know if you and Kevin can escort me to the nurse?"

"Of course, you ok?"

"I don't think I should have eaten those eggs" Hans smiled sheepishly.

"I told you." Kevin accused "Cereal, that's the only safe breakfast."

I laughed.

The nurse's office was on the far side of the building. Personally I thought it was asinine to put it so far from the kids. We had to stop once along the way as Hans felt he was going to vomit again.

"Morning" Ms. Perez greeted us. "Who is my patient?"

"Me ma'am" Hans sighed "My eggs made a comeback on my desk."

Ms. Perez looked at me.

I smiled "He was answering a question and it just came up, their teacher already has moved them and called for a janitor."

"Alright, well he will be fine. Mr. Williams get Master Roberts back to class.

At 12:30 I switch to watching Kyle nothing really changed but the person I was watching. I was very impressed with Kevin; he had behaved all week so far. I would have to speak to his consoler again. Kyle ate his lunch in silence.

"What's wrong?" I asked.

"They said I am getting a new roommate." He sighed "And that Curtis is going back to the C-hall."

"That's not so bad is it?"

"What if it's someone worse like Buddy?" He winced as Buddy sat down in between him and Kevin.

"Buddy find a new seat, please" I said.

"Why?" He said tauntingly.

"Because I asked you to and because that is my seat."

"Well you find a new seat."

"Buddy, find yourself a new seat or you will find yourself in trouble."

He made a face and moved to a table of girls.

"Thanks Alex" Kevin said.

"Your welcome" I sat in between them so no one else tried to get any bright ideas. "So Kyle, other than the roommate thing, how are things going?"

"Good I get to go home this weekend" He smiled from ear to ear.

"How are your grades?"

"Ok, Kevin has been helping me with my math."

"That's good."

Before the start of their afternoon lessons I made a quick call to check on Paul.

"Come è? Non hai fiducia mia capacità di prendersi cura di (How is it? Do you not trust my ability to care for) . . ."

"No, sorry Uncle Christian, I just don't want him to be too much trou . . ."

"Non sarà mai troppo disturbo, è chiaro(he will never be too much trouble is that clear)!"

"Yes sir" I laughed "Give him a hug and kiss for me" I hung up my cell.

"Who did you call?" Kyle asked me.

"My uncle to check on my son."

"What's his name?"

"My uncles name is Christian, My sons' names are Paul and Anthony."

"How old are they?"

"They are six and three."

"Oh."

Kevin smiled and showed Kyle another math equation. "Kyle, Anthony is the little boy down by the time out room."

"Wow! Really Alex, that boy's your son?" Kyle said.

"Yep" I said. "The adoption was final yesterday."

"After lessons I took Kyle back to his room and helped him with his homework. Around three thirty Jared came in with Curtis telling him to collect all his personal belongings.

"Hello Alex" Jared addressed me. "I hope we haven't distracted you, Curtis is moving back to the C-hall."

"I heard; Kyle is worried he won't get along with his new roommate" I smiled.

"Awe Kyle, don't worry I bet you will be just fine" Jared said.

At four Quentin came in with Kevin. I looked up at Kyle he was still reading his science chapter, I motioned for them not to say anything as Kyle was very easily distracted.

"I'll be right back, Kyle; I'll be right outside the door."

He nodded "Stomach acid . . ." He mumbled finding his place.

I stepped out in to the hall to speak to Quentin and Kevin. "Good the room request went through" I said.

"You" Kevin looked at me stunned.

"I told you I have brothers" I smiled at him "But I wanted you with Anthony."

"I like Kyle" He smiled.

"I know"

"Ralph says to tell you" Quentin looked like he had had the eggs for breakfast also "Anthony and Kevin are too far apart in age to be roommates."

"Ok cool" I nodded. "What's wrong Kevin?"

He pulled me down and whispered in my ear "I don't like Quentin."

"Oh I'm sorry, well I spouse he wants to go to the family room if his homework is done and I have to get back to Kyle."

"The family room?" Quentin made a face as if he had smelled something awful.

"Yes Quentin, the family room, he likes cartoons and board games and loves National Geographic."

Quentin looked at me like I was crazy "But . . . never mind come on Kevin let's go."

I walked in to the room muttering.

"What's wrong?" Asked Kyle.

"I encountered Quentin."

Kyle winced "I don't like him."

"Neither does your new roommate."

"Who is my new roommate?"

"Kevin."

"Awesome."

"Ok, Kyle have a good day I have to go to the girls halls."

He looked at me shocked "Ok Alex, see you Friday."

Tiffany looked quite different without her makeup, jewelry, and dark clothes

"Good after noon" I greeted her.

"Whatever, why are you here?" She growled.

"I work here, why are you here?"

"Because my mom's a wench."

"Really those band-aids say otherwise."

"What do you care?"

"If I didn't care why would I be here?"

"Money" She shrugged.

"If I wanted money I would work for my uncles."

"You're gluten for punishment."

"Yeah, but there are a lot easier ways to get punished then this."

"What do I have to do to make you go away?"

"I am not leaving, until seven-thirty. Your homework done?"

"Yep"

"Do you wish to go to the family room?"

"No."

"Do you have your schedule?"

"Yes."

"May I see it?"

"Fine" She shoved it at me.

"Did you go today?"

"No."

"Fine we will sit here in silence but you may question or speak to me at free will."

"How did you get the shiner?"

"His name is Jack Roberts the fourth but everyone calls him Buddy."

"I met that dork; he's still in 7th grade."

"What grade are you in."

"10th not that you care."

"If I didn't care I wouldn't ask."

We sat for a while with her glaring at me "What do you wear when you're not in that?"

"Clothes."

"That's good you would be ugly naked."

"Well I'm glad you approve of me wearing clothes" I laughed.

We sat in silence again. "Can I go outside?" She finally asked.

"Not in the rain and only level two and up."

"What level am I?"

"One."

"This place sucks!" She punched the wall.

"I don't suggest you do that, I will have to place you in the time out room."

"You know how queer that sounds?"

"No, because I don't think like that, I was not raised to be rude, intolerant, or prejudice."

"You're odd."

"Thank you."

"Are you a prep?"

"No, I dressed in a school uniform before and now I have this uniform."

"You wore a uniform?"

"Yes, I went to a privet school."

"Prep."

"No I wasn't and I wasn't Mr. popular, or Mr. School spirit neither. I had two friends, my girlfriend and my physics lab partner."

"Why didn't you have friends?"

"I was different."

"Like how? Like gay?"

"No, I just told you I have a girlfriend, my mothers are though and I didn't learn how to control my panic attacks until about 2 years ago. My arms were always covered in blood and I was meaner than Buddy."

She just looked at me in disbelief "But you look so . . ."

"Normal?" I offered.

"Yeah."

I laughed "There is no such thing as a normal look only a hidden inner self. Yesterday I saw my physics lab partner in school he had a rainbow colored Mohawk and more piercings then I could count, when I saw him yesterday he had no piercings and I finally saw his real hair color."

"Why did he change?"

"Army reserves."

She sat in her chair "What do you do for fun?"

"I play keyboard, piano, and drums. I watch TV, I hold my girlfriend, I go to her uncle's pool hall and . . ."

"Your girlfriend's uncle owns the pool hall!"

"Yes."

"That place is awesome."

"I haven't been in a long time."

"Why?"

"Crowds."

She nodded "Are you going to leave yet?"

"Nope."

She grabbed at her neck then swore and punched the wall.

"Something wrong?"

"Too many haters in this place."

"Explain please?"

"My necklace."

"You get your jewelry back at the en . . ."

She pointed at my pendants "Your Wiccan?"

"Er no, this my mom gave me and these were my father's."

"Do your parents wear anything?"

"My mama wears a gay pride necklace."

"Does she ever take it off?"

"No I think she would kill someone if they tried."

"They took my gay pride necklace."

"For your safety but I understand and I will see if they will let you have just that necklace back."

She leaned back and sighed "What's it like to have two moms?"

"Like having a mom and dad, it's just the same you have two loving parents, only they are both women."

She nodded; and kicked at her shoes.

I looked at the clock it was five thirty. "Penny for your thoughts, and are you ready for dinner?"

"My girlfriend isn't family she . . ."

"Friday from eight to four thirty if she . . ."

"School" she frowned.

"I'll find away."

"Why?"

"I told you I care, now the cafeteria may not serve blood but the curly fries are . . ."

"Who said I drink blood?" She snapped.

I smiled "I was trying to make you laugh."

Hot dogs and French fries I chose to wait Mama always saved me dinner anyways. Tiffany refused to sit with anyone. Buddy tried to sit with her and I had to take him a side and persuade him that he wanted to wait a few more days to sit with her she was still getting use to the center. Kevin wanted to sit with us because he couldn't stand Quentin; I just wanted the two hours to be over.

I called again to check on Paul. He was fine, he was eating dinner. I would not get to see him today he was sleeping when we left and would be in bed already when we got home. Ana came over and hugged me.

"How is he?" She smiled.

"È benissimo io non sono(he's fine, I'm not)" I laughed.

"Who's she? She's hot" Tiffany said.

I blushed "Er thanks, this is my girlfriend Ana, Ana this is Tiffany."

Ana smiled "Nice to meet you. Thank you; you are an attractive young lady yourself." Ana turned to me "I have to wo . . ."

"It's ok I need to spend some time with Anthony."

"Alex" Ana said "I'm sorry Honey, tomorrow is our short day."

"Its fine baby" I was watching a scene I didn't like unfolding. I grabbed my walkie-talkie "Dave Quick Buddy and Curtis in the Café." I kissed Ana "Stay with her please and thank you she won't give you any trouble." I ran and grabbed up Kyle and Kevin and put them with Tiffany, she would have to deal. I ran back and scooped up Anthony and the trays of food. "Daddy loves you, I'll see you later." I kissed the top of his head setting him with the others. I went back and grabbed hold of Buddy. "Jack. Calm. Down." I shielded him from Curtis' punches "Ok Buddy, it's ok Buddy."

"He's crazy" Tiffany shook her head watching me protect Buddy.

"Buddy? Yeah" Kevin said.

"Curtis? Definitely" Kyle said.

"MY DAD IS NOT CRAZY, HE'S PERFECT!" Anthony snapped.

Ana smiled "Anthony come sit in my arms?"

Anthony crawled up in to Ana's arms.

Tiffany shook her head "Alex is your dad?"

"He adopted me yesterday, my brother too."

Tiffany looked at me again stood up and marched right over to Curtis. Then looked him straight in the eyes and yelled at him "YOUR SPIOLED THREE YEAR OLD TEMPER TANTRUM IS SPOILING MY DINNER. KNOCK IT OFF!"

I would have laughed if I hadn't been pinning Buddy. "What took so long?" I growled at Bruno.

"Billy was fighting with Cory sorry." He grabbed Curtis and forced him into a straight jacket "What happened?"

"I don't quite know." I rocked Buddy "Shhhh Buddy it's ok."

"Kevin ok?" Bruno looked around for Kevin.

"He's fine; he might know what happened though."

Dave came in and took Curtis. I was still holding Buddy who was now crying instead of trying to swing.

"Save Kevin, where's Kevin" He sobbed in to my chest.

After dinner I walked Tiffany back to her room.

"Why did you put your son here?" She asked accusingly.

"I didn't the state did before he was my son and I cannot take him until he completes the program; or he would not be here."

"How come you grabbed Buddy and not Curtis?"

"You can't 'grab' somebody swing like Curtis was the way I pined Buddy, besides Curtis had already blacked out and Buddy hits harder."

She laughed "You look like a walking bruise."

"Better than the mess under those band-aids."

She made a face.

"Make any face you want I saw your arms Monday. I may have been sick but I am far from blind and stupid."

"What are you going to do about it?"

"Nothing only you can fix that."

She scowled "Are you leaving yet?"

"Nope."

She growled at me.

I laughed "You won't scare me; nothing you say or do is going to unnerve me."

She stomped to her bed "I had dreams of making out with my roommate last night."

"Did you enjoy them?"

She scowled again "Yes Genevieve is gorgeous."

I smiled "Maybe you should tell her then?"

She blushed "NO WAY SHE'S STRAIGHT!"

"So says you. Good night Tiffany see you on Friday."

I was sore and stiff; I clocked out and walked down to see Anthony.

Dave caught me outside the room "Eight to four thirty tomorrow."

"Ok that's cool two extra hours."

"Yep" Dave looked at me ice those bruises your with Buddy tomorrow."

"Thanks" I groaned; and walked in to Anthony's room.

"DAD" He jumped, he was drawing at his desk.

"Hey little man what are you up to?"

"Waiting for you" He sat his crayon down.

"Well I'm here; tell me about your day, please?"

"It was ok. I have one less band-aid."

"That's great."

"I guess, Daddy how did you stop cutting?"

I held him tight "I wish, little man, I could let you do that; but it is not very healthy and you would be here a very long time Paul would not like that he misses you. He constantly asks when I'm bringing you home. He has lots to tell you on Friday."

"Where is he if you are here?"

"He is at home with my parents, I haven't found him a preschool yet, the one I went to was in Italy."

His eyes went wide. "Is he coming Friday?"

"Yep."

"Will you be here Friday?"

"Yes, and I will be here tomorrow as well, I think Dave is trying to kill me or at least completely exhaust me so I don't try and work on my days off."

He giggled "D-hall is cool."

I shook my head "I would tell you not to call him that but he would scold me."

He giggled more "What does Paul's room look like?"

"His half looks like a fire station; boy does he love his fire trucks."

Anthony laughed "I know it's the only toys savable after the baby sitter caught the house on fire trying to cook."

"Well Ana and I have gotten him clothes, books and toys. And my uncle and my mothers never have set the stove on fire."

"She said she was saving me and Paul. I think Santa sent her because me and Paul were trying to be really good this year, will I get new stuff too?"

"It's Paul and I, and of course you will."

"Can I have my side of the room be a space ship?"

"Absolutely your nana will love painting that."

He gave me a confused look.

"My mama, your nana is an artist."

Ana joined us "You don't worry so much pumpkin, little men of six shouldn't worry so much its bed time" She hugged and kissed him.

"Night Ana."

I scooped him up "She's right bed time" I kissed him and tucked him in. "You need us tell Dave, he won't deny any child in this hall me."

"Night Daddy" He rolled over and curled up closing his eyes."

We closed his door quietly.

"You worry too much Alexander" Dave laughed "What happened at dinner with Curtis and Buddy?"

I laughed "I wish I could answer that. Kevin and Kyle might know."

"All right go get some rest."

"I'm going to learn about my parents then to bed."

"Alex, my boy I wouldn't dig to deep your mama don't . . ."

"My dad's going to talk to him" Ana smiled.

Ana drove I was too sore to drive Curtis was no light puncher. About half way home I called Mama.

"Ti amo e mamma ed i miei zii(I love you, mom, and my uncles). How is my son?"

"He is fine, he is sleeping relax; Ana called earlier your food is waiting for you."

"We're going to stop at her house she needs to get a few things. Dave raised my hours I'm out at four thirty tomorrow."

"Ok see you when you get in" She hung up.

I sighed "How was your day, Dear?"

"It was good. How was yours?"

"Well, Kevin thinks I'm the best thing since I pods because I don't see him as a hideous beast, Kyle thinks I rule the world because I have the power to request room changes, and Tiffany has a chip on her shoulder the size of the empire state building. I miss my son and my other son doesn't want to follow the program he wants to do it my way."

"You haven't meditated today have you Honey" She laughed.

"No, I wouldn't have had time to talk to Anthony if I did and he is more important."

She gave me a look "Are you sure you want to do this tonight?"

"I'm sure, how bad can it be?"

"It may not be bad just time consuming."

"Its fine" I opened the door to her house for her.

"Hi Daddy" She called "Are you busy."

Her dad and her Uncle Ken were in the kitchen "No dear just talking to your uncle."

"Uncle Ken" She squealed.

I laughed. "Hello sir, hello Mr. Wittson" I gulped.

"Hi Alex, how are you?" Ana's dad asked.

"Good sir" I choked.

"Daddy, Alex wants to know about his parents' pasts."

Mr. Wittson laughed "I think we can help you with that, what do you want to know?"

"Kork hush" Ana's dad laughed "JJ new this day would come Alex sit down and tell us what you already know."

"I don't know much just that Mama went to Crimson like us and Mom only went there for her last year and a half of school."

"That place hates me" Mr. Wittson laughed.

"Shush Kork, you have dad's ill timed talking problem" Ana's dad shook his head "I'm sorry Alex continue."

"Uh I know her and Uncle Chris and grew up in that house."

"Sort of, my father and grandfather built them that house the summer after your grandfather died, your Mama's real dad. That house has many memories" Ana's dad smiled.

"Bad?" I asked.

"Some good, some bad some indifferent" Mr. Wittson shook his head.

"Witch room was Mamas?"

"Yours."

"And" Added Ana's dad "About half way through your mama's senior year it became your mom's as well."

"It did?"

"Yes" Mr. Wittson shuttered "To this day I have no desire to talk to your mom's mother . . ."

"Ken shush that's his . . ."

"Don't worry I know she doesn't like Mama and that her and Mom don't get along to well."

"Well anything specific you would like to know?" Ana's dad asked.

"Where did Kenny get his name?"

"Not me" Mr. Wittson laughed.

"Let's see" Ana's dad said "When we had Davie, Jess and Tina got all he's so cute we want one, but I assume your parents taught you where babies come from. So it took a while, discussing ways, and then your daddy . . . well you're a smart boy. You're named after your godfather, he was your mama's best friend in grade school I think the only reason they are still friends is because he remembers to call her. When Kenny was born he was suppose to be a girl so your mom told your mama to name him so she named him after her grandparents Kenneth was her dad's side and Joseph was her mom's dad. Tina told her you and he would have the same middle name and Jess told her you two wouldn't care because you would know you had good names."

"I never went by Kenny; and if he were named after any Ken in my family he'd be Kenneth William not Kenneth Joseph, Besides Jessi always called me Kork." Mr. Wittson added.

"Why?" I asked.

"I prefer it." He laughed.

"What is Mama's birth name?"

"Boy is trying to get us killed" Mr. Wittson choked.

Him and Ana's dad exchanged glances.

"It is Jessica the second JJ is because she use to stutter."

"The twins are named after my uncles . . ."

"Yes, and oh are they just like your mama and your uncle Chris" Anna's dad made a face "Nick was just a name they liked, and Colt well I think you're ready to see this."

I followed them in to the living room. Ana's dad pulled out an old VHS and old VHS player "This should kill some of that curiosity."

I sat on the couch as the picture came in to view. It looked like a younger much younger Mama standing in the middle of the living room. "Mama?" I asked.

"Yes she's fighting your uncle Marc, Henry give that some sound."

"NOOOOOOOOOOOOOO!" The Mama on TV yelled. What appeared to be Uncle Marc moved in to view and picked her up "Let's go princess."

"She never did like doctors" Ana's dad laughed.

The screen flickered and it showed a tall blue haired boy yelling at Uncle Mike "I said no I mean no Michael."

"Oh Henry you did not edit this well" Mr. Wittson groaned "I still can't believe I dyed it that color all those years."

"Well don't worry now, your almost as bald as Popi" Ana's dad laughed. The screen flicked again and it showed Mom hollering at a tall boy with short hair that looked just like me "Not on your life Colt that's my girlfriend we are going." "But milady" Colt said . . . He sounded like me as well.

"Mom?" I looked at Mr. Wittson.

"Yes, Miss Tina chewed him up daily about the care of Jessi." Mr. Wittson looked at me. "You look more and more like your daddy every day. Alex sometimes I think I'm seeing a ghost."

"That's my dad?"

"Yes, just watch."

The TV flickered and I saw Auntie Kate staring at Uncle Chris "Don't you dare tell me you just said that." "So what if I did." A hand grabbed him from the side and yanked him out of view. The TV flickered and a tall boy with two toned hair stared at me awkwardly "This one's my favorite."

"Ewe Hen that hair hurts; you haven't dyed it like that since Ana was born." Mr. Wittson laughed.

"Well hell Ken" Her dad laughed "It scared her."

"Vedo perché(I see it)" I mumbled.

The picture changed and it showed Uncle Christian chasing Mom around and old mustang with rainbow flames painted on it and with the two boys in the car kissing and laughing at Uncle Christian. "Milady please, please take your medicine" the younger version of my uncle begged. She ran behind the blue haired boy that Mr. Wittson had said was himself; he looked at Mom and said "Miss Tina I will not have sick and or psycho children in my house or in my care take your medicine" Uncle Christian looked like Mom had beat him up. Then the blue haired boy looked at Uncle Christian and said "Take a deep breath and join me in a chess game."

Mr. Wittson laughed "Good times huh Hen?"

Ana's dad just looked at his feet the scene had changed a very short girl with magenta bangs and plenty of piercings pounded on a door with some really old poster promoting a band for some time in the 1980's "JJ, JESS, Jessica, Jessica Marie." She yelled as she pounded the door. The boy that mirrored my image opened the door and the girl pushed past him and ripped Mama's headphones off.

I laughed "Uncle Christian still has . . ." The room had gotten really quiet.

"Sorry," Ana's dad said "That is Nalanie. JJ, AJ, and Nalanie were best friends Alex"

I looked at the screen it looked nothing like Ana's mom, but neither did Ana's dad or Mr. Wittson.

The picture changed flickered and it showed Ana's uncle Kyle hanging upside down off a stage singing pop goes the weasel severely off key.

Mr. Wittson laughed "I am so glad he has stopped doing that, see Ana that is why I call him deranged when his true hair color started to show he would do things like that or dance with the bar stools."

Ana gave me a look that said both her uncles were deranged and I tried not to laugh.

The clip switched and it showed Uncle Christian with the blue haired boy playing chess. "What was that?" The blue haired boy laughed "That was Jess and Nalanie dragging Colt." "What did they say" "I don't know, check mate." Uncle Christian threw his arms in the air and the blue haired boy just laughed "Play again?" "No! I need to take a deep breath and check on milady because her girlfriend and her girlfriend's psycho best friend just dragged Colt off"

Mr. Wittson laughed "Boy did he ever hate my method of relaxation. He was a good player but I could always count on something to distract him so I always won."

"He still does hate it" I laughed.

The scene changed and it showed Uncle Chris putting worms in a shoe and Mama holding a blow up doll and itching powder with Mr.

Wittson's wife Crystalline glaring at them "What are you two doing?" "We are . . ." ". . . Having fun."

"Twins" I growled.

"So it was those fools that did that to my shoes" Mr. Wittson laughed "They blamed Kyle."

"Twins" I growled again.

"Yes, I told you, your brothers are just like your mama." Ana's dad laughed.

The scene changed and Uncle Marc and Uncle Mike were sitting in a snow bank wearing nothing but there boxers.

"Do I even . . ."

Mr. Wittson laughed "I bet those two goons they couldn't go an hour in the snow bank in just their trousers."

I looked back at the TV Uncle Mike looked like he was turning blue and Uncle Marc just looked angry. The picture switched and it showed Uncle Chris and Ana's dad chopping wood "Pig strips and foreign burnt bread." "Henry if I didn't know better I would say you were on crack."

Ana laughed "Daddy still does that when he is mad, sometimes."

The picture flipped again it was a scene of the pool hall and everyone was on stage singing. Ana's dad and uncles and all of my uncles were teaching my dad and my Uncle Christian to back flip off the stage. My dad landed face first on the floor and my mom poured some liquid on his head.

I laughed "That had to hurt."

"I think it was the Pepsi bath she gave him that was bad" Ana's dad laughed.

The next few clips were of every one goofing around and having fun everyone looked so happy and care free. And with every shot of Ana's mom, her dad looked closer and closer to tears.

"Mama had a good child hood?"

"Yes Alex, your Uncle Marc and I took excellent care of her anything that made it bad came from within her or outside of the home" Mr. Wittson said.

"Why does she hate her birthday so much?"

"I don't know, that's something no one can answer I don't even think she knows why" Ana's dad shook his head.

"The next clip showed Mama, Uncle Chris, Ana's dad and her uncle Kyle in football jerseys then one of my dad playing the key board.

"That's my keyboard" I pointed at the TV.

"Actually it is mine but since I haven't played that one in almost twenty-three years I guess you can keep it" Ana's dad laughed.

The picture flipped and Ana's dad appeared on the screen in front of the brunt out gas station at the end of our driveway "Hi Alex if you're watching this you have started to ask questions. This is where your dad died he was getting gas but something happened and the tanks blew up. Your mom was eight months pregnant with you. His death hurt us all very much." The scene flipped and it showed my father's funeral. Ana reached up and wiped a tear from my cheek. The scene changed and it showed my dad sitting at a drum set smiling ear to ear in small letters at the bottom of the screen it said "In loving memory of Colt 1984-2005."

Ana's dad got up and shut it off "That last picture was the day he found out about you, it was the biggest smile I had ever seen on him. Any more questions?"

"Why doesn't Mama and Nana get along?"

Mr. Wittson shrug "I don't know I always got along with her mom, Juliet loves her children very much I'd go with a personality clash your mama and your Uncle Chris are very much like their father."

Ana wiped another tear away "Alexander, blink someone is going to think something is wrong, you scare people when you do that not blinking thing."

Her brother laughed.

I laughed "Sorry, I'm fine I was just really focused."

"Did that help?" Mr. Wittson ask "And don't forget to blink near your mother she will swear I taught you that just to unnerve her."

"Yes it did, and she already does know about my lack of blinking, but didn't she have friends?"

"Just the ones you saw in the film and your Godfather." Ana's dad smiled "JJ is herself."

"Thank-you very much Sir, but I best get home" I said.

"I'm coming too, Baby, just give me a minute to get a few things." Ana ran her hand along my shoulder sending chills down my spine.

"So when do you plan on returning my daughter?" Ana's dad laughed.

"Sorry Sir, Ma . . ." I choked.

"Hush, it's fine, I'm just teasing, Alex are you ok?"

Mr. Wittson grabbed and pinned me like Uncle Christian did.

"I'm fine, I'm just cold" I objected.

"Uh huh, fever" He said checking my shoulders for cuts.

"That fever hasn't gone yet" Ana frowned coming back down stairs.

Mr. Wittson released me and looked in to my eyes and ears, up my nose and in my throat "Uh-huh thought so you have a sinus infection."

I groaned "No way, no, Mr. Wittson with all due respect I can't be getting sick I have to work tomorrow and I have Paul."

Ana took my hand "Night Uncle Ken, night Daddy, night Davie." She looked at me "Your sick get over it, if you don't believe my uncle you can always go ask my granddad.

I muttered a few ungentlemanly phrases then said "Night sir, Night Mr. Wittson thank you both very much; Night David." He handed me a drawing of my father, I wondered how much time with my dad he got to spend when our parents were touring.

In the car I showed her the drawing "He draws like Daddy" She smiled "I wish I could draw that well."

"I wish he wrote as well as he draws and I wish your uncle wasn't always so right" I shivered more.

"Well maybe if you wore a coat . . ." She looked at the bottom of the paper "It says Colt he drew a picture of your father."

"I knew who it was he looks like me. Your brother doesn't like me does he?"

"If Nick were a girl would . . ."

"No, no I get that I mean in general?"

"He does he just has a lot of Mummy in him" She smiled and looked like she might start to cry.

When we got in my parents were in the kitchen playing cards.

"Alex, you alright?" Uncle Christian automatically pinned me.

"I'm fine I'm just cold."

"He has a sinus infection, sir," Ana laughed "And thought it fit to argue with my uncle Ken."

Uncle Christian laughed "Boy, even I don't argue with him."

"That's why you will play a game of chess with me" Mr. Wittson pushed the door open "Ana you dropped these." He handed her a pair of socks.

"Ever hear of knocking old man?" Uncle Christian laughed hugging him.

"Not in my own house" He laughed. "C.J., Miss Tina, Princess good evening. I have come to see my great nephew."

"Kenneth William Wittson the 3rd how dare you even assume he is awake this late" Mama scolded hugging him.

"He is down in the guest room Kork" Mom said receiving her hug.

"Don't you dare wake him" Uncle Chris took a his hug.

"I won't" Mr. Wittson laughed.

I escorted Mr. Wittson down to Paul's room. I covered him and kissed his forehead.

"I assure you" Mr. Wittson said "He has already been tucked in."

"But he is my son, it is my job" I whispered back.

"And your father would be very proud of you."

After I ate Mama handed me a note from Ms. Meyers. Stating that she had come by to check on Paul and found his room, clothes and living area suitable and that he was adjusting well. Uncle Christian made disapproving noises at the chess game. Uncle Chris had gone to bed and Mom and Mama were in the living room talking to Ana.

"Alex" Uncle Christian frowned at me "Go to bed your sick.

"I'm fine."

"Alex don't argue"

"I promise I'm fine."

"Alexander, do I have to tuck you in?"

"No sir" I blushed "I will go soon."

"Check mate, you will go now, Alex" Mr. Wittson said.

"Mama . . ."

"Don't look at me, I'm not fool enough to argue with him" She laughed.

"Mom?"

"Night dear, sleep well." Mom smiled.

I sighed "Did the state lady say anything?"

"Oh that yeah, Friday" Mama answered me.

"Inferno andrò a letto(The hell I will go to bed)."

"Would you like to be tucked in?" Mr. Wittson asked.

I blinked at him as if to ask am I three.

"I do Uncle Ken" Ana smiled grabbing my arm; I raised my eye brow at her.

"Of course you do sweetie, but your Romeo here looks like he wants to suck his thumb."

"He might" Uncle Christian laughed "Boy gets up at 4:30-5:00am."

"Hmm works all day and tonight he had questions."

"Alex?" Mama looked at me.

"Don't worry Princess, Hen just showed him that video" Mr. Wittson moved his rook, Uncle Christian was about to lose again.

"Oh, ok" Mama breathed a sigh of relief.

"Mama," I objected "I'm not Kenny I don't need that much help."

"Hey!" He chucked a couch pillow at my head he was less focused on his homework than I thought he was.

I laughed chucking it back to him "I just wanted to know a little more about you and mom and, and" I gulped "And my dad."

She nodded "It's ok, that's not even close to what I thought you were asking; Henry is a bit squeamish."

"*A bit*, little one?" Uncle Christian raised his eye brow.

"Hush you or I will make you play another game." Mr. Wittson laughed "Besides Henny Penny has gotten much better with that kind of stuff since David's accident."

"Probabilmente desideri non lo denominereste penny di Henny affatto più lungo anche (you probably don't want to call him Henny Penny any more)" Uncle Christian muttered under his breath.

"Well" Mama said "I still know two things that would . . ."

"No Mama" Ana laughed "I am not pregnant and Al hasn't purposed to me yet."

"WHOA NO!" I said shocked "We haven't been . . . no . . . We just . . . I . . . long enough."

Everyone laughed.

Ana hugged me "How long have you loved me, Alex?"

"Kindergarten" I mumbled blushing

"You know how long it has been obvious, dear?"

"No."

"Kindergarten."

"Oops" I blushed harder.

"You know how long I have loved you?"

"Last Friday?"

My Uncle stifled a laugh and Kenny hit me in the head with the pillow again this time I just let it fall to the floor.

"Kindergarten, but you went emotionally blind on me for a long time, so I waited for you and tried to tell you every chance I got. I turned many guys down for you even Wilson because I have never wanted anyone but you."

I hung my head blushing "I . . . I . . . I . . ."

"Shhh" She kissed me and I staggered backward, more from being dizzy and tired than anything else.

"Hahaha" Mr. Wittson laughed "Ok let's get him to bed before he passes out where he is standing."

Mr. Wittson tucked us in I set my alarm and wrapped Ana in my arms; and he shut the lights out. I forgot how good it felt to be tucked in at night.

"That boy of yours is definitely his father's son, Miss Tina" Mr. Wittson said to Mom.

"I know, Kork, even the way he hugs" Mom smiled a little.

"Unfortunately neither my niece's socks nor my great nephew were why I am here."

"Never is Ken" Uncle Christian gave him a concerned look.

"I got a call from Marc."

"And?" Mama said.

"Sasha is pregnant."

"That's Awesome! Well not for Jr. Marc probably wants to kill him, but still that's great" Uncle Chris laughed.

"And the bad news, old man?" Uncle Christian asked him.

"Hold your horses you old fart I'm getting there." Mr. Wittson laughed. "No one has heard from Kyle and we are getting worried."

"Mmm" Mama said "Henry said something about that last night."

"I contacted his supervisor over there and she said he was in surgery but she would have him call me back; that was two weeks ago.

"I wouldn't worry too much, Ken, he will be fine" Mama said.

CHAPTER 9
BUDDY

IT WASN'T THAT I HAD to work long hours, and it wasn't that I had had no sleep. It was Buddy! Jack Edward Roberts the 4th, or as most people called him Buddy, was mean plain out bully style mean. He was Fourteen and in seventh grade. He was five feet of pure evil, not including his actual blacking out and like I had told Tiffany he hit very hard.

"Morning Buddy" I smiled at him from the door, he was laying in the time out room.

"Morning Alex" He looked up at me.

Do I even want to know?" This wasn't my first time with Buddy it would hopefully be an easy day he would hit someone and spend the rest of day in the time out room.

"Probably not I punched Quentin, I didn't like the way he was talking to Kevin."

"That is not a reason to hit, Jack. You really need to learn to use your words or instead of set free at eighteen they will just switch you to the state correctional psyche ward." I sighed we had had this talk about a million times in the past month.

"Oh well that is my brother."

"I have already gone to Ralph about Quentin, as *your* brother was complaining about him yesterday. Now come on it's time for school."

"Lucky me" He sneered.

"Want to tell me what happened yesterday at dinner" I asked him as we walked down the hall. "I took quite a few punches for you."

"Well that was dumb that where you get the shiner?"

"No that was you first thing yesterday morning."

"Well I don't remember that."

"I didn't expect you too."

"I don't remember dinner either."

"It's ok I was just wondering if you did."

"Sorry."

"Its fine, Buddy, I promise."

I opened the door to the classroom. Buddy wasn't aloud writing paper in class because he made spit balls; he wasn't allowed a chalk board because he bashed them over peoples' heads. So he had to do all his work orally and his teacher or chaperon for the day had to write it down for him. So I sat writing out his work, which was fine until he saw Kevin and Kyle laughing and talking. His eyes switched to cold and he started to shake. I set down the paper and crayon and grabbed and pinned his arms and pulled him in to a close and tight hug rocking him.

"What are you doing? I'm fine, you do not need to pin me" He objected trying to pull away.

"I bet you are fine I'm just making sure you going to be fine later on." I said.

No one was affected by this it was an everyday occurrence with Buddy, some of the kids from the b-hall or the detox wings would take bets on how fast he'd be moved to the time out room. They were also the kids Buddy would hit first. I had more than once suggested the kids in the detox wings get their own teacher as they weren't nice to the other kids constantly picking at them to set them off they saw it as a way to get out of a few minutes of class or group. Dave told me no and rolled his eyes at me every time I brought it up.

After about twenty minutes he stopped fighting and just let me hold him. By then it was lunch, once again I called home to check on Paul. I was really missing him, but he was fine. Mama told me not to worry so much. I sat between Kevin and Buddy to eat my PB&J. Kevin tapped my arm and pointed at Buddy. Buddy had taken his shirt off and was starting to get his pants down. I caught him and forced his shirt back on.

"No, no, no, no, no get it off me, get it off" He tried to get his shirt back off "There's spiders in it."

I took Buddy back to the time out room and went to get a medic and nearly ran in to Ralph.

"Hey Alex, how are you?" He smiled.

"Good . . . I guess . . . I have to go . . . need a medic . . . Buddy" I stammered.

"Ok well stop by my office later."

I nodded and kept running to the medic lounge. I closed my eyes and pushed through the door. "Need a medic . . . Buddy . . . D-hall . . ." I panted keeping my eyes shut as tight they would go.

"Dude" Greg laughed "It's ok slow down and open your eyes Valeriano and Chelsea aren't in here."

"Few" I opened my eyes.

"So, what's going on down in the D-hall?"

"Buddy."

"Who?" He said washing his hands and putting clean examining gloves on.

"Jack Roberts."

"Oh, yeah him, who did he hit this time?"

"No, he's ripping his clothes off telling me there are spiders in them."

"Hmm" He ran his finger down a check list "Ah ha." He pulled up a bottle "Come on I don't pin anyone, I would end up looking worse off than you. I am haven't made very many friends here."

I laughed he was right the medics did not make friends well. "So where are Chelsea and Val?"

"Well Val had the day off and Chelsea is supposedly sick so who knows what freaky things . . ."

"Man I don't want to know what they do in here is bad enough."

He laughed and shook his head like all work places we had our dramas I tried to stay out of them, Chelsea and Val was something no one could avoid they used the medic lounge as a make out and extensive groping room. Ana and I were not like that at all. If we kissed in public it was a quick peck or a quick peck to the cheek. Greg was single his girlfriend had left him for his friends brother last year so he wasn't fond of it either. He shuddered again.

By the time we got back to Buddy he had stripped, I knew he would. His clothes were in one corner and he was balled up in another on the other side of the room shaking. I tapped his shoulder and Greg handed him some thick liquid in a dosage cup. He took it willingly and curled back in to the corner. Greg went back to the medic lounge and I quietly took a chair from Dave's office; as he was sleeping on a stack of paper work. I sat down in front of the time out room and filled out the incident report.

Buddy knocked on the door around three he was redressed and his shoulder length hair was all in his eyes he looked tired and irritated.

"Ready?" I smiled opening the door and leading him back to his room.

He nodded.

"Good you have homework."

"Lucky me" He groaned.

"Are you feeling any better?"

He nodded.

"That's good," I smiled.

"Did I hit you?"

"Nope."

"Did I hit anyone?"

"Nope, gave some off the ladies a nice view of your chest though."

He groaned "Did she see me freak out?"

"Who?"

"The new girl um . . . Tiffany; I think is her name . . . the gothic one."

I laughed "I don't think so, do you have a crush?"

"What's it to you!" He snapped at me.

"How about we do your math?"

"Science."

"Pardon?"

"Science I have more trouble with science, so I do it first."

"Ok, no problem . . ."

He wasn't kidding the simple cell diagram took him forty five minutes. Then he went on to his English, which was spelling. That took him thirty minutes. When I left he was still working on his history.

Dave caught me out side of Anthony's room "Buddy Ok?"

"Fine, he is doing his home work."

"Good, Greg apologized again for the mistake this morning."

"It's alright."

"Oh and he is in the family room." Dave smiled pointing towards Anthony's room.

I found Anthony in the family room with Ana. I kissed Ana and hugged Anthony in a tight bear hug. "Hey, bud how was your day?"

"Fine, Dad I miss Paul."

"Well you can see him tomorrow, he misses you too. How many band-aids?"

"Twenty-three Still" He looked at his feet.

"It's ok little man, it will go fast."

"Who is coming tomorrow?"

I looked at Ana. "Well my uncle Christian, Mom, Mama and Paul."

"And my dad said he and Davie would try to stop by" Ana smiled reassuringly at him.

"Who's Davie?" He wrinkled his nose.

I laughed "I think he'd prefer you call him Uncle David, he is Ana's brother."

"True" Ana laughed "He does make that awful face when I call him Davie in front of some one. Anyway kiddo we have to get going I have school tonight."

"Mmm and I haven't seen Paul since Tuesday. See you tomorrow, I love you." I hugged him again and kissed the top of his head. He hugged Ana and we left.

Tomorrow is an easy day I told myself as I drove home as fast as I could.

"Hot date, dear?" Ana asked after the third time I nearly ran a red light.

"Er do we? That would be fine if we did but I . . ."

"No silly but you are nearly speeding."

"Oh sorry you have school and I have my on-line classes and I want to see Paul before he is a sleep today."

She looked at me "Ok super dad, just slow down a bit you're no good to them dead, you know."

"Miele spiacente (Sorry Honey)" I slowed down, admittedly I did have a bit of a lead foot.

"DADDY!" Paul jumped in to my arms the second I walked through the door. I hugged him tight and set him down. I hung up my coat and put my shoes away.

"Daddy! Daddy! Daddy!" He pulled on my arm. "Eat Uncle Christian played ire uks with me and Grandma read to me and Nana colored with me and grandpa here."

"Er ok" I nodded walking in to the kitchen "Hello sir" I gulped. At the site of Ana's granddad. I hugged and kissed my mothers.

"How was work dear?" Mama asked.

"Long and agonizing," I sat next to Colt; Paul was sitting in between Mama and Uncle Christian.

"I hear I have another great grandson?" Ana's granddad asked.

"Ehm, yes sir, Anthony" I choked.

Uncle Chris came flying through the door "Sorry I'm . . . DAD!" He choked.

"Chris" Ana's granddad nodded "How was work?"

"Good sir."

I shook my head and then remembered that Mama and Uncle Chris called Ana's grandparents; Mum and Dad as they were their Godparents and their father had died when they were young. Ok maybe Dave was right I wasn't getting enough rest. Uncle Chris served himself and sat in between Mom and Nick.

"Chop sliver" Paul smiled.

"Hi squirt" Uncle Chris smiled at him. "So, Dad what brings you state side?"

"Kyle" He said.

"We haven't . . ."

"Kyle is fine, but he won't be home for a while."

"Why for Daddy?" Mama asked.

"Liz is due in two weeks."

"Really that's great."

"His name is to be Kyle Mathew Wittson Jr."

"You never know with him Dad," Uncle Chris sighed "First he tells us he's headed over to help with a surgery and then we don't hear from him. Henry is afraid he will get the plague or something and come home in a body bag."

Ana's granddad laughed "No, no he is just fine he is back there driving your mum crazy. Marc and Kate are doing well also Savanna is a joy to have toddling around."

Uncle Chris smiled from ear to ear he was still slightly floating on cloud nine. Savanna was my cousin Kimberly's daughter and Kimberly was my Uncle Marc's oldest child. She had named Uncle Chris Savanna's God father. "Did he send any pictures?"

"No just said to tell you everything was good, they are enjoying their vacation and will be home soon.

After dinner I had my online classes it was easier for me than regular classes at a collage. I was majoring in child psychology and in a music course that I didn't really need this semester by June I would have a bachelors in special education. I groaned at my music expressions assignment. I tapped irritably at the key board as if it were my key board or drums.

"Having trouble?" Mama asked me.

"Having a headache" I sighed "Pick one song that describes your father?" I read the essay question.

"Well just use me for that one and your mum for this one" She smiled pointing at my next question.

I sat and typed in "Who you'd be today" by Kenny Chesney.

"Yeah, honey, that works too" Mom smiled it was almost a wince.

"What was he like?" I asked.

Mama laughed uneasily and looked at Uncle Christian who looked as if he might cry, Mom sighed "He was . . ."

"He was like your Uncle Christian, but less high strung, a bit shorter and he was just a genuinely nice guy" Mama's smile was more forced than she wanted it to look.

I nodded and returned to my work answering the question with a song from Mama's band called "Dream Mum." The next question was harder it was to describe two people in the house using only one song. I thought hard looking around the living room and kitchen. Then typed in "My brother Kenny and my son Paul 'wild thing'" I didn't know who it was by hopefully my professor wouldn't take points for my being too lazy to look it up. Then I added another song from Mama's band titled "A precious gift (Davies's song)".

"Good choice" Uncle Chris said "Your Uncle Mike use to sing that all the time to Davie."

"Aye bloody fool couldn't carry a tune to save himself" Mama sputtered picking up a trail of pencil shavings.

"1 . . . 2 . . ." Uncle Chris stifled a laugh.

"CHRISTOPHER MICHEAL, CHRISTIAN JAMES!" Mama bellowed up the stairs.

"Uh . . ."

". . . Oh." I heard the twins gulp.

Sir chuckled "Just like someone else I know."

Mama Blushed.

The twins looked up at Sir. "Did she . . .

". . . Really . . ."

". . . Leave . . ."

". . . Shavings . . ."

". . . Everywhere?" They asked.

"Her and Henry both" He laughed "And everywhere was an understatement, your Uncle Marc use to find her by following the shavings."

"Dad that was more Henry than me," Mama scowled "And you two clean this mess."

Mom laughed "Jessi, dear, your erasers did and still do make such a mess that Christian vacuums our room as many times a day as you shower."

"Well excuse me" She laughed kissing Mom.

I looked at my parents and down at the list of songs on the CD case, in my hand, that Mama had wrote. I typed in "Happy in love" I had never heard the song but a side note had said it was her and mom's song back then.

"I told you your mothers will never change." Uncle Christian sat next to me with Paul on his lap; Paul was driving a matchbox fire truck up and down him.

"One song to describe yourself or your significant other" I read aloud "Ana" I typed in "An American girl" By Trisha year wood. My last question was to describe Ana and mine's relationship. I chose a song off the sound track to Disney's <u>The Lion King</u>.

By the time I finished it was seven and Paul had already been put into his Pajamas. He was in the kitchen at his easel drawing on the chalk board side.

"Can I play with you?" I smiled at him.

"No work?" He added a few more slash lines to his drawing.

"No work, no school, just you and me time."

"IRE UCKS!" He set his chalk on its tray took his smock off and showed me his hands; I grabbed a wipe and wiped his hands clean. He had defiantly been spending a lot of time with Uncle Christian. He hugged my leg and ran off to his room; he came back with two huge fire trucks. I sat on the kitchen floor and played fire trucks with him until 7:30.

"Bed time Paul" I handed him my truck.

He picked up his truck and stated to cry.

"I'm going to put you to bed tonight" I smiled at him. "Let's put these guys in their garage for the night" I pointed to his trucks.

"NOOO!" He cried.

"Oh someone is tired" I picked him and the trucks up and carried them to his room I set him on his bed and the trucks in their garage and then picked him back up. "You need rest tomorrow you have a big day you get to go to work with Ana and I."

"Where's my Ana?" He cried burring his little face into my chest.

"She is at school tonight, Sweetie." I turned down his covers and laid him down wiping his tears. I picked up his fairy tale book and opened to where it was marked

"No" He closed the book "Me and Grandma only" He crawled off his bed sniffling back his tears; he went to his book shelf and brought me back four other books.

I read him his books and tucked him in then went out to the living room and sat in the recliner to watch some T.V.

Ana shook me around 10:30 "Uncle Ken told you, you had a sinus . . ."

"Shhh, così ha fatto il vostro nonno(So did your grandfather)." I stood up yawning and hugged her tight. "Tempo della base(bed time)?"

"Yes, dear, most defiantly bed time" She snuggled my chest.

CHAPTER 10

FRIDAY DECEMBER SECOND

I STARTLED AWAKE DRIPPING SWEAT and shaking. Ana was still asleep. I silently grabbed clean under clothes and a clean uniform, then head down stairs to shower. Nightmares no longer bothered me, too much. They startled me awake and then depending on the time I would just get up or roll over and go back to sleep. Today it would have been pointless as the alarm would go off before I even reached the bottom of the stairs.

I was right at the bottom of the stairs Ana jumped on my back and started kissing my neck. "Good morning, dear" I laughed "Good dreams?"

"Very" She smiled and jumped down "Showering?"

"Normally" I laughed "You're full of energy?"

After my shower I ate breakfast happy we didn't have to be in early today.

Paul toddled out yawning "Uncle Christian I is up."

"Morning Paul" I smiled at him.

"DADDY!" He jumped in to my arms.

Christian and Christopher were getting ready for school. Christian popped a waffle in the toaster and Chris poured orange juice in his cup. "Good morning Paul, what is the proper crayon brand?" Christian asked him.

"Ayola" He smiled *"Uncle Chris"* He giggled.

"Ok Paul, Good morning, what direction must brush strokes always go in?" Chris asked him.

"No irection they give the painting feelings." Paul smiled stretching for his breakfast.

"I see you two have already started torturing him" I shook my head.

"We are doing no such thing . . ."

". . . We are teaching him . . ." They objected as they set his food down.

Nick fell down the stairs followed by Colt. Colt ran a hand through Paul's hair and crawled in to my arms. Nick sat down and pulled out a Stephen king book and stared reading to Paul as they ate. When I finished eating I picked Colt up and set him on the couch shoving a thermometer in his mouth. Then I combed Ana's hair.

Uncle Christian and Mom came out of their room laughing followed by Mama who was laughing just as hard.

"Uh oh sick solider" Mama frowned.

"Mmm" Uncle Christian said looking at the thermometer "No fever get moving Colt history test flu is not going to save you from school, should have studied."

Colt muttered and grumbled under his breath dragging himself into motion, I could hear the twins and Nick trying not to laugh as I was stifling a laugh myself. We had all at tried to get out of our pre holiday history exam in sixth grade. All with the same symptoms after the twins Uncle Christian started calling it history test flu.

I dressed Paul and told my mothers I would see them later. As a promise to Kevin I made sure just his mom came by picking her up myself. And for Tiffany hoping she would be less cynical today I went looking for her girlfriend . . . I found her, slightly wished I hadn't. She was a frightful looking child about the beasts' age.

"What do you want?" She glared at me shutting what must have been her younger brother and sister in the house.

"ER, hello my name is Alex, I work at the center your girlfriend is at, she wants you to . . ."

"How is she? Is she ok?" The young lady looked like she was about to cling on to me and start to cry, this made her look twice as unbalanced.

"She is ok, well as ok as she is going to be until she is out of there."

"Oh, then why are you here." The drastic switch was unnerving and sent up red flags in my head.

I swallowed hard "She would like you to come visit her."

"When?"

"Now."

"Fine." She opened the door and yelled in at someone "Hey Maggot do that trick with your voice and call me out of school." She slammed the door shut again.

"I could have gotten you an excused absence."

"Oh well" She climbed in my car and looked at Paul.

Paul looked back at her "Daddy she didn't wash her face."

I tried not to laugh, Ana and Mrs. Roberts did laugh.

"No Paul, she is wearing makeup," I tried harder not to laugh.

"Like Halloween?" He asked.

"Yes Paul, like Halloween."

"My think she smudged it Daddy."

I laughed "It is ok, Paul"

"She go see Anony too?"

"No dear", Ana laughed "She's going to see her girlfriend."

"Oh" He looked inquisitively at Tiffany's girlfriend "What her name?"

"Her name is Tiffany" Tiffany's girlfriend said; a chill went through my spine when the young lady spoke.

"What you name?"

"I'm Sadie."

"Oh my go see Anony."

Sadie looked at Ana.

"Anthony is brother" Ana smiled.

"You no school today?" Paul continued to chatter "Uncle Nick have School so we finish Cujo. Tomorrow, Nana says he can't take it to school because Grandma had to go get him from school three times for reading in class."

She smiled which was scarier than her frown "I'm taking the day off. I think I know your Uncle Nick." She looked at me "Nick Williams, right?"

"Yep, that is my little brother" I nodded.

"My sister has a huge crush on him," She got out of the car at the center.

I laughed "Has she tried to talk to him?" I lifted Paul out of his car seat.

"She's too afraid to talk to him."

Ana laughed "Nicky is a sweet heart, she shouldn't be afraid of him."

"Nicky?" Sadie's eyes widened as if she had discovered one of the world's greatest secrets.

"Nick!" I said sternly enough to make Ana jump and give me a questioning look.

I sent Sadie and Mrs. Roberts through the mess of visitor metal detectors, as Ana and I took Paul through the employee security. Paul ran back and forth through the metal detector his overalls setting it off every time until I caught him, Harry just laughed. Ana showed Mrs. Roberts and Sadie to the family room, while Paul and I went to see who I was with.

"Anthony, Kevin, Kyle, Tiffany, and Becca" I read to Paul.

"ANONY" Paul squealed.

"Yes Paul, Anthony"

"E-all" Paul squealed hugging Dave's leg as I put our stuff in my locker.

I shook my head "Dave I really wish you wouldn't . . . ."

"Hush" He scolded.

I sighed and slung Paul up on to my shoulder. Kevin and Kyle had their noses pushed to the window on their door.

"Morning Alex" They both said. Kyle had an ear to ear grin "I get to go home this weekend."

"Good job Ky" I gave him a high five.

Kevin looked at his feet.

I lifted his head "I have a surprise for you as well."

"Who's the baby?" Kyle asked.

"I no baby I a big boy" Paul objected.

"This is Paul."

"He's small" Kevin said.

"Yep, let's get Anthony then the girls."

Kevin and Kyle ran as fast as they could racing to Anthony's door. Anthony had his face against the door in anticipation.

"Can we let him out, Alex?" Kevin asked.

"Please?" Kyle begged.

I handed them the keys "Ok, ok."

"DAD" Anthony shot into my arms nearly knocking Paul and I over. I hugged him and set him down catching my balance. "Look! Look!" He lifted his shirt "Twenty-two, dad twenty-two."

"Awesome" Kevin said giving him a high five.

"Go Anthony" Kyle hugged him.

"I am very proud of you." I hugged him again "And so will everyone else be."

Dave tapped my shoulder "Your mothers are here and your mama is demanding to see her grandchild now."

I smiled "Tell Mama I am coming and to hold her horses."

Dave shook his head "As you wish Alex but death by stupidity is still no reason to miss work."

"Ok let's go get the girls before your nana has a cow, Paul."

Paul giggled.

Kevin laughed too "Which girls?"

"Tiffany and Becca."

"Becca!" Both Kevin and Kyle gasped.

"Yeah."

"Can we stop in the wash room really quick, please?" Kyle asked.

"I don't see why not."

My mama could wait so I took them to the wash room. Kyle picked up a tooth brush, and attacked his teeth; the label said it was his. Kevin straightened Kyle's shirt and took a comb to his hair.

"Boys?" I questioned letting Paul down to hug Anthony.

"Yes?" Kyle said mouth full of spit and tooth brush.

"Something I should know?"

"No" They laughed.

"Uh huh, well, let me see." I said taking the comb and fixing Kyle's unruly hair. "There perfectly handsome."

We got Tiffany first as usual she greeted us with her dismal attitude. "Why do I have to go?" She growled at me.

"I have a surprise for you" I sighed trying to keep form showing my exhaustion.

"A naked girl?"

"Nakie" Paul giggled.

I shot Tiffany a look and tried hard not to laugh "No Paul no one's naked."

"Then I am not going" Tiffany argued.

"Then Sadie will be very sad, as she is very worried about you."

"Yeah right."

"Sadie" Paul smiled "She smudge her Halloween make up to come here."

I laughed "Paul come here" I lifted him back on to my shoulders.

"Fine" She growled

We got Becca and Kevin and Kyle got all shy and Kyle tried to flirt, it was cute. Although Becca wasn't even paying attention to them, she was focusing on the floor tiles.

"Something wrong Becca?" I smiled down at her.

"You mean other than her being in this sh . . ."

"Tiffany, don't even finish that" I cut her off.

Becca looked up at me and stretched her arms up.

"Hold on, Becs" I pulled Paul down, he grabbed Anthony's hand and started to chatter away to him. I picked Becca up.

"My mom here?" She trembled.

"I don't know yet" I watched the boys chase each other down the hall.

"I made a mistake" She showed me her band-aided arm.

"It's ok" I smiled at her."

She jumped down and ran to her mom as we entered the family room.

"TIFFANY" Sadie squealed flying in to her arms.

"Well then" I nodded rubbing my ears "That, yeah." I shuddered Sadie was scarier looking happy then upset.

Kyle joined his family and Kevin hid with Anthony behind my legs "Is Dad . . . ."

"No Kevin, just your mom" I pulled him forward, he smiled and ran to be with his mom.

I picked up Paul and whispered "Go find Nana" I set him back down.

He giggled running full force in to Mama's arms. Anthony stood next to me kicking his feet studying the floor tiles. I picked him up.

"Come meet your family." I walked him slowly over to the corner of the room where my mama was sitting, Uncle Christian was with her.

"Where is Mom?" I asked

"She is in the bathroom, now let me see my grandson."

I sighed "Anthony this is your great uncle Christian and your . . ."

"Nana" Paul cut me off "Anony."

"Excuse me, Alex" Tiffany tapped my shoulder.

"One second Mama, stay here Anthony." I turned "What's wrong?"

"With me" She shrugged "Nothing, thank you for bringing my Sadie but um . . ." Tiffany pointed to Becca balled up on the floor crying.

I nodded "Thanks, go enjoy your time with her she was really worried about you and as Paul pointed out she smudged her Halloween make up to be with you."

She laughed "He's cute, how old is he?"

"Three."

I went over to Becca and knelt down beside her "What's wrong Becs?"

"Mom doesn't love me today; she left because I was bad."

I gritted my teeth and picked up my walkie-talkie "Dave" I choked.

"Yes" He answered "What do you need?"

I laughed "Want a list? No um can you come here a minute."

"Yep."

"Thanks" I said; turning back to head back to my family, just in time to see Ms. Meyers entering the room, talking with Mom.

"Daddy" Paul clung to my leg.

"Paul" I said picking him up.

"Anony have twenty-two band-aids not twenty-three, he come home now?"

I laughed "Not yet, little guy." Anthony was playing chess with Ana's dad. "Sir, I am glad you and David could come today."

"Wouldn't miss time with my grandchildren for the world" He smiled.

"Ana" Anthony excitedly ran over to her and lifted his shirt "Look one less band-aid."

"Awesome" She hugged him.

"And Papa said when there all gone he will give me five dollars."

"Dad." Ana made a disapproving face "Don't spoil them.

Anthony went back to playing chess and Paul crawled up Uncle Christian.

"Take it easy on him Anthony he is getting old" Mama teased Ana's dad.

"Ok" Anthony said moving a rook.

"Good morning Ms. Meyers" I gulped.

"Good morning, Alex, you got my message."

"Yes Ma'am."

"Excuse me Jules I need to speak to Al a moment" Dave said as he entered the room. "You needed me?"

"Yes, Becca."

He looked over at Becca balled up under an end table. "I see, no problem I'll take care of this."

"Thanks." I said "Is it just me or is it like a million degrees in here" I stared to walk around the room.

Tiffany shrugged "I'm fine."

"No Alex, I'm actually a bit cold" Kevin smiled.

I nodded and went back to my family "So, Ms. Meyers, how can we help you this morning."

"I was checking on the boys" She smiled "Dave" She caught his arms as he was carrying Becca out. "You always make your employees work sick?"

"No ma'am, Alex works on his own sick, tired, frustrated, stressed and even on his days off."

Mama laughed "Ms. Meyers it would take an earth quake forced miracle or worse to get my boy to call out of work."

"Well, Alex you should rest you look ten times worse than you did last Friday."

"Thank you ma'am, I will."

She sat and talked to the boys I sat near Mom and laid my head back against the wall, it was pounding, I was over heating and I was in server need of sleep. Ana and I both had classes tonight and tomorrow was the charity breakfast at the school. I felt Ana's hand on my shoulder I opened my eyes; her brother was glaring at me.

"Davie" She frowned "Don't give me that look; you are too much like Mommy"

David smiled an evil crooked smile, before his accident he always smiled like that and was very scary when he was mad. Anthony crawled up in to my lap and whispered in my ear "Daddy get her away from us she thinks we are babies or something."

I choked trying not to laugh and hugged him "I bet your Ana can fix that."

Ana gave me a suspicious look and went to her office for a second. I got up and walked around the room again Kevin was playing checkers with his mom, she actually looked happy this visit. Kyle sat with his mom and step dad discussing his overnight trip home, he was biting his nails.

"Hey you" I smiled at him "Stud like our self shouldn't be so nervous."

"I'm ok" He smiled back.

"Oh Alex while you are here" His mother said "I'd like to thank you for getting him a different roommate he seems much happier."

"Oh you're welcome, but it was more Ana than I." I neglected to tell her that an angered lion would have been an improvement to sharing a room with Curtis.

"So when are you two tying the knot and starting a family?" Kyle's step dad teased.

I blushed and stammered "I uh am um not sure."

"*Brian*" Kyle's mom laughed "Stop your making him blush."

"No, no it's fine; I hear it daily from her dad."

"How long have you two been together?" Kyle's step dad asked.

"Unofficially eight years on and off, officially three and a half on and off."

He laughed. "So can we take him now or . . ."

"He is free to go just sign him out in the office" I said good-bye and headed over to Tiffany and Sadie snuggling in the recliner.

"Geese, you ever going to leave me alone?" Tiffany stuck her tongue out at me.

"I am just checking on you, to see if you need anything."

"Chocolate sauce, satin ties, privacy" She smiled evilly.

I choked not expecting that answer and Sadie blushed making her twice as creepy looking. "Funny" I nodded "I'll bite you prove to me you're into staying clean and I'll give you privacy."

"How about you just get me my necklace back."

"That I am already working on, it isn't something I exactly have say on."

By the end of lunch I was done! My nerves were shot and I had passed physically and mentally exhausted hours before and I still had three hours to go. Mom and Mama were enjoying the boys; Uncle Christian was talking with Ana's dad and David. I sat down and put my head in between my knees, hoping it would help, right as my walkie-talkie went off.

"ALL HANDS, ALL HANDS D-HALL! I REPEAT ALL FREE HANDS"

I groaned and replied "Sorry hands tied visitation supervision."

"Your excused Alex" The voice that came back sounded like Bruno. "ALL HANDS ALL FREE HANDS" He repeated again.

Mama looked at me I shrugged.

"Alex" Ms. Meyers addressed me "I shall see you next Friday; everything seems to be going well. I hope you feel better."

I stood "Yes ma'am thank you." I shook her hand and she left. I sat back down and sighed.

Uncle Christian looked at me "Hmm Henry" He said to Ana's dad "I don't know about you but to me Alex looks rather sick."

Ana's dad nodded "Very much so."

"Uncle Christian I swear I am fine." I objected.

I sat and watched my boys play and talk. About two Paul crawled up in to my arms and yawned. Anthony talked with my parents and Ana's dad. Paul fell asleep around two thirty; Uncle Christian lifted him and took him somewhere I was so dizzy I didn't even argue. Finally it was four and every one said their good-byes. I asked mom if she could bring Sadie and Mrs. Roberts home then I took Kevin to his consoling appointment and Anthony and Tiffany back to their rooms.

"Thanks again, even if we couldn't make out it was nice to see her" Tiffany smiled.

"Remember our deal" I winked locking her in.

"Yeah, yeah" She laughed flopping down on her bed.

I picked up Anthony and carried him to his room hugging him tightly "I will be back Sunday, be a good boy and if you need me or Ana we are a phone call away."

"Ok dad" He smiled and sat at his desk to write in his journal.

"Love you Anthony see you Sunday."

"Love you too Daddy."

I left the room and Dave caught me by the arm "Go home your sick."

"I'm headed home, I swear."

"Where is Paul?" Ana greeted me at the car.

"Uncle Christian . . ."

"Ok honey I'm driving."

I nodded and sprawled out in the passenger's seat laying my head back. I woke up at home in the drive way, more like Ana woke me as she had school and so did I. Mama greeted me at the door with Tylenol and water, I reluctantly took them and looked in at Paul whom was still sound asleep.

"He will be up any minute" Uncle Christian smiled "You go rest."

"Yeah, so."

"And this is from the young lady with the temper unbefitting her."

I took the note and laid back in the recliner to read it "Dear Alex, thank you for taking me to see Tiffany. I apologize for any trouble she gives you. I hope you feel better see you next Friday sincerely Sadie." Then at the bottom it listed her number and said "Please call me, if you get a chance." I folded it over I would call her later. Uncle Christian put a hot cloth over my eyes.

"Dove è il(where is) Mama?"

"She is at A.J's and your mom is working you are stuck with Paul and I."

"Oh, ok that's not a bad thing."

Nick came in around five thirty followed by Colt; the beasts had a foot ball game.

"Ugh Al you look like dog food" Colt said hugging me.

"Thanks rodent love you too, go do your home work."

"Uncle Nick read more?" I heard Paul ask.

"I will Paul let me finish my math."

"Ok, I paint for Uncle Chris."

Around six thirty the beasts came in hooting and howling "We . . ."

". . . Won . . ."

". . . Oh . . ."

". . . Yeah . . ."

". . . . Crimson . . ."

". . . in the . . ."

Uncle Christian clamped his hands over their mouths "Congratulations on your win but Alex is sick and your mothers are working dinner is late I just ordered it. Get your gear off and your uniforms in to the wash." He sighed "Alex, keep that on your eyes."

"It's cold and I wish to be with my son" I objected.

"He is reading with Nick and I will make it hot again."

I stretched back out in the recliner and closed my eyes again admitting defeat.

I woke to the smell of Pizza and Kenny shaking me.

"Dinner" I said before he could.

"Yeah, and I was wondering if you had seen Andreios' food I can't find it."

"Fridge its lettuce" I growled.

"Never mind Al, but its d . . ."

"Dinner I caught that" I stood and stretched walked over to the fridge grabbed out the romaine lettuce marked Rei and shoved it at Kenny. I lifted Paul in to his chair, pushed in Nick's seat, pulled straws out of Christopher's nose and Christian's ears, then took my place near Colt.

Uncle Christian smiled "And they said you had no Tina in you." He hugged me "You sure you are up to dinner?"

"No" I muttered.

"You want to go lay down."

"No."

"Want some pizza?"

"Sì."

"Ok."

"You can't get sick Al, breakfast with Santa is tomorrow" Colt whined at me.

"I'm not don't worry" I lied.

"Don't lie Alexander it's unbecoming of you" Uncle Christian Handed me my plate.

"Who is lying" Mama frowned joining the table "Chris . . ."

"Wasn't us . . ."

". . . This time . . ." The twins automatically objected.

"For once they are telling the truth, it was me Mama" I said.

Mom frowned at me "Alexander at nearly twenty-two I should not have to tell you not to lie."

"Sorry Mama, sorry Mom, I was trying to believe I am not sick."

Kenny snorted; "Sure Alex and the twins truly are aliens."

"Sono (they are)" Nick muttered.

"That is enough, time to eat" Uncle Christian stopped our bickering.

After dinner I went to take my online course. I checked the grade on my last assignment. "C: expand your taste in music, try something made in the last five or even ten years" I growled to myself; then checked my new assignments for all courses. The new music one was about composing our own music and the psyche was about my end of term paper. I Groaned and laid back down in the recliner.

"Well dad's home for Christmas so I suggest . . ."

"He's as stubborn as my little one," Uncle Christian cut Ana's dad off.

"No, he is as stubborn as his mother" Mama laughed and hugged Mom.

"Ana kissed my forehead and I opened my eyes all the way "I wouldn't mind waking that way every day" I smiled at her.

"Hey sweetie" She laughed "Paul in bed?"

I nodded and stood up stretching "Hello sir" I greeted Ana's father.

"Hello you are coming to the pool hall with me" He responded.

I sighed "Yes, sir, but with all due respect I mus . . ."

"Non discutere (Do not argue)" Mom cut me off.

"Sì signora (yes, ma'am)" I gulped.

I knew what this was about. I knew it was a battle I could not win and I knew without a doubt that slamming my head into the Ana's dad's minivan window would not make things better. David put his hand against my head to stop me "No!" He barked at me.

"Davie" Ana frowned "Don't yell."

"That's my fault baby I was banging my head on the window" I sat up in my seat.

Ana's dad sighed "Out and straight into me dad" He frowned.

"Yes sir."

The pool hall pulsed with loud in style music, teenage girls who knew better wearing too little clothing, Samantha, Jeremiah, and Kenneth the fourth were running around like crazy, Mrs. Wittson was helping them. Mr. Wittson was cooking and Sir was in the bar.

I walked over to him "Good evening Sir."

"Hello Alex, how may I help you tonight?"

"Check up, Sir."

"Well if my boys told you, you have a sinus infection, than you probably do . . ."

"Dad" Ana's Uncle Ken frowned "Just check him he's twice as stubborn as Tina."

Sir laughed "Ok, ok, come here what are your symptoms?"

"Fever, dizziness, congestion, extreme migraine" I sighed reluctantly knowing that I was sick.

"You know what I am going to say?"

"Yes, that I have a sinus infection, I need to increase my fluids and rest."

"That and go home and go to bed."

"Yes Sir."

I climbed into the Van and laid my head back.

"And?" Ana's dad looked at me.

"You were right I'm to go home and rest" I sighed.

CHAPTER 11
PAUL AND SANTA

"SOME DAYS IT IS NOT worth biting through the straps in the morning." That is what Nick's shirt said and that is exactly how I felt.

"More pease, Daddy" Paul showed me his empty plate and I cut up one of my pancakes for him.

"Alex" Someone said.

I jumped nearly out of my skin "Hullo Katharine" I glared at the girl standing near me.

"Who's your little friend?" She gestured to Paul.

"My son" I said through gritted teeth.

"Our son" Ana said holding me closer to her than usual.

"Oh" Katharine stuck her nose in the air and walked away.

"OOO I hate her" Ana bristled.

"Hate Who?" Kenny sat down next to Paul.

"Katharine Smith" Ana growled.

Uncle Chris shuddered "That apple didn't fall far from the tree."

Ana laughed "I love my Alex, and that little thing needs to stay away from him."

"Honey can you watch Paul for a moment I need to . . ." I vomited all over the table "Move Paul, move Paul I tried to say before I vomited again. Ana must have understood me because she and Kenny moved him over to sit with Mama.

"Daddy ok?" He asked.

"I'm fine Paul" I swallowed down hard "I'll be right back." I ran to the nearest boys' bathroom.

Uncle Christian was right behind me "Well, that was impressive."

I looked at him "I'm sorry Uncle Christian that was not . . ."

"No worries" He cut me off "Christopher and Christian went to find a janitor."

"I'm sick."

"Yes you are" He chuckled "Don't worry Paul is fine."

"That's good; I didn't vomit on anyone other than myself?"

"No, but I suggest this when you're done cleaning yourself up" He handed me a handful of breath mints.

"Thanks" I tried to smile.

"No problem let's go see how Ana and Paul are doing? She put him in line for Santa."

When I got back to Paul he was three people away and talking a mile a minute to Ana. I stood next to them looking like I wasn't so sick; I felt dead.

"Daddy, I going to ask Santa for Anony" He smiled at me.

I laughed and smiled at him "Well I don't know if Santa can do that but I know he will try."

"Here" Colt shoved a bottle of pills and a bottle of water at me "Sir, says take two every six hours and David says next time aim it so you hit the twins."

"DAVIE!" Ana glared at her brother who was still sitting at the table with Mama.

"I agree with him" Colt smiled.

"Colt" I growled "It wasn't funny."

"Yes it was and Mama says you have to take those now and make sure you get a decent picture of him and not just on your phone.

"Fine" I scowled pulling out my wallet.

"On me" Mr. Wittson handed me enough money for six pictures "Make sure they give you at least two frames."

"Thank you, Sir." I said.

"You're welcome, now take that medicine."

"Yes, Sir."

I took the medicine and watched the little boy about five in front of us flip out at the sight of Santa. I hoped Paul wasn't afraid of Santa. When it was Paul's turn he crawled right up in to Santa's arms and started to ramble.

"Hello Santa how is you? Me and Anony must have been really good this year cause you did give us a new mommy and daddy who loves me and Anony. But can you make Anony better so he can come home for Christmas please pritty, pritty please, I be a good boy, my new daddy says I'm a good boy.

Mr. Johnson the man who played Santa just laughed "Ho, ho, ho. Well, Paul I will do my very best and your dad is right you are and always have been a very good boy. And I must say you have grown an awful lot in the past year. Can you smile big for the camera please?"

I paid the violent looking girl that looked to be around Nicks age "Six please and two frames, I have crazy parents."

She laughed "Does he talk?"

"Who Paul? Did you just miss him nearly talk Mr. . . . ."

"No Alex, Nick" She smiled.

I jumped.

"I don't look familiar?"

"Slightly" I gulped.

"I'm Sadie's sister I answered the door yesterday morning."

"Oh yeah" I choked at the thought of running into Sadie "Yeah he talks, watch."

"Ok" She shrugged.

"Nick come here" I called to him.

Nick sat his book down and came over to me "Yes Alex?"

"This young lady would like to speak to you."

"Er morning Margaret Ann" He mumbled and kicked at his feet, blushing at the floor.

"It's um just Mag" She winced.

"Um ok morning Mag."

I laughed "Well, I will leave you two to figure out what langue he speaks. I have to go apologize for Paul's blunt requests." I walked away from them laughing to myself and walked right in to Wilson.

"Eye's open then walk mi amigo" He laughed at me.

"Sorry Will, have you seen Mr. Johnson? Paul . . ."

"I saw" He tried hard not to laugh.

"Hmm, well have you seen him?"

"Last I saw he and Ana's granddad were talking over by the vending machines."

"Thanks Will"

"Yeah sure, no problem" He called after me as I ran a crossed the room.

Wilson was right Sir and Mr. Johnson were talking by the vending machine.

"Sir, Mr. Johnson" I gulped "I apologize for interrupting but Mr. Johnson I am so sorry for what Paul said I had no idea . . ."

"No worries, you're probably the best thing to happen to those boys. Last year that woman had them here and Anthony asked me for new parents, I thought she was going to kill him then and there and the look on his face said he thought so too. Where is he now?"

"C.H.T.D.C." I choked out.

"Oh, I see." He smiled sadly "State had their way all kids would be in centers like that."

After the breakfast Colt had basket ball, the beasts had piano lessons and Nick had karate. Ana and I took Paul home. She and him played and bonded while I got some more rest.

When I woke up Paul was in my lap "Arg Daddy hand over me treasure."

I smiled and laughed, he had one of Mama's bandanas tied around his head, a sock over one eye to make a patch and a paper sword. "Well

aren't you a sight, but I don't have any treasure, I have cuddles though."
I wrapped him tight in my arms and cuddled him.

"Hello Paul . . ."

". . . Hello Alex . . ."

". . . We got . . . ."

". . . Hair cuts."

Paul stared at my brothers and his face said it all. They both had the underside of their hair shaved. I shook my head "I see."

Colt came in his hair was cut long and shaggy like mine was at his age. Nick's was trimmed short do to his curls his hair grew out not down so he liked it short.

"I see Mom took you to the barber." Mom didn't get Kenny and I for haircuts any longer at almost 22 and 19 we were in charge of our own hair. I liked mine long and had Uncle Christian trim the dead ends when necessary and Kenny kept his short and neat.

I looked around and found a note from Ana "Down doing laundry, Kenny and Juliet are upstairs and your little pirate has a treasure for you." I picked Paul up "Where is my treasure huh?"

He giggled and kissed my cheek then ran off to his room.

"I see you got your treasure" Ana laughed carrying a basket in.

"Hmm, he kept telling me I had the treasure. Can you please pass me the phone?"

"Sure dear" She handed me the phone "Calling any one good?"

"Returning a call actually?"

"Oh?"

"Sadie asked I phone her if I could."

"Oh OK. I was going to sleep at my dad's tonight if you don't mind?"

"Ok Baby doll" I said. I pulled out the number and dialed.

"Hello" A young boy said.

"Hello is Sadie available?"

"SADIE" The child yelled "*IT'S FOR YOOU!*"

There were some scratchy sounds and a loud yelp of pain "Hullo?"
She finally said.

"Hello Sadie, this is Alex, you requested I call you?"

"Er Yeah can you meet me at the pool hall tonight around nine this is an unsecure line." I heard slight giggling "See" She growled.

"Um hang on" I looked at a clock it was only four thirty "Sure."

"Ok thanks see you there" She said and disconnected fast probably to go attack the poor little boy again.

The phone started ringing the second I disconnected "Hello?"

"Hi is Colt there?" A young girl beamed.

"May I ask who is calling?" I asked.

"Danni."

"Hold please" I passed the phone to Colt "Danni" I smiled. He blushed, took the phone and raced in to the bathroom locking the door.

Ana raised an eye brow at me laughing.

"First girlfriend" I smiled.

"Awe how cute."

"Right cute" I sighed.

"So what did Sadie need?"

"Me to meet her at the pool hall, because she couldn't discuss it on the phone; are you going to come with me?

"Yes, you rest some more I'm going to take our pirate sledding it has been snowing and I want to go play in it."

I smiled "Ok Honey, you two have fun."

"I didn't say he did!"

"Calm down, please" Uncle Christian pleaded.

Half asleep I heard my parents talking but I couldn't make out any one but Uncle Christian, whom sounded really close by me.

"He spent all day resting?"

"He is sick!"

"He needs to call out."

"You know he won't, he has your sisters work ethic" Uncle Christian sighed; I felt a hand on my forehead.

"He still have a fever?"

"He is burning up definitely your son Tina."

I opened my eyes and couldn't see. I freaked out and fell off the couch.

"Whoa easy there killer" Uncle Mike helped me stand and pulled the wash cloth off my eyes.

"Thanks" I blushed.

"Yep" He said.

I looked around "Wha . . ."

"Seven thirty-five" Mr. Wittson said "Paul is down having a music lesson, and my niece is down there watching . . ."

I nodded "Um ok?"

"Your mother? You know beautiful lady long blonde hair, blue eyes, evil as all sin, taught you how to play the drums too even if you like your keyboard better" Uncle Christian laughed "You ok?"

"Disoriented."

"It's showing" Kenny threw a pillow at my head.

I threw it back with twice the force.

"Don't you two start" Mom growled "Al, honey come eat something."

My stomach churned at the thought of food "No thank you Ma'am" I gulped "May I please have some water instead."

She made a face and handed me a glass of water as Mama came up with Paul, he was already in his pajamas.

"Daddy, daddy" He jumped into my arms "Boom, boom, bang" He smiled at me from ear to ear.

"Nana teaching you how to play the drums?"

"Left, left, white."

"Yep left, left, right" I hugged him tight "or in Italian di sinistra, di sinistra, di destra" I hugged him tight. "Where is Ana?"

"Mommy with Papa."

I looked at him lost "Paul bring me to Ana, where is your Ana?"

"Mommy with Papa" He said forcefully.

I looked at my mommy and set him down "Ok Paul we will . . ."

"Stupid" Kenny hit me "He is telling you Ana's at her dad's."

I looked at Paul "Are you calling Ana mommy?"

"Ana is my mommy she love me and take care of me like the book" He showed me one of his books.

"I'm gone" Nick bolted up the stairs more like tried as Mr. Wittson caught him.

"Yeah, Nick, he is good at that" Uncle Chris blushed rubbing his shoulder.

"I didn't do it I swear Al, all I did was read him that book and he kept asking me like Ana . . . and well I wasn't going to lie . . ."

"Hush Nick" I picked Paul back up it was eight o'clock. "Ok monkey time for bed, little men need lots of rest."

He made a face "Daddy read?"

"Of course" I scooped him up and carried him to his room.

"Hey honey" I said coming back out to the living room "You ready to go?" I asked Ana.

"Yeah, babe you?"

"Almost I just have to . . . never mind it can wait."

"Ok" She raised an eyebrow at me "Come here" She kissed me.

"I love you" I choked out.

"I love you, too" She laughed at me smiling evilly.

The room spun and I nearly fell "Let's go and get this over with, beautiful."

"I'm driving, you are still sick."

"Good idea" I handed her the keys.

The pool hall was packed, lines to get in everywhere. "Hey Auntie Crystalline; can we get in without the wait?" Ana smiled.

"Of course, dear" Mrs. Wittson smiled letting us in.

I gulped the pulsing lights, loud music, smells of food and all of the people made me dizzy and I had to stop and sit at the bar.

"Just because you are twenty-one, Alexander, doesn't mean I'm going to serve you. Granddad, Mum, and Daddy would chew you and I both up for it."

I looked towards the sound of the voice "I don't drink, Sam, and you know it!" Sam was Ana's cousin she was six months younger than I was and six times more annoying than my brothers ever could have dreamed of being.

"Well then what do you want?" Her voice was grating and she was glaring at me "Granddad told you to rest."

"Buzz off Sam! Don't you have a table to wait or dishes to wash?" Ana glared at her; they did not get along and many family events end with pulling them a part.

"Daddy has me working the bar to night and Jer's latest fling waiting tables" Sam smirked.

I stood and walked over to Jeremiah letting the girls fight I was not fool enough to try and break them up. "Hey Jer."

"Hey Al, why are you out of bed?" He looked cautiously toward the grill area no doubt making sure his grandfather had not seen me.

"A four foot frightful looking child with temper to back the . . ."

"Sadie" He groaned.

"Uh yeah that's her name."

"No she is coming towards me" He ducked behind me.

"Hey Alex thank-you for meeting me" Sadie smiled pulling Jer out by his arm "Tiff is not here you don't need to hide."

"Do you always make it a point to scare my girlfriend's family?" I raised an eyebrow at her.

"Don't flatter yourself, pencil neck there tried hitting on Tiffany and she nearly killed him" Sadie growled.

"Mmm" I nodded "I see. Well Jer do you have a table for us I don't allow minors in the bar or near my girlfriend in a bad mood."

Jeremiah laughed "Sam can put any one in a bad mood, Justin told her off again and dad told him what he could do with his temper near Sam; follow me."

"SADIE!" Kenneth jumped "Alex I um . . . ."

"Chill dweeb" Sadie growled at him "She isn't here."

"I know but you are and I . . ." He stammered.

"And I already told you it is cool" She snapped.

We walked closer to the stage and passed a cute little girl juggling plates. "Cindy!" Jeremiah gasped catching her in a hug and steadying her balance. "Careful."

Sadie started to laugh.

"Something I should know?" I raised my eye brows.

She pointed towards Adam. Adam was Uncle Marc's son he was the beasts' age.

"What that is my cousin, Adam?"

"I'm sorry" She gulped.

"It's fine he does look dumb in that apron." I chuckled "What's wrong Mr. Wittson making the poor baby work?" I called to him.

"Shut it Al" He glared at me. He had been arrested for defacing public property or he would be in Germany on vacation with Uncle Marc.

Jeremiah sat us down near where Adam was bussing tables and muttering under his breath.

"Thank-you again for seeing me, I know you are sick and busy."

"Like I said it's not a problem, I enjoy getting harassed by my girlfriend's evil cousin."

"Sorry" She blushed.

"Why? It is not your fault Sam has permanent p.m.s."

"So does my Tiffany" She sighed.

"I have noticed, no offense, but she definitely hates me."

"No she doesn't, you have no broken bones."

"Oh joy thank you for the warning" I shook my head.

"Spoiled wench" Ana slammed down next to me.

I raised an eye brow "Pardon dear?"

"Sam" she growled.

"Yeah" Adam growled in agreement "She needs to change her tampon and . . ."

"Don't you dare finish that in front of the ladies, Adam; I know my uncle raised you better."

"Sorry Al but . . ." He started to stutter "Never mind."

"Anyway" I turned back to Sadie "What can I do for you?"

"Um" She gulped picking at a scab on her wrist and turning almost transparently pale. "I . . ." She started to shake.

"Adam can you get me rubbing alcohol and a band-aid."

"As you wish but sir . . ."

"Farlo appena(just do it)!" I growled at him he looked lost but did as I had asked him.

"It . . ."

"Stop and slow down whom is your physician?"

"Dr. K-Kyle Wittson."

I handed her a fork "Slow down it is going to be ok."

She slammed the fork in to her hand "Sorry" She started to cry.

"It's ok, I figured this is what you wanted to tell me, you were very nervous today in the center and had a knife up your sleeve when you went through security that you forgot was there. And you're not in trouble but you aren't going home."

"No, she shook her head I want help."

"I know it is ok, does Tiffany know?"

"No, oh please don't tell her, I told on her" She sobbed harder "Because she was scaring me, talking about killing herself because cutting just wasn't doing it any longer"

"You did the right thing."

She took a deep breath "I need help; I know I do, but I need it without my mom finding out about Tiffany and I dating."

"Er here Al" Adam gulped "Wasn't me."

"Hush Adam and be of some use, go get Granddad" Ana growled at him.

"But . . ."

"Ora(now)!" I growled startling several of the tables near us and Jeremiah's girlfriend.

Sir came back with Mrs. Wittson and Adam. Adam's bright blue eyes looked like horrified little beads, he ran his hand thought his greasy mousey brown hair and wiped it on his filthy apron.

I carefully lifted Sadie's arm so Sir could inspect the stab and other cuts.

"Mm" He said dabbed at the wound with a napkin, Sadie just kept crying "I know exactly what this is, your mama use to . . ."

"I know Sir, does it need stitches?"

"No, maybe a band-aid, it isn't too deep."

"Ok, thank-you, Sir" I poured rubbing alcohol over her hand, she winced and gave into a fresh set of tears.

"I'm sorry" She sobbed again and again.

"It's ok" I yawned, Sir evil eyed me.

"You best not be working . . . ."

"No Sir, not yet give me a few minutes."

"Oh no you don't young man you are sick, Ana is going to take you home I will take care of this young lady and if you do not believe I can . . ."

"No Sir, just . . ."

"Just nothing go home!"

"Yes Sir good night Sir" I sighed defeated I could hear Adam a couple tables over laughing happy it wasn't him in trouble.

"Night Alex, Good night Ana" He said escorting us to the door.

"Night Granddad" Ana stifled a laugh.

"Oh and Alex . . ."

"Yes Sir?"

"You aren't working tomorrow I already called Dave."

"Yes Sir" I sighed.

"Alex" Sadie sobbed.

I looked back "I know your, sorry, don't worry I already told you it is no big deal, and how did I know 'I been there that's why I'm here'" I quoted one of the songs off of one of Mama's old country CD's.

"Don't leave" She looked scared.

"I have no choice, don't worry Sir will take good care of you."

"That's . . ." She gave back into a fresh set of tears.

Sir picked her up and carried her to the car, he looked down at me with his piercing blue eyes "She needs you; I'll be by tomorrow to check on you and talk to her and I EVER SEE YOU POUR . . ."

"Sorry Sir" I leaned my head on the window getting dizzy "Peroxide would have hurt more."

He shook his head, shut my door and looked at Ana "Night princess you tell my sons and my daughters they are not above manual labor and we are too packed for them to be home gossiping, Jeremiah, Sam, and Kenneth can't do it by themselves."

"Yes Sir" Ana laughed. "Love you Granddad night."

When we got home I carried Sadie into the house, she had cried herself to sleep. Uncle Christian met us in the studio and took Sadie from me. We had Jeremiah call her mom and tell her something.

"And . . ." Uncle Christian raised an eye brow at me.

I lifted her sleeves and showed him "She will be fine, but Sir wishes . . ."

"He called that is not why I said and."

"No sir I am fine just sick"

"Fine" He took her to the guest room, but didn't look like he fully believed me.

I hugged Ana "Night baby see you at some point tomorrow and by the way your period is no reason to pull away from me."

"She blushed "I um . . . I""

"It's ok Honey."

"I um night, I'm sorry."

I pulled her close to me and kissed her deeply "No need to be sorry."

She looked at me wide eyed "Honey?"

I blushed "I love you."

She laughed "I love you too good night see you in our room."

"Um ok" I nodded and walk down to Paul's room. Uncle Christian was tucking Sadie in what would be Anthony's bed.

"You alright, you look a bit lost" Uncle Christian whispered.

"She um I'm fine I got a *good* night kiss" I blushed.

He chuckled "Well come on he is fine and she needs her rest."

The beasts were out on a date, Nick was on the computer, Colt was at a friend's and Kenny was up in our room working on something. I sat down near Mama who was playing Scrabble with Uncle Chris.

"Appendix" I pointed at Mama's tiles.

"No helping you" Uncle Chris laughed.

"What's wrong with your appendix?" Uncle Christian started to check me.

"Nothing, Mama's tiles can spell it" I took a step back looking at my uncle like he was crazy.

"Uh huh, when you were little you use to spell out what hurt on you."

"If that were the case now I'd be looking to spell head ache and sinuses."

Every one laughed at me.

"Night Mama, Night Mom I hugged and kissed my mothers goodnight "Oh Mr. Wittson, Sir . . .""

"Dad called, Kork and I are going down and so is David" Ana's dad smiled "You go get some rest."

CHAPTER 12
KEEPING PROMISES

I HAD PROMISED SIR I'D rest but I also promised my son I would see him on Sunday and today was Sunday. Sir called to say he'd be over around three, Mama and Mom had taken the big and little boys as they put it and Paul to Nana's, the beasts were at work, Kenny was at Juliet's and Ana and Sadie were at Ana's dad's house doing something girly with string and hair and beads. So I snuck out to see Anthony.

"ALEX!" Harry jumped as I stormed through security.

I had left everything in the car so I didn't have to fuss with my locker or anything else. "Not now I have to see my son."

"But . . ."

"MOVE!" I growled.

"Ok your . . ."

"ALEXANDER JOSEPH" Dave growled at me "GO HOME YOU ARE SICK AND YOUR SON IS FINE!"

"I . . ."

"I already spoke to him, don't make me call your mother."

"Dave please, trust me on this I need to see my son."

"Go home Alex, I am calling your mom."

"No one's home, I am fine." Ok that one was a lie. I was freezing, pale, and couldn't breathe through my mouth or nose due to being congested.

"Don't lie to me, it won't help you." He picked up the phone and dialed "Hello, yes, Henry Anthony is fine. Can you please tell Ana to come get Alex? He thought he would work today anyway . . ."

I glared at him "I can drive myself home."

"Oh ok thank-you" He hung up "Don't give me that look, your girlfriends says you have an hour and five minutes to get you rear-end home."

"Cinque minuti (five minutes)!" I grumbled "It takes five minutes just to get to the d-hall."

"He is in class, go home."

"Not till I see him, just because . . . ."

"You can't spoil him Alex; he has to run the program like everyone else."

I sighed Dave was right. I wrote him a quick note saying I love him and that I am sorry and would see him when my doctor said I could return to work. I handed it to Dave and stormed out.

"Take care of yourself, kiddo" He called after me.

"Your late" Ana practically dragged me out of the car.

"Traffic I swear"

"Yeah right, Alex, you put up a fight."

"No, well yes, but that isn't why I'm late there was a two car on the highway."

"Fine let's get you inside. You know Granddad he runs early."

"Yes dear" I gulped

Inside Sadie was doing homework "I want to graduate" She smiled, her long black hair was natural, and her skin was pale and her makeup dark she wore a leather spiked collar and a dragon pendant. Her clothes were all black.

"Want to talk?" I asked as the phone rang.

Ana answered it "Williams re . . . oh hi Mama yeah I found him . . . no . . . yea work . . . no . . . sure"

I took the phone and put it to my ear "YOUNG MAN" My uncle's voice startled me.

"Yes sir" I gulped it took a lot to make my uncle Chris angry.

"If you cannot follow the house rules I am sure your cousin would love your help at the pool hall."

"Yes sir, Clear sir I will behave, tell my mothers I am sorry and I love them."

"I bet you are sorry now hand the phone to Ana and go rest."

"I love him anyway Mama" Ana laughed and I got lost in her beautiful hair and gorgeous eyes. She hung up the phone and puttered around making lunch.

"Er Alex . . . ?" Sadie waved her hand in front of my face.

"Oh don't mind him, sweetie" Ana laughed "He does this every time he looks at me, has since kindergarten." She bent down and kissed me.

"MMMM" I smiled ear to ear.

She laughed and playfully smacked me.

"Che cosa (what)? I want another kiss."

"I know" She laughed.

"Is that bad?"

"No your just cute, now hush your voice is getting all raspy."

Sadie started to laugh.

"Glad to see a real smile" I said.

"Do you hate me?" She gulped.

"No."

"Does the big guy with the British accent hate me.?"

"No, he was mad at me, that is Ana's granddad and my doctor."

"Does anyone know I'm . . ."

"That you cut? My parents, that you're dating Tiffany? Not unless you told them, that you're here? Yes."

"Does *she* know?"

"Your mom, not unless you told her."

"Phew" She sighed.

Ana raised her eye brows at me.

I nodded "She's a bit close minded?"

"That is an understatement I cut my hair short and she freaked out. I needed to cut it I work at a day care and got lice from one of the kids before they realized they had it."

I choked hard.

"Sorry"

"No, it's ok but in the future don't say lice, my mama goes into a full blown panic attack over it."

"Ok?" It was silent a few minutes as she watched her feet "I miss Tiffany."

"I am sorry."

"I want to cut."

"Not happening, thank you for your honesty."

"You suck."

"Yeah but only good things" I smiled waiting for a more aggressive come back. "Not feeling so tough anymore?"

"No, I just don't fight with ghost."

Ana looked at me "Yep your fever is back, eat your soup and we will cuddle on the couch."

"Ok that sounds great, I love cuddling you."

Ana laughed "Forgive him, Sadie, he is not normally so out spoken I believe this is the fever talking, for my Alex is excessively shy and extremely prude."

"Oh my, poor man, my Tiffany must be having a field day with him" Sadie looked embarrassed.

"Nah" I smiled "Mainly she just tells me to go away and leave her alone."

We ate and Sadie went back to her school work, while Ana and I cuddled on the couch.

"Get up!"

I jumped and bowed unsteadily "Sir"

"You don't listen well do you?"

"Pardon, sir"

"Oh sorry, Alex, I had not meant to awaken you I was talking to your mutt, he's lying on my foot I did not mean to startle you."

"It's ok, Psycho" I whistled "Here boy" I offered him his bone he got up lazily and walked to me as graceful as a drunk "Fool" I muttered giving him his bone. "He only likes Mama and Kenny."

Sir laughed "She asleep?"

"Yes Sir" I ran a hand through Ana's beautiful hair."

"How are you feeling?"

"I cannot answer that there are young ears and ladies present" I heard Sadie laughing from the kitchen.

"That good?"

"Yes Sir."

"When I come back tonight we will discuss your working."

"Yes Sir" I groaned.

He stood and walked in to the kitchen to talk to Sadie, I laid back down.

"Shh, Juliet no one is home except for Al and Ana and they are both asleep."

"Are you sure?"

"I'm positive."

"I'm nervous."

"Don't worry we won't get caught."

I groaned "I am not a sleep and not that I care, but discuss it up stairs so I can sleep" I rolled back towards Ana not bothering to open my eyes light hurt way too much.

"Sorry Al," He chocked "Don . . ."

"Just shut up, be smart about your actions and go into our room I am trying to sleep!"

"Ok" I heard Kenny wince.

"But . . ." Juliet squeaked.

"What, but what!" I sat up aggravated "You two want to have sex right, I don't care at all won't tell don't want to hear the details, not going to think about it I just want to rest!"

Kenny involuntarily jumped back and flinched.

"He . . ."

"Sock draw under the tank tops" I growled at Kenny

He flinched and took another step closer to the stairs. "S-sorry Al."

"Che cosa ci vorrà per riposare(what will it take to get some rest)!" I laid back down and the phone rang. "Hello"

"Hey Al can you . . . tell mom we . . . are out at . . . nine not ten?"

"Benissimo (fine)" I growled at the twins "When I see her."

"Thanks Al, hope . . . you feel better."

"Yeah whatever" I hung up the phone and laid back down. Kenny taped my shoulder "CHE COSA(what)!"

Kenny jumped nearly dropping everything he was holding he handed me two notes and two Tylenol. "Here and Any su . . ."

"Listen to her you'll know when she's happy and zitto e lasciami riposare!" Wow I had never missed my uncle so much. One note was from Sir with the instruction to take the Tylenol and that he took Sadie with him. The other was from Mama telling me they would be home around four it was three thirty. I laid back down and the phone rang again. "Hullo"

"Alex it's me Tavi, Mom needs to . . ."

"Call back about 4:15" I hung up not even waiting for a response and closed my eyes.

"Baby doll you alright?"

"Sono benissimo(I'm fine)" I held her close and finally fell asleep.

When I woke again the house was not empty but no one had bothered me "I love you Uncle Christian" I said automatically.

"Love you to, Al" He chuckled "Have you seen Kenny"

"Yes sir, in our room with his girlfriend."

"Doing?"

"I can only imagine and I don't really want to know or think about it."

"I see" He winked at me we knew what those two did out of sight, they weren't quiet and they weren't smart.

"Where is . . ."

"Daddy! Paul flew in to my arms.

"Never mind."

Uncle Christian laughed "Your mothers are . . ."

"Out on the porch listing to Uncle Chris play guitar, Colts riding his snow mobile and Nick is chopping wood. Ana is at her dad's doing laundry."

"Exactly that's my boy."

"Oh, the beasts say to tell you they are out at nine not ten."

"Ok, they have their bikes."

"Don't look at me."

"I don't understand them either."

"Did you and dad work at the pool hall?"

"Yes."

"Did you like it?"

"It was honest pay I preferred to work at the stable with your mama."

"Did dad like it?"

"No, he had a lot of trouble, and your mothers didn't make it any easier for him."

"I take it he was a bit of a klutz?"

"No, it was his first manual labor job ever."

"Oh."

"He found taking care of your mama easier."

I looked at my uncle wide eyed as if he had just told me he gave birth to a pink hippo.

"Yeah" He laughed "That's what I thought too. So what is with the twenty questions?"

"Curiosity, sorry, Sir."

"It's ok" He chuckled.

"Mommy" Paul leaped in to Ana's arms.

She looked at me "When did he start this?" She asked hugging him.

I shrugged "The other night when you were at your dad's."

"Ok" She set him down and hugged me "What is he watching?"

"I am" Uncle Christian said "Watching a video tape of an old soccer game but it is a commercial."

"Wow that's old" I said.

"Thanks I love you too" He laughed.

"1994 that was last century."

"Your point?"

"That's old."

"Actually it was 1993 the commercial was advertising new car models for the next year I was nine and my father use to watch it with me."

"Did . . ."

"No, he liked hockey and your mothers."

"Ok"

"He was miserable, Al, he also liked to surf, swim, play Frisbee, and volley ball."

"Was he Wiccan like you and Mom?"

"No vampire, similar beliefs."

"Mama?"

"You're going the right way to get your uncle Marc after you and I'm with that one."

"Sorry" I blushed.

"Honey" Ana laughed "We playing twenty questions?"

"He has been since he woke up" Uncle Christian chuckled.

Dinner was chicken cordon blue, mash potatoes, broccoli, and fruit salad. I helped my uncle set the table. "Why don't you work now?"

"I have no need to; unlike your mothers I am content with my earnings and royalties from before, as well as my guard duties."

"Dad?"

"You have your mother's work ethic, he was lazy."

"Oh"

"Now go tell your mothers it is cena (dinner)."

"Yes sir." I went to tell my mothers it was dinner."

"Oh my, Ana, that boy digs too deep . . ."

"I know Uncle Christian Who is the extra plate for? She asked putting Paul into his seat.

"Your grandfather."

"Oh great."

"Papa?" Paul squealed.

"No sweetie" Ana tickled him "My papa you'd call him . . ."

"He'd call me granddad just like you" Her granddad came in.

"Sir" Uncle Christian hugged him.

I took my seat; everyone else came up stairs slowly.

"Jessica weren't you cold?" Sir asked her.

"No daddy, I love the cold."

He shook his head "Alex you may return to work Tuesday."

"Yes sir" I gulped.

"Provided you rest properly."

"Rest?" I started to object "Come diavolo posso supporre di riposare(how the hell am I suppose to rest) . . ."

"I will be home tomorrow" Uncle Christian started to laugh.

"Oh yeah" I nodded.

"When are you leaving dad?" Uncle Chris changed the subject.

"After the holiday, are you trying to get rid of me?"

"No sir, just wondering."

The phone rang and Uncle Christian scowled "Who would be calling during dinner?"

"Christian let the machine get it" Mama frowned at him.

"As you wish mio piccolo(my little one)."

Every one was quiet while we waited for the machine to get it, it picked after six rings. "Christian it's me . . . pick up the phone I know you are there . . . it is dinner time . . . milady ple . . ."

Mama picked up the phone "Donavan, are you alright? Uh . . . Ok . . ." Mama handed the phone to Uncle Christian, who excused himself from the table to the back porch I could see him pacing and he looked thoroughly annoyed the longer he was on the phone. Donavan was Uncle Christian's brother. Mama and he didn't get along, something to do with after my father died.

"Christian is everything alright" Mom asked Uncle Christian as he sat back down to eat.

"È benissimo(it's fine)!" He said sharply changing the subject immediately "So, Sir any more from Kyle?"

"No not yet any day now though" He said looking concerned.

"Good, good."

"My rock it's unbecoming of you to lie to us" Mama frowned at him,

There was a round of stifled laughs around the table as Uncle Christian was always telling us that it was unbecoming of us to lie.

"Il mio piccolo un Donavan è benissimo(My little one Donavan is fine)" Uncle Christian gave her a look.

"Donavan does not call un . . ."

"Mio piccolo not now!" Uncle Christian Said sternly.

"As you wish my rock."

Mom gave them a questioning look; Kenny must have seen what I saw because he stood up and excused himself. Nick and Colt followed suit.

Ana who had not quite finished eating looked at me "Did Mama tell you Paul is checking out a preschool tomorrow?"

"Good, good" I said a lesser man would have bolted instead of trying to help change the atmosphere in the kitchen "Sir, did you know my father?"

"Of course I did."

"Am I anything like him?"

"Yes, you are."

"Alex, Honey come on you need to rest" Ana smiled finally finished with her meal and saving me from having to sit in the kitchen with the tangible tension between my parents.

"Oh I know I do, but I have a son" I lifted Paul "And we are going to go play a board game."

"Ooties, Ooties" Paul jumped up and down in my arms "Ooties please"

"Ok, we can play *cooties*" I emphasized the "c" hoping he would soon call it cooties. We went into his room and got his game and played until his bed time, when I put him to bed.

"You call this nothing!" Uncle Christian muttered as I came out of Paul's room "Note" He growled at me and pointed to the table.

"Yes, Sir." I gulped and read it "Dear Alex, I went with your parents to Wal-Mart, I needed a few things please rest so you feel better. I love you-Ana"

"Colt?" Uncle Christian's older brother squinted at me.

"Hush, Che cosa stai dicendo che è suo figlio Alex di Bella (what are you talking about that's bella's son, Alex, You are just lucky they aren't home" Uncle Christian growled at him.

"Sir" I gulped greeting Uncle Christian's brother.

"Seder! (sit)" Uncle Christian said.

I obeyed he was in too much of bad mood to argue, so I sat and looked at them Uncle Christian was sewing a gash in his brother's leg."

"What on earth where you thinking!" Uncle Christian growled at him.

"Stavo pensando(I was thinking) . . ." He attempted a response.

"Non anche, sciocco(don't even, fool), you aren't twenty-four any longer" Uncle Christian was so angry he was having trouble staying in one language.

"What did you tell vostro (your) piccolo?"

"Nothing now hush!"

"You sure that isn't Colt he looks like . . ."

"Sir" I gulped "With all due respect my father is dead"

"Pay him know mind Al, hand me that peroxide, he knows your dad's gone. He and I were both there when it happened, he hit his head and I think he has been drinking" Uncle Christian sighed.

"Sono spiacente(I'm sorry)."

"No need to be sorry, please hand me the blue bottle."

I picked up a small squat bottle with a white top "Sulfur silvadane" I read.

"Sulfur silvadine" My Uncle Corrected me "It is for burns and this sciocco(fool), has many." My uncle was definitely irritated he didn't normally go around calling his family members fools in Italian unless he was mad at them.

"Am I allowed," I gulp "May I ask what happened?"

"He forgot he is not a bambino(child)!"

I gulped taking a closer look at Uncle Christian's brother he had long blonde hair and shocking blue eyes and looked more like Uncle Chris than Uncle Christian. He was built like Uncle Christian though, tall and broad shouldered. The splits on his lip, eye and arms had already been sewn up. His entire left arm was singed and his right arm had a bone sticking out of his hand. I winced "Uncle Christian should I get Mr. . . ."

"No"

"Can I help you?"

"You already are."

"Um . . ." I gulped "Sir . . . , Sir . . ."

"Let him sleep."

"Concussion?"

"I might give him one."

I tried not to laugh "Ok."

"Hand me that cast equipment." He took the objects from me then looked at me then his brother then back at me "Distract him."

"Er, Uncle Christian, he is asleep."

"Not for long." Uncle Christian kicked the chair out from under his leg.

"Owwww" His brother howled in pain.

"I'm setting your breaks, sciocco(fool), talk to Alex."

I stared at my Uncle in disbelief and gulped "Hello, Sir"

"You've grown more?"

"Pardon?" His accent was thick.

"Have you grown more?"

"No Sir, still seven feet." I had been the same height for five years.

"Hmm" He nodded "See you let your hair out."

"Stay still you, sciocco(fool)" Uncle Christian growled at him.

I gulped.

"You still with Henry's girl?" He continued ignoring Uncle Christian witch I felt was a fool thing to do.

"Yes, Sir" I held my breath.

"I hear you have a son now?"

"Yes sir, two?"

"What are their names?"

"Paul and Anthony, Sir."

"Don't ignore me Donavan, it will not benefit you" Uncle Christian's tone had only been that icy one other time in my life and that was the day we met Nick's dad.

"Chill icy" His brother growled back "I am staying as still as I can with you prodding me?"

Uncle Christian placed his arm in a sling and lifted his leg. "Where?" He breathed arguing with what looked like Neosporin.

"Pardon?" His brother said.

"Not you, Alex is signing."

"Sorry" Sir I gulped.

"No. Tell me where?" Uncle Christian insisted.

"Il mio cuore(my heart) . . ."

"I can fix that later for now hand me the air cast and go lie down on the couch and rest some more."

"Prideful, arroganti(arrogant) . . ."

"Do not go there Donavan it will not help you any." Mama growled entering through the back door. "I knew you weren't well."

"Miladies how are you?" He greeted Mama, Mom, and Ana.

"I have been better, what did you do now?" Mom said.

"My wounds are insignificant, Bella, what ails you?"

"Never you mind him Bella," Uncle Christian growled "He forgot he wasn't un bambino insensato affatto più lungamente(an insane child any longer)."

"What ails me is my wife" Mom shook her head and sighed.

"Tina, My Bella, I told you she is fine, I just checked her earlier."

"English?" I choked.

"Boy," Ana raised her eye brows at me "You are sick, that was English."

"Yeah sorry that isn't what it sounded like."

"It is ok Alex" Mama said sitting next to me "He is just agitated with Donavan." She kissed my forehead "It has dropped a bit."

"Yippee" I groaned sarcastically.

"What's wrong?"

"Nothing Mama, Sono benissimo(I'm fine)."

Ana kissed me and sat on the other side of me "I am going to shower and go to bed I still have work tomorrow."

"Ok" I stared at my feet, then at Uncle Christian and Uncle Chris who were inspecting something that had been bought at the store today.

"We will talk later, Alex, relax" Uncle Christian said.

Uncle Christian's brother was sitting in the recliner "Bella, please pass me the remote"

Mom looked at Mama and shook her head "I should hug you but for being so stupid" Mom handed him the remote "I might just kick you instead."

He chuckled "I am fine, Bella, just a few minor bruises"

"Yeah minor" Mama scowled "Minore confrontato al fuoco (minor compared to the fire). I'm going to shower."

Uncle Chris winced as Mama slammed her bedroom door and then her bathroom door. "I see she still loves you, mate."

"Always" He sighed flipping through the channels.

"Um Sir" I choked "Uncle Christian says you knew my father?"

"Of course I knew him he was . . ."

"Donavan, it is getting late, and Alex needs to rest and so don't you. Come Al we will have our talk in the studio" Uncle Christian cut him off.

"I . . . but, yes Sir" I stammered following him to the down stairs studio.

"Bella, did I say something wrong?" Uncle Donavan asked.

"Not your fault, Donavan, Christian still has a lot of trouble talking about Colt sometimes" Mom shook her head.

"So what does Al know?"

"Only that he was a good guy played piano, keyboard, and drums. Was Jessi's body guard and died in that fire."

Donavan shuttered "That's a bad memory, Bella."

"I know it is bad for all of us."

"Talk to me" Uncle Christian's voice was short and brisk as we sat in the studio, he was staring at me hard as if any second I was going to collapse or vanish.

"She's pulling away" I sighed.

"It happens."

"More than usual; but not more than when her mum died."

"Have you tried talking to her?"

"No . . . I don't know . . ."

"Just say what's wrong?" He chuckled "Now straight to bed with you, you're sick."

"Yes sir, night Uncle Christian."

"Notte (night) Alex."

After saying good night to everyone I went up stairs. Ana was in the bathroom in our room, it was just a toilet and sink, it sounded like she was crying.

I knocked on the door "We need to talk when you get out."

"Real sensitive" Kenny sneered from his side of the room.

"What!" I growled "Share or shut up."

I heard him flinch and drop what ever he was holding "She has cramps you fool, she won't let me help her back to bed."

"Well why didn't you come get me?"

"I did but mom said you were with Uncle Christian."

"Great" I picked the lock and picked Ana up and put her on to the bed. "Quit pulling away from me." I said a bit gruffer than I intended to and I wrapped my arm around her falling to sleep.

"I swear he gets any blinder . . ." Kenny sighed "Would you like Tylenol?"

"Mama?"

"Ok I will get her."

"No Kenny, my Mama."

"Um Ana s . . ."

"I know" She sobbed harder.

"Will my Mama do?"

"Always has."

"I hope it helps, because he is no prince he is a foolish blind . . ."

"Toad" Uncle Donavan cut in.

"Hello Sir." Ken stood and bowed "With all due respect, Sir, shouldn't you be resting?"

"I am fine just as he is."

"He is not fine Sir, he is sick and blind."

Uncle Donavan chuckled "Sometimes people heal better with less rest and as for his 'toadness', he isn't all Bella he has some Colt In him, as well."

"His father was a toad?" Kenny asked.

"If he had gotten any more toad Bella and Princess may have been ok but his girlfriend wouldn't have."

"Whoa wait a minute his dad had a . . ."

"Yes, but she knew Princess and Bella came first."

"Wow, so toadness is genetic? Kenny beamed.

"In his case" Donavan laughed "Although your father can be quiet unsavory."

"I didn't like him, I am glad I have my mothers."

"They love you boys very much."

Ana made a whimpering noise.

"Can you walk Ana?" Kenny asked.

"No" she sobbed "Ooff, dope, he is holding me tighter."

Donavan chuckled "Because you are crying. Is there anything I can get you?"

"Mama or Uncle Christian."

He smiled "Well my little brother is out on the front porch muttering to the stars how foolish I have been and Princess is . . ."

"In the shower." Kenny guessed.

Donavan laughed "Well yes but I was going to say *il suo* piccolo does not favor me, but I will tell her you need her."

"Thank you, sir" Ana sighed as Donavan left.

"Wake him" Kenny glared at the back of my head.

"He is sick" Ana objected.

"You need him, wake him, he won't object."

"Ok, Alex, Alex honey, wake up."

I rolled "Is it Morning already, oh no did I forget to set the alarm for you?"

"No sit up and cradle me?" she asked.

"Uh ok do you sleep better this way" I adjusted for her and she snuggled close to me and started to cry "I uh . . ."

"Cramps you dope" Kenny snapped at me.

"Ok, uh Tylenol?"

"No stupid she wants Mama." He growled.

"Oh ok, well that's easy" I stood up and carried Ana down to the living room."

"Dove si trova la mamma(where is mama)?"

Uncle Donavan said something in Italian.

I blinked "Pardon?"

"On the porch" He repeated himself "Got mud in your ears to night, son?"

"No, sorry Sir thank you . . ."

He made a grunt of consent and went back to channel flipping.

I carried Ana to Mama "She wishes you Mama."

"What's wrong?" Mama looked shocked.

"I uh well I don't know I was asleep" My face flushed and I sat on the porch swing between Mama and Uncle Christian holding Ana as tight as I could still cradling her.

"Ana what's wrong?" Mama asked again.

Ana looked at me and started to cry harder, buried her face in my chest and sobbed "Cramps".

"Still?" Mama said softly.

Ana nodded.

"Well come with me I can fix that."

Uncle Christian lifted Ana out of my arms "Andare a letto(go to bed)." He barked at me.

"Yes, Sir" I gulped and headed back to bed.

Mama gave Ana some patch thing that made the cramps better.

"What did he do?" Uncle Christian asked her.

"He growled at me to stop pulling away" She sobbed harder.

"Mm, he mentioned concern of you doing that to me."

"I'm not trying to, but what if I bleed on his sheets?"

"He will get up and change them."

"He won't be upset?"

"No, he loves you. And despite his silence he understands. His father was a quiet man, Colt could roll with it, Alex can't."

"Is he mad at me?"

"No he is worried." Uncle Christian laid her in my bed next to me and moved my arm around her. "Shouldn't you be sleeping Kenneth?"

"Working on it, Sir" He answered.

"Something on your mind?"

"He is so stupid he can't even treat her right."

"Pardon?"

"Alex."

"He is sick you wait and see the difference when he is healthy."

"Yes, Sir."

"Good night, Kenny."

"Night, Uncle Christian."

CHAPTER 13

PAUL'S PRESCHOOL

I WOKE TO A HORRIFIC night mare and looked at the clock, 8:30. I headed down stairs for a shower. When I came out of the shower Paul was painting.

"Breakfast?" Uncle Christian offered.

"Yes, Please."

"Come ti senti (how do you feel)?"

"Much better thank-you."

"Glad to hear it, anything else wrong?"

"Paul's appointment is around noon correct?"

"Sì (yes)."

I looked over at Uncle Donavan "How do I address him, Uncle Christian?"

"Fool, come here, Alex, wishes to speak to you." He called to his brother.

I choked on my waffles trying not to laugh.

"You find him amusing?" Uncle Donavan asked limping into the kitchen.

"Spiacente (sorry), Sir" I gulped.

"It's fine. What do you wish of me?"

I gulped and looked at my Uncle Christian.

"It's alright, Alex, his growl is the scariest thing to him; especially since he's broken." Uncle Christian chuckled.

"Don't push it, you are still my *fratellino(little brother)*."

I gulped again what do you say to someone you have only seen two other times in your life; Once when you were born, and once because you were an unstable teenager who needed a baby sitter. I gulped harder. "Buon giorno (good morning), Sir."

"Good morning, how are you? How did you sleep?" His demeanor was not calming like Uncle Christian's; it was harsh and gruff like sand paper.

Ok, Sir." I choked. "Have you met, Paul?"

"Yes, he is well spirited and full of life."

"Thank-you, Sir" I spilled orange juice on myself from shaking so hard.

"Easy Alex, Donavan take it easy on him he is more Bella than Colt sometimes. You probably looked more sociable last night on the morphine." Uncle Christian laughed.

I said don't push it CHRISTIAN!"

"Irritabile. Irritabili, andare a rispondere alla porta(irritable. Cranky go answer the door)."

"Why don't you. I am speaking to *our* nipote (nephew)."

Uncle Christian hollered, "Come on in Henry."

"Mike, but close enough."

"Morning Uncle Mike" I smiled.

"Whoa, stop the presses Alex is actually listening to the doctor."

"I have no other choice" I frowned.

"What can I get you Mike?" Uncle Christian asked.

"No delivery for Jess actually."

"Bella and Suo(his) Piccolo are up at the stables" Uncle Donavan growled

"Hey ogre, I heard you are broken, and trust me I know where my little sister, is, she asked me to leave this with you and Al."

"I may be an ogre but at least I have manners and taste."

"OK, take the paint so I can go."

Uncle Donavan pulled the bottle of ink out of his hand "Arrivederci (bye)"

"And good riddance" Uncle Mike slammed out the door.

Uncle Christian glared at his brother "Real mature."

"He is still an obnoxious snob" Uncle Donavan set the ink on the table.

I swallowed hard "I um . . ."

"Yes" Both Uncle Christian and Uncle Donavan looked at me.

"I um . . ."

"You going to vomit on the t . . ."

"No Uncle Christian," I laughed "I'm done with that. I um I'd like to see my father's grave today I haven't been in a while."

"As you wish right after Paul's appointment."

Paul crawled into my arms "Hi daddy, I go school today"

"Yep" I hugged him.

"I scarred you going wit me."

"Yep."

"Can teddy come?"

"Sure."

I took Paul down to the studio with me to finish some of my homework.

"Tu e le signore hanno sollevato bene (you and the ladies have raised him well)." Donavan helped Uncle Christian.

"Mostly me Don, He spent a lot of time with me with his stubbornness."

"He'd make Colt proud."

"That's for sure, he makes me proud."

"Bella says he has been asking a lot of questions."

"Yes, I think he is worried about being a good father."

"I assume the child is being raised same as he was?"

"Yes, and so will Anthony."

"Whom?"

"He has two sons."

"Oh ok, hmm so when do I meet Anthony?"

"Friday if you are here."

"Do I look like I'm going far."

"No."

"Boom boom bang" Paul giggled all the way up the stairs. He was covered head to toe in stickers.

Uncle Christian laughed "You have fun."

"Boom boom bang." He giggled.

"He got in to . . ."

"I see." Uncle Christian cut me off "Go get a wet wash cloth."

"I got it" Donavan said.

"He's just like you." Uncle Christian laughed "You got into the same stickers when you were little your mama laughed so hard she almost cried."

We got him cleaned up and headed to the preschool. He clung to my leg, snuggling his stuffed animal, looking around. Some kids played with paints others were playing dress up.

One little boy looked at him and said "It's not share day you can't bring toys from home."

Paul looked up at me and I picked him up. Most of the kids just stared at Uncle Christian and I.

A little girl pulled on my leg "Wow mister you're tall. Can he come play trucks with me?"

I set him down "Do you want to go play?"

He nodded "Teddy too"

"Ok" I smiled at him.

"Hi I'm Emily, I'm four" The little girl beamed.

"I Paul. I is three." He held up his fingers.

I spoke to the director and head teacher and received a large amount of paper work. Paul came flying over to me and clung to my leg I picked him up. "What's wrong, bud."

"Teddy" He pointed at his ripped puppy on the floor.

"What happened?"

He buried his face in my shoulder and pointed at a boy sitting playing with play dough. "Teddy" He cried.

I picked his dog up "I can fix him" I sighed.

"Excuse me ma'am" Uncle Donavan's thick accent was barely understandable. "Someone owes my great nephew compensation for the damage of his toy."

"Don, it's ok" Uncle Christian smiled "Alex said he can fix it."

"Ma'am That child wrecked someone else's property" Uncle Donavan persisted "I have requested some form of compensation."

"I am sorry the dog was ripped, but I am sure it was an accident they are . . ."

"I have heard enough, come Alex" Uncle Christian said.

"Yes, Sir" I followed him out.

"Ma'am I would like to speak to the child?" Donavan asked pointing to the little girl.

"Sir, like I said . . ."

"That's not why ma'am; I did not mean the irresponsible one I'd like to thank the young lady whom was nice to my nephew's boy."

"Um ok I will tell her."

"As you wish ma'am have a good day."

"You too and I am sorry about his dog. I hope we see you again soon."

"Highly unlikely ma'am."

"Are you done acting like a belligerent fool?" Uncle Christian glared at Uncle Donavan.

"I was not belligerent nor am I stupido(stupid). If a child is not taught responsibility then they will . . ."

"It's fine, Sir." I gulped turning on to the high way.

"Whe . . ."

"Stables, Uncle Christian."

"Daddy?"

"Yes, Paul."

"Where's Mommy?"

"Ana is working."

"Oh."

I whipped into the parking lot and out of the car grabbing Paul. "Mom! Mama!"

"Al?"

"Alex? What's Wrong" Mama looked out of the stables at me.

"He's not going there! Dove è Lizzy (where is Lizzy)?" I spat, Lizzy was the smallest horse she was actually a Shetland pony. "Out grazing?"

"Are you feeling well it's winter, she's in her stall." Mom glared from the other side of Wilbur where she was brushing him.

"Ok, is the sm . . ."

"Yes" Smiled Mama.

"Good Paul's learning to ride." I took Lizzy out of her stable and put on her saddle and reigns and set Paul on her.

"Me big now" He smiled.

"Hold here and here" I told him handing him the reins and tucking his feet into the stir ups. I lead Lizzy into the gated track with Paul on her back.

"Problems Bella? You are going to brush his hair off" Donavan asked.

"How do you tell an eleven year old his father is dead?" Mom shook her head.

"Same way you told the twenty-one year old eleven years ago."

"Colt knew about Al, He left Al a trust fund, He didn't know about Colt jr." Ma'am sighed.

"He left the sperm knowing you two would use it I have Colt's money" Uncle Christian said "It's not quite as much but I think 33,000 is still quite a bit."

"His royalties from the second album?"

"Yes, little one, It was his wishes."

"How do we tell Alex?" Mom sighed.

"I will" Uncle Christian said, "I think he already knows any way."

When Paul was able to ride around the small circle without help I went to clean out Lizzy's stall and left Uncle Donavan to watch him.

"I'm going to talk to Paul" Mom said.

"Me too" Mama added.

"I swear I didn't do it, Uncle Christian."

"I know, I need to talk to you about Colt" He sighed "He started to ask about his father."

"That's good when do we tell him?"

"Um well that's just it Colt, um, Colt is named . . ."

"After our dad I know."

"How long?"

"At least four years you didn't think I needed to know so I didn't say anything, besides Colt looks just me and I look like Dad."

"I will take you to see your father when we are done here."

"Ok? You alright Uncle Christian?"

"Yeah, here I got this you go get Thunderbolt he's waiting for you."

"Cool, I'll take Paul with me."

Thunderbolt was my horse he was a black stallion and despite his name he was a loving gentle horse. He whinnied as I put the saddle and reigns on him. I put Paul on and then hopped up myself. "Let's go boy" I said, he took off slow. "Faster boy, it's ok" He speed up a little when we got out to the track he walked around the hurdles which was fine with me I didn't think Paul was ready for that. Paul giggled running his hands through Thunderbolt's mane. When we got back to Mom, she took the reins and told me she would bathe him. She sent Paul and I to talk to Mama.

"So, what happened at the day care?" Mama inquired.

"He was mean hurt teddy" Paul cried.

"Some kid ripped his dog in half, I can fix it, but the teachers didn't make the kid apologize or anything told us they were just ki . . ."

"Stop."

"I know, Mama, that's why we left."

"Why does the boy need Day care any way?" Uncle Donavan asked.

"Speech and social interaction" I gulped.

"Horse feathers, that kid would talk to a tree stump if it could hold a decent conversation and as for his speech I can fix that."

Mama frowned at him "There's one other place we can check before. Donavan has him playing with his cheerios."

Uncle Christian laughed.

I tried not to laugh, too "I am afraid ask."

"Kenny use to have similar speech patterns as Paul" Mama sighed "Believe it or not Donavan has a job, he's a speech pathologist, and fluent in three languages."

"It worked did it not" Uncle Donavan's sharp tone made me jump.

"He still plays with his cheerios" Mama frowned.

"Well we must go mio piccolo (my little one). I told Alex he could visit his father" Uncle Christian hugged her.

"Want me to keep Paul?" Mama asked me.

"No, he needs to meet his papa" I said.

"His papa would love him" Uncle Donavan smiled "But if the ladies do not mind I wish to stay with them and the cavalla (horses)."

"Sì" Uncle Christian said "Come Alex."

"Coming" I picked up Paul.

"Horsies" Paul cried stretching for Lizzy.

"Mmm . . ." Uncle Christian nodded "Maybe it is best at least this time for Paul not to join us."

"Ok" I sat Paul down "Mama do . . ."

"Go Hunny" She smiled.

"Thanks" I sighed.

"I am driving, you are resting." It wasn't a request or a question, it was a harsh command.

"Yes, Sir" I handed Uncle Christian the keys and sat in the passenger seat. I slept the entire ride. When I woke up Uncle Christian was knelt in front of my father's grave, so I waited as he spoke to my father's tomb stone. I was taught at a young age our loved ones hear our thoughts for them.

"Oh Colt I don't know anymore, what I can say or do to reassure him he is making you proud and doing fine. Little brother it has been twenty-two years and Donavan is still foolishly chasing arsonist. Alex helped me patch him up the other night. Colt jr. has started asking questions, Tina fears it will upset Al. I am not worried Alex loves his brothers, and already knows. He may look and sound dead on you but when push comes to shove he is all Tina. We just fear he is cutting again he has been more moody than usual."

"Ehm" I pretended to stir awake.

"You don't lie well" Uncle Christian glared at me.

"Sorry Sir" I gulped.

"It's fine, visit your father then we will talk, and for the record when you wake you jump about three feet, sit bolt upright and shake the sleep from you."

"Yes, Sir" I blushed. I knelt by my father's grave "Hello Dad I'm sorry it has been so long, I have been very busy. I am sure Uncle Christian has told you about Paul and Anthony. That probably means he has told you about Ana too. Well Dad I just wanted to say hi. I now must go answer for my poor judgment earlier." I stood and walked over to where Uncle Christian was clearing off a double headstone that read Wittson.

"This is Ana's great grandparents they died when you were . . ."

"Twelve, I remember, kind of."

"They were good people."

I nodded and stood waiting for my lecture.

"How much did you hear of my conversation with your father?"

"Enough" I gulped "To know you worry more than you say and Uncle Donavan is as you said a fool."

"Yep"

"Dad was murdered?"

"No his death was an accident; he was not the target nor was the fire an accident like all the papers said. Don and I heard things we should have spoken up about back then and never did. And Don well I have never seen anyone hold a grudge as well as he does."

"How old was Dad?"

"My age, well nine months younger."

"Oooh."

"Si(yes), si(yes) I know I am old. Don't make that face at me."

When we got home Uncle Christian and I were the only ones home so I took a well need nap to kill my migraine. When I woke I felt a hundred times better and the living room was a thousand times louder. I opened one eye, every one was home. I stood up and picked Paul up and carried him down stairs.

"Wheee" Paul giggled when I picked him up.

I sat him on my drum stool and I knelt near him "What did you do this afternoon with nana?"

"I ride horsies"

"You rode the horses, was it fun?"

"Yeah, it was awesome" He beamed.

I chuckled "I'm glad, what else did you do?"

"Bathe horsies and sing Christmas moosic all way home and read wit Nick."

"What did you sing?" I deciphered half of what he said.

"Donkey" He smiled and grabbed my drumsticks "Me play"

"Sure" I lifted him and sat down on the stool placing him on my lap and let him play. I am glad the studio was sound proof and no one could hear him, he was defiantly no musician yet. I ran my hand through his blonde hair.

"Dinner!" Mom called down to us.

"Ok we are coming." I called up the stairs.

"Tacos" Paul smiled.

"How do you know monkey?" I carried him up the stairs.

"My did ask, while you were sleepy."

Who ever invented the taco never had a three year old. It took me an hour to get all the meat and cheese off the floor, table, and chair after dinner. Then I joined my family outside in the snow. Paul looked very cute in his snowsuit. The snow was falling thick and heavy; it was perfect for snowballs making a snowman and uncountable snow angels.

After I put Paul to bed and collapsed into in my chair to watch some T.V. Kenny was playing an old school Mario game; the graphics were weak compared to our new games, but he seemed to be having serious trouble beating the game. The double mint beasts were drawing each other Christopher had a stack of Paper balls building up near the wall and Christian's were building up near the T.V. Colt and Nick were still outside with Mama and Uncle Chris. Mom and Uncle Christian were at the table talking with Uncle Donavan.

My cell rang "Williams" I answered it.

"Hunny" Ana Cried "Come get me."

"What's wrong? Where are you?"

"The on ramp to the highway near work."

"On my way, battery dying talk later, love you."

"What's wrong with . . ."

"Don't know yet I'll be back, watch Paul for me" I cut Nick off.

Kenny blinked at me "Umm . . ."

"Not now!"

I flew down the stairs and into my car my normal 45 minute drive took 20 minutes. I'm glad no police caught me. I found Ana sitting on the side of the rode with a small child.

"He jumped out in front of my car." She shook "I swerved and hit the rail."

I picked Ana up and held her close and looked at the boy for the first time "MOHAWK!" I barked. Mohawk was Wilson's little brother who chose to live on the streets. Occasionally he turned up at the center, his given name was Samuel.

He looked up at me slowly "I didn't see the car I swear."

I held Ana tighter. Mohawk's eyes were glazed over and he was shivering. It had to be about ten degrees fifteen at the most; at least the snow had stopped. I put Ana and Mohawk in my car and turned the heat on full blast. I covered Mohawk with my jacket. I called triple A. We waited for them to come haul Ana's car away. I checked her over she was fine other than a bit scared and very rattled.

"Where is Tiny?" I asked Mohawk, Tiny was a girl he ran with I think they were dating too.

He shrugged "Said something about scoring money."

"Can, I take you home yet, Mohawk?"

"NO!"

"Well I'm not letting you stay outside its too cold."

"So, I was fine."

"Yeah, ok whatever; I am putting you in the center at least for tonight."

"But . . ."

"Mohawk home or center?"

"Center."

We didn't speak after that just waited for triple A. He was asleep by the time I got him to the center. I picked him up and carried him straight to Dave.

"Oh my" Dave gasped "Is that Samuel."

"Yeah" I sighed "He won't go home and I don't know how to reach Will at his new place yet."

Dave took Mohawk and laid him on the bed in his office. "He has lost more weight, where's the girl?"

"I don't know, he didn't know either, I can work again, by the way."

"I can see that you don't look so sick any more, seven to five tomorrow."

"Sounds good" I smiled. Mohawk coughed so hard his whole body rattled "So um may I . . ."

"You know where he is; I have to get Sam down to the hospital wing."

I shot a crossed the hall and peeked at Anthony, he was sound asleep I smiled.

"Why do you insist Sam at least come here?" Ana asked wrapping her arms around me.

I made a promise to Wilson to check on him, he is only fourteen well almost fifteen now." She was still shaking so I held her tighter "Alright dear?"

"I thought I was going to hit him, and then he slipped and fell. Daddy is going to be very angry I crashed my car, good thing I was wearing my seat belt."

"What? I thought he just ran in front of you?"

"Yes, he did but then he fell and the ice was messing with my breaks and I swerved I was so afraid I hit him . . ."

Anthony had started to stir "Night mares" I said.

"You had some bad ones . . ."

"I know, come on lets go home."

"What about Sam?"

"He's fine, Dave will bathe him, change his clothes, feed him, detox him, get rid of his cold and release him to the world again."

She gave me a "don't be heartless" look.

"I'll bring him a book tomorrow."

"'What's your name kid?' The officer glared at her through the flash light beam. 'Blade' She growled shielding her eyes from the light." Mohawk read aloud Tuesday morning.

"Newest one" I smiled.

"You read it yet?"

"Nope it's not even in print yet."

"Oh" He was sweating and shivering all at the same time.

"But you can read it until Dave lets you free again."

"Find Tiny for me?"

"Where would I look? Mohawk every time I have seen her she was with you."

He shrugged and looked at his feet "She's . . ." He started to choke.

"See the . . ."

"Bronchitis" He wheezed "She was headed up to 18th and Simon." He gulped barely audible.

"Alright" I sighed "You already know what I am going to say so I am just going to shut you in here and see you at lunch." I shut and locked his door the detox rooms were plain a bed and a side room with a toilet and shower, and a video system on the ceiling in the main room.

"Long, agonizing, hellacious, painful, and absolutely worth it" I answered Tiffany's question.

"Man, I thought my weekend was bad" She laughed.

"Still dreaming of your room mate" I raised an eye brow teasing her.

"No, that dumb Buddy couldn't take the hint and kept hitting on me."

I tried not to laugh "I'll speak to Buddy, but call it a complement, Buddy doesn't normally speak to any one kindly let alone like anyone."

"Gross" She grimaced.

"Yeah, yeah, back to class. Lunch is over and I need to go catch up with Kevin and Kyle before they pull a hostel take over on Quentin and end up in the time out room."

"Ok" She sighed and went to class.

I walked down to Kevin and Kyle's class they were working on math. So I quietly switched with Quentin. He looked more than happy to leave. He only got a job here because he was Chase's nephew. Chase was the head of the janitorial department. I felt Ralph was being too kind. I had to apply with a resume and a state back ground check just like everyone else. He just had to have the back ground check.

After their classes I brought Kyle to his consoler and Kevin with me to check on Mohawk. He was laying on his back staring at the ceiling. The bed had been torn apart his book in the corner near the entrance to the side room. He looked like death and was barely awake. I unlocked the door and we entered quietly.

"Is he dead?" Kevin peeked around me.

"No, just sick."

Mohawk started to cough, his entire body shook and his lungs rattled. "Owe" He wheezed.

"How you doing?" I asked.

"How the hell you think I am?" He pulled himself to his feet and started to choke again.

Kevin jumped and hid behind me "H-hi S-Sam."

"Oh hiya Runt didn't see you there." Mohawk smiled.

"How's the book?" I asked him.

"Haven't read more than I read aloud this morning" Sam answered.

"He gets a book, unfair" Kevin objected.

"He won't hurt himself or anyone else. He doesn't leave this room everything comes to him." I said starting to put the bed back together.

"How about you read to me Runt?" Sam suggested

"Can I Alex?" Kevin was more than excited at the thought.

"I don't see why not, it's not a text book though."

"Awesome!" Kevin grinned ear to ear.

Mohawk's body rattled as he coughed and shivered. I wrapped him in a blanket and propped him up on about four pillows on the floor till I could get the bed remade. Kevin sat next to him with the book.

Ana knocked on the door "Delivery for Alex" She smiled letting Anthony in.

"Thanks sweetie, can you get me two or three more blankets, please?"

"Sure babe" She smiled and kissed me.

"Oooooooooo Ana and Alex up in a tree K I S S I N G . . ." Kevin taunted laughing.

Anthony scowled "Don't tease my daddy."

"It's ok, Anthony, he is about to read how about you go sit with them while I fix the bed."

He looked at me confused; I walked him over to Mohawk. "Anthony this is Mohawk, Mohawk this is my son Anthony."

"Nice to meet you squirt, your dad's one of the coolest guys on the planet."

"T-thanks" Anthony gulped "Your mommy named you Mohawk?"

I laughed "No, his given name is Sam."

"Oh, that's a better name."

Mohawk laughed and went in to another coughing fit. Anthony jumped back and sat next to Kevin.

"I am going to start reading now" Kevin said.

"Sounds brilliant" Sam wheezed.

"'What's your name kid?' The officer glared at her through the flashlight beam. 'Blade' She scowled shielding her eyes from the light." Kevin read "It was a new cop; Blade had never seen her before. Most cops left her alone as she had made a deal with them. 'What's your real name, kid?' Boy this officer wasn't very smart. Blade rose to her feet. 'I told you I am Blade and you are a new cop. I have permission to be here.' 'I doubt you have permission to be sleeping in central park at two-thirty am how old are you anyway?' Blade sighed 'I am sixteen, I wasn't sleeping I was meditating, and I would like to go back to it.' 'Joan' Officer Johnson called running up to them "Morning Blade, Joan this is the young lady Tom was telling you about.' 'Officer' Blade said thoroughly annoyed 'You need to train your new cronies better."

"What's a crony?" Anthony asked.

"A follower" Kevin said and continued to read "Blade was lean and muscular. She stood five foot six with piercing blue eyes and strawberry red hair down to her knees. She wore heavy steel toed black combat boots, tight black wranglers and an even tighter black tank top. Across her back was sheathed a katana . . ."

"What's a katana?" Anthony interrupted again.

"A huge sword," Mohawk smiled weakly. He was doubled over holding his stomach "Your nana has one."

"Cool" Anthony's eyes went wide "Read more Kevin."

"In each boot was a small knife, in her left pocket was a pocket knife, taped to her right wrist was a switch blade, and holstered to her shoulder was a dagger. She hoisted her back pack and glared at the new cop 'Don't interfere in what you don't know.' Blade walked towards west central park and 108 west. 'Blade' several homeless kids jumped at the site of her. Blade wasn't homeless, she could go home whenever she wanted or needed too. And she did she just preferred to lay in central park and watch the night sky. She walked up to a group of guys dressed like her only difference was the weapons. 'Fire Ball' She growled. A tall boy with a rat like face and tattered Mohawk jumped and turned. 'Yes blade, must you be so icy.' "Damn cops, I don't see how we're suppose to protect their little park from rouges if they're trying to pop us on loitering and concealed weapons!' Kevin stopped to take a breath; he looked at Mohawk "What's he on this time, Alex?"

"I don't know my guess is heroin or cr . . ."

"Heroin," Sam choked cutting me off "Was addicted, I haven't used in about six months drugs take money."

"Drugs are bad for you!" Anthony piped up.

"Yeah. Squirt that's why you won't do them" Mohawk started to choke again "Did you call the school Al?"

"Yep" I answered "I'll have your work for you tomorrow. Does Tiny still attend school?"

"If she feels up to it, but not if she's out working . . ."

"Alright," I picked him up and laid him down I'll get you a real doctor this isn't bronchitis and as for you two" I looked at Anthony and Kevin. "You can read more to him later It is dinner."

"Yes, Alex" Kevin said dog earring the page.

As Anthony and Kevin ate I made a quick call to Ana's granddad I didn't believe for a minute that Sam had bronchitis. Kenny had it almost every winter and it never looked that bad. After dinner I took them to their rooms. Kevin told Kyle about Mohawk being back and reading to him. Anthony sat to do homework, draw and write in his journal. I hugged and kissed my son good night and went to meet Ana.

"We have to go to Eighteenth Street" I muttered, grabbing my coat.

"WHAT!"

"18th" and Simon where . . ."

"I know what it is but why?"

"Mohawk's girlfriend or friend that's a girl however you want to put it."

"Ok, why the cranky face?"

"Because, I have thirty seconds to get from here to the detox hall, or Sir will give me a lecture on being prompt" I said starting to run.

"Granddad's lectures are enough to make me cranky too" Ana laughed.

We got there just in time "Sir" I said catching my breath.

"Hello Alex, Ana."

"Hi, Granddad" Ana smiled hugging him.

"So where is Sam?" He asked.

Sadie stood behind him looking absolutely miserable.

I smiled at her "Third hallway on the right tenth door." I winked "Tell her you two have ten minutes, so make it count and no scaring my Genevieve."

Sadie took off like a lightning bolt and I showed Sir into Mohawk's room.

"Samuel" Sir woke him.

"Sir" Mohawk smiled starting to cough.

Sir sat him up "Have you been taking your Z-pack I sent you?"

"I was until my *tunnel mate* sold them as drugs so we could get food."

"Mmhmm" Sir scribbled something down. "How is your tunnel mate? Last I heard you and him were cleaning up?"

"Yes Sir, we have been clean for about six months. We drop in that NA meeting at the Baptist church on sixth on Tuesdays."

"How's Miss Amelia?"

He shook his head "We got in a fight and she took off to work the streets down on 18th and Simon."

"What were you fighting about?"

"My meeting I should be at right now, she doesn't see why I'm cleaning up."

"Ok, but your tunnel mate does?"

Mohawk broke in to another coughing fit. "He is all for it."

"Wait you go to school, NA meetings and the doctor but not home?" Ana looked at him confused.

"I can't" He wheezed.

"You know Wilson is worried about you?"

"He wouldn't understand he didn't hear what they said. Sir, does and Mrs. Williams did but I can't stay where my parents can get to me."

"Ok" Ana shook her head.

"Hey, wait you told my mom and not me, when I am the one continually saving your butt" I objected.

"Yeah, sorry, Al but your Wilson's best friend" He stared to choke again.

"You haven't told them about your tunnel mate" Sir frowned at him.

"I haven't had a chance yet, I will."

"Now is as good a time as any, Sam" I sighed.

"Spike" Sam smiled ear to ear "He is sooooo gorgeous."

"Got it bud, I'll find Spike and Tiny tonight, ok?"

"Thanks Al"

"Don't thank me, that's your brother he had me promise to look after you."

"Let me listen to your lungs one more time" Sir smiled and pressed the stethoscope back on his back. "Deep breath."

Mohawk wheezed in and out "It's just a cold."

"It is pneumonia" Sir corrected.

"Ugh" Mohawk groaned "I will miss so much school."

"We'll tell them. Good night, bud, try to get some rest" I said and left to fetch Sadie.

Genevieve looked up at me when I walked in. "Knock much, Dog Breath?"

"I don't have to knock" I laughed, I wasn't always Genevieve's favorite person. "Alright, Tiffany give her back, she has to go."

"I want to keep her" Tiffany whined.

"And I want a full night of sleep, now let her go."

"I hate you, she's not here anyway"

I looked at the shaking lump under Tiffany's blankets "Let's got Sadie, Sir will not be . . ."

"Coming" She shot out of the blanket and back down the hall to Sir.

"You suck" Tiffany growled "I was going to get what I wanted."

"Well you will see her Friday."

"I want congical visits" She hissed.

"Take it up with Dave" I laughed "Night Genevieve, lights out."

"Night Dog Breath" She smiled.

"Good night Tiffany."

"Yeah whatever" She growled.

I was sure I heard Genevieve laughing as I left.

Spike paced back and forth in front of the Baptist church on 6th and Evergreen Terrance. He was tall bone thin he had a spiked collar and spiked hair; he was pale and shivering.

"Spike I presume" I greeted him.

"Who wants to know?"

Ana and I got out of the car and walked over to him "My name is Alex, I work over . . ."

I know who you are; my tunnel mate speaks of you. What do you want I'm busy . . ."

"Mohawks not coming tonight."

"Why? What's wrong? Did he give up? I know he has a bad cold . . ."

"Shh relax, uh . . ."

"Spike it is my given name."

"Ok, Spike, he's fine, he wants to see you."

"Where is he?"

"He is at the center I work at."

He thought for a moment "If I go do I get to sleep in the same room?"

"I . . . uh . . . I'll see I need your help though. Sam wants me to find Tiny."

Spike frowned a little.

"What's wrong?"

"She runs with a gang and some of them aren't too fond of Mohawk and me. And uhm . . ."

"Hun" Ana smiled "You see Al, he only looks stable and his uncles are twice as unstable and twice as mean, no one will hurt you."

He looked at the church and then back at Ana and I "I have a meeting I promised Mohawk. I missed last week I was sick, I need a meeting."

"Hold on." I made a phone call "Mom I am going to be late, Anthony says hi, love you, night." I looked at Spike he was shivering "Let's go to your meeting."

"Uh ok" He stared at me like I was some sort of alien.

At nine a clock we walked back out of the church, Spike seemed to be feeling a little better. He walked to my car and waited.

"It's unlocked" I smiled "So 18th and Simon."

"Uh yeah" He gulped.

I swung through McDonalds all the way to the pull up window not bothering with the speakers. "Wilson" I called into the window.

"Yeah?" He smiled when he saw it was me.

"Two number threes one large with a coke the other medium with a vanilla shake. And whatever Spike wants."

"I have . . ."

"Shut up and order" I laughed.

"A large number one with an orange juice" He squeaked.

"Ok I'll have that for you in a minute." Wilson smiled.

"Will, Spike here lives with Sam" I said making sure he understood it wasn't a convenience thing.

"Sam! You've seen Sam? Where is he? How is he?"

"He is at the center, be there eight am Friday morning."

"But uh . . . ok. Here's your food have a good night."

"Thanks, I'll tell Sam you say hi." I drove toward the other side of town.

"He was cute" Spike smiled happy to have food.

"It's bad form to make eyes at your boyfriend's older brother" I laughed.

"That's Sam's brother?"

"Yes."

"Oh" Spike grew silent as he ate.

I pulled up to a corner with a group of tall boys all wearing leather jackets.

"Excuse me" I called to a boy about my height "I'm looking for someone I was hoping you could help me?" Spike had practically dived under the seat and my coat so I figured I was in the right spot.

"That depends on who you are looking for" The boy sneered.

I got out of the car I stood two inches over him if that "I am looking for a young lady named Tiny."

"You're in the wrong neighborhood trying to push your weight around rich boy" He snickered "Hey Will," He called to another boy, this one my height exactly "This guys looking for your girlfriend."

"What!" The boy growled walking up to me.

I stuck my hand out to shake "Hi my names Alex, I am looking for a young lady who goes by the name of Tiny."

"Willful is my name, what do you wish with my girlfriend?"

"Willful?"

"My mom is a hippie" He sighed

"Right, mine are Wiccan and vampire but anyway one of her friends is very sick and worried about her."

"She's fine, she is up in my mother's house warming up."

"Ok?"

He looked me up and down "I'll get her, you tell the shivering fool in your back seat to come be social Carter's looking for him."

I walked over to the car and told Spike to come out it was ok I wouldn't let anyone hurt him.

"There's my cutie" The boy Willful called Carter gushed "You give up your mama's boy boyfriend yet, Sweetie?"

"I-I l-love Mohawk" Spike shivered.

"Oh ok, well when you two want a real man let me know I'll be there. Are you going to introduce me to y . . ."

"Alex" I said shaking his hand "And asleep in the car is my girlfriend Ana."

"She's very pretty."

"Carter!" The first tall long haired boy made Carter and Spike jump. "What are you doing . . . oh if it isn't weasel . . ."

Spike kind of hid behind me "He isn't with me."

"What's wrong scaredy runt, where is your boyfriend?" The boy taunted.

"Jesse let him be, he has nothing to do with Sam's debt" Carter objected.

"Look ya fag, I . . ."

The last boy came over and slammed their heads together. "Enough, you two make us look like violent fools." He stuck out his hand "Names Alex."

"So is mine" I laughed shaking his hand.

"Great minds" He smiled "I apologize about these two; they don't play well together when they mix business and pleasure."

I laughed "It's fine, how much does Mohawk owe?"

"Thirty dollars" Jesse sneered rubbing his head "And I am going to pound it out of . . ."

"You only think you will!" Willful returned carrying Tiny "She is just asleep, please bring her back I don't want her sleeping outside or doing any more drugs. I love her."

"I will bring her back once she is detoxed and healthy. Until then you can visit her . . ."

"At the center on Friday's" He nodded "Sam there too?"

"Yeah" I recognized him, he had come with Tiny to visit Sam the last time, I had found and caged him.

"Thanks" He smiled.

I glared at Jesse and looked at the post behind him "Willful please put her in the back seat, Spike go back in the car . . ."

Carter looked like a broken puppy "Can I walk him to the car?"

Willful and I exchanged 'someone save me' looks.

"Uh . . . that's up to him" I sighed "But he needs to be in the car its very cold out and he has inefficient clothing.

Carter hugged Spike and took off running towards one of the houses.

Willful laughed "He will be back."

"I figured" I said walking towards Jesse, who was slowly backing up. I backed him in to the telephone pole. "Here is your thirty dollars stay away from Spike and Sam, chiaro(clear)!" I growled in his face.

Sometimes you know what some one is saying no matter what langue it is and Jesse was smart enough to catch on. "Clear" He gulped, taking the thirty.

Carter came flying back to me "These are Spike's" He smiled showing me a pair of black jeans and a black long sleeve t-shirt. "And these are his baby's" He showed me a pair of khakis and a gray dress shirt. I hope they fit right. I have been trying to reach them for two weeks, but I couldn't find them."

I drove back to the center, it was ten thirty when we got there, I shook Ana and Tiny.

"Alex!" Tiny yelled "Where's my Will? Where am I?" She panicked.

"Breath, Willful will come visit you on Friday, you're at the center. Mohawk said you could use checking on, he was worried."

She woke up more and saw Spike and hugged onto him "Carter's looking for you, he has warm clothes for you and Mohawk and don't worry, Will and Alex won't let Jesse hurt you."

I chuckled and showed her the clothes in my hand and walked them to Mohawk's room.

"Sam . . . Sam . . ." Ana gently shook him. "Sammy . . . Spike is here." His eyes flickered open.

"Hi handsome" Spike smiled.

"Oh Hunny, you look so handsome" Mohawk hugged him tightly.

I had let spike shower and put on the clean clothes and put Tiny in her room before waking Sam.

Mohawk started to choke.

Spike held him close "Thank you sweetie, you look cute in that."

Mohawk made a face "Alex wouldn't let me keep my shorts and t-shirt."

"*Alex* took them home washed them and patched them." I corrected, "You as well have new clothes and a note from a very bubbly young man. Also your debt to Jesse is paid."

"Thanks Alex" He wheezed, looking at his feet "I had to replace my science book it fell in the river last month."

"Thank your brother; he will be getting my bill." I smiled handing Spike the center clothes, everyone else had so he would have pajamas.

He went back to the bath room to change. Dave had said because Sam was not in a treatment program Spike could stay with him as long as they behaved.

Mohawk read his note allowed. "Hey JR. cutie hear your sick hope you feel better. I'll be checking on you and super cutie on Friday as Will is dead set on seeing Amelia. Hope you like your new clothes. I gave your buddy the receipt in case they don't fit. You got a good buddy there; got right in Jesse's face and made him back down but good. Take care of our boyfriend for me.—Carter" Mohawk rolled his eyes "He hits on Spike all the time" He tried to laughed and end up choking. Spike crawled in the bed next to him. I turned the light out and Ana and I went home.

CHAPTER 14

NEVER ENDING WEDNESDAY

AFTER ONLY FIVE HOURS ASLEEP both Ana and I were exhausted. Dave was not helping as my rounds were everywhere in the morning I was with Tiffany and Buddy, Buddy was in the time out room and had been there all morning. Tiffany was still mad at me for taking Sadie away.

"Bite me" She hissed.

"No thank-you, please just finish your work and we will go to lunch."

At lunch I called home to tell Paul I loved him. He was playing with Uncle Chris. After lunch I was with Kyle and Kevin whom nearly blew my ear drums out asking to go see Spike and Mohawk. After their classes and homework I took them and Anthony, who was not happy for some reason, and we checked on Tiny and then went to check on Mohawk. He was sound asleep witch up set Kevin and Kyle. So I took Spike and we all went to play cards in the family room. But the clock seemed to be going three minutes backwards and one minute forward, to the point where five minutes seemed like an hour.

"Daddy who's coming Friday?" Anthony asked.

"Uh . . . Ana, me, Grandma, Nana, your Great Uncle Christian, Paul, and possibly, your Great Uncle Donavan."

"Oh."

Kevin frowned "He is really loved."

"So are you, your mother will be here. My parents make their own hours and my uncle doesn't work. Therefore their schedule is more flexible. Also Ana and I have to be here we work here. There is no need for you to be jealous and ungrateful."

Kevin sat miserably watching cartoons after that.

"I get to go home again" Kyle beamed.

"I don't see what he's so unhappy about" Spike scowled at Kevin "I don't have parents or a home, I may be free to come and go as I please but I would rather stay here where I am cared about and there is heat and plumbing, a real bed and real meals; instead of in the cold construction tunnel, I think he needs to count his blessings again."

It was the most I ever heard Spike say but it was real sobering for everyone. I looked at the clock it was only four. "Let's go see if Sam is awake."

Spike looked at me odd.

"Sam you know you call him Mohawk."

"I know who you meant it's just they gave him something strong to help him sleep, he will be out for a while."

"Oh, ok."

Kevin watched cartoons while Spike and I helped Anthony and Kyle build a card castle. By five it was done I brought them all back to the cafeteria for dinner. Spike ate in silence, Kyle and Anthony talked about Christmas, and Kevin sulked.

"Kevin, eat please" I pleaded.

"What for?"

"You aren't hungry?"

"Maybe if I starve myself to death dad will notice me."

Buddy smacked the back of his head "Eat before I notice you . . ."

"Buddy move on" I growled, he had been downright mean all day. "Kevin although I do not agree with Buddy threatening you, he is right you need to eat, I am sorry your dad hurt your feelings but it won't change or help anything by not eating. If you would like I can take you to your consoler after dinner."

"Fine!" He started shoving the food on his plate around.

A mattress can be soft or the world's worst enemy, tonight they were my best friend. I had returned Kyle and Spike back to their rooms, Kevin to his consoler, tucked Anthony in, came in here and just laid here waiting for Ana more exhaustion then meditation. I yawned and stretched.

"Let's go sleepy I'm driving" Anna smiled down at me.

"Sounds Great" I stood up and we walked towards the punch clock.

"Alex" Dave called me "Anthony!"

I turned back so fast that my own head spun, Ana on my heels. Anthony was clawing at his arms. I separated his hands and looked in to his eyes, they were dark and stormy "What's uneven?" I asked him.

"I am never getting out of here am I?" He cried.

"You will in time."

"They won't heal."

"What wont?"

"The dumb cuts won't heal" He cried harder starting to sob "I am a good boy I talk to my consoler, I do what Mr. Dave tells me to, I don't act like the other boys, my home work is always done. I want to go home with you and Ana, I want to be with Paul and you . . ." He broke down sobbing hard in to my shoulder I rocked him back to sleep and tucked him back in.

"He was up at three this morning" Dave sighed "He will be fine, I'll see you *tomorrow*, Alex."

"Night Dave" I sighed and followed Ana to the car.

"Mommy" Paul squealed as Ana and I pushed through the door around eleven.

"What are you doing still up?" She picked him up.

He hugged tight to her "Antony come home."

"Not yet why are you up, Hunny?"

I looked around the lights were on in his room and the bathroom. "Let's go sit in Nana's rocker, Paul, mommy needs sleep."

Uncle Donavan limped out of the bathroom "Your dinners were saved. He is up because we just got in ourselves. We had to go to the clinic, Nikolas broke Christian's arm. Not that we all didn't see that coming."

"I'll pu . . ."

"He has been read to, his prayers have been said, and he was tucked in" Donavan looked at Paul "He needs to stop getting out of bed."

Paul squiggled out of Ana's arms and ran back to his room giggling, I followed and tucked him back in.

"Sit" Uncle Donavan said indicating the chair next to him at the kitchen table.

"Yes, sir" I gulped looking around for Ana.

"You hath no need to fear me boy, and Uncle Donavan will do you just fine."

"Si . . ."

"Hush and listen to me, your father is was my brother . . ."

"I kn . . ."

"Silence your tongue or I shall silence it myself, tis rude to interrupt. I know you know better, I may not agree with everything my little brother does but I know his stand on manners." He stirred a cup of coco. "Colt, was a decent man and a hard worker and wished nothing more than to make Christian proud of him." It was the first time I had ever heard my father's name used so freely, I was shell shocked. "It still hurts Christian too much, they were very close."

"Then . . ."

"Ooo boy you listen like your father, I'm not finished. I tell you because I feel you and Colt Jr. have a right to know. I have no problem, no problem at all answering any and all questions you have about your father. Don't hold it against my little brother he loves you very, very much but this is one thing he just can't do."

"I love my uncle, Sir" I shook my head.

"Ugh well at least your manners hath returned. To bed with you, Buona notte, mio nipote più vecchio(good night my oldest nephew).

"Good night Si . . . I mean Uncle Donavan" My head was swimming like the sinus infection was coming back.

CHAPTER 15

SOMEONE GIVE ME THE TIME OUT

IF WEDNESDAY WASN'T ENOUGH AND Thursday wasn't torture Friday was defiantly both. I hadn't slept well Wednesday from my head swimming and Thursday Paul for whatever reason felt the need to climb in our bed and kick my back all night. So I was already over tired and Paul did not want to get up, get dressed, or go. It was a forty minute fight to get him dressed and ready.

"I no want to go I mad at Antony" He said crossing his little arms. I had to look up to keep from laughing.

"You can be mad all you want, Sweetie" Ana said.

"But he is your brother you are going to go and show him you love him and that you are there for him" I added.

"NO! I no love him no more he stay way too long."

"Not by his choice, he's cried for you almost all week."

"Then bring him home you bought me, Nana love me. She love him too."

"There is no doubt in my mind that your grandparents love you both very much but we cannot bring him home until he stops purposely hurting himself.

Paul sat in his car seat pouting. Sir had dropped Sadie off and she sat next to him pouting.

"Don't make that face at me" I looked at her in the rear view mirror "Not my rules."

"I know" She pouted more.

Thursday I had talked to Kevin's consoler about his outburst on Wednesday; only to find out neither of his parents would be able to attend and he had finally earn a weekend out and his parents said not this weekend. When I checked my rounds I had tiffany, Kevin, Kyle, Mohawk, Spike, Tiny, and Anthony with a see me note taped to it. So I slugged down to Dave's office.

"Yes" He looked up at me from his breakfast.

"You . . ." I started to say.

"Oh I meant after work?"

"Two?"

"Three but only, because I will leave you on the clock for what I need you for. Are you getting sick again?"

"Physically? Nah, just haven't been sleeping well. Paul kicked my back all night."

"He loves you."

"I noticed he's mad at me right now; because *his* Anthony can't come home.

Dave chuckled "Well everyone but Sam and Amelia should be in the cafeteria. Oh and Kevin's mom called . . ."

"I know won't be able . . ."

"Actually wanted to know if someone could bring him there as his dad is fixing the car or they would have come themselves."

"Yep I will."

"Boys" I snuck up behind Kevin and Kyle.

"Ahhhhhhh" They both jumped.

"Morning boys ready?"

"Yep" Kyle smiled.

"No" Kevin sighed.

"Come on let's get the others" I smiled.

"State lady" Kyle pretended to cough.

I turned a small blonde lady in a skirt and blouse was standing there.

"Mr. Williams I presume" She had a nasally voice.

"Yes, Ma'am" I said extending my hand "I'm Alex Williams. How can I help you?"

She pushed her glasses up higher on her nose "I'm Violet Brown, I am filling in for Ms. Myers today."

"Ok" I smiled "Kevin here will show you to the family room." Kevin started to object then thought better of it "While Kyle and I get everyone else."

"Ok, thank you" She said.

Kevin yanked on my sleeve for me to bend down so I did "You owe me" He breathed.

"You'll thank me later" I whispered back.

"Come on, Spike lets go Wilson will be there and Sam has to go too" I pleaded. Tiffany rolled her eyes at me.

"Mohawks still sick" Spike pouted.

"Know he will be."

"And Tiny . . ."

"Not now bud, see me at lunch for that ok, we're running late." I scooped up Anthony who objected.

"I know how to walk Dad" He complained.

"Love you too dear, take the shoulder ride." I took a deep breath and unlock Sam's door. "Sam let's go"

"No"

"Don't make me carry you too."

"Fine" He walked out and unlocked Tiny's door "Only if . . ."

"Thank-you, she already was."

"Is Sadie here?" Tiffany asked.

"Yes, and no you . . ." I tried to answer.

"I wasn't going to ask, the other night she said she had something to say."

"Go ask her" I said opening the door to the family room. I sat Anthony down, and told Kyle I'd see him Sunday. Tiffany hugged Sadie tight I looked at Tiny "Go sit by the TV."

"You suck" She glared at me.

"On occasion I might but only good things." I sighed and told Sam and Spike "Take Anthony to my mom I need to speak to Kevin."

"Ok Al" Mohawk said; both him and Spike were dressed in their new clothes from Carter.

"Paul!" Anthony ran over to Paul and tried to pick him.

"Me maa at you!" Paul pulled away "I want me Antony home!"

I groaned and took Kevin aside "Let's talk."

"About" He groaned.

"Why didn't you tell me you . . ."

"It was supposed to be surprise but it got all messed up they're not coming."

"Their car broke down your going to them you are free to sit with Amelia and watch TV."

"How . . ."

"Me."

"Thanks, Alex" He hugged me.

My radio went off "Alex, there's a Wilson Needle . . ."

I cut him off before Mohawk heard "Yeah, Send him down."

"Will do."

"Thanks Harry" I walked over to my own boys and sat down near my uncle's.

"Paul won't talk to me Daddy" Anthony looked hurt. Then he noticed Uncle Donavan and crawled in to my arms. "Who's he" He whispered.

"Anthony this is your great Uncle Donavan."

He nodded "Hi."

"Hi" Uncle Donavan smiled at him.

"You have a lot of boo boos"

"I was in a car accident."

Uncle Christian made a disapproving noise; I tried not to laugh and covered by checking on Tiny. Sam and Spike had joined Tiny and Kevin over near the TV. Paul came over "Daddy, Antony no wants to see the cavalli."

"I don't know what you're saying and I think you said you loved them more than you love me" Anthony objected.

"Me do the cavalli aren't here the cavalli know they not suppose to go bye-bye."

"Horses, Paul?" I tried not to laugh "And don't tell Anthony you love the horses more than him."

"Ehm" Wilson stood in the door.

"Cost you thirty bucks" I smiled standing to greet him, setting Anthony back down."

"What did he do?" Wilson's eyes went wide.

"Lost a school book."

"Phew thought . . ."

"He's clean, did it on his own but he has something to share with you."

"Ok?"

"Still thirty . . ."

"Yeah, yeah I owe you."

"Sam come here, just you" I called to him.

"Sam" Wilson crunched him in a bear hug "You're so thin and you . . ."

"Will" Sam gulped then started to choke.

"He has pneumonia" I offered.

"Ana's granddad still here . . ." Wilson started.

"Already done" I smiled "Sam you need to tell him about Spike and then tell me when Spike turns eighteen so he can fix that."

"Spike?" Wilson raised an eyebrow.

"I didn't name him" Sam laughed walking Wilson over to Spike.

I went to sit down again as Ana walked in so I gave her my seat.

"Mommy" Paul crawled into her arms "Mommy Antony no want to see cavalli, he said they ugly and I tupid."

"That's not our mom Paul, our mom didn't love us she's in jail."

I crouched down between them Paul don't tell your brother you love the horses more than you love him and Anthony please don't call Paul stupid, neither one of you are stupid or unloved or ugly. Please boys, please don't fight." I walked over to talk to Mrs. Brown.

Paul came flying into my leg "Daddy, Antony say Ana can't be our new Mommy because she no married to you."

I sighed "Excuse me one moment Ma'am" I picked Paul up "So today you want me every other day you want Ana or Uncle Christian. Let's go talk to Anthony." Again I knelt between them "What's going on you two love each other."

"He keeps calling Ana, mommy." Anthony made a face.

"You call me daddy"

"Well yeah you adopted us you're my new Dad."

"I never said you had to call me dad did I?"

"No I wanted to."

"Well, Paul feels he should call Ana mom you don't have to she will understand."

"Well, she can't be our new mom, you aren't married to her."

My parents started to laugh.

"This isn't funny" I said to Mama and sighed "You don't have to be married to be someone's mom or dad. Also go tell Paul Mommy's Christmas ring he will tell you all about it." I stood back up "I am sorry Ma'am they normally can't stop hugging each other, today they fight."

"It is fine" Mrs. Brown smiled "I have four boys myself, they will fight and your mothers have every right to laugh if you have a brother."

"Yes Ma'am, I am the oldest of six"

"Oh my, your parents have their hands full."

After lunch Wilson asked when he could take Sam home.

"Sam is free to go just stop and get his belongings and medicine on the way out."

"I'm not going without Spike."

I looked at Wilson

"I never said he couldn't come Sam, I didn't know if he had to stay" Wilson sighed.

"Want to trade?" I laughed.

"Oh no, I am good I know who my mommy is and so does Sam" He laughed.

"I'll see if Mom can drop Spike off and I will bring Sam home when I get out of work."

"Ok thanks, I have to go, work."

"I'll probably swing by later for a couple of trees."

He laughed "I'll see you then and I'll see about fixing that speaker."

Right after Wilson left Carter and Willful showed up "Where is she?"

I pointed.

"Long day" Willful asked.

"Don't even ask, you don't want to try and know"

"Dad" Anthony whined "Paul said he is going to tell Santa he doesn't want me to come home anymore or I think that's what he said."

"Yes dear I know, his speech, we are working on it, and tell Paul Santa is doing his best" I sighed.

Carter looked at me.

"Yes? You want to wine at me too?"

"No," He laughed "Just won . . ."

"Follow" I walked Willful and him over to Tiny, Sam and Spike.

"You Suck" Tiny looked up at me.

"Yeah, I know, I suck. I told you I only suck good things and today maybe my thumb" I sighed.

"He sucks too" She was looking at Carter.

Carter laughed "Yes I do, baby girl, all the time."

"And so does he" Tiny slammed her fist in to Willful's chest.

"I told you, only Carter and only on Thursdays." Willful blushed.

"Oh, Oh wow, too much info for me" I laughed and walked over to Kevin.

"Hi Alex" He looked up at me he was laying upside down in a bean bag chair.

"Can you please go tell Dave I need a new walkie-talkie battery?"

"Sure" He smiled "By myself?"

"You are level four now aren't you?"

"Awesome." He jumped up and ran for the hall.

"You suck" Tiny said as I passed.

"Oh, my Amelia, must you tell me that every time you see me?"

"Yes"

"Why?"

"Because I don't want to be here; I want to get something and go earn some money."

"I have your money" Willful said "And NO DRUGS!"

I sighed it was only one o'clock Paul and Anthony had finally stopped fighting and were playing with Lego's. Mom had agreed to take Spike to Wilson's for me. Carter had brought them their school things and more clothes.

Kevin came back with my battery and looked at my Uncle Christian. "Is that your dad? You look like him."

I laughed "I told you I don't have a dad, I have two moms. This is my uncle Christian. Are you feeling well?"

"I am a bit tired."

"Ok, go rest on the chair over there" I shook my head.

At two Anthony and Tiny went back to their rooms.

Willful shook his head at me "Alex, she means the world to me."

"I understand." I looked over at Ana talking to Paul.

"Please, I will sign anything I have to don't let her leave until she is healthy and clean."

"I won't let her, but you aren't her legal guardian or I would let you sign anything you wanted to."

"Oh and are you really changing Spike's name?"

"Uh he has to be 18 and that's his choice. Are you changing yours?"

"I checked in to it once, a while ago, but I am good with Willful David Moore. At work they just call me Will though."

"Understood, see you next Friday."

"Yep, Friday, maybe by then we won't suck."

"I think you and Carter still might suck."

"Like I said only Carter and only on Thursdays."

"That's still too much info for me."

"Well at least I am honest, Friday Alex."

"Friday" I nodded. "Spike come here" I called to him. "I would like you to meet my mothers and my uncles Christian and Donavan."

He gulped looking up at them.

"They are going to take you home, to your new home not a construction tunnel. I will bring Sam a bit later." I hugged my mothers good bye. I looked at Tiffany and Sadie "One hour in this room Sam and Kevin stay here, nothing inappropriate, thank you for not whining.

"Uh ok your welcome, did I miss . . ." Tiffany started.

"My children" I sighed.

"Oh ok" She laughed.

Dave was watching some court show when I got there.

"You rang."

He looked at me and laughed. "Have fun?" He handed me two Advil.

"Loads" I rolled my eyes.

"Sit down."

"I'll fall asleep."

"Ok stand, I am pushing to have your son released on grounds that he is too young."

"Dave he . . ."

"You can clean him up the way you choose you are his father."

"Quando (When) . . ."

"No later than the new year. Speak English in my building!"

"Thanks that's great news."

"Go home."

"See you Sunday."

"I better not see a minute before seven am Sunday."

"Yeah, yeah" I laughed headed toward the family room.

Sadie evil eyed me.

"What, I know I said an hour . . ."

"SHE HATES ME!"

"Oh Please" I sighed rolling my eyes "You two can work it out, Genevieve is moving and you two get to share a room your welcome, get over it, good night and Tiffany don't bite Quentin."

Quentin looked at me "S-She bites?"

I shrugged "I don't know she might." With that I took Kevin and Sam and met Ana at the car. Paul was in his car seat already. "You're driving" I said handing her the keys "Ok? As long as they get to the right spots I am sleeping."

"Sounds good to me don't forget the ball is tonight."

"Ugh" I ground.

The winter ball, my parents chaperoned every year. It was a charity ball and they insisted we go every year. Normally I wouldn't mind but today was not my day. And it was all money, gossip and politics between the adults at the ball.

"Don't ugh me, we are going last date you took me on was our senior prom, and don't say the movie because your little brother was with us. Dad said he and Davie will watch Paul."

"Ok, ok" I laughed "Goodnight." I laid my head to my shoulder and was out.

Ana woke me at home "I can barely lift our sons there is no way I can lift you."

I laughed and kissed her "I love you Ana; I have all of my life."

"I know sweetie, I love you too just as much. Let's go eat dinner, and wake Paul or he won't sleep tonight."

"Dinner sounds good." I shook my head and woke Paul. As we walked toward the door, I watched Paul try to step in my foot prints and fall in the snow every time. I picked him up "Legs need to be longer handsome ready for diner?"

"What we eat?" He yawned.

"I don't know. We will find out."

"Baked Mac and cheese" Uncle Christian slopped some on my plate. "If you're hungry you will eat it." He glared at Colt.

"Colt have bad day?" I asked him.

"Dani doesn't want to be my girlfriend because she thinks Tommy is cuter than me. She just wants to be friends."

"Well, it happens you will be fine, you still have to eat dinner" Mom sat down at the table.

He made a face, Colt didn't like baked Mac and cheese and we had it at least twice a month for dinner.

"Do we . . ."

". . . Have to . . ."

". . . We look . . ."

". . . Like penguins." Christopher and Christian whined about their hair and ties.

Kenny walked by smelling like he bathed in the cologne bottle.

"Shoo Kenny, you reek, you're not supposed to bath in the cologne" I started to gag.

He turned and glared at me "I didn't bathe in it I spilled it I have to re-shower after dinner."

"Uncle Christian" Paul stretched his arms out to Christian.

"Hey little Guy."

"We look like penguins" The twins picked him up and hugged him.

"Nick" I frowned.

He was making faces at Uncle Donavan "What?"

"You know what."

Ana and I showered and dressed for the ball. I bathed Paul and put him in his pajamas and packed his overnight bag. We dropped him off with Ana's dad. David was chopping wood, he glared at me. I picked up the other ax, and let Ana take Paul in.

"She loves you." He growled.

I jumped "I know, David."

David didn't talk to me much the accident had left him disabled and quiet. "When are you purposing?"

I looked at him "Uh . . ."

"My nephew speaks to me."

"Oh Christmas dinner." I was scared he hardly talked much and now he was talking to me. I finished splitting the log I had. "It's a small diamond with a hear . . ."

"My nephew draws with me" He unfolded a piece of paper. His speech was slow and slurred slightly and he could not move his right arm. He was still learning to use his left hand for everything. He handed me the drawing.

I smiled "Its close the purple should be in the shape of a heart."

"I figured it is the one at the jeweler near the book store?"

"Yeah."

"Don't hurt my little sister!" The words sent chills down my spine.

"I-I won't."

"Have a good night, Ana" He said as she came out.

She gave a puzzled look "Ok Davie?" She looked at me "Everything alright?"

"We were just talking" David said.

"Ok talk to you later" Ana smiled and we got in the car.

"I have good news to tell you, but you can't tell anyone yet because it is not a definite" I said as we drove towards the school.

"Ok" She eyed me.

"We may have Anthony by Christmas."

"Oh Hunny" She jumped on my shoulders hugging me I had to stiffen my arms so I didn't lose control of the car. "Sorry" She blushed.

"It's ok baby I understand" I smiled "Dave is pushing the he's too young theory."

She frowned "You . . ."

"He says I am his father it should be my choice how he is treated for it."

"Oh, ok.

"I won't let it go uncared for, Ana."

"I know."

"Ana, baby, talk to me."

"You were emotionally blind for years. I cried for nights, praying you'd be ok, praying you'd open your eyes and stop, praying to know what was going through your mind so I could help you."

"Anthony may be ok out of his mother's house. Especially if his cutting was an attempt to get out of there in the first place. Anthony is very smart and advanced for his age."

"I know I just worry."

"Well don't, tonight is for fun" I smiled pulling into the parking lot. My family was already there. I straightened my suit, it was light gray to match Ana's sliver Christmas gown. She looked absolutely stunning in it.

Wilson was there with Debbie and Spike "Hey Alex, the thirty I owe you." He handed me the money. "Ana" He bowed and shot Spike a look.

"Uh sorry" Spike bowed "Thank you both again."

"It is fine bud, it is my job. You just take good care of Sam and Will for me Debbie can't handle those two by herself" I smiled.

"Sam was too sick to come" Spike looked at his feet.

"He will get better I promise, Sweetie" Ana soothed.

"Uh oh" Debbie sighed "Vindictive wench approaching two O'clock."

"Katherine" Ana chided emanating hatred form every pour in her body.

"Williams, Needlemyer" Her date greeted Will and I.

"Glassman" Wilson spat.

"Drew" I hissed.

Poor Spike looked very lost.

"Debra, Ana" Katherine flashed a vindictive grin.

"Katherine" Both Ana and Debbie growled as they passed. It was a very tense moment as they passed and the tension between the girls was almost tangible.

Mom glided over in her gown; it was odd to see Mom or Mama in a gown or skirt as they mostly wore jeans and t-shirts. "Everything ok" She smiled "You look like something smells."

"Katherine" Ana hissed.

Mom laughed "She's just like her mom."

"Mrs. Smith isn't a back stabbing nasty whore, Mrs. Williams" Debbie looked lost.

"She use to be . . ."

"Be what?" Mama and Uncle Chris joined us.

"Krystal White" Mom said.

"Bloody tart ne . . ."

Uncle Chris covered Mama's mouth "Why on earth are you bringing her up, Tina?"

"The kids ran into her daughter."

"I told you" Uncle Chris looked at me "That apple does not fall far from the tree she stemmed from."

"Neither did her niece" Mama sighed through Uncle Chris hand. "Whatever Davie saw in her . . ."

"I can't believe Melanie still blames Davie for Sierra's death" Uncle Chris shook his head "Sierra was driving not Davie."

Ana clung to me.

"What kind of goodies are at the snack table, ladies you want some punch?" I changed the subject.

"Your mother made her divinity fudge and I am waiting for your uncle to be distracted so I can steal me a piece" Mama smiled.

"Not a chance Mio Piccolo you are allergic to that." Uncle Christian said joining us; he was never too far from Mama. "Bella your son is with a young lady and wishes his mother to meet her."

"I have six sons wi . . ."

"Hmm Mom I can answer that he's about Mama's height, he has brown curls and reads all the . . ."

"Hush you, don't tease your mother" Mama swatted me.

"Ms. Williams when you have a moment Sam wanted me to introduce you to Spike, but I see he has found the snacks and punch bowl" Wilson laughed.

"Of course" Mama smiled "Let him eat first."

"Owe" I hissed something hit the back of my head.

"Sorry . . ."

". . . Alex."

"Twins" I growled.

"Hunny they didn't mean it" Ana said grabbing my hand to dance. I watched my parents dance. Mama was a graceful dancer, very elegant and poised. A mother child song played Mama danced with Ana. Mom and I danced.

"I am proud of you, Alex" Mom said as we danced

"Thank-you" I said not quite sure why she was proud of me.

"Everyone says I have an honest good boy with a big heart."

I blushed "I . . ."

"We did our best with you as we are with your brothers, granite you were much harder to care for . . ."

"Sorry."

"Alex, don't be sorry; Sweetie, I knew one of if not more of you would get a few recessive traits from your Mama and I. I am sorry you never met your father, you or your brother."

"It's ok, I understand Mom. I am one of the luckiest guys here. I have the best parents any one could ever ask for an understanding patient girlfriend who knows everything about me and still loves me, a house to come home to every night two smart awesome sons. Yeah, I would have loved to have met Dad but I am happy the way I am."

"You look and sound like your daddy; and you are very much like him as well."

"Is that good?"

"Well yes and no, he was stubborn . . ."

"So are you Mom."

"You have his nervous energy though."

"Yeah, that tends to get me in to trouble."

"It did him too. Tomorrow you ask Donavan about your father."

"Ok Mom . . . Mom why does Mama hate Uncle Donavan?"

"She doesn't hate him I doubt she truly hates anyone. She is just stubborn and prideful like your Uncle Christian."

"Oh ok."

The song ended and Ana came to me in tears. I held her tightly; I knew exactly what was wrong this time, she missed her mom. I held her close and I wiped her tears away and held her until she pushed me away.

"Let's get a drink and some of Mom's divinity before it is all gone" I smiled.

"Sounds good" She sniffled a bit.

There were three pieces of Mom's Divinity fudge left. I grabbed them, two glasses of eggnog and some Chocolate chip cookies.

"Psst Mama" I whispered while she danced with Mom "Come see me and Ana when you're done" I walked with Ana to a table.

Mom raised an eye brow "Are you sure that one is mine?"

"Positive, beautiful, he is yours do you not remember telling the doctors not to drop *your* son."

"Ha ha, I love you Jessi bear."

"I love you too, Hunny."

"You think he knows yet?"

"Knows what there are so many things we tried to keep from our son's to make their lives easier."

"I don't know . . ."

"You worry too much."

"I worry too much? With you as a wife I don't worry enough."

"Oh really how is your heart?"

"You have gorgeous hair."

"Yeah, I thought so, you can hold my gorgeous hair back for me later *your* son has a piece of *your* fudge for me" She kissed mom and headed toward me.

"My fudge dear?" Mama wheezed.

"You sound like a space man Mama, take your inhaler" I frowned.

"I'm fine, but you won't if your uncle catches you giving me that fudge."

I sighed "Here, take your inhaler please" I handed her the last piece of divinity fudge.

"Thank-you" She kissed the top of my head "Now I must return to your mother before someone else does."

I laughed my parents were head over heels in love with each other when they were young time had seemed only to strengthen their love.

"His little one and Bella look beautiful together" Uncle Donavan sat near us.

"Huh . . ." I looked up.

"Your Italian that weak?"

"No sir. Sorry, sir I just didn't hear you."

"I said his little one and Bella look beautiful together. Out in your own world?"

"When isn't he" Ana laughed.

"I was thinking about you" I kissed her standing up to clear the plates and cups as my cell went off "Williams . . . yeah . . . , yeah . . . ok we'll be there right away Sir."

Ana looked at me "Wha . . ."

"Paul" I said I ran and told my mother's I had to leave then lifted Ana so we could run.

"You know I can walk, Hunny. What's wrong with Paul?"

"He did something to his finger; they are at the ER with your Grand dad."

"What do you mean something?"

"I couldn't hear clearly."

"Oh"

"Alex, I told you it would be fine" Ana's dad greeted us.

"What happened? The school has bad reception."

"He got his fingers stuck in a door we are just making sure nothings broken, he's in x-ray now."

"Why wasn't he in bed, Dad?" Ana frowned "I told you he isn't to stay up parting with you and Davie."

"Partying my foot I was nodding out in the lazy boy, but I allow people in my house to use the bathroom when they need it even if it is past their bed time."

"Oh ok."

We waited and I held my breath, Ana paced.

"His speech is getting better" Ana's dad broke the silence.

"Thank-you, sir, Uncle Donavan has been working with him."

"Cheerios?"

"No captain crunch."

"Ok?"

"Mama told him she wasn't going to have another boy playing with his cheerios, so he is using captain crunch."

He laughed "How is your Mama doing?"

"Oh I'd say about right now she is spiking a fever and getting cold chills."

"She ate Tina's divinity fudge? She never could pass it up."

"Yes, Dad and my dumb boy friend gave it to her."

"Hunny, it was a small piece, she will be fine" I objected.

"Alex, your daddy use to sneak her white chocolate all time" He laughed harder.

"See, I told you she'd be fine, I have seen Uncle Chris do it on their birthday."

Ana frowned at me "Still."

"MOMMY" Paul Squealed "Look boo-boo finger" His little hand was red and swollen.

"Not broken" Sir said walking into the room "Definitely bruised but not broken ice it down and be mindful of it."

"Thanks dad" Ana's dad said.

Sir glared at me "I see you over there; I can hear you wheezing take your inhaler." He looked back at Ana's dad "Your welcome Henry."

"Yes, sir" I gulped.

"Go back to the ball, you two, I told you he is fine" Ana's dad sighed.

"It's fine, I would rather stay with him" I said.

"Me too dad, Katherine was there."

"Ana . . ."

"I know, I know, I should feel sorry for someone so shallow."

"That and she is no reason to hide from the ball."

"I know Dad but I am tired and I know Al is exhausted."

"Hmm alright but he's still staying with Davie and I."

I laughed "Yes Sir, come on Hunny lets go home" I smiled at Ana.

CHAPTER 16
TWO MANY QUESTIONS

I WOKE ABOUT 7:30 MY body no longer slept past eight unless I was sick, Ana was still asleep. I could hear someone chopping wood outside. I threw my boots and coat on and ran outside. I had expected to see Uncle Christian but it was Mama.

"You ok Mama?"

"Yes dear I am fine"

"Is Uncle Christian ok?"

"He is fine; he is sleeping, as you should be. It is your day off."

I picked up an axe and started to help Mama "I'm not tired."

"Well neither am I, which is why I am out here. No one makes your Uncle do all the house work he does it by choice."

"I know."

"Aren't you cold?"

"Slightly" I blushed my boxer pants were thin and I had slept without a shirt or socks.

"Go shower and dress then come talk to me."

"Ok good idea."

She laughed "And she had to ask if you were hers."

When I got out of the shower Uncle Christian was making breakfast. "Morning" I said tying my hair back.

"Good morning, Alex."

"Where is Mama?"

"She is in the studio."

"Thanks, see you at breakfast."

"Your welcome."

Mama was sitting on the washer staring at the instruments. I stopped on the stairs; she was crying. I ran back upstairs.

"Uncle Christian Mama's . . ."

"Relax I know she doesn't just go down there to play her drums, Alex she feels she talks best to Nalanie there as Henry takes Ana and David up to the cemetery."

"Oh phew."

"Set the table, and then go wake your brothers, your girlfriend and your mother."

"Whe . . ."

"Chris and Donavan went to the store and I will take care of Mio Piccolo, I always have."

"Yes sir" I went up stairs to wake my brothers, I would wake Mom last.

"Mio Piccolo?"

"Hey my big rock, I was just talking to Nal."

"I know Mio Piccolo you do every morning you ok or do you need a hug." Uncle Christian said wrapping his around Mama. "What brings your tears Mio Piccolo. Has been a long time since you cried for her passing."

"Ana" Mama sniffled "I have seen the same 'will I be an ok parent' look in her as I have in my son."

"They will be fine, Mio Piccolo."

Uncle Chris and Uncle Donavan came in and stomped their boots off.

"Tis rather cold . . ." Uncle Donavan stopped mid sentence, "Something wrong with Il tuo piccolo?"

"Sta bene, go warm up."

"I will take Paul to the stables tomorrow, too cold today, Chris and I fed them though."

"That's fine go check on Bella" Uncle Christian curtly dismissed Uncle Donavan.

"J.J, you ok?" Uncle Chris asked Mama.

"Yeah CJ, I am fine" She gave him a teary smile.

"Ok see you at breakfast" He headed up the stairs.

"She'd be proud of Ana, Ana has stuck by Al and she works and goes to school and she insisted to be marked as Paul and Anthony's adopted mother." Mama cried into Uncle Christian's chest.

"Shh, shh, shh Mio Piccolo. She would not want you all worked up over this she can see for herself how strong, polite, smart, and awesome Ana is 'there are holes in the floor of heaven and . . .'" Uncle Christian Sang a line from an old country song and rocked Mama a little. Mama started to sniffle as the tears slowly stopped.

"Shall we eat?"

"Yes, my rock."

"We didn't . . ."

". . . Do it, Alex."

"Swear it wasn't us . . ."

". . . We were asleep."

The twins and I were fighting over who broke the picture of Mom, Mama and all their friends when they were younger. "Then who did."

"I did Hunny" Mom took the picture out of the shattered frame "It's ok I got it a new frame."

"Sorry guys" I apologized to the beasts.

"Told you . . ."

". . . So, Alex." They stuck their tongues out at me.

"Real mature guys" I sighed.

Breakfast was extremely silent; Mom broke the silence it seemed to be making her nervous "Dinner and a movie tonight?"

"Sounds good to me" Mama said.

"What movie?" Kenny asked.

"Does it matter?" Nick interjected.

"Hush rodent . . ."

". . . You injured us." The beasts whined.

Nick rolled his eyes.

"Something family oriented Paul will be with us . . . ok?" I half asked.

"Sounds good" Uncle Donavan said limping to the table.

"Morning Uncle Donavan" Colt and I said.

"Morning boys, Bella, I believe this is for you and Il suo piccolo" He handed Mom a note "Found it taped to the back door."

Mama read it aloud "Twenty minutes to the woods two hours to the high way one donut and a slim Jim is the toll."

"Jake!" Uncle Christian hissed.

"Hush, big dumb rock" Mama laughed, reading the rest to herself.

"Christopher, Christian did you wish to see your . . ."

"No thank-you."

"We are no longer . . ."

". . . Curious of . . ."

". . . Our hair." They smiled.

I stifled a laugh, watching Christopher put Christian's broken arm in its sling as they headed in to the hall.

"We are off . . ."

". . . To fetch Paul . . ."

". . . There is lots . . ."

". . . Of fresh snow."

"Be careful with him" Ana called after them.

"Nikolas, just because you think I don't see that face doesn't mean I don't. Make that face again and I am sure your mama will freeze it there for you" Uncle Donavan said.

Nick gulped "I um I told Mag I'd call her I, Mom excuse me please."

"Your excused, mind yourself young man" Mama said.

Mom looked at Kenny "Juliet may come with us this week."

"Thank-you Mom, Thank-you Uncle Christian breakfast was good, m . . ."

"Shoo" Mom laughed as he tried to beat Nick to the phone.

"Well, dear I think I am going to go join the boys out in the snow, I had Mike wax my sled runners" Mama kissed Mom's Cheek.

"Oh wait for me that sounds good" Mom said clearing their plates.

"I have laundry to do" Ana smiled and kissed my head as she headed for our room.

"I guess I will call the movie house to see what is playing, but I will go to Ken's do so as the boys are fighting over our phone, besides I told them I would go with him and Henry to help Dad arrange Mum's flight."

I gulped "I um . . ."

"Yes" Uncle Christian said.

"Colt . . ." I tried again.

"Yes."

"Uhg, so because him and I have the same dad we have to have a private talk" Colt groaned.

"Yes" Uncle Christian sighed your mothers felt you to should be allowed to ask questions."

"Ok fine, How if he was pushing up daisies before Al was born is he my dad too.

My gut wrenched I had been raised to respect my father as if he were still alive. "You don't have to say it like that. That is our father and these are his brothers our uncles you know his blood, our uncles."

Colt backed down.

"Alex breath" Uncle Christian said, he looked like his gut had wrenched too. "Colt, usare le buone maniere."

Uncle Donavan cleared his throat "Yes, Colt manners would be appreciated, Your father had the doctors save some of his sperm in case your mothers wanted more than Al when he did it he thought Al was actually a Laci but that's beside the point."

"Oh wait Al would have been a girl?"

"Well there was a chance all of you could have been girls but your mothers were blessed with boys" Uncle Christian laughed.

"But, Laci eww who picked that."

"Your mother"

"Oh" Colt raised his eyebrows and ran to join the others outside.

"That one is all Tina" Uncle Christian shook his head.

"And that one is all you" Uncle Donavan said watching my head spin.

"No he is Colt; that is the look Colt would give me until Mio Piccolo accepted him as her guard."

"I thought . . ."

"I was Alex, but C.J. wasn't always into guarding his sister from wild fans he was into his guitar and girls."

"Uncle Chris with a steady girlfriend ha-ha-ha, Uncle Chris doesn't date . . ."

"Miss Nikki is his girlfriend."

"Only lady dumb enough to put up with him this long." Uncle Donavan laughed.

"Don, be nice" Uncle Christian shook his head stifling a laugh.

"Any questions about your father, Al?" Uncle Donavan smiled. His smile was scarier than his frown.

"You look like Kenny."

"No way, that fool is all your Mama and she hated me from the start; told me Colt's genes better not be as defective as mine because if they were her and Bella would have to sell you."

I laughed "No that wasn't a question, sorry I know, I have met Kenny's father unfortunately."

Uncle Christian made a disapproving noise and face "I didn't like him the second I saw him."

Uncle Donavan laughed "Any real questions or odd thoughts?"

I thought "Only of Mom and Mama."

"That is a ship you can't sail without them" He shook his head and laugh "La curiosità uccise il gatto e la paura ha rilevato per scalpitare di profonde nel passato (Curiosity killed the cat and fear took it over for pawing to deep in the past)" He looked out the window "Your Mothers are an enigma I will not irritate."

I looked at Uncle Christian.

"Don't look at me I won't cross them either go meditate" He laughed.

I did as I was told, I knew better than to disobey my uncle other kids had a mother and a father. I had my mothers and my uncle Christian. I meditated in the studio.

Meditation was to clear one's mind not congest it with more unanswered questions, but that was what it did today. When I felt it would no longer help I checked out side no one was out there. So I went back up stairs loud old country music blasted through the house. The number one reason I hated my parents arguing, when they argued they blasted every radio in the house. I turned off the bathroom Paul's room and kitchen radios. Turned down the TV in the living room low enough so I could actually tell what the words were after turning off the computer music. I followed the music to Mama's room I knocked.

"Come in" Uncle Christian's voice sounded far away.

I looked at him "U . . ."

"They are up in the attic."

"Oh" I nodded.

"I thought I told you to . . ."

"I did."

"Tell that to your eyes they are a pretty shade of black" He turned down Mom's radio.

"Mama isn't the one blasting the music is she, you are?"

"Pretty hair, your Ana has pretty hair."

I laughed 'pretty hair' was Uncle Christian's way of ignoring a question. "Dad seemed like a great guy, he took care of Mama that doesn't sound like it is easy."

"You're telling me!" He laughed.

"Well I am going to go see . . ."

"What's your question?"

"Uncle . . ."

"Your uncle, you're not that dumb they are twins. You know that already though I told you before . . ."

"No, no but thanks for confirming they are twins again," I looked at him he was way off today, "Uncle Mike . . ."

"He's your uncle too."

"No, he said something about Mama having friends . . ."

"Donavan told you not to dig to deep but if you think it's necessary your mama is up stairs in the attic; don't say I didn't warn you."

"Thanks Uncle Christian."

"Your welcome" He laid back on the bed and sang softly to the music, sulking. I rethought talking to my mothers.

The movie was funny it was the newest animated Disney flick and as always Saturday dinner was at the pool hall. Mr. Wittson put Paul up on a bar stool with a chocolate milk.

"Thank-you Ate Uncle Kork"

I laughed his speech was improving thanks to Uncle Donavan. Uncle Christian took the seat to the left of Paul as I was on Paul's right. Ana was on my right and Uncle Donavan was at the other end of the bar. My brothers had mingled into the crowd and my parents were dancing.

"Hey you old fart, what's up" Mr. Wittson said hugging Uncle Christian and handing him a soda.

"Deep breaths and board games of pure evil, and who are you calling an old fart?" He laughed "Tis you and Don that are old farts."

"Nay not I, I am young in spirit and you have been an old fart since . . ."

"The day he was born" Uncle Donavan laughed cutting off Mr. Wittson.

"Penny for your thoughts Alexander" A deep voice said behind me.

"Uncle Marc!" I jumped and hugged my uncle "How was your vacation?"

"It was fine, where's my nephew, my brother and sister? And why are you giving people headaches?"

"I . . ."

"Marc Ramon Williams" Mr. Wittson smiled cutting me off.

"Kenneth William Wittson the third" Uncle Marc said back hugging him tight "It has been too long."

"That it has. How are Mum and Ky?"

"Mum is herself and Kyle is a frantic wreck, quiet hilarious though."

"Dad's here driving me batty."

"How's Adam?"

"Drove him batty too."

"That's not what I asked Ken, I know my boy."

They talked as if I wasn't there.

"Yeah he has too much of you in him" Auntie Kate said joining them. "Hey old fart how's my baby brother?"

"Damn chess games. Hey! I am not an old fart" Uncle Christian laughed.

A memory of being Paul's age hit me, of the best thing in the world being to sit between my uncles drinking chocolate milk. I watched Paul his eyes got huge with excitement as he took everything in.

"I asked you a question" Uncle Marc remembered I hadn't answered.

"I was um . . . Witch nephew oh Paul I . . ." I was lost my uncle Marc was about six foot two broad and strong he was an honest, kind hard working family man. He had three children Kimberly, Adam and Marc Jr. When he spoke you listened, although he always spoke too fast never making any sense or giving you time to answer any questions let alone find the questions.

"Where is my nephew?"

"Witch one?" I cut him off.

"My Great nephew . . ."

"Right here this is Paul." I had to cut him off it was the only way to talk to him.

"He's cute ho . . ."

"He is three" I sighed happy I cut him off in time.

"Where are your parents?"

I pointed to Mama dancing with Mom near Uncle Chris and Miss Nikki; happy he caught on and slowed down.

"Why were you digging up old graves?"

"Huh? Oh Mama's past, curiosity."

"Yeah, don't get to curious."

"Yes sir" I gulped.

He walked over to Uncle Chris and Miss Nikki and whispered in Uncle Chris' ear. He smiled and came over to us and whispered something to Uncle Christian. Uncle Christian laughed and whispered something to Mr. Wittson.

"What is he up to boys?" Auntie Kate asked.

"Nothing Kate" Uncle Chris gave an evil grin.

"Real convincing C.J" Uncle Christian rolled his eyes.

Uncle Marc returned with Mom and Mama.

"I called Henry he's on his way" Ms Nikki smiled.

"Papa!" Paul squealed at the top of his lungs.

Uncle Marc jumped "Well, I see Hen's finally made a friend" He laughed, Mama swatted him and they laughed harder.

Adam finally noticed Uncle Marc and came over. "Hey Dad."

"Hello I doubt your work is complete."

He looked at his feet "Mom . . ."

"Don't whine at me I worked here from the day it opened until your uncle took over" Aunt Kate glared at Adam.

"But Sam . . . ."

"Adam, tell Sam dishes she will shut up." Mr. Wittson sighed "I swear that one's too much like Chrystaline's side of the family."

Uncle Christian pointed at Kenny "All Mio Piccolo."

Mama swatted him laughing "Well it could be worse."

"Alex you ok?" Uncle Chris said as I stared at a couple of guys I didn't now walking toward us.

"Down boy" Ana patted my back; she looked at Uncle Chris "I have a guard dog not a boy friend."

Uncle Chris laughed and pointed at Uncle Christian who promptly smacked him.

"Hey, no fighting in front of Paul you two" Mom objected.

"This is a pool hall not an arena, C.J. leave the old fart alone" Mr. Wittson added.

"This band blows" I said absently.

"It won't soon" Uncle Marc said.

"JJ, Tina" The men I didn't know greeted them.

"Travis, Kevin" Mama smiled hugging them "How have you been?"

"Good, good" One said.

"Troy says hello him and Ben were unable to attend" Said the other.

"Where's your daughter?" Mom asked.

"Oh Izzy is out there in that mess, but I don't see how she can stand this awful music. Kork don't you regulate the music any longer?" The second one said.

"Kevin" The first one shook his head "Please dear don't embarrass yourself."

Mr. Wittson laughed "What to drink boys?"

"I'll have an apron and an order pad" The one called Kevin said.

Mama laughed "That leaves Travis dishes."

The one called Travis laughed "I don't mind JJ, only you and CJ hated those things with a passion."

My head started to spin and I nearly fell off my stool as I had another memory this one of Mama taking orders here and there yelling at uncle Chris not to put dish soap in her hair.

"What's wrong with you Alex?" Uncle Christian asked balancing me.

I shrugged "I don't know, I'm fine."

"Wow, this is Alex? Has it really been that long?" Kevin asked.

"Yes" Mom said.

"Wow, he looks like, well how old is he now?"

"Twenty-two almost."

I wasn't there again having another flash back of being little as I watched Paul.

"Ken that Sam?" He gestured towards Ana.

"With all due respect sir," Ana objected "I am not Sam, I could never be that caddy."

Uncle Marc, Uncle Christian, Uncle Chris and Mom all stifled laughs.

Mama looked at the ceiling. "No, Kevin that's Ana"

"Wow" Travis said.

"And the little Guy is Ana and Al's son Paul" Mom added.

"More Milk pease Ate Uncle Kork" Paul smiled as Mr. Wittson filled his glass.

"So where is Hen and Davie?" Travis asked.

"On their way" Mama said.

"Did you two do what I asked you to?" Mr. Wittson asked.

"Yes" Travis laughed "Oh and Mike says although he is on his way he says he doubts 'the old fart' can still do it after a year off."

"I'm not an old fart." Uncle Christian Sighed.

"I don't know" Uncle Chris laughed.

"Forty-three almost forty-four" Mama laughed.

Colt Climbed Up on the bar top and eyed Travis and Kevin "Mom who are they?"

"Manners much?" I shook my head.

Mom frowned "Your brother's right some manners would be nice, now what's wrong?"

"She won't dance with me."

"Whom dear?"

"Danni won't dance with me."

"Come on, let's talk where I can hear you" Mom lead him to the kitchen.

"That one . . ."

"That is Colt Jr., Kevin, but he is all Tina" Uncle Chris laughed.

"Excuse me, Daddy, Dad there is this or these I can't . . . but he or they are . . ."

"Twins" I growled before she could finish.

"Izzy, dear" Travis said turning her around "This is Ms. Williams."

Izzy curtsied "Nice to meet you ma'am."

"She's a Doll Travis; it sounds like she has encountered my beasts."

"It was awful" She shook her head in disbelief.

I spotted them in a corner laughing "Excuse me I'll be right back."

Kevin shook his head "Sure that one isn't Christian's I remember both Colt and Tina being more relaxed than that."

"He's Colt's but he . . ."

"I heard, your mom talks to Troy, he misses you a lot." He cut Mama off.

"I wish he could be here."

"I know"

"I pulled Christopher and Christian back to Mama by their ears.

"Is this them?" I asked the young lady.

"Yes" She smiled at them.

"This" I swatted him "Is Christian and this is Christopher" I swatted him. "Apologize now" I growled at them.

"We're . . ."

". . . Sorry."

"We were . . ."

". . . Just having . . ."

". . . A little fun."

"Well, you guys are kind of cute" She blushed.

"Gag me" Nick and Mag walked up to Mama.

"Manners" Mama frowned.

"Those idiots are nowhere near cute, they are barely tolerable."

"Nikolas, behave tonight, please."

"Where is Mom?"

"Talking to Colt."

"I hate this band."

"It's about to change."

"Ok, Kenny and Juliet are . . ."

"We know" Mama sighed.

"So how many all total? I know you wanted six" Kevin asked.

"There is six Alex, Kenny, Christopher, Christian, Nick and Colt Jr."

"Isabella" Uncle Donavan smiled "Very beautiful name."

"Thank you sir" She curtsied "May I . . ."

"Go on dear" Mama laughed "My goons should leave you alone they are afraid of their brother."

Uncle Mike came in" It's snowing again."

"Well, it is December you block head" Uncle Donavan growled at him.

"Wasn't telling you Ogre, was telling Kork so Jr. or Adam can shovel" Uncle Mike Scowled.

All of a sudden the pool hall was flooded with people about Mama's age.

Ana's dad came in with David "Where's . . . Kevin, Travis nice to see you."

"Over here Daddy" Ana Smiled.

"Henry" Travis smiled and hugged him.

"Our condolences Joker, I am sorry we couldn't be there for you" Kevin said.

"It's fine I understand. Has Marc lost his mind, or does he realize Kyle is still in England."

"I haven't lost my mind we can play man down Kyle has more important things to be doing right now, besides unless the old fart lost . . . ."

"I am not an old fart, and I haven't lost my mind either." Uncle Christian objected to Uncle Marc dragging him in to their banter. "But Kevin and Travis better go help Crystalline and the kids before she yells at you and Kork."

"I say we get going before this bands music kills everyone." Ana's dad laughed.

Mom, Mama, My uncle's except Uncle Donavan, Ana's dad and Uncle all jumped up on the stage and then I caught on they were going to perform tonight. It had been a long time since I heard them perform. I avoided the pool hall for a long time I hadn't been here on a Saturday night passed eight pm for more than fifteen minutes at a shot in months. The other band stopped and moved aside. The older generation cheered the younger generation looked lost.

Uncle Marc, once the other band had fully left the stage and everyone was settled with their instrument, yelled into the microphone; "GOOD EVENING POOL HALL."

Auntie Kate whistled. I tried not to laugh. Marc Jr. sat looking miserable.

"What's with him?" I whispered to Ms. Nikki.

She whispered back "I believe they said his girlfriend is pregnant."

"Oh" My eyes got wide Marc Jr. was only 15. I focused back on the stage.

"I CAN'T HEAR YOU" Uncle Marc was yelling.

Kenneth passed muttering about snow, I laughed I agreed with him Adam or Marc Jr. should have to shovel.

Mama counted off and the music started. The music was strong and intense. It wasn't a song I recognized. It had a strong bass and the lyrics were hard hitting and deep, Mama's voice sent chills down my spine. It was defiantly a song I had not heard enough to recognize it.

"Those eyes of fear hide your lies" Uncle Chris sang as if the song was killing him.

At the end of the song Uncle Marc stepped forward again "That was "Blinded" and we are M2CJ." The Adults in the crowd went wild.

Kenneth passed by again muttering that the customers could just break something on the Ice.

"Hey K-4, What's up?" I asked him.

"It's hailing, bloody ice pellets! Jr. can shovel." Kenneth growled

"Well tell him, but I think he can't leave Uncle Marc's sight."

"I told him and he is a . . ."

"Kenneth William Wittson the fourth get out there and shovel right now!" Mrs. Wittson cleared all questions about who was to shovel.

Uncle Marc finished a spiel about some can and introduced the next song as "Lost Soul".

"She's all alone in a darkened world . . . not a single soul to consol her broken heart . . . Band-Aids empty on the floor blood pouring out for the war. Tears fill the hurt one's eyes. All she ever does is cry. Crrrrrrrrrrrrryyyyyy! Cry out in pain for everyone but her unselfish and kind, she's gentle and mean in ways no one has ever seen.

They turn their backs as if they don't care, glass shards softer than their fears. She's the one they fear the most, Androgyny their favorite host. No label, box, or prefabrications to hold her in her place.

Band-Aids empty on the floor blood pouring out for the war. Tears fill the hurt one's eyes. All she ever does is cry.Crrrrrrrrrrrrryyyyyy! Cry out in pain for everyone but her unselfish and kind, she's gentle and mean in ways no one has ever seen.

The cold chills she sends down their backs warmer than the creepy thoughts, that fill their heads. As the truth unravels exposing all their shallow minded acts. A fallen angel they will never know a broken hearted soul that will never show . . .

Band-Aids empty on the floor blood pouring out for the war. Tears fill the hurt one's eyes. All she ever does is cry.Crrrrrrrrrrrrryyyyyy! Cry out in pain for everyone but her unselfish and kind, she's gentle and mean in ways no one has ever seen."

I was stunned frozen to my seat as the song ended the crowd went wild. "Wow" I whispered Mom Hadn't sang like that in a while.

Auntie Kate laughed at me "That one's nothing."

The next song they did was the song they wrote for each other they didn't just sing it though they preformed. They alternated verses and started with Mom.

"Write me pretty love songs and send me romantic poetry; that tells me how much you love me. Because I'm in love with you deeper than the canyon goes longer than the river flows. I'm in love with you." Mom stopped and then there was instrumental break.

Mama turned to face Mom and Mom turned her back to Mama and faced the Audience. Mama began to sing "I dream of romantic insights, candle lights, dancing in the bright moon light. All . . ." They switched again Mom making almost pleading gestures.

"Because I'm too shy to tell you I'm in love with you. I love you deeper than the canyon goes longer than the river flows. I'm in love with you."

I looked way from the stage I had heard this song a million times over. I watched Nick and Kenny dance with their girlfriends. I looked back Sam was talking to Justin and Ana was watching the stage.

"Alex" Mom said into the microphone. "Bring Paul up here."

Paul heard his name and then spotted her and squealed "Grandma!" and started trying to get off his stool. I helped him down and he took off running for the stage. For the most part the crowd parted for Paul, those who couldn't catch on parted when they saw me running after him. I lifted him on to the stage and he jumped right in to mom's arms.

"This is our grandson Paul." Mama took the microphone. "And we are going to sing a special song just for him." The crowd cheered. Mama kissed Mom and headed back to her drums and counted off.

The person my parents called Travis came up to me "That Davie's song?"

I nod

"Your Mama doesn't talk about us much does she?"

"Sir, with all . . ."

"Travis, just Travis, Hun. I work for a living. And don't worry I know your Mama doesn't."

"Yes, Sir."

He shook his head "They told me you were all your uncle and barely any Tina. I hear you're with Nal's . . ."

"Yes sir, she is dancing with Colt so he doesn't . . ."

"Are you taking good care of him?"

"Travis how dare you even assume" Ms. Nikki growled "How about instead of scaring him to death tell him about Colt.

"Ms. Nikki you knew my dad?" My eyes widened.

"A little; he was oddly private and always standing in a door way or next to your mama. He was quiet, fidgety and always trying to impress your uncle Christian."

"Oh" I nodded "Sir you knew my . . ."

"Travis, and yes I knew Colt I lived with Colt. He was kind, considerate, really quite, Kept to himself and his sworn duty to protect your parents and was forever trying to impress his brother."

"Hunny" Mr. Travis' husband came over "Your daughter would like permission to dance with Tina's boys or one . . ."

"Twins!" I shuttered.

Mr. Travis laughed "He sounds like his uncles. Tell her she may."

"You're boring him, Trav," He stuck his hand out to me "Kevin, I know better than to assume your parents told you about us."

I smiled "Alex sir, nice to meet you."

"I know your Colt's boy; you look just like him, besides your Mother's smile looks nice on you."

"I uh . . . thank-you Sir."

"I wasn't boring him; I introduced myself and told him about Colt."

"Tina said he was curious of that not much to say though, really, he was quiet and very private." Mr. Kevin returned to the crowd.

"Curiosity killed the cat" Uncle Donavan joined us.

"And satisfaction brought him back" Ms. Nikki growled at him. "There is nothing wrong with him knowing about Colt."

"Nay I never said it would, He keeps asking of his mothers."

"Mmm" Mr. Travis shook his head "Only a fool wishes to pry in to JJ's past, he wish to know of his mothers he has to ask them himself."

I looked at Ms. Nikki.

"Don't look at me, Sweetie, I don't cross JJ and Tina; learned that a long time ago."

"Actually I was going to ask why you never married Uncle Chris?"

"He never asked" She smiled "Besides we are content as we are."

Mr. Travis snorted.

Ms. Nikki glared at him. "So Alex, tell me of your sons."

CHAPTER 17
BLURRED DAYS

The week past as many did up, work, home, school, sleep with very little time to spend with Paul. They state lady had checked on Paul on Wednesday; she had left a note saying how well adjusted he is and how good his speech is coming along but that day care is still strongly suggested for social interaction with children his own age. Ana was either extremely over tired or strangely distant. Kevin had come back with a cold and could not leave his room all week consequently he was mean and uncooperative for Quentin. Dave had me everywhere and anywhere and no one was happy with me. Kyle missed Kevin in meals and classes and Genevieve was unhappy about having to switch her room for "spoiled brats".

"I don't see why I have to move" Genevieve hissed at me "I am a level three and a half!"

"I know, I know" I sighed carrying her school books.

Genevieve was about five foot three with icy green eyes and waist length dark hair, darker than mine. "Dog breath! It's not fair they shouldn't share a room they won't ever progress that way."

"Sadie will or she will be very miserable." I thought back to when Sir said he knew what to do thanks to Mom and Mama, I wondered if he would tell me about them.

"I'm serious Dog Breath" She added as we checked on Amelia.

"You suck!" Amelia yelled at me as I opened the door.

"Whatever dear" I rolled my eyes relocking her door she was fine other than miserable.

"Dog Breath did you hear me?!?"

"SI! Yes Genevieve I hear you, I heard you quite clearly you wish to either keep your old room or have your own but I do not have control of that so for now you are placed with Latrice."

"No way she is a homophobe let me stay in with the spoiled brats they can share a bed!"

"You can take it up with Dave at dinner, dear. I must go check on my son."

"Night Dog Breath" She hugged me.

I hugged her back "Hang in there kiddo maybe Andrea will visit you Friday."

Sadie cursed my every move and Tiffany was violently insubordinate. Even my own son wouldn't talk to me. He wanted Paul and he wanted to go home "NOW" and he didn't care what any state personnel said about it. The only one who seemed to be acting himself was Buddy.

Things at home weren't going much better. Mom and Uncle Donavan were always disagreeing over something. Colt was moping about over some girl turning him down. The twins were busy with work and Nick with his girlfriend neither of which made Paul happy. With the colder weather Paul couldn't go with Mama up to the stables for hours on end witch made him even crankier.

I could not wait for Friday, Thursday after a long day of arguing with Buddy to behave, Dave called me in to his office. "I didn't do it, I don't have say in the cafeteria foods, level changes, Ana's granddad, the color of band aids, the rules of this establishment, or someone else's personality so if you're going to whine at me I quit."

Dave laughed "long day?"

"Si. Long day, week, month, year your choice."

Dave laughed "English. Go tell Anthony neither did he, tell Kyle real middle school food is worse, tell Tiffany she has to put effort in to earning outside, tell Sadie neither do I" He laughed "and I can't quite say much to him she is here much as Amelia is. Tell Quentin to grow up or by his own Band-Aids. Tell Buddy if he would follow the rules he wouldn't have such an issue with them, and tell my Genevieve her and I will talk later."

I groaned.

"Are you going to argue with me?"

"No" I head out the door and ran in to Ana and tired to hug and kiss her.

"Ugh Al don't paw me" She pushed me away. "What has gotten into you?"

"Nothing I thought I was hugging the person I love."

"We are working and that's like the seventh time this hour."

"Fine, don't worry I won't do it again!" I slammed off to the time out room to talk to Buddy.

"Oooh that boy" Ana bristled.

"Him" Dave looked at her.

"Yes him" He has been all touchy feel in work today and he knows how I feel about that. And it's just not him, I mean he will cuddle and hold me but he isn't clingy like this."

Dave shook his head "He is reacting to you my dear just tell him what's wrong."

"I will I'm just not ready yet I came for more level report sheets."

"Ok" Dave shook his head and handed her the papers.

I opened the time out room door and told Buddy Dave said to knock it off then I went to Anthony as they were closet to Dave's office. Anthony had a long list of questions for me.

"Dad are you getting sick again?" He greeted me.

"No, I have stress induced asthma" I answered.

"Do I stress you?"

"No, Buddy hit me in the ribs today causing me to breath irregularly."

"Oh, why?"

"Why does it . . ."

"I know what rib injuries do Dad; I mean why did he hit you?"

"I don't know; he is a bully."

"Oh" He looked at his feet.

"I am waiting."

"You don't get mad at me for it?"

"No. I enjoy my time with you."

"But I take time from Paul."

"I have two sons and no one and nothing come before them. I try to spend equal time with both of you."

"Christmas is coming . . ."

"I know Ana is already on me about last minute shopping."

"Will I still have Christmas?"

"Of course Dave makes Christmas special, you guys are people just like everyone else; you just are here instead of somewhere else."

"Can I ask Santa for something?"

"Go for it I will hand deliver the letter myself."

"I have tried that it didn't work."

"It might this time, try again."

"Did Paul write Santa?"

"I believe so. I know at breakfast with Santa he asked for you."

"Does Ana celebrate Christmas?"

"Yep."

"Who is coming tomorrow?"

"Uh . . . Me, Ana, Paul and um . . . . Well at least us. Wow, am I tired tonight."

"Are you sure you're not sick?"

"Yes dear, I share a room with your uncle Kenny and he snores really loud."

"Oh, kind of like the boy with the Mohawk?"

"Yes, like Spike, but louder?"

"Wow I'd be tired too. Do I have to call Ana mom?"

"No, that choice is up to you, she will understand either way."

He nodded "Why did Paul start calling her mama?"

"Well I am not entirely sure, I was sleeping. I had that cursed sinus infection. When I woke up I asked him where his Ana was and he told me that Mommy was at Grandpa's and it took us several minutes to figure out he meant Ana. I think that's more a question for him."

Anthony looked lost as I had when Paul called Ana mommy. "Yeah" He agreed. "Does Ana really love us?"

"To the best of my knowledge but those are questions for her."

"Did my old mommy love me?"

I sighed "To the best of my knowledge she loved you in the only she knew how. Sometimes no matter how hard one tries not all their actions turn out the way they planned. Child abuse often is a hard cycle to break." I gulped "We learn to be parents by watching our parents. I have been very fortunate I was blessed with two very awesome mothers, not everyone has that opportunity, some people like you and my Godfather are not so lucky and draw the short straw and their parents don't quiet do everything they should or like they should. As much as we'd like, children don't come with instruction books or step by step manuals. Um . . . Am I making any sense?"

"More than Tiffany did."

I laughed "Tiffany is mad at her mom because she sees nothing wrong with cutting and her mother can see it is wrong and it is hurting her to see her child hurt if her mom didn't care Tiffany wouldn't be here."

"Does that mean my mom cared?"

"Did your mom know you cut?"

"No she thought they were from her and told me to cover them better or I would be in bigger trouble."

"Unfortunately although I am sure she cared about you, I don't think she would have put you some place like this. She probably . . ."

"It's ok Daddy I get it, she would have hit me because she wouldn't know what else to do."

"More than likely, little man."

"Will you ever hit me?"

"Hit you? No, I don't believe it is entirely necessary."

"What about Ana?"

I stifled a laugh "I doubt she will; she is soft on your brother letting him sleep with us. I have bruises to prove it."

His eyes went wide "She hits you?"

"No" I laughed "Your brother kicks in his sleep."

"Oh, do you hit her?"

"Never, I don't hit ladies, and something tells me if I ever entertained the thought of hitting her or any lady or disrespecting any lady in any way my uncles would make sure I knew I was wrong." I shivered knowing I would be dead on the spot if I hit a lady for any reason.

"Oh, Ok" The relief that swept over him scared me a little. "What is the other language you speak to your parents; that they are teaching Paul?"

"Italian."

"Oh will they teach me?"

"Of course there is no way around it if we don't teach you, you will not understand most of what is said in the house."

"Can Ana speak Italian?"

"Of course she can, she has been my best friend for as long as I can remember and my girlfriend since we were old enough to date."

"My mom said my daddy was sick so that is why he wasn't there, said he died of something called A.I.D.S. after Paul was born."

"I have seen that we have state files on everyone here saying who their parents are and where their parents are and why they are here and not with their parents."

"What does mine say?"

"It says your name your, date of birth, your age, your height, and weight. Also Your mother's name, date of birth, and location, Your father's name, date of birth, date of death, and on a sheet stapled to it says a case number, your social workers name and office number and that you and Paul were placed for adoption and then under that it says adopted and it has my name and Ana's name and our dates of birth, and your new address and contact numbers."

"Oh when is your birthday?"

"Febuary 22."

"Oh. Why did you adopt us?"

"I" Why did I adopt them hmm it filled the missing something in me. I looked at him and smiled "I wanted to be a daddy and it seemed like a good idea to have you and Paul."

"Was it?"

"Best thing I have ever done."

"So that means Ana can have babies?"

"Er yeah to the best of my knowledge."

"Phew, so I may get more brothers and sisters?"

"Er . . . maybe?"

Ana came in "Hey kiddo looks like you finally stumped him."

"No I am good." I objected "He is just asking things I can't give a plan yes or no to."

"I knew that would happen, come here Sweetie, let's talk." She lifted Anthony out of my arms. "What's on your mind?" She sat down on his bed near me.

"Are you mad at me?"

"No should I be?"

"I did something wrong. I yelled in some ones face?"

"It happens we all make mistakes, doesn't mean we need to be severally punished or we need to punish ourselves."

"Would you ever hit Daddy?"

"Ha-ha-ha" Her laughter rang happily in my ears. "I doubt I would but even if I did he's all strong muscle, I think he would just laugh at my weak punch."

"Would you ever hit me?"

"No I will never hit you, I will never see a reason good enough too."

"Do you really love me and Paul?"

"It is Paul and I and yes I love both of you with all my heart."

"Why did you and Daddy adopt us?"

"Because we love you and feel you need a safe loving home with loving parents."

I grimaced her answer was much smoother.

"Do you love Daddy?" He smiled.

"Have all my life."

"Why aren't you and Daddy married?"

"I don't know. *Daddy,* why aren't we married?" She laughed and smiled at me.

"I uh OK now he has stumped me" I laughed.

"I we aren't ready yet" Ana laughed.

"Does that mean you can't be my mom?"

"Marriage doesn't make someone a parent."

"Oh, do Paul and I get more siblings I like being a big brother."

"Maybe someday, but these are big thoughts for a little man all of six. How about I bring you and Kyle to the dining hall and you two can throw mash potatoes at the ceiling while I do my paper work so daddy can finish his rounds."

"Ana, Mash potatoes?" I raised my eyebrows.

"I forgot my lunch and had to eat their food today."

I laughed "Ok have fun, don't get caught."

"Oh they will but only by me" Ana smiled.

I shook my head and hugged and kissed Anthony. "Have fun, and remember she is letting you do something that is inappropriate we don't normally get to throw food at the ceiling because it doesn't taste good." I didn't bother trying to hug Ana this time I just said "See you after work, Hunny."

"Um ok?" She looked lost.

I walked down to Sadie and Tiffany's room. Sadie was balled up under her bed crying and Tiffany was sitting on hers glaring at Sadie.

"She's been there all fu . . . ." Tiffany started to fuss.

"Rephrase that or don't say it" I sighed.

"She's been under there all flipping week, all she does is cry she won't graduate if she doesn't do her homework. She needs to graduate so she can get her big flashy job and we can . . ."

"Slow down, how about you just worry about you right now, you want outside you need to start by taking the right steps to get there.

And she needs to focus on feeling better herself and if crying makes it better let her cry. College and big flashy jobs will be there when she's ready for them."

"I don't want to get there without her."

"This is something both of you need to both do on your own. Sadie is only here until her birthday or Ana's Uncle Kyle returns state side and says otherwise or she wouldn't even be in this room. She has to do it on her own too. Sometimes no matter how much we want to help someone we can't because we are to emotionally attached to them and it blinds us because we don't wish to think of our loved ones in any way where we aren't all they need."

"You sound like a shirk."

"I apologize, but this is how life works and my uncle will be happy my college classes are sticking and not just the music ones."

"Well at least make her see I love her."

"I can't show her you love her, only you can do that. Get healthy for you, because you want to, if she truly loves you she will be there once you are both healthy and if it is meant to be it will be."

She pouted at me "You suck."

"Yes, I know Amelia points out about seven times a day I have that skill."

"At least he gets to taste her . . ."

"Young lady" I cut off Sadie's muffled protest "I strongly suggest you rethink that sentence."

"Sorry, but Ana loves you."

"That's currently debatable but as always my love life and or lack thereof at the moment is never up for discussion. The best advice I can offer you, Sadie, is talk to Tiffany" With that I left.

"I didn't do it" Dave raised an eye brow at me as I stomped back in "But can you . . ."

"Sì, va bene, qualunque sia (Yeah, fine, whatever)." I stomped back out and tossed the keys to Ana "Kiss Paul for me Vado a piedi a casa. (I'll walk home)."

She raised her eye brows at me "Hunny?"

"I said I would walk home."

Dave Came out behind me "Go down to Amelia's room, Alexander"

"Fine" I stomped down to her room.

"He needs to meditate, Dave" Ana sighed.

"No he needs to relax, and he needs to know he is loved, but when the girl he . . ."

"It's not that Dave, I swear" Ana shook her head.

"I didn't think it was I am here if you need to talk though. Go home to your son he's out at ten thirty if you wish to obtain him instead of letting him walk home."

"Thanks Dave, please tell him I love him."

"Of course.

"You Suck"

"And you have a displeasing attitude, young lady, to the point we have contacted your parents, Will and Will's parents."

She groaned and slammed down on her bed. "I wish I could be emancipated, my parents don't care about me Will cares about me and Mrs. Moore cares."

I sighed "What makes you say your parents don't care?"

"They are drunk all the time; I bet they were too drunk to notice I left. Mohawk had someone looking for him and Spike had Carter but . . ."

"You have Will, and you have Sam and no matter what you will always have me."

The meeting with Amelia's parents went alright. They weren't happy she wanted to be emancipated but they signed the forms on the agreement she finished her treatment at the center. Witch wasn't hard as she had no other choice. Dave would not let her leave as she like Sam had pneumonia, so she was stuck there until she was healthy any way. At ten thirty I flopped down into Dave's desk chair.

"Get up. You know better."

"I . . ."

"Get up and don't argue with me."

I sighed and reluctantly moved I did know better. Dave was the reason I was ok, alive and had a job and two kids. He was as my mama put it an answer to her prayers.

"Feeling brave?

"Not really, actually I am feeling . . ."

"It was rhetorical, sit" He pointed at his bed.

"Wow I'm dizzy"

"I'd imagine so you took a good hit there."

"What is my uncle going to say?"

"About?"

"About me walking home like this."

"You aren't going anywhere till Ana gets here you have a concussion."

"Well, yeah Curtis decked me in the temple and tomorrow won't even realize he did it."

"You tired?"

"Yeah"

"What happened today you were short with me, you were short with Ana, and you were even short with the kids?"

"I don't know, what happened everything felt like it was my fault and I was left in charge of the universe and no one told me I was in charge of it today." I sighed "I don't know. I just . . . I guess it's just not my day. I am sorry."

"Ana says you're scaring her all of a sudden your Mr. Affectionate."

"I was thinking that's why she started to pull away, because unlike the other guys I wasn't all touchy feely."

"How long have you been with her?"

"Uhh . . . I think you know that."

"Then why after this long would she want you to drastically change like that."

"I DON'T KNOW!" But I did know this was a bad cutting withdrawal that I was trying to fight on my own without telling any one

"She doesn't!" Ana stood in the door way "I have always loved you just the way you are, Al, I don't know what is causing this odd behavior but I'm not liking it and I don't like being pawed and you of all people should know that. I don't need you to show off for me and if you hadn't gotten hurt I probably would have let you walk. And if you keep this up I am taking Paul and we are going back to my dad's until you are you again. Now let me see where he hit . . . Never mind, oh my gosh Alexander Joseph Williams why aren't you icing that?"

"I . . ." I looked at Dave.

"It's bruised kiddo, really well. You go wait in the car SHE is driving not you, you already told me you're dizzy and no sleeping yet."

"Yes sir, good night see you tomorrow" I made my way to the car.

"Ooo he is just so . . . just so . . ."

"Alex, Ana, he is Alex."

"I don't hate him."

"I didn't think you did, if you're going to confide in me how about telling me something I don't already know, instead of something the whole world knows."

"Sorry, he's just been acting so odd. I mean he's not acting like *MY* Alex at all. I want *MY* Alex."

"Well think about this for every action there is an equal and opposite reaction, maybe Al's behavior is the reaction to something in his world that he feels isn't *acting* quiet right to him. But for now just go home get some rest odd or not you both still have work tomorrow."

"Yes sir, Good night Dave." Ana sighed "And this too shall pass."

I laid against the window all the way home.

"He asked for you" Ana tried to talk to me.

"At least some one still loves me."

"Alex . . ." She gave up.

I knew it wasn't the right thing to say but I wasn't feeling right. The car stopped abruptly. I ignored it knowing she was trying to get me to look up at her. I didn't want to she'd basically all but told me it was over, so I didn't care how immature or self centered I was acting.

"We can sit here all night or you can respond to me" She sighed after about five minutes of her rubbing my back.

"It feels fine you're putting me to sleep" I said probably way too gruff.

"Ok I tried, I'm going up stairs to bed, you can follow or whatever I don't care but I can't do this with you again, Alexander, I love you but I promise if your cutting again I am taking our sons and we are through."

"COSA(WHAT)!" I slammed out of the car and up the stairs taking about four at a time. I let off a loud long stream of profanity mixing in English and Italian all the way up to the attic and started violently attacking the punching bag.

"Aiming to wake the whole house?" Mama stood with her hands on her hips at the top of the stairs.

"Well at least I don't blast twenty-two year old music at the top volume when she hurts me!"

"Twenty-three year old music and my aren't you flippant tonight." She frowned, whatever higher power you believe in well they blessed my Mama with the loving heart of a saint never once did she screech scream or hit us for any reason she told us that there were more effective ways starting with calm conversation, open ears, open mind and an open heart. "Would you like to talk or would you like your uncle."

"I'd like not to be accused of things I didn't do or the girl of my dreams walking out on me all because I . . ." Another string of angry hurt pain filled English and Italian profanity filled the air as I rocked the punching bag harder.

"Whoa there slow down your going to knock it off the hook" Uncle Chris steadied the bag joining Mama at the top of the stairs. "Davie's here to see Al and I don't think it's to be social."

"Well did you let him in, C.J.?" Mama glared at Uncle Chris.

"I'm right here Ms. Williams." Davie's tone sent ice down my spine.

"Ok well it is late you two try not to wake the whole house." With that she and Uncle Chris descended the attic stairs.

I gulped. "Alright then get on with it; get it over nice and fast I will stay still."

He made me a "give me a break, drama queen" face and growled "Take your shirt off and sit you're too damn tall." That sounded funny as David was at least 6'4" But I listened confused but I listened. I sat on the window sill bracing myself to be pushed out it.

"Spread your arms out" He knelt down near me looking over my arms and chest carefully "Didn't think so you still have enough brains to fear me."

"Well hell David I maybe taller but I'm not as strong as you and I don't doubt you'd kill me that's your sister."

"I know who she is, I also know four years ago you wouldn't have cared who you picked a fight with and you wouldn't have care if you won either, Alex. I lost my arm and I think and speak a bit slower, but I didn't lose my memory."

"I . . . I . . ."

"Hush, she came to me crying you've changed and it's scaring her you were short with her and have been acting so odd. She says you are scaring her and she is going to take my nephews and turn you over to Dave." He tossed me a pocket knife "Prove to me you're safe to be with my sister."

I gulped, I wanted to cut but I wasn't going to; I open the knife and slam it into the window sill "NON TAGLIARE PIÙ! (I DON'T CUT ANY MORE!)"

"And you yell at me again you won't have any teeth" David glared at me.

I gulped.

"Well, since you aren't cutting, what is going on with you?"

"WRONG WITH ME?!? Other than tired I have had a long day and your *precious* Ana keeps pulling away from me not me from her."

The blow was hard sharp and fast it left stars and white lighting pain before I even had time to think what it was.

"Watch your bloody tongue, mind you" David growled.

I reset my jaw and shook my head; I thought Curtis hit hard.

"She says you're not acting right."

"She's the one pulling away not me!'

"She says you have been all over her."

"I thought that's what she wanted. I thought I wasn't being affectionate enough. COME DIAVOLO DEVO SAPERE COSA FA LEI MI ODIA (HOW THE HELL SHOULD I NOW WHAT MAKES HER HATE ME)!"

Again I was seeing stars.

"You learn so slow" He sighed "Stick to English it's late and I'm tired."

"I switched languages" I tried to feign that I had no knowledge of my bad habit of switching languages when I was angry.

"Don't play dumb with me, Alexander. I'm not stupid." He sighed sounding completely exasperated. "Go apologize to my sister and you better mean it or you will be the sorry one. Good night AL." He picked me up off the floor from where his last hit had left me unable to move, wiped the blood off my face with my shirt handed it back to me and left.

CHAPTER 18

NO ONE SAID LIFE WAS EASY

"Ooff."

"Wake up" Ana belted me a crossed the chest, not hard just startling.

I jumped slamming my head in to the head board "Sorry" I chocked "I didn't hear it go off."

She made a 'please Alex' face "You didn't hear it because it didn't go off. You were screaming unmercifully as if you were being beaten brutally."

I slid down in the bed dislodging my head from the headboard "Sorry babe. I'm fine, go back to sleep."

"Al what were you . . . ALEXANDER YOUR JAW!"

"Huh, oh yeah that, I'm fine go back to sleep my love."

"For a whole three minutes?" She rolled her eyes and shut our alarm off. "Come on its Friday we have a day off tomorrow" She tossed clean clothes at me.

"Wow it's been two and half hours already, yeah me."

She frowned at me "Go shower."

"Fine like you were going to join me any way" I stomped down stairs clearly the lack of sleep had not improved my mood.

"Dumb toad" Kenny, pushed open the divider "Can I get you anything Ana?"

She gave him a teary smile "A driver's manual to Alex."

"Never tattle on him, or make him mad or . . . well you know what, I want one too. Mom swears he never came with one."

She laughed a little and wiped her eyes "I am sorry we woke you."

"*You* didn't wake me *his* nightmare woke both of us. I would love to know what he was dreaming."

"He wouldn't tell me."

"Never does."

"Do you know what happened to his jaw?"

"Not the slightest, but by the sound of things you might want to be showering before he is eating breakfast."

"I know" She sighed "Have a good day Kenny."

"Yeah you too Ana, hey listen to him he will show you what's hurting him.

A shiner, a bruised ear and temple, a bruised and swollen nose and a fat lip between Buddy, Curtis and, David I didn't need to cut if pain is what I wanted I had plenty of it. I took another deep breath feeling for a split rib where Buddy had hit me.

"Hey Gorgeous George lets go we still have to get Paul ready." Ana came in and started to prepare for her shower.

"Shall I cover my eyes so you call me prude or can I hug and kiss you good morning?"

"Alexander . . . ." She started to object.

"I got one better" I grabbed my shirt "I will go eat and wake your son seeing as your taking him and Anthony!" I stomped out into the kitchen and tied my hair back.

"Alex, you know the rules shirt on at the table" Mama said setting out her kix and my apple jax.

"I'm working on it" I snapped pulling my head through my shirt.

"My aren't you happy this morning. What happened to your lip?"

"He's about six foot seven and calls Ana sissy" I growled headed towards Paul's room.

"My isn't he cheerful" Mom kissed Mama good morning.

"Definitely not" Mama shook her head "He said Davie hit him. I wonder if Ana and him are fighting."

"I hope not he is not smart enough to say sorry" Uncle Donavan limped to the table "Bella mattina, Il suo piccolo mattina(Morning Bella, morning His Little One)."

"Morning Don" Mama said "How is your leg doing?"

"Fine Il suo Piccolo, Bella fetch my coffee, would you please?"

"Of course" Mom shook her head.

"NOOOOOOOOOOOOOOOOOOOO" Paul wailed.

"Sorry guys I guess he's not a morning person." I laughed carrying Paul into the kitchen.

Paul's eyes finally opened and he wrapped his arm around me "Daddy! Daddy is it Friday? Do we get to see Antony today? Can I ride Lizzy yet? I missed you Daddy."

"Wow Questions yes, it is Friday, yes you are going to see Anthony. No riding Lizzy again until spring it's too cold out for you. I missed you too, eat up" I sat him in his chair. "Where is Uncle Christian?" I asked Mom.

"I am behind you" He frowned at me "Do I truly wish the knowledge of why Davie hit you?"

"Can I take a ten hour rain check on that?" I asked putting Paul's shoes on him while he ate.

"Or I can go ask him."

"Sound good but I still need a lecture approximately ten hours from now and even more so when you speak to David please and thank you Sir"

I wiped Paul's face threw his coat on him, pulled hat, scarf and gloves on him I hated running late. I got him buckled in and my Cell went off. "On my way Dave I swear"

"Breath you're not late yet and I am going to make you late so I will clock both you and Ana in on time. I need you to stop and get Band-Aids"

"Ok?"

"There for your son, him and . . ."

"On my way now!"

I belted up the stairs and pounded on the bathroom door "Ana, Dave just called we need to go something about Band-Aids for Anthony. Ana you hear me?

The door swung open "I can hear you just fine, Al, I am almost sure my father could hear you." She grabbed her shoes and coat and I grabbed her. "I can walk you know?"

"Yup, but I can walk faster and our son needs us."

"I caught that" She sighed as I sat her in the car. "Where is your coat?"

"Not that you actually care if I a freeze or get sick, I left it at work on accident last night."

It was a thick tension filled silence all the way to work.

"Where is he? Is he ok?" I panted sliding through Dave's office door twenty minutes late.

"Slow down did you get the Band-Aids?"

"Yeah right here. Where is he? Is he ok?"

"Whom?"

"Anthony."

"He's fine He is eating breakfast. You listen like a brick the Band-Aids for Paul."

"Paul's fine he's right here in the hall with Sam and Spike, talking their ears off." Ana said looking lost.

Dave laughed "I know he is fine it's an art project now why is Sam out of bed?"

"He swears he needs to see Tiny and speak to you." I sighed; Sam had called me while I was in the pharmacy demanding I pick him up.

"Fine, send all three of them in and you two go to work. I swear only thing wrong with your sons are their parents are neurotic, don't listen well and won't talk to one and other."

"Fire ball blinked 'blade did you attack a . . .'" Mohawk sat with Spike reading to Kevin.

Kyle had already gone home for the weekend. Amelia sat on Mohawk's feet waiting for Will and Carter. Tiffany and Sadie sat on different sides of the room as Tiffany visited with her mom. Genevieve sat Indian style on top of the book case, I hoped for her new roommate's sake that her girlfriend finally showed up, and my boys were fighting again.

"'No fire ball I didn't. I was meditating when she interrupted me' Blade glared off in to the distance, her twin brother staring back at her from the distance without her knowing." Sam had no clue how happy he was making Kevin by reading to him.

"Daddy" Anthony pulled on my leg. "Paul said something I don't understand."

"He told you Lizzy is his horse, horse in Italian is cavallo." I sighed.

"Are you and Ana fighting?"

"Slightly."

"Does this mean you're going to give Paul and me back to the state lady?"

"It's Paul and I. And never our fight has nothing to do with you and everything to do with being over tired. Now go play with Paul, he missed you a lot this week."

"Ok, Daddy."

I walked over to Genevieve "Day is still young" I smiled hopefully at her.

"So is your son Dog Breath but Andrea will not come."

"Have a little faith, she said she was coming."

"She's come once in two years and that was to bring me in."

"And that stack of letters . . ."

"She won't come Al, she made it perfectly clear when she dropped me off."

I sat back down between my family and Sam.

"Fire ball blew a heart shaped fire ball and wrapped his arms around Blade 'Feeling him again aren't you?' Blade just stared in to the distance." Sam's reading had seemed to capture every ones attention except Genevieve. "Fire ball wished he could find Blades twin brother for her. It was well known vampire twins were close and need to stay close to function."

By lunch even my boys were listening to Sam read. Tiffany's mom left but instead of requesting to be brought back to her room she stayed to listen to the story.

"Hey Mom got another best seller" I hugged her as her and Mama came in.

"Good to hear" She smiled "Where are my grandsons?"

"Nana, Grandma" Anthony flew in to their arms as if on cue. Anthony dragged Mom and Mama to his lunch table.

I walked over to Genevieve who chose to site by herself "You need to eat." I towered over her.

"I did Al scouts honor I had a sandwich" She gave me a weak smile.

I sat next to her "Ok talk to me you haven't insulted me much today I am starting to feel loved here, Ana might get jealous."

She laughed and flung her arms around me "Six months Dog Breath six months and I am free!"

"And I will miss you, but . . ."

"I know, I know take it one day at a time. I didn't make level three by ignoring you."

"Can I see your last letter?"

"Sure" she handed me the letter.

I read it to myself "My dearest Genevieve, I miss you to the extent of unbelievable. I am sorry but this is how it had to be. I kept my word one letter a week. I feel that from what your consoler last told me it is safe we see each other; so I will attempt to attend your Friday event. I wish I could promise but I do work. Love you—Andy"

"Do you wish to talk?" I asked Genevieve.

"Dog breath she made it very clear two years ago she loves me and always will and is mine forever and will never leave me but until I am level five and leave here she will not come see me."

"You wish to go . . ."

"So Latrice can torment me? No way!"

"Ok, but have faith in your girlfriend she may have changed her mind."

Willful and carter got there around one. "Hey Alex" Willful greeted me.

"Hey guys"

"We still suck?"

"Something tells me Carter will suck no matter how many times I eat a lollipop" I laughed.

"Only the very best" Carter laughed.

They joined Spike and Sam on the floor with Amelia; Kevin was watching animal planet. Tiffany was staring at the ceiling and Sadie was staring out the window. Genevieve was up on the book case and my boys were playing with Uncle Chris. The absence of Uncle Christian meant he had spoken to Ana's brother. Ana was talking to the state lady I would have to thank her for that later.

"Genevieve I bet you can help me with something."

"Treating Ana better."

"Funny. No, maybe you could talk to Sadie and Tiffany?"

"Those brats!"

"Genevieve do you remember when you first got here?"

"Yeah I had some butt face telling me he was sorry but I couldn't go outside and my wife . . ."

"Wife?"

"Wistful thinking fine my ex girlfriend . . ."

"I truly hope that isn't so."

"Sorry Al, I am just feeling a bit down today, I will go talk to that one over there the other one you can't get two words in edge wise without getting sworn at, I am not into non civilized conversation today." She jumped down and headed over to Sadie.

"Daddy, what's Paul saying about Papa?" Anthony tugged on my arm.

I knelt down "Paul come here what did you say to Anthony?"

Paul ran and tackled Anthony in a bear hug "I say Papa and Uncle Davie no come to day." Paul kissed Anthony and Anthony rolled them over and started tickling Paul. I watched them happy they weren't fighting.

"Ehm"

I looked up "Can I help you?" I asked standing up.

"I am looking for my girlfriend . . ."

"Andrea?" I asked.

"Yes" She smiled.

"I'm Alex, will you be taking her for the weekend or . . ."

"I don't know I wish to see how she does."

"I understand, I will get her she is helping me with something I don't want the young lady she is speaking with to scare you."

She nodded cautiously. Andrea was tall and elegant, but defiantly a Goth. She was exactly what Genevieve had described to a tee. I walked over to Sadie and Genevieve.

"It's not the end of the world." Genevieve was saying "Dog Breath is pretty cool and if you're so sure you're only here for a few months Dave will probably leave you with Dog Breath."

"It's not that I am here, I told Al I cut because I knew I needed help." Sadie's eyes filled up with tears, "It is that she hates me. I am the one who told her mom she cut, but she was scaring me talking about suicide and stuff." She swallowed down some more tears. "I don't blame her for hating me." Even crying and make up free Sadie looked frightening and mean.

"Excuse me ladies" I said "Genevieve may I see you in the hall."

"Sure" We walked out in to the hall "She is hopeless unless she talks to the other one."

"Andrea is here, are you ready?"

"She really came this time?"

"Yes, she is standing with Ana."

Genevieve looked like she was going to vomit "Is she still pretty?"

"Just as you described."

"Alex, I think I am going to panic, it's been two years."

"And there are 104 letters that say you are still everything she wants."

"Come with me Dog Breath?"

"Of course."

We walked back into the family room and over to where Ana and Andrea were talking.

"She has come a long way" Ana was saying.

"That's what they tell me, I check once a month, but I really wish she would have written me back."

"Excuse me" I spoke up "Ms. Andrea I have someone here to . . ."

"GENIE!" She squealed grabbing Genevieve in a tight hug "You look marvelous, Dear, How I have missed you."

"Then why didn't you visit me?" Genevieve muttered off handedly.

Andrea ignored the jab "I did not wish to hinder your recovery, my love."

"Andy?"

"Yes dearest?"

"Do you really still love me?"

"Till the day I die, Beautiful."

Ana leaned her head to my shoulder "Genevieve, sometimes it may seem like our loved ones don't care, but when in fact there love is very true."

Genevieve looked up at me as if to say 'What do I do'.

"Andrea as I said before she can go home for the weekend and it is suggested for normal functioning life."

"I know but, like *I said before* we will see how this visit goes for as much as I love her our home has a large amount of swords, knifes, and daggers."

"I . . ." Genevieve started then changed her mind "Dog Breath I . . ." She started to cry, Andrea held her tight.

"Mr. Ellsworth told me this might happen" She leaned down and kissed Genevieve's head "It's ok Genie, I am right here I am not leaving, I'm not mad at you. In fact I am very proud of you and I am sure if it were the other way around you would have done the same thing." Andrea looked up at Ana and I again. "Mr. Ellsworth said I have to set up a time . . ."

"You can do that with me at the front desk when you leave", Ana said, "Just worry about her right now."

"Genie is my world I have been so lonely and lost without her" Andrea smiled.

"Andy, how's Jethro?" Genevieve asked.

"Your snake is fine probably eating the rat I fed him at breakfast this morning."

Ana startled hearing that as we headed back to our boys, I just chuckled I had heard all about Jethro before.

"Mooommy" Paul pulled on Ana "Antony no WRITE SANTA YET." Paul had picked up a bad habit of random yelling.

"Inside voice, Paul" I corrected.

"He will", Ana smiled "He still has time."

"Can I have a hug or will I be told not to paw you?" I asked, with more edge than necessary in my voice.

"Alexander" She frowned.

"Never mind" I sighed "I will save you the pain I have to go check on Kevin." I growled and stomped off towards Kevin.

"Dumb boy" Ana sighed "Come here Anthony what's wrong?"

"Are you and Daddy going to break up?"

"No dear, he's mine for a long time. Why the worry, little men of six should worry of trucks and books and Santa Claus."

"But you're fighting."

"Your daddy becomes really grumpy when he's over tired or in pain and with the bruises he received yesterday and the fact he went to bed late, I'd say he is both right now" She hugged him tight "Don't worry about us, I plan on being with your daddy a really long time."

"Can I call you mommy?"

"That is entirely up to you little man, if you want to you can if you don't want to you don't have to it doesn't change my love for you."

"Am I going home this weekend?" Kevin asked me.

"What do you think?" I was shorter with him than I meant to be.

"Yes?"

"Then if you know why ask?"

"Because Mom's not here yet."

"She will be, be patient."

I walked over to Amelia and Sam. Sam looked hideous but Amelia's cough was worse than his. "You should be home" I shook my head.

"And you should be kinder to Ana" He said.

"Yeah, yeah, and Wilson's prince charming."

Willful looked up at me "Will that agreement stick, I will sign anything I swear."

I laugh "It will stick, Will."

"You suck" Amelia punched Willful.

"Only Ca . . ."

"Pause I'll walk away and then you can over share with each other."

They all laugh, Tiffany laughed too.

"Hey, what do you find so funny."

"You."

"Me, well me says you should go hold Sadie don't say anything just hold her."

"What good will that do?"

"A lot trust me."

"Oh and maybe you should tell Ana Sorry."

"I will when I need to."

"Ok yeah" She went to do as I told her.

With Tiffany, Sadie, Amelia and Anthony safe in their rooms; Kyle and Kevin at home for the weekend, I asked again. "Ms. And . . ."

"Andy, please" She smiled.

"Ok" I shrugged "Ms. Andy, are you taking Genevieve for the weekend?"

"That is up to her, I am very proud of her. I would love to have her for the weekend."

"Oh sorry" Ana smiled "Can I steal him for a moment?"

"Sure" Andy smiled.

She dragged me out in to the hall, and wrapped me tightly in her arms "WE need to talk when you're done. Paul is with Dave I'm afraid to ask what he's up to, but we NEED to talk I'll meet you in the car." She kissed me and slowly pulled away running a hand down my chest.

I stood stupid starring at Ana as she walked away.

"Ehm" Genevieve clung to my arm.

I looked down "Ok I know why my sons do it and I know why Kevin and Kyle do it when Buddy is chasing them, but you have never seemed to be a clinger your seventeen years old and your clinging . . ."

"Shut up and carry me to my room like you did when Buddy hurt me, Dog Breath."

"I spoil you guys way too much" I picked her up "I'm going to make you pay a toll."

"How much?"

"All."

"I'm scared; Andy has been my guardian since I was fourteen and my girlfriend since I was twelve. Two years! Two years, Dog Breath I bet she's changed and I know I have. What if she . . ."

"Genie do you think I don't know you have changed? People change and grow when I left you here you were a stubborn, selfish, child; today I see a young lady" Andy soothed.

"The two matching claw sets digging in to my back says either she doesn't like being called Genie or she didn't realize you had followed" I laughed.

"Oh my I didn't even think of that, Honey, I am so sorry. Do you wish I call you something other than Genie", Andy looked hopefully at Genevieve, "Or are you still my Genie in a Bottle?"

"The claws are lessening Ms. Andy" I shifted Genevieve.

"You need to speak to me, Genevieve, we discussed this in your T.V. Room, nice and slow you take your time. When you're ready, there is no rush. I am still *your* Andy, I still work twelve hour shifts a day, I haven't changed your room, I have no new friends, and Jethro, Jeremiah, and Icy are all right where you left them."

"I want to go Andy I'm just scared" Genevieve gulped from her spot buried in my shoulder.

"Come on you, you got your ride I said full payment" I shifted to open the time out room door.

"Andy can't go in there Al."

"There you go with the calling me Al again making me think you might actually like me."

"You're my Dog Breath" Her grip on me tightened "But An . . ."

"You're in the time out room, I am not letting you go until you talk to me and if you fight I will interrupt Dave whom is playing with Paul. You thi . . ."

"No, I just thought . . ."

"Do you think I am that dumb?"

"I don't know you are still MY Dog Breath" She clung tighter as I tried to set her down.

"Ok fine a feather ways more any ways" I said regaining my hold on her.

Andy had been looking at me as if studying me "Hey I know you, Your Alex Williams."

"The one and only, Ms. Andy, I am hard to forget," I laughed, "I am seven feet tall."

"You don't remember me?"

"No more than Genevieve will remember anything she cut away." I sighed Andy looked slightly familiar like she had gone to my school at some point, but I didn't like discussing me all that much, especially me in school.

Andy looked shocked as if the mere mention of it would Cause Genevieve to start cutting instantly. "She won't remember"

"Some things not all and not that well it's an addiction like drugs or alcohol." I sighed again I could see Andy was trying but it was hurting my head I was not in a good mood and I was stressing over what Ana wanted to tell me.

"Oh" She looked lost in memories she would want Genevieve to remember.

"I'm all right, Andy, I want to go home and be with you. I'm just scared those dumb boys they have nothing to lose they screw up they just come back here. That Jack Roberts will be here till he is eighteen no matter what. Me I have something to lose, you, and I don't want to lose you. I love you, Andy."

I shifted Genevieve; I knew that feeling all too well.

"Genie I am going to go get those dates for your counseling thing and when I come back if you are ready we will leave if not I will see you next Friday. I don't expect perfection. I expect you to try your very best if you mess up shame on me you weren't ready, you mess up again shame on you, you know better you were here to work on it."

I looked at Genevieve as Andy walked out and toward the main hall.

"She means well Al, honest."

"You don't think I know that?"

"Don't tell her I can't go."

I raised my eyebrows "What makes you say that? I had no intention of stopping you; I feel it will be good for you. Now if you had Kevin's dad . . ."

"I saw your face."

Oops maybe I had shared one to many of my opinions on state regulation and how it should work with them. "I had your claws in my back, dear; Ana may call me on cutting."

She laughed wiping her eyes "Cutting not cheating?"

"She knows I am hers and no one else's, no one else could handle me I am not as great as you all think I am."

"I know your awesome, Dog Breath," She wiped more tears, "I love Andy, but I am scared."

"It will be ok, just remember what I taught you."

"Ok" She rolled her eyes, jumped down and ran to her room making me chase her.

I waited outside her room the exchange between her roommate and her was more than I could handle right now and I knew it.

"This place is huge" Andy greeted me, when she caught up with us.

"Tell me about it, it is almost a mile long and I walk it no less than three times a day."

"Wow, that must be how you keep in such good shape" She laughed. "You know I wouldn't trust anyone else with my Girlfriend. I remember you; you were mean, quiet, shy and normally bleeding and when that guy tried to harass me you saved me."

"Bleeding? Yeah I bled a lot in high school."

"I know and I know why."

"Um ok."

"But I never got to thank you, so thanks."

"No offense, but I don't remember, I have only been clean for four years, And like you said I was bleeding there for I had just cut."

"Also as I have said I wouldn't trust anyone but you with my Genie. I do not like hypocrites, Genie and I spoke while you were running crazy."

"I am always running crazy. Here" I handed her my cell number "Any problems call me don't hesitate, don't wait, and don't second guess. If she panics, cuts, you think she has cut, is panicking or wants me call. She hasn't wanted me in a year but you never know."

"For people to request you and only you, you must have made a large impact on their life, especially my Genie. I know if you had not saved me from that brute I would not have remembered you."

"I may not remember what happened, but if it was what I think it was let me help you out I am Alexander Joseph Williams oldest son of Christina Marie and Jessica Marie Williams. If I had seen and not done anything I would not be standing here to tell you, squat."

She laughed "Glad to here you say it with pride finally. You were continually defending me."

"Thanks it took me a bit I had to grow into it. I am serious though you call me. She needs me you have questions anything anytime just call me."

"Thank you; can I ask you what happened to your face?"

"Face, ribs, back it is all bruised. The back is bad sleeping habits and the ribs, ear, eye, and temple are from work."

"Here?"

"Yes, here this is my job. The lip and nose . . . well I am not quite the prince charming you feel I am I angered my girlfriend's brother."

"Hmm if Ana is still your Girlfriend I fear you will be angering him again."

"Yeah well it won't be at midnight this time so he won't hit me again."

"Or you could try hearing her out and saying sorry."

"Thanks" I rolled my eyes.

Genevieve jumped on my back "Dog Breath, I really get to go?"

I looked at Andy "It's up to your lady."

"Are you ready my Genie?" Andy smiled "And you never answered are you still my Genie in a bottle?"

Genevieve jumped down and into Andy's arms "DOG BREATH! Close your eyes!"

"Sorry" I laughed closing my eyes, so she could kiss her girlfriend.

"OK Dog Breath" She hugged me tight "See you Sunday."

"Best of luck, I am off to get lectured, enjoy your weekend."

"I am sitting I am too tired to do anything else" I rolled my eyes.

"Stop talking until you can be something more than rude, sarcastic and flippant!" Ana sighed, "I need to talk to you."

"That's . . ."

"I said shut up ALEX!"

I slammed my head harder on the back of my seat as I had been for the last half hour, this was not going well. "And as I said if you want out Paul, Anthony and I will be fine on our own."

She sighed again "Would you just shut up and listen, Al! I told you I am keeping you, you are mine, and I love you."

I slammed my head into the seat and fist into the dash board.

She sighed "Alex I want you tested both your mom and . . ."

"I do ok I do, I was diagnosed in high school I thought you knew that I had asthma."

"Not that, I knew that, I want your heart tested"

I slammed my head extra hard "Mom makes us have our hearts and lungs checked every three months."

"I don't believe you go, Alex; I know how you feel about doctors."

"You argue with my uncle Christian and then tell me I don't go. What has gotten into you? You pull away from me so I try and love you more and you sick David on me. I don't know what you want but I am just me and just me use to be good enough for you" I went to get out of the car.

"Ho detto siediti e stai zitto(I said sit down and shut up)! You know, Alexander, you listen like a brick!" She sighed "I am sorry if it felt like I was pulling away and yes I don't want you 'pawing' me but I didn't and never would 'sick' Davie on you. I assume that Davie is what happened to your face and yes just you is what I want, I don't want you to change other than this current mood you're in which I am sure your uncle or my brother is just waiting to fix when you get home. I am sorry it felt like I was pulling away I am not trying to there is something I should tell you."

"And cause you . . ."

"Shut up, Alex, your uncle thought so too, you are scaring people."

"Lack of sleep will . . ."

"HO DETTO ZITTO (I SAID SHUT UP)! I wonder if your mom had to shut your dad up like this, I have never seen her argue back like this."

"Geese thanks" I shook my head "I wouldn't know either I never met the man but yeah my mom and mama can argue just fine."

She flinched only slightly she wasn't that afraid of me it was more like what she had said caught up with her "Hush, you know I didn't mean it like that, it's just very frustrating when you keep interrupting with rude comments when I am trying to tell you . . . Are you sure your heart is good?"

"My hearts fine my heads spinning a bit but I am fine, spit it out."

"My last doctors . . ."

I wrapped my arms around her wiping the fresh set of tears "Shush" I rocked her "I am here talk to me, is it cancer?"

"They don't know" She sobbed so hard "They are pretty sure it is just cysts."

"Ok baby this is going to be ok, I am sure of it."

"I am sorry, Al."

"It's ok don't worry about it lets just get Paul and go home." My temper started to defuse something only Ana could make it do but I could feel the withdrawal at the back of my mind just waiting.

"LOOK, DADDY, LOOK!" Paul ran between a picture of Anthony and me.

"What is this little man?" I knelt down to him.

"Antony get better."

Dave laughed "I don't know if his English is getting worse or his Italian is getting better."

"Good question, neither do I" I laughed.

"This is a countdown for Paul and I, it will help him wait for Anthony to come home. I did it with your cousin, Tyler, when he was Paul's age."

"Ok" I nodded "Dave, you could be brain washing him and I wouldn't know it because if you tell me it's good for him I believe you."

Dave chuckled "Go put Paul in the car; I need to talk to Ana."

"Yes sir, see you Sunday."

"Not a minute before, Alexander."

"Yeah, yeah" I lifted Paul.

"Bye-bye E-hall see you iaday" Paul called over my shoulder as we left.

"If I didn't know him better I would say he is too trusting" Ana sighed.

Dave frowned at her for trying to avoid the subject; she knew what he wished to talk about. "How did he take it, Ana."

"Well . . ." She looked at her feet "He turned into my Alex when I told him, but something tells me no one will see him until tomorrow, except for Paul and that I might tell his Uncle to strip search him for cuts anyway something didn't feel right."

Dave nodded "Al's not cutting the kids would pick up on it and tell me, how are you?"

"Scared to death, I haven't even told Daddy or Davie yet."

"You will, when you are ready. Go home and enjoy your weekend; if by Monday Alex is still acting 'weird' tell his Uncle that we need to talk."

"Thanks Dave if Anthony . . ."

"Anthony is fine, now go before I give you a room."

Ana laughed "Not me Al" and with that she left.

The ride home was silent; dinner was steak I didn't speak to anyone. After dinner I went down stairs to the studio with Paul. Around seven

Ana came down, kissed the top of my head and took Paul for his bath and bed. I buried myself deeper in to my music so deep that all I could see were my drum sticks and all I could here was my drums. Time past and I became aware of another physical presence in the room with me. When I heard a guitar I Stopped and looked up.

"Why stop, it sounded good?" Uncle Chris asked, "Don't think I know that one? Of course I do its 'The I Had A Bad Day Blues'."

"How about the 'my girlfriend may have cancer and I was the south side of off a north bound mule to her all week blues'?"

"Yep that works too, same sheet music, your mama use to have a similar one just best friend instead of girlfriend. So have you said you're sorry yet?"

"No I couldn't say anything I was stunned stupid."

"I suppose half those bruises are from Davie and not work?"

"My nose and mouth, I got flippant with him."

"Get you anywhere?"

"No."

"Feel good?"

"No."

"Going to repeat that action?"

"Not if I can help it."

"Then I guess you learned your lesson."

"I suppose I have."

"Your mama use to be so flippant that Christian, Ken, and Marc all forbid her from talking for weeks on end."

"Really?"

"Yes, really, and your father would just laugh at her when she got like that, your mom too."

"Did my dad know how to say sorry?"

"Well if he didn't, J.J. and Tina made him know how and if not them, Nalanie sure did. Ana's mom was crazy as they come. I swore she was certifiable but only once to her face." The inflection in his words implied he had gotten beat for it. "She was mean and quiet like Davie; only person your mama would not pick a fight with."

"Did mama get in a lot of fights?"

"She fought with anything and everything."

"What did Nana say?"

"She didn't know we didn't live with her. We lived here with our older brothers and Ana's uncle Ken. Also several of our friends stayed on occasionally. Marc cursed the stars every time the school called and your mama spent ninety percent of high school grounded."

"Really?"

"Yes."

"You willing to tell me about Mama?"

"A bit, J.J. is too private for her own good sometimes."

"Did mom get in fights too?"

Uncle Chris laughed "Yes they both did but Jess more than Tina. Your uncle would yell at them 'It's unlady like to fist fight."

I laughed "These really Mama's drums?"

"Yep had them since she was thirteen, she took good care of anything she called hers your Mom included."

"They make it look so easy?"

"Who make what look easy?"

"Mom and Mama, they never fight like Ana and I do."

"Oh they use to fight awful, both of them too stubborn to say sorry. Marc would have to interfere."

"I bet the way they blast music."

"No that is the improved version. They would scream and yell and throw things up and down the stairs and around the house, mainly J.J."

"Why do you call her J.J.?"

"Nick names, they stick with you."

"What's the other 'J' for."

"Nothing you need to know, now before that old fart your avoiding finds me going against your mama's wishes go get some rest, you have a busy day tomorrow."

CHAPTER 19
MALLS ARE DEADLY

"Get up"

"Ahh" I jumped and a rough hand cover my mouth

"Hush" Uncle Christian Growled.

I rubbed my eyes "What's wrong?" I whispered shivering; I added more blankets to Ana.

"I said get up, are you that dumb to question me?" A flash light hit my eyes.

"No sir" I stumbled to my feet shivering.

"Go add a blanket to Kenny and get yourself down to the studio clear."

"Yes, sir."

"I also suggest you get more clothes on."

I looked down and covered myself "I am sorry sir I swear I went to bed with my . . ."

"Tis fine twas your brothers being spiteful your trousers are in the freezer."

"I'll just grab clean ones."

"I figured."

I covered Ken after I redressed; I hated when the fire in the wood stove went out. I went to the studio. I looked at the clock it read 2:30. Uncle Christian and I loaded the wood stove in silence. I knew that his waking me instead of Uncle Chris or Uncle Donavan or even who ever had forgotten their chore was my punishment for being rude to my girlfriend, my mother and my elders.

"Sit" He pointed at Mama's drums.

"I know I am an imbecile, trust me I am feeling it on my own."

"I just wish to make sure he didn't break your nose and I am glad David actually does have some of Henry in him, although I truly would prefer he not draw blood on my nephew." He dabbed my lip with witch hazel and poked at my nose "Not broken."

"Hurts like he broke it."

"I bet it does. Marc would upset Kate, when we were kids, and she would go home crying and Ken would beat Marc hard enough to knock him out. However ungraceful your words may have been they were not uncommon merely ill timed."

I nodded. My phone rang "May I . . ."

"You are dismissed."

"Thank you" I sighed knowing my phone saved me. "Williams" I answered.

"Alex, I am sorry for disturbing you at such an hour and I know it is most unflattering of me but can you come over at some point this morning."

"Um it's fine, I was awake any way, but I am sorry I have no clue who I am speaking with, old English does not compute at three am."

"Andy, you, s . . ."

"Ok I am on my way 10th and evergreen right?

"Yes, I'm so sorry, thank you so much."

"No problem, I'm on my way" I hung up.

"That was?" Uncle Christian looked at me.

"Can you drive me to 10th and Evergreen, its work related?"

"As you wish, notify your love as I will notify mine."

"Is that Mom or Mama?"

"Your mother, your mother has always and will always be my only love."

"Uh . . ."

"It wasn't supposed to help, now move."

"Oh thank-you so much for coming so soon" Andy answered the door. She was wearing a black velvet bath robe.

Ana had frowned at me for not going back to bed but had wished me a safe trip. "No problem, this is my uncle Christian."

"I have seen him before with your mothers" She smiled.

"Tis the only job I take pride in, Miss" My uncle gloated in reference to caring for my mothers.

Andy looked toward the back of her house "She woke up screaming and swinging. I had to leave the bed to avoid being hit. I triggered my alarm to wake her. She is in the living room on the couch."

"Did she request me?" I asked.

"I'd say so, I am afraid you are the only one she does call Dog Breath."

"No need to be sorry I know I am Dog Breath" I smiled.

"May I ask why she deemed you that?"

"You may, but only she can answer that" I laughed, Uncle Christian stifled a laugh.

Andy led us down a corridor, the walls were black marble, the floor was white tile and as she had said there were different types of swords hanging on the walls. The living room had white marble walls and plush black carpet with black leather furniture. A T.V. and computer were adjacent to one and other in one corner. The room was decorated with dragons, weaponry, fairies, pixies and tigers.

"Mio Piccolo would be very, very happy here" Uncle Christian remarked to himself.

Genevieve was curled into a ball on the couch; she was wearing black satin pajamas.

I smiled at her "Do I have to beg or are you going to cut me some slack to night?"

"Nightmare" She muttered. She lifted a long thick black object "Want to meet Jethro?"

My eyes went wide Genevieve was playing with a ten foot black boa constrictor. "I'll pass, why are you a wake it's three am?"

"I had a night mare, Why are you awake?"

"Why am I now or why was I when Andy called me?" I knew this game it was the best way to get Genevieve to talk to me; question for question and pure honesty.

"When Andy called you."

"My uncle and I were loading wood into the wood stove and resetting the breakers the storm knocked everything out. He was also talking to me about my uncle Marc being as foolish as I am. Why didn't you go back to sleep?"

"Jethro and I tried but we couldn't it was a bad dream."

Andy offered my uncle some coffee and the arm chair which he took both of and thanked her.

I knelt near the couch forcing Genevieve to look me straight in the eyes and tell the truth. She had, had three months with a sign saying that she had to tell the truth. I thanked Andy for my coffee and told her a caffeine drip would be more effective. She sat near Genevieve, cautiously, watching the large snake.

"Genie, you wouldn't tell me what you dreamed of" Andy sighed.

"You wouldn't answer what it mattered" Genevieve said defiantly.

"Hunny, I really wish you wouldn't do this."

Uncle Christian laughed "I really wish I could tell you she will grow out of that but Mio Piccolo has not."

Andy looked at me lost.

I laughed "He told you my mama does the same thing. Mio Piccolo is what he calls my mama it is my little one in Italian."

She nodded.

"Come on Genevieve I know you won't answer me unless I answer something."

"Does that spoiled brat I gave my room to really get to leave before me, weather she is clean or not?"

"Yes, but she is not going home she is being released to a doctor for more treatment. What were you dreaming of?"

"Witch dream?"

"If there is more than one obviously the one keeping you awake."

She looked at Andy, then at her feet. "Remember the first one I had in the center?"

"I remember it was my first and last attempt at over night." Genevieve had cried for hours I had to carry her with me everywhere trying to take care of the others and keep her from clawing her arms, consequently after that I told Dave he was never allowed to be sick again, I clipped her nails so short she couldn't scratch anything and added my name to the list of staff willing to adopt. "Was it that one?"

She nodded "Have you and Ana . . ."

"Just about, does Andy know how to get you to sleep?"

Andy shook her head she was always so active, so hyper she use to just pass right out if she had nightmares then I didn't know it."

"Her arms and thighs did" I sighed knowing I'd have one pain of a question for what I was telling Andy "Dreams don't just appear especially ones like hers, most addictions are a way to cope with painful or stressful things. Nightmares are our subconscious showing us our pain and stresses. That is why it is best to get our thoughts and feelings out in a productive way" I looked straight into Genevieve's eyes.

"Dog Breath you sound like a shrink" Genevieve groaned.

"Good he is actually learning something through that online course" Uncle Christian had made it very clear more than once that he would have preferred I attended regular classes at a university.

"Go ahead Genevieve I will answer any and all questions you ask me, if you tell her what you were dreaming of."

"I . . ." She set Jethro in a glass tank and crawled in to my arms.

"Ok you haven't done that in a long time."

"Andy doesn't like my parents" She whispered in my ear.

"With just cause, Genie" Andy said, Genevieve blushed.

"I . . . I dreamed of why I don't live with them." Genevieve choked.

"Oh Genie, come here I'll hold you" Andy reached for her.

"Dog Breath, hold me!" She clung to me.

"I um ok" I stammered, I felt tears landing on my shoulder and I started to rock her.

"Ok you can ask him now, I will tell you if he lies," My uncle said trying to help, it didn't.

She clung tighter to me, with her nails witch Dave no longer let me clip. He said she had to learn on her own; she had, she wasn't trying to claw herself. "Dog Breath do you have nightmares?" She asked my shoulder.

"All the time" I choked; I knew where this was headed and it wasn't boding well for me.

"What are they about?"

"I dream about Paul and Anthony's birth mother coming for them and or hurting them, I dream of work A LOT . . ."

"I have that problem too" Andy smiled.

"That is what you two get for working ten or more hours a day" Uncle Christian glared at me.

"Yeah, yeah you want to share about your dreams I recall just last week you woke every one in the ho . . ."

"Hush yourself and finish answering tuo piccolo(your little one)."

Genevieve giggled.

"Not funny you" I shook her a little still holding her tight. "I dream of Ana leaving me, I . . ." I took a deep breath, I was not raised to lie or omit or break promises "I dream of cutting and occasionally I dream I am with my father."

"But you have two moms."

"I know, my father's belongings and pictures of him still reside in my mothers' house he was one of their friends."

"His spirit is checking on you, Alex" Uncle Christian yawned "I as well dream of my brother those are welcome dreams. Ms. Genevieve nightmares are very common things I have yet to meet a single person in my entire life whom is exempt from their own subconscious."

"Dog Breath what are your triggers?" She had finally removed her claws from my shoulders.

"Crowds and panic attacks" I stopped.

"Ehm" Uncle Christian glared at me.

"I was getting there; people harassing me about my mothers."

"I remember that" Andy said "We were in the band room I was packing up my violin and this kid was bugging you . . ."

"I don't remember and I am willing to bet Genevieve doesn't remember a few things."

"I don't remember the trials . . . or my birthdays, or school. I mean I remember but it's really foggy" Genevieve gulped. "How old were you when you started cutting dog breath?"

"I was nine" I felt my uncle tense behind me.

"Tell me about it?" she yawned.

"You only want the world tonight, ok" I rocked her gently.

"Alex" Andy pointed to a rocking chair.

Graciously I sat and rocked her "We were at one of Mama's gay pride events by then there were five of us all dressed in our best summer suits. Nick was almost two, the beasts were five and Kenny was just about seven. Uncle Chris and Uncle Christian were up at the micro phones with Mom and Mama. I was listening to what they were saying. I was with my Uncle Marc and Aunt Kate and there children; Kim was ten, Adam was almost five, and Jr. was three. I was watching Ana and her brother play with Tonka trucks . . ."

"You liked Ana back then?" She yawned.

"She was and still is my best friend. All of a sudden I got separated from my uncle Marc and was highly aware of all the people surrounding me, pushing past me. I started to panic and scream for my uncle, but there was so much noise he didn't hear me. I broke out in hives and started to claw at the hives; eventually I broke the skin and realized it had caused me to stop panicking. Ana's dad found me and told me not to scratch my hives; it would only make them worse. Later we realized that those hives were an accident with the laundry, my clothes had hit the wrong hamper. You see all of Mom's boys are allergic to Tide and all of Mama's boys are allergic to everything but Tide, anyway as the addiction developed I discovered its power."

"Did you actually save Andy from some boy?" Her eyes were closed.

"I suppose I did, now weather that was my intent or I was picking a fight with someone I don't know I don't remember."

"What's the big scare fr . . . ." She was asleep before she could finish her thought. I laid her on the couch; Andy covered her and kissed her.

"Next time you will know what to do."

"She wouldn't let me near her, she screamed for you" Andy shook her head.

"That's the first time in a year I slightly expected it do to her reaction at the center, though."

"Maybe it was too soon" Andy frowned.

"No, that would have happened no matter what. Two years away from her, fear you'd tre . . ."

"I'd never do that I love her."

"It shows; if I didn't think she'd be ok I wouldn't have let you take her." I yawned "May I have a piece of paper and a pen? I still have one more question to answer."

"Sure" She smiled, handing me a note book.

"Did I save you or was I just picking a fight?"

"I believe you saved me, Alex" She sighed like she was trying to think back "You came around the corner and saw him or heard me, you pulled him off me, and started pounding him. When he called you a filthy comment and you said 'You got that! I am Alexander Joseph Williams first born to Jessica Marie and Christiana Marie Williams.' May I add you said it like it was the worst thing to be?"

"Being me back then was bad that me was not who I am."

I wrote the letter and reread it to myself. "The 'big' scar if from when I hit rock bottom. See you Sunday. If you need me I am a call away, be patient with Andy she can't help you if you don't help her." I handed the note to Andy and we said our good-byes. We got home around five thirty.

"Andare a letto (Go to bed). I will wake you when you are needed" Uncle Christian was still not happy with me but I could tell he was proud of me and mostly just tired.

"Yes, sir" I crawled to my room and into bed. Ana rolled over and watched me strip to my boxers "Your being awake is unnecessary, love, return to sleep."

"Unnecessary to whom I am enjoying the view and the show it is my favorite" She smiled.

I blushed.

"Oh, please" She rolled her eyes.

"May I hold you tonight, what's left of it anyway?"

"I like that idea very much" She laid her head on my chest. "Is Genevieve alright?"

"Yes she had a nightmare; sweet dreams love."

I woke up five hours later to someone pulling at my eyes. "Hi" I opened my eyes. Paul was sitting on my chest poking at my eyes "That's not always a good thing Sweetie, Daddy, has bad dreams a lot and sometimes wakes up rough."

"I sorry, Mommy say to get you up we go to . . . I in touble"

"Huh," I rubbed my eyes and lifted him and my clean clothes. "No you're not in trouble bud, let's go find Ana."

"Mommy in the kitchen."

"Cool, how was your morning?"

"Goood, laffles were bakefast. Me play with Uncle Colts and Nana. Then Mommy say go wake Daddy."

I sat him on the couch and took a shower. When I came out there were three notes for me on the table. One from my uncle saying he would like to speak to me and one from Ana saying she was outside talking to Auntie Kate. I sat Paul on the toilet lid and took a fast shower then cleaned the tooth paste mess he made. When we came out Ana was sitting at the table drinking a cup of coco she looked to be in deep thought.

"Penny for your thoughts beautiful?" I sat Paul down.

"Christmas list."

"What have you got so far?"

"I don't know what to get your parents or uncles; you or Nick and I drew Bonnie at work for secret Santa."

"Uh Mom likes white gold and dolphins, Mama likes tigers and markers, Uncle Chris needed a new ratchet set, but I'd check with Mama on that, and Uncle Christian Um . . . what did . . ."

"Gift card."

"Yeah that sounds good."

The mall was severely packed; Paul bounced up and down, in his mall stroller, excitedly. I was clutching the handle of the stroller so tight my knuckles were white and I couldn't feel my fingers.

"Relax Al," Ana wrapped an arm around me, "It's just a mall."

"It's normally why I pay Adam or JR. to shop for me."

"Oh hush you'll be fine, call Dave and see what Anthony wants."

I muttered and pulled out my cell phone, I knew what he wanted without asking, he wanted to be out of the center.

"Alex why are you calling?" Dave growled.

"Were Christmas shopping Ana wants to . . ."

"I'll call you back in ten with it" He cut me off and hung up.

"And . . ." Ana stared at me.

"He'll call back in ten."

"Relax, Alex, Sears is right here."

I looked down at the other shopping bags; the ratchet set was the last thing we needed from the mall.

Three hours later all the Christmas shopping was done, I was exhausted and never wanted to see a store again in my life. There had been people everywhere. The stores were too packed to breathe or move in, I helped Ana wrap and hide all the presents while Paul played with his art easel. After dinner I went straight to bed by order of my parents and girlfriend. I woke five hours later to find Paul sound asleep next to me and Ana rubbing my back.

"Mmm hi" I smiled.

"Just watching you sleep" She smiled back.

"How about we cuddle instead, my arms feel empty?"

She smiled and crawled into my arms, both of us wrapping an arm around Paul and falling sound asleep.

CHAPTER 20

INSERT TITLE HERE

SOME WHERE BETWEEN FALLING ASLEEP and my alarm going off Paul woke up and found my old box of crayons and left a decorative trail all the way down to Mom's room. Mama just laughed and told me I had done worse with ink. I corrected Paul, soaped up a sponge and made him clean his mess; while I got ready for work.

"You look like a steam roller hit you" Dave greeted me.

"I feel like it Paul kicks in his sleep."

"He loves you."

"Yeah, yeah . . . you wanted . . ."

"Don't get smart with me you're with Buddy and Curtis all day they are both at breakfast"

"I hate you too."

"This has nothing to do with hate and everything to do with the state inspectors."

"Like I said I hate you too."

Curtis and Buddy were in breakfast alright but not eating they were already fighting thankfully not with each other. Buddy was fighting with his clothes so I took him straight to the time out room and told a medic to get him his meds; I felt bad for him when that happened. Curtis on the other hand was terrorizing the cafeteria workers. I moved Buddy to his room and put Curtis in the time out room. I filled out both sets of paper work and waited for Buddy to feel better."

Around lunch, Buddy was feeling better and Curtis had calmed down.

"If it makes you feel better, I caught you before you took your shirt off" I smiled at buddy.

Buddy looked like he'd been dragged through a tornado "Great" He slammed down his lunch tray next to Kevin's "Hey little brother."

I didn't stop him. He didn't look like he was out to cause trouble; but the action startled Kevin and Kyle causing chocolate milk to spill. Witch all three boys scrambled to clean up laughing. Curtis on the other hand sat with some of the other boys from the c-hall; thankfully despite the look in his eyes he did not start another fight.

On Monday I was out at three, so I told Ana I would be back at seven to pick her up, as it was my short day. I swung by home and picked Paul up and went to the Jewelers to get Ana's ring.

"Morning, Sir."

"Morning, Alex it's afternoon" He laughed "You here to pick up the ring?"

"Yes sir how much is it?"

"Your left over total is two hundred and fifty seven dollars and fifty three cents."

I swallowed hard and hand over the money reminding myself Ana was worth every penny and then some. The ring was not a diamond Ana did not like diamonds. The ring was white gold and the stone was onyx shaped like a heart. It was also engraved with "I will forever love you, Ana—Alex". I went home changed in to jeans and a t-shirt and took Paul sledding.

Seven thirty found me sitting in bumper to bumper traffic; in a cell phone dead zone. Paul asleep in his car seat, me slamming my head into the top of the steering wheel. We had been stuck here for an hour an oil tanker flipped causing a huge mess. I was worried about Ana. Around nine we started to roll slowly, I didn't complain I was too happy to be moving to care about speed.

CHAPTER 21

TUESDAY

TUESDAY I SPENT WITH PAUL having pre Saturday panic attacks. Saturday was the big family dinner and that's when I was going to purpose to Ana in front of everyone, her family and mine. I was nervous and it made Paul giggle to see me pacing and talking to myself. By noon I was a complete nervous wreck and Uncle Christian and Kenny were laughing at me.

"Calm down Alex, it's not like she is going to say no" Kenny laughed at me.

"She could, you never know" I shoved my inhaler in my mouth.

Paul was at my feet playing with his fire trucks and watching cartoons. His chart said lunch and free play was right now and in a half hour was quiet/slash nap time for two hours.

Uncle Donavan sat down next to me "What is worrying you? That she may say no? Or that you have chosen to ask her in front of everyone."

"Both I guess I mean everyone will be there what if she says no?"

Kenny went into another laughing fit "Dude she isn't going to say no."

I sighed and scooped Paul up.

"uup"

I laughed I supposed that was what it felt like when I pick him up. I sat him down at the table.

"Put a bib on him" Uncle Christian scowled at me.

I rolled my eyes and tied a bib on Paul "Lunch time handsome" I smiled at him.

"What for lunch oggi (today)?"

"Soup and grill cheese and apple sauce" Uncle Christian Answered Paul as he set his plate and bowl down in front of him. "You too?" He offered me.

"Yes please, Sir" I nodded.

I sat and ate with Paul. After lunch Paul went down for a nap and I helped Uncle Christian wrap presents for my brothers and other family members. I called Ana's Grandmother to if she was flying in for Christmas dinner, she said yes she was and so was Kyle. That was fine. Ana's Uncle Kyle didn't scare me as much as her father or her Uncle Ken.

Paul woke around three as Ana came in. "Mommy, Mommy; Daddy make Zio (uncle) Kenny laugh."

I laughed; I wondered if I spoke like that when I was little half English half Italian in the same sentence, I defiantly did now.

"He did?" She laughed hugging Paul tight.

That night I went to talk to Ana's dad to ask permission to marry his daughter.

"Of course Alex; so when are you asking her?"

I gulped "Saturday at the holiday dinner."

"You ok?"

"No"

"Want to talk?"

Mr. Wittson was a good man but I was too scared to think straight or make coherent conversation. "No thank you."

"Ok tell your Mama to come see me, I drew the short straw."

"Yes, Sir."

I left it was only nine I had an hour and a half till I had to be at the pool hall. I walked home and crawled the back porch to the roof to stare at the stars. The snow was cold on my back and legs. I laid there watching the sky for an hour then went inside to tell Mom I was leaving and that Ana's dad wished to speak to Mama.

I sat at the bar with my ears covered, Kenneth sat watching me like any second I would self combust.

"K4 must you stare?"

"Sorry, dad said to watch you; you looked like you're going to explode."

"Might."

"Where is Ana?"

"Home with Paul probably getting ready for bed."

"So why are you here?"

"Business meeting."

"Oh so you came here?"

"Not my choice K4, please just stop and go look for Mr. Travis and Mr. Kevin they are my ride to the business meeting." I had arranged to visit with my Uncle Troy per Uncle Chris' suggestion.

"Ok."

I focused on my inhaler. Kenneth returned about fifteen minutes later with Mr. Travis and Mr. Kevin.

"Let's get you out of here," Mr. Travis said, "I meant for you to meet us out front."

I followed Mr. Travis out to their car and climbed into the back seat we drove for about two hours.

Uncle Troy was sitting at their kitchen table smoking, when we got there and his husband was watching TV. He looked up at me "Your mama know you're here?"

"N-no sir" I gulped.

"That won't be good she finds out."

"I-I don't know, Sir."

"I do sit down I don't bite."

I sat down the last time I had seen my uncle I was three months he sent cards on holidays and birthdays and occasionally called my mama to 'check' on her. "H-How are you?"

"I'm fine, how are you? You look like Travis chewed you up and spit you out."

"G-Good, Sir, he didn't."

"I no he didn't he doesn't even swat mosquitoes."

I raised and eye brow "Why does . . ."

"Differing opinions" My uncle was tall and thin. He looked and acted nothing like Uncle Mike. "I hear I have a great nephew?"

"Yes two, Paul and Anthony."

"Christopher James said you had questions?"

"Yes, Sir . . . Why did you call Uncle Chris his full name?"

"No his given name and because it is his name, most of us have either two middle or two first names."

"Oh what about Mama?"

"I won't go against Marc, Alexander even here he would hunt me down and beat me. I will tell you she has four names but I will not call her, her given name."

"Who else has four names?"

"Joseph and Danny."

"Oh"

"There are nine of us Tim was a wow didn't know he was coming, cool."

I nodded "What was Mama like?"

"I don't know on a daily bases but mean as a rattler on a good day and more like a pit viper on a bad one, when I got to see her."

"Mmm" Mr. Kevin said "Mean fits, mean miserable, and not friendly."

"My mama?"

"Yes" Uncle troy said "She has mellowed since, and she no longer cuts so I bet that improved her mood too."

"I looked at my arm."

"I know about those too; I call her we just don't spend a lot of in person time Alex, better for us. We are siblings, you and Kenny fight."

I nodded

"It is late you need to go home and rest next time be honest with your mother and come earlier in the day so we can have more than a few minutes."

"Yes sir."

Wednesday came fast and snowy, I drove slowly over the slushy roads. Ana was sitting next to me riffling through her purse and wallet. "Are you ok?" I glanced over at her.

"What time did you come in?"

"Um somewhere near three" I yawned.

"Did you get anything you wanted from it?"

"Kind of, he says hi."

"I figured he would. Has Dave found out anything about the boys dad yet?"

"Yes actually, he found out, that their father died of A.I.D.S., he was born with it; he gave me a picture." I riffled through junk in the glove box at the red light, and then showed it to Ana. "Dave says he never knew about them or if he did he never told his family."

"He looks like Paul," Ana smiled, "You going to show the boys?"

"Yes, Anthony asked I will answer."

CHAPTER 22

WEDNESDAY

"Tiffany life does not end just because your girlfriend is mad at you" I sighed, we were sitting at her desk waiting for class to start.

"It hurts" She whined.

"Yep fights hurt, but life goes on, talk to her she will cool off."

"But . . ."

"But nothing, you are making this harder on yourself. Refusing to cooperate, eat, and or do homework will only hurt you. It will not make Sadie love or not love you any more or less. Enjoy your time with her now, by the New Year her doctor will be back and she will be removed from here for the treatment he feels is adequate. This is not the way to show her you love her, want her and or forgive her."

After a morning with Tiffany refusing to do anything but cry over Sadie in a protest of love, I welcomed the afternoon with Buddy.

"Are you sure she only likes girls?"

"I am sure, Buddy, she only likes girls."

"Man, she is so hot her girlfriend is so lucky."

I chuckled "I am sure she would *love* to know that."

"No, I told her last Saturday and she told me if I ever came near her again she would kill me." Sarcasm was lost on Buddy, unless he was the one using it.

I laughed "Yeah she is a bit of a 'treat'; what are you reading?"

"Beowulf, it's taking me forever."

"Homework?"

"No, Dave brought me a stack to read in my spare time but only when I am with you or him."

"Is it any good?" I had never read Beowulf; my class had voted on some other book, which was old enough to cough dust.

"Eh, I prefer mysteries. I hear Kevin gets to go home on weekends?"

"Yes, he is doing very well."

He smiled slightly "I do love him."

"I know you do, Buddy. Enjoy your book; I have to go check on Tiny."

"Night Alex, hey Alex?"

"Yeah?"

"I . . . never mind tell her hi for me."

"I will you know where I am if you need me."

"I hate you!" Amelia yelled at me.

"I like you too, darling, how are you feeling?"

"How do you think I am feeling?" She balled up holding her knees.

"Wish to talk to me? Dave says you won't go to group or sessions?"

"So?"

"So, your parents and your Boyfriend's parents agreed that if you wish to live with Will you need to complete the program here."

"Do you have any candy?"

"No, but I can talk to Greg to see what I can do about getting you candy."

"Can you get a message to Will for me?"

"Yep, hold on" I went in the hall and flagged down a nurse for a pen and piece of paper.

"You can read if you want" She said handing the paper and pen back to me.

"Not mine to read, Amelia."

"Alex?"

"Yes?" I sighed, Amelia on a good day was exhausting, and on a long day I prayed for it to be the end of my day.

"Does Ana really love you?"

"Yes. I like to believe she does."

"Even though you use to . . ." She trailed off.

"Yes, even thought I use to cut. You don't have to be afraid to say it or to ask me anything ever."

"Do you ever still want to some times?"

"Yes but I sit and I mediate, I remind myself that I do not want to or need to and it is not the life style for me. Although lately for some reason I am having a tough fight with it."

"But what if someone is bugging you?"

"It is still ultimately up to me, I am solely responsible for my own actions, reactions, behaviors, and decisions. Short of taking my hand and holding it to a blade and physically making me cut it is no one's fault but my own. Clean and sober is a choice and action only you can make for yourself and something only you can do for yourself."

She balled up tighter "Oh, yeah" It was not the first time her and I had this talk we had it about four times a week. "Can you give this to Dave?"

"Sure" I took the form.

"It's my Christmas wish list."

"If you asked for congical visits Tiffany already tried and got told no."

"Uh no I didn't" She laughed.

"Ok then I will pass this to Santa."

She rolled her eyes at me.

I gave her wish list to Dave and went to talk to Anthony.

"He never knew about us?" He asked as if I had eight heads.

"No he didn't; but he has passed away, he was very sick."

"Oh."

I gave him the picture of his father.

"He looks like Paul."

"Is that bad?"

"No, I know I look like my old Mom. I saw him once, He took my old mom to the movies and I stayed with the neighbors. How come she didn't tell him?"

"I don't know that is something I can't answer."

He nodded studying the picture and then gave it back. "Is your Uncle Chris coming this week?"

"I don't think so, he works on Fridays, but Paul, Ana and I will."

"Grandma?"

"Probably."

"Has Dave given Santa my letter yet?"

"I am sure he will but I think he is waiting for every ones so the post man has to make only one trip up to the North Pole."

"Daaaad the post man doesn't do it alone they take it to the post office and then the post office ships it by plane to a post office up there."

I laughed "Ok smarty pants but I am sure Dave is still waiting for every ones so that our post man has to make only one trip with the extra mail here, I think Curtis scared him yesterday when he barked at him."

He just looked at me like I was nuts again "Last year Paul and I asked Santa for a new mommy and daddy and he gave us you and Ana."

"I heard, Paul told me" I blushed slightly remembering breakfast with Santa, Paul had told almost every one.

"Do you still get to be my daddy even though you found my real daddy?"

"Yes, unless you would like to go back to state custody until someone else adopts you."

"No thank-you, I love you Daddy" He wrapped his arms tight around me; it was the best feeling in the world.

"I love you too."

"What did Paul ask Santa for?"

"You and toys for you and um . . . more tracks for his cars or something like that, he said it in split languages again and I was sick when he went to see Santa."

"I can have toys?"

"Well of course, I just haven't gotten anything for your side of the room yet when you come home we will go together and get your clothes, school things, toys and everything else you need."

"Coooool" His eyes lit up.

"Dave can I see Anthony's Santa list now?"

"Of course, Santa can't fix his but you might be able to."

I raised my eye brows, "Do I even . . ."

"You might want to sit."

I sat on the edge of Dave's bed and read it aloud "'Dear Santa, I have tried very hard to be a good boy this year. Thank-you for giving me and Paul new parents'," I shook my head, "Paul and I, Ana is forever on him about that"

Dave laughed.

"'Dave says I am to ask you for the top ten things I want, He says it is not greedy, it is so you have a decent idea of what I want, in case your elves are out of stock on something.' Nice Dave," I shook my head, "That is greedy and you know I . . ."

"Hush I tell all my kids top ten it's not greedy I am just not a mind reader, but I had to tell him something he nearly refused to fill it out because he didn't want to be greedy."

"Good he does listen occasionally" I continued reading "'So most of all I want to be home with my new daddy and Paul. I also would like a game system, please, Kevin has a game boy and Kyle has a PSP.

I like Kevin's game boy sometimes he lets me play, and I don't know what it's called but the big boys in the B-hall kick it at each other when they are allowed outside. I like comic books, and I like action figures but not girl action figures boy action figures. I want daddy to marry Ana and I like to read a lot and I want daddy to teach me sports and a swing set please. Also I want more brothers and sisters I like being a big brother. Please remember Paul and me again this year. Love Anthony ~~Kineston~~ Williams. P.S. I think Kevin deserves his books and national geographic.'" I looked up at Dave "Ok what are they . . ."

"Just a hacky sack, Al, the boy isn't an axe murder, he's too sweet, besides axe murderers aren't afraid of being greedy."

"I thought so" I ignored the jab at my worry over what the teenagers were doing that he wanted.

He tossed me the keys "I need to go talk to Buddy, go get the tree, leave the tree in the truck and the keys on the desk see you tomorrow."

"Ok," I held the door for him "I know big and full like last year."

"Hunny you ready, it's three?" Ana caught us in the hall.

"Not quite got to go pick up the tree" I kissed her and jogged to the door.

"He hates Christmas" She laughed "Well, I'm going back to the family room to play checkers with my son."

"You do that" Dave laughed.

"Mmm" Ana nuzzled me in the car "You smell good like pine."

"Ha—Ha—Ha thanks" I rolled my eyes, stopping for the train. "Here read Anthony's Christmas wish list."

She read it to herself and then started laughing hysterically "Well isn't he sweet maybe we should practice getting him that sibling tonight."

I choked nearly backing in to my uncle's truck "Paul needs a bath and I um Kenny um . . ."

"Alex, why are you blushing" She laughed and kissed me. "You know I was joking right?"

"I . . . um . . ." I was blushing so hard I could feel the heat in my face.

I spent the afternoon playing with Paul, he liked his board games. He showed me his flash card sets; he had numbers, letters, shapes, colors, and Italian words. He showed me his schedule and his sled. We ate dinner; I gave him a bath and put him to bed. Earlier I had left a message for Uncle Christian asking if we could talk; so I went down to my drums to practice. I lost my self in my music and soon I heard him playing with me. I could always tell Uncle Chris from Uncle Christian. Uncle Chris' notes were sharp, harsh and had a creepy edge to them where Uncle Christian's were Soft, mellow, and calming. I stopped and allowed him to place a song tab in front of me, I didn't recognize it.

"Just play and listen."

I obeyed and counted off, he played with me; he didn't need the paper he played as if he had known the song for a long time. It was soft music and he started to sing the song was slow and soft and defiantly intimate. It seemed as if the song switched from one point of view to the other, back and forth. When the song had finished he laid his guitar back on it's stand.

"It's pretty is it new?"

"It was a duet but not meant for any radio, CD, or performance."

I nodded "Mama's work?"

"Not quite, it was actually a letter between your mothers."

"But . . ."

"Sometimes poetry sounds good to music, and makes it easier to communicate."

I nodded this was a gentle reminder to me make sure I let Ana hear my feelings and thoughts too. "I got Anthony's Christmas list."

"He wishes more than to come home?"

"Yeah, more siblings."

He laughed "What did Ana say?"

I blushed hard "She said we should practice getting him that tonight."

"I presume that is why you left me the message."

"Er kinda"

"Ok I am listening."

"Tell me about my mother? Er me?"

"You mean when they decided to have you?"

I nodded.

"Hmm well let's see your were defiantly planed for" He chuckled. "Your mama said me and I said no."

"Why not?"

"I wouldn't, couldn't, I was very jealous and stubborn. I said not unless my love and I were together and raised it together. Looking back it was foolish and immature. Your father willingly agreed they both said they wanted the donor to be someone they knew, so that they didn't have too much trouble with the history of health issues."

"Did they always want six of us?"

"Mio Piccolo wanted seven."

"Another one!"

He laughed hard "Yes a girl, but your mom has that thing about even numbers and your mama has a thing about your mom."

I laughed "Trust me I noticed, they make it look so easy."

"Twenty-six years they have had to perfect its look, but it is not easy, and it is not always fun or stress free. Love is not a secondary emotion that will fade in a day or so. The stubborn jealous anger that causes you to be Colt's son and not mine is a secondary emotion, but it was for the better and both my love and I are very happy."

"But who is . . ."

"Your mother."

"I have two mothers."

"That is the point my love knows whom she is and it is unnecessary for you or your brothers to know.

"Why do Colt and I have the same father and not Kenny and I?"

"Pain, your mothers missed Colt so badly that they didn't care what he had left them. You could have all been Colts son's but they wouldn't talk or think about anything having to do with him so they found other donors until they couldn't find one they liked and were forced to think about it."

I nodded

"Anything else?"

"Why do they call Mama J.J.?"

"It's a nick name."

"I know but what's the . . ."

"When Mio Piccolo is ready she will tell you."

I gulped at the sharpness

"Letto (bed) Alexander you have work in the morning and it is now late."

"I know, night, thank you Uncle Christian" I took the steps two at a time leaving him to his music and memories.

"You ok sweetie?" Ana asked me.

"Thinking."

"About?" She rubbed my back and shoulders laying her head on my chest over my heart.

"A lot of things, such as why you doing that takes my breath away and stops my train of thought."

She giggled kissing and nuzzling my neck.

I caved and held her tighter "Friday, if Paul is not in here." I felt her grip tighten and her breath become slower and even; she was tired and falling asleep.

"I love you" She breathed.

"I love you too" I gently rubbed her back watching her drift off to sleep. She was drop dead gorgeous. She was smart, funny and could have any guy she wanted, but for some crazy reason she only wanted me.

CHAPTER 23
WINTER

THE FIRST DAY OF WINTER brought enough snow that Ana and I had to take one of the snow mobiles to work. I should have listened to Uncle Chris when he told me to park near his truck at the bottom of the hill. I knew this would happen it always did too much snow to drive down the drive way.

I shook the rest of the snow off me slamming "the see me" note on to Dave's desk.

"Didn't listen to your Uncle again?" He looked at me.

"Yep" I sighed.

"Here take my truck and the lists plus whatever else you feel you need, and keep it under five thousand this year will you."

I laughed last year I had spent one penny over five thousand. We only bought for our hall and anyone else Dave was in charge of, like Tiny. "Please tell me none of this is at the mall" I grimaced.

"I can't I didn't read them all just glanced, that's what I have you for, now scoot I have to call and make sure Santa is still coming tomorrow it is suppose to snow again tonight."

I groaned my car would be stuck till spring at this rate. "I hate you too, don't say that, I need my car. Can I at least take someone with me?"

"Level three and up only" He gave me that look.

I laughed "I wanted to take Genevieve, Serena wants hair things and yeah I am a guy."

Dave laughed "Yeah that's fine she will like that and it will make Jarrod's day easier."

"The store dressed like this!"

"So?"

"No! No, real clothes or I am not going!"

"I don't have your clothes, Genevieve" I sighed.

"I do, I have my clothes."

"Ok, then Dress and meet me in Dave's office."

She slammed the door and I walked down to Dave's to be lazy and use the calculator. There were fourteen children and five thousand dollars which came out to $357 and change for each child. I shook my head and just did the math out by hand and got the same answer so I guessed it was right.

"Ana said I could barrow her coat" Genevieve was wearing tight black jeans and a tight black top with a dragon on the back of it.

"Yeah, it's snowing" I gave up on the math.

"Can I where make up?"

"No sorry I can't help you there I would let you barrow my blush but . . ."

"Dog Breath!" She giggled.

She followed me to the staff locker room and then stopped "What?"

"It says . . ."

"Oh yeah, that's fine ignore it your with me."

I handed her Ana's coat and shrugged back in to mine. We stopped in the office; I kissed Ana and signed Genevieve out. She stood spinning in circle catching snowflakes on her tongue while I opened the truck doors.

"Is this your truck?" She asked.

"It's Dave's" I frowned "The snowmobile is mine."

She looked at my snowmobile and laughed.

"Hush, my car is snowed in, and if you must know it's a 1998 Buick and I am just happy it runs."

She giggled "Can we stop and see Andy."

"Your spoiled you, know that."

"Oh well."

"Where does she work?"

"She's a journalist for the news paper."

"Genevieve . . ." I frowned.

"It's the building on Callaway and 4th."

"Ok if there is time, you are spoiled."

She smiled triumphantly, "Have you read them?" She pointed at the lists.

"Only Anthony's, can you do me a favor?"

"Yes?"

"Read them and separate them in to three piles: Store, mall and neither."

"Ok" She took them "You don't looks so well?"

"Ana has a lead foot and *loves* the snowmobile; also I am still terrified of malls.

"Ooo Corey wants a tool set."

"Wal-mart . . ."

"I know, did I tell you I get to go home for Christmas, Andy said so in her last letter."

"Cool!" I was focused on the car riding on my tail, "Hit play on the mp3 drive please?"

"Sure, why did you take me, because I am almost level four."

"No, that's why no one objected to me taking you. I took you because I needed help and you won't fight me."

"Ooo that might be hard."

"What?"

"Sorry, I was listening; Kevin wants a subscription to National geographic."

I looked at the paper at a red light "See the check mark, it means Dave has already taken care of it."

"Cool, where's mine?"

"Nice try, I still have yours."

"Did you read it?" She blushed.

"Not yet" I pulled in to the parking lot and read the new list for Wal-mart and Genevieve's list "Play boy?"

"No!" She smacked me, "Your cruel dog breath."

"I am honest," I laughed, "You asked for Andy naked several sex toys by name, a whip, dragon statues and three new bra's. I can't get you Andy so how about a play boy?"

She swatted me and blushed harder "I um . . ."

"It's fine, breathe, other than making me go to the mall . . . good thing I did take you I don't know your size, nor do I wish to."

"They sell bras here" She blushed.

"I have two mothers, eight aunts, a girlfriend, cousins, grandparents and friends I have been trained that a good bra is important."

"Can I pick them?"

"Yep just act surprised and you can pick everything that's yours."

"Ok there's no . . ."

"Dave does stockings, he shops off line."

"So," She grabbed a cart, "Where do we start?"

"One name at time and you are in charge of writing down all the prices so I stay on budget this year."

"Ok, who's first?"

"Serena: Hair ties, lip gloss, brats dolls, nail polish, a purse, a new dress and matching shoes." I dialed Dave "Dimensioni sarebbe bello (Sizes would be nice)!"

"Alex, English! Serena is a junior miss' ten in clothing and five in shoes. You have Genevieve with you, relax."

Genevieve laughed "This way, Dog Breath" She pushed me in to the junior miss department and picked up a red and black spaghetti strap dress. Then dragged me to shoes and picked out a pair of black strappy things.

"Um ok"

"$15.99 and $24.95"

"Er ok" I wrote it down.

She laughed, "$3.99, $4.99, $7.95" She read the prices as she tossed earring packages.

"Having fun?" I asked writing down the prices.

"$9.99, $13.99, $3.49" She added a hair bush hair ties and some girly make-up kit thing. "Yes I am what next?"

"Nail polish, purse and Brats doll."

"Ooo" She dragged the cart hard and fast I almost had to run. She threw in a purse it was a tiny girly thing, then she threw in four nail polishes "Ten, Six, sixty-two, fifteen, forty"

"Er . . ."

"Gosh, Dog Breath, you're clueless! I hope you never have a daughter."

"Soorry," I rolled my eyes, "What do you expect I have five little brothers." I shook my head and gripped the carriage tighter trying not to notice all the people around "Kevin?"

"Nope he is all mall."

"K-Kyle?" I stuttered.

"Maybe check."

"Yeah mp3 and 'good' head phones."

"Can you or are you going to look at me lost?" She smirked at me.

"Oh you little . . . . Here these are the rest of the girls remember no more than two hundred and twenty each person."

"Really! All by myself?"

"Yep."

"You going to be ok?"

"Sure."

I grabbed Kyle's head phones and mp3, Buddy's snow board and everything on Corey's list. I met Genevieve back in toys she put an arm full plus in to the cart.

"What's left?"

"Anthony."

"Well, Ana is back at the center . . ."

"Oh hush you! Action figures, a bike; I got a letter they're talking about making him a level two. Helmet, roller blades, foot ball, base ball, glove, bat, and fishing rod. Um . . . hacky sack?"

"Mall"

"Comics"

"Mall."

"Hush I am thinking . . ."

"You think I will shop, I bet Ana hates taking you shopping." She left me debating over bikes; I was stuck between a blue one with nice strong, sturdy mountain bike tires and a red one with a horn. Fifteen minutes later I was still staring at the bikes, gripping the cart and shaking. Genevieve put an arm load of things into the nearly over flowing cart. She looked at me and shook her head "Witch bike?"

"The blue one with the good tires there, the sixteen inch."

"I thought so; did I get a good fishing kit."

I looked at it "Yeah, it's perfect, let's check out I am hungry and we have more sh-shopping to do."

"Yeah lunch sounds good."

We checked out and I called Dave "Ch-Checks still mean . . ."

"Yes are you ok?"

"Grande, io sono appena Grande(Great, I am just great), I just got insulted by a shopaholic. I hope her girlfriend has a lot of money, this kid can shop" I was speaking at the speed of light again and not completely in English.

He laughed "Glad it's going well."

"Not funny!"

"Breathe, Alex."

"Can I actually get Genevieve her list?"

"Yeah I don't see why not as long as she doesn't have half of it here or see it till Christmas unless you wish to teach your son . . ."

"Oh no, no thank you try again in twenty years."

He laughed "Have fun, I have to water the tree."

We had McDonald's for lunch she got excited over the idea of French fries and I had my normal fight with the speaker system. I blessed out the manager again; it didn't fix the speaker but our food was free. She had Salad and French fries I had my normal meal.

"I let you have junk food and this is what you eat?"

"I am a vegetarian, Dog Breath, meat and I don't agree."

"You didn't even order a chocolate shake."

"I was being kind, Chocolate makes me hyper."

"I think I could have handled it." I pulled into the mall parking lot and we got out. I gulped "Let's get this over with."

"I take it this isn't divide and conquer?"

"No and if I were off work it would be hell no, I take it large crowds aren't one of your triggers?"

"I am a teenage girl, Dog Breath; the mall is my mother ship."

"Being tough?"

"Yep."

"Try not shaking first."

She swatted me "You could cause earth quake tremors with the way you shake."

"Not funny, let's start with the store wear Ana got Paul's riding gear and end with your bras."

"Dog Breath, your red" She laughed.

"What, I am not use to bra shopping, ok."

"Whatever."

We started with Anthony, because most of it for him was now my money not Dave's. When we were finish and about to move on to the next person, I had to stop in an empty corner of the mall and panic for a few minutes.

"Do you get to bring him home?" Genevieve was trying to distract me.

"I hope so, I don't think so, but if my mama has her say . . ."

"I met your mama once; I wouldn't mess with her or her family."

"Dave just laughs at her."

"He laughs at me too."

"So do I" I laughed.

"Hey!" She swatted me until we were shopping again.

I didn't stop again until the only thing left were her bras. Both of us were shaking enough to cause earth quake tremors, I was trying to find a sales representative in the bra department of Victoria secrets. I thought bras were all Victoria secrets sold I was wrong. After fifteen minutes an encounter with something that set my asthma off, something that so rarely happened it caused panic attacks. I finally found the sales rep and Genevieve described to the lady what she was looking for. After being properly fitted she picked out the three she liked I stood staring at the ceiling.

"Done" Her voice trembled.

"You sure that's all you . . ."

"Yep I got myself some books in borders and some quills in the art store."

I nodded "H-How do I get you in to V.I.P.?"

"You were serious!" She blushed.

I nodded "Dave just said you can't have it at the center and I don't want to see or know, other than the whip."

"Ooo kinky."

"Hush like I told Sadie you can ask me all you want but my sex life or lack thereof is never for discussion, but I feel the need to clarify that one I like you like whips, knifes, swords, and crossbows."

She laughed "Are you Goth?"

"Er I wouldn't call it that, but I do enjoy dragons . . ."

"Are you vampire?"

"Could you not laugh like that my parents are vampire Goths as disturbing as that sounds, but I am . . . I am Alex."

"What's your animal sprit I can't see the pendent clearly."

"I don't know this is a wolf it was my father's necklace."

"You where a pentagram."

"It was a gift from my mother; she is Wiccan we all get one on our sixteenth birthday." I blushed "I don't know what I am other than I am

Alex. So how do I get you into V.I.P.? You are not 18 yet?" I changed the subject.

"Andy can help. Is your mama Wiccan?"

"I don't know I never asked, I know she was raised some form of Christian."

She started to laugh.

"Hush or no Andy It is not funny."

"Yes it is you look so confused."

"Please Genevieve, let's just get out of the mall."

"Ok sorry, but it is funny to see you make that face."

Genevieve and I tucked the bags tighter into the truck bed and went to the news paper office on Callaway and 4th. Andy was on the tenth floor. Genevieve curled up in the crowded elevator and started to rock. If I weren't working I might have joined her. Instead I picked her up.

"What's wrong? Is she ok? Andy panicked at the sight of us.

"She is fine, Ms. Andy; just way too many people in Wal-mart, the mall and the elevator" I answered.

"Oh look at you, you're both shaking" She fussed "Here let's go in my office it is quite in there."

Her office was stark compared to her house; on her desk sat a picture of her and Genevieve, as well as one of just Genevieve. I set Genevieve down she handed Andy the rose I let her get when I picked up Ana one for my bad judgment of the snowstorm.

"Thank-you Baby Doll, it is beautiful" Andy hugged her tight "Oh look you're in civilian clothes, look at you, you are so gorgeous." Andy fussed over her and held her close, I saw Genevieve start to relax.

"Can you get a way form work for a moment?" I asked her.

"Yes if she needs me."

"We have been Christmas shopping all day and her last few gifts are at an 18 and older store."

"Need to get her in to V.I.P.?"

I nodded, blushing.

She laughed "Sword or whip?"

Genevieve whispered in her ear.

"Genie, you're going to hurt Alex."

"I am fine, I think Ana took care of that for her last night" I blushed harder.

"Dog Breath already knows and Andy do you have make-up on you? Dog Breath doesn't have any."

I blushed more.

Andy laughed "You know I do but I have no mirror sweetie."

"Bathroom?"

"Um yeah . . . This way I think, this place is too big."

We followed Andy to the ladies room, Andy handed Genevieve the make-up and looked at me nervously as Genevieve headed into the bathroom. I smiled and looked at my watch.

"Should I . . ."

"Nope" I cut Andy off "Just trust her" I smiled "Fussing over it makes it worse."

Genevieve came back out "Andy can you help me with my mascara please?"

Andy helped her completing her makeup and we went to V.I.P. Genevieve picked a cat of nine tails that made my knees weak and several other things. I grabbed things in case Ana actually heard me last night promise we could do things Friday night.

We carried everything down to Dave's office after we got back to the center, except for the things from V.I.P. that were Genevieve's.

"Under?" Dave asked.

"By four pennies" I handed him five hundred dollars, laughing.

"Good go see your son and go home his mother is already with him in the cafe."

I left Genevieve with him.

"He spoils you Genie Jelly Bean."

"I know" She smiled "Andy kisses sooo good."

"He let you see, Andy?"

"Payment for my help; he is so clueless when it comes to girls, I hope he has all boys."

Dave laughed "How was the mall?"

"We made earth quake tremors from shaking, I made him turn bright red and he gave me chocolate a big bar and let me eat it in one shot. It was awesome."

"Let you pick your own?"

"Yep, and a few things for Andy" She smiled dreamily.

"Got your whip?"

She smiled ear to ear "He was soooo red in V.I.P. they carded him."

"Did you get the object I asked you for?"

"Yeah, and he was so oblivious he didn't even notice he spent fifteen minutes staring at the bikes shaking. It was like he was a level one not smart enough to remember how to cut."

Dave laughed "He was trying to remember how not to is more like it but I am sure you made him feel better. And I know he was oblivious, he always is on Thursdays I think his mind is elsewhere."

"Ana" Genevieve laughed.

"Probably; ok, you, go get back in your center clothes."

"DADDY, ANA SAYS SANTA IS COMING HERE TOMORROW!" Anthony jumped into my arms.

"Oof; yes, kiddo, he is coming here tomorrow" I sat him back at his dinner table. "How was your day?"

"I hate Quentin!"

I nodded "I am sorry, other than Quentin how was your day?"

"Good, I was with Dave. Where were you? You weren't with me, and Kevin and Kyle said you weren't with them and you weren't in the cafeteria at lunch or in the family room after classes."

"I was running errands for Dave."

"Ana said you and her drove here on a snowmobile."

"Yep, when you see our drive way you will see that it is just safer until My Uncle Marc Can plow us out and I can get my car to the bottom of the hill."

Ana stifled a laugh.

"Anthony, are you finishing your lima beans?" Kevin asked.

"EWWWW NO!" Anthony crinkled his nose.

"Can I have them then, please" Kevin's eyes lit up.

"Go for it, Sweetie" Ana handed Kevin Anthony's plate. "Alex I got a note from his consoler today."

"What? Why? What happened?" I picked up Anthony holding him in a tight bear hug, fearing the worst.

"I don't know, it just asked us to stop in after work."

"Oh ok" I set Anthony down. "Night Anthony love you see you tomorrow."

"Night Dad . . . . Hey Dad?"

"Yes?"

"I love you."

"I love you too."

Ana hugged him and said good night about ten times making him giggle.

Ana wrapped her arm around me as we walked. "Had to be in the mall today?"

I nodded "Way, way longer than I wanted to be."

"It will be ok, baby."

I doubted it but I didn't tell her otherwise just knocked on the office door "Steve, it's Al you said you wanted to see us?"

"Come in take a seat" He called out to us.

"What did he do?" I asked as we walked in.

"Nothing, Alex, Relax; I just wanted to show you something." He handed us piece of paper labeled 'fears of my new family.' On it had a big stick figure hitting a little stick figure and two big stick figures giving the little stick figure to two other big stick figures.

I gulped "Maybe if I come in earlier, stay later and try to come in on my days off . . ."

"Alex, relax," Steve looked at me like I need the consoling. "I personally think he is too young to be in here but he is very smart and advanced for six. He knows what he did, why he did it, and why it was wrong to do it. He is progressing very quickly and doing well I feel he is ready for level two."

I nodded breathing slightly and then looked at the drawing again.

"On Wednesdays I would like to set up a session for you two and him. He has a strong desire to learn and take everything in; I think it will help him."

"Yes, of course, I will tell Dave right away."

"Alex, relax, please; if you can't clam down I will have Dave give you a room. He sent you to the mall again didn't he?"

"Yeah, sorry" I blushed.

"Don't be sorry just relax; just go home and relax." He took the picture back "And, Alex, don't worry about these, these are normal fears for kids from that kind of back ground. I would have been worried if he had no fears."

I got off the snowmobile shaking; Ana defiantly had a lead foot and liked the snowmobile. I looked at my half buried car and shook my head.

"It's not quite six, I am going to get Paul and go sledding with him until dinner" Ana said trying to get my attention.

"Ok, I'm . . . I've" I pointed at my poor car."

"Going to learn to listen better when almost everyone tells you not to park up here."

"Yeah" I sighed "I guess I will join you guys sledding."

After dinner I was playing play dough with Paul and my cell rang. "Williams" I answered it. I added more play dough to my deranged clay lump waiting for Dave to stop coughing or laughing or both. My clay lump was suppose to be an elephant, but my normal clay skills included lumps, balls and rolled pieces that could make cylinder shaped things such as snakes, logs, snails, and worms; unless I had a mold.

"Did you know Kevin was the only one that didn't ask to go home?" Dave finally asked "Even Amelia at least wanted to go to her boyfriend's house."

"I know I figured he already knew or he didn't want to be near his dad. I don't blame him holidays are too stressful and too much family; but I told his consoler."

"Your car still stuck?" He laughed.

"Yes, thank you very much, even if I unburied it I can't get it down the hill without taking out trees and houses mainly Dr. Witson's and Uncle Mike's."

He laughed "Your Mama use to toboggan all the way here; I don't suggest it now that your uncle built his house at the base of the hill and that interstate they put in when they 'modernized' the town." Dave had told me in the 1990's the town was very small and not busy at all; I had seen a few pictures of it. He had also told me he had wished that it had stayed that way. "So you taking the . . ."

"She is taking hers and I am taking mine and yes I know stop and grab the candy canes."

"Actually no, I remembered them this year or well Greg did. I was going to suggest Paul ride with you. Ana is sweet but she loves the speed on those dangerous toys."

"Tell me about it I am still car sick from this morning not to mention tonight. So how is my son?"

"He is fine; Kevin, Genevieve, and he are playing board games and Kevin is telling him how Santa comes and brings the Christmas tree. What are you up to?"

"Paul and I are playing play dough" I grimaced I hated play dough even as a kid I hated play dough. Play dough and I had a strong hate, hate relationship. I hated it and it hated me.

"You and play dough" Dave laughed "I want a picture of that."

"Over my dead body or shall we discuss finger paints" I laughed. Dave had a similar relationship with finger paints but where as mine was straight at the play dough his was more towards the idea of children and what they can do with finger paints.

He laughed harder "Alright Al, see you tomorrow."

"Later" I hung up. I looked over at Paul's creation it was a lump too but it was a flat lump looked more like a steak than a lump.

"It a kating rink, Daddy" He was proud of his skating rink; I could tell he had been playing with Colt. Colt had my hate for play dough; skating rinks were his level of experience.

After I put him to bed, I sat at the puzzle table in the living room working on some puzzle Mama had going. The twins were doing homework and Nick was reading. My parents were down stairs playing music, they still played a lot they just no longer toured and had not played at the pool hall in about six months before last weekend. Ana was doing home work for one of her classes I had already done my homework for my online class. I had worked so hard on my end of term paper that I thought I was going to self combust.

Colt came flying up the stairs and jumped on my back "I have a half day tomorrow."

"Ow" I breathed hard he had slammed my ribs into the puzzle table."

"Mom says Uncle Christian is picking us up and taking us to your work to see Anthony."

"Either you are getting heavy or I am getting old or both and yes, you are, and it will make Anthony very happy."

"What did he ask Santa for?"

"To be home, most kids there want nothing more than to be home."

"Even that Kevin kid?"

"Yes, Colt even Kevin doesn't want to be there."

CHAPTER 24

CHRISTMAS AT THE CENTER

CHRISTMAS AT THE CENTER WAS always held the Friday before Christmas and Dave always went all out; a tree, presents pictures with Santa and any one level three and up went home until the New Year. I had decided to talk to Dave about letting Anthony come home just for Christmas. I dressed Paul in his suit.

"We go to Mr. Tomp son's Office?" Paul smiled up at me.

"Nope it's Friday; Anthony gets Christmas today."

"Me too?"

"No Santa comes to you Sunday night when you are in bed and fast asleep."

"I comb me own Capelli, papa (hair, Daddy)." He pulled the comb from my hand.

Ana laughed, she was laying out his snowmobile gear "He riding with you or . . ."

"Me I love you but you have a speed thing" I kissed her.

"Morning" Uncle Christian handed us breakfast. "si guarda scosso Alex (You look rattled, Alex)."

"Sto bene(I'm fine); I am not rattled."

"He is right Hun, you look rattled" Mom stretched to kiss the top of my head when I bent to hug her. "Donavan . . . Donavan! DONAVAN WAKE UP!"

Uncle Donavan had fallen asleep in his morning paper again "I am up, Bella, I am up."

Uncle Christian and I stifled a laugh; Uncle Donavan was always falling asleep in his news paper or coffee at breakfast.

"Come on Al we are going to be late" Ana said.

I grabbed Paul's helmet and mine "Coming" I said grabbing Paul.

"Coat" Uncle Christian growled at me.

I sighed and put my coat on over my snow gear.

I pulled in next to Ana's Snowmobile, it was purple with her name in light blue. Paul went with her into the office after he had been stripped of his riding gear and she of hers. I went to the locker rooms and then down to Dave.

Genevieve caught me half way down the hall she shouldn't have been roaming without a staff member but she was so close to level four most staff mainly Dave and I let her. "Dog Breath go get a medic, Buddy is sick and choking and . . ."

I took off down the hall at top speed in the other direction "Greg . . . Greg . . . Greg buddy's inhaler fast . . ." I was yelling in to my Walkie-talkie headed to the cafeteria. We both ran to the cafeteria "Ok Buddy" I said. Buddy had asthma worse than almost anyone I knew; sometimes I felt bad for him.

Greg handed him his inhaler, I still thought that the inhaler was something that he should be allowed to keep on him but the state law said no.

After getting Buddy calm and breathing I went to the family room because Jarrod told me Dave was there.

"Morning, Buddy is in the . . ."

"I know, Greg told me" Dave looked tired.

"Ok I got to ask, where's the tree?"

"In conference room B with Santa."

"I have . . ."

"Kevin, Kyle, Anthony, Tiffany, Sadie, Genevieve and Amelia in here; at 2:30 per parental request."

"I . . ."

"The room spun."

"Al?"

"Motion sick, we raced Ana."

Dave laughed "Alright go get your creatures."

"Creatures fit."

I went back to the cafeteria and told my "creatures" as Dave put it, that I was getting Tiny then them so finish up there breakfasts.

"Dad I'm already done can I come with you?" Anthony asked.

"Me too?" Kyle and Kevin both said.

I sighed "Fine ladies we will be back."

"Ok Dog Breath" Genevieve yawned.

I took the boys down with me to get Tiny, Kevin and Kyle chattered the whole way.

"You suck, go away!" Amelia rolled over facing the wall.

"You have a potty mouth!" Anthony yelled at her.

I shook my head, trying not to laugh "Amelia, now get up and moving or I will tell Will you aren't going home for the holiday."

"You suck" She scowled flopping into a sitting position.

"We have established that fact already, now let's go!" I very rarely lost my temper with the kids at work, but ever since Sam had introduced her to me she did everything in her power to get me to lose my patients.

Kevin held his breath staring at the ceiling and Kyle kicked the door jamb looking anywhere but at me.

"Amelia you have the count of three or I am relocking this door."

Jarrod tapped me on the back "Can I see your little man Dave wants to talk to him and your parents are here they wanted to talk to Dave."

"GRANDMA!" Anthony yelled and took off down the hall.

I laughed.

"Er" Jarrod smiled and ran to catch Anthony; Jarrod did everything by the book so the sight of the six year old level two running down the hall alone nearly sent him in to a panic attack.

Greg laughed as he passed on his way to the medic station.

"Oh, hey Greg can you bring these two back to the cafeteria Amelia and I need to talk."

"Sure, they can tell me about their Christmas plans, make me feel better about mine."

I laughed "I will trade with you I have to talk to Ana's Godfather."

"Nope I am keeping my empty one room apartment" He laughed and took the boys for me.

I sat on the edge of Tiny's bed "Ok runt let's talk."

"No!"

"What's wrong?"

"I don't want to go just come get me when . . ."

"You know I can't or I would."

"FINE!" She threw the blankets off and stormed out.

"Thank-you" I sighed.

"You're not welcome."

I rolled my eyes sky ward sending silent prayers to the powers that be; to help me get through the day. What I truly needed was about four more hours of sleep a night.

Anthony was still with Dave when I got everyone to the family room. Paul was instructing Sadie on how to play cars; Tiffany was adding Blessed Yule to the sign that said Merry Christmas. I laughed because in our house we said both. I don't know what Yule was but Mama said it to Mom and Uncle Christian. Genevieve was up on the bookshelf, again; only this time she was meditating not reading. Kevin and Kyle had taken over the legos and were building something large. Amelia was sulking on the couch and telling me she hated me and anything else she could think of every time I passed her.

Ana came up behind me and hugged me tight very un Ana like but I was not about to complain I just turned and hugged her back. "Ms. Meyers called; she will be here at 2:30 and wants . . ."

"I know what she wants" I cut Ana off "Can you find Greg and tell him I need an Advil, please."

She raised an eye brow "Already?"

"I don't want to talk about it."

"Ok" She said and left.

Tiffany's mother arrived first she brought her a stack of books and was all emotional; and left fast. Tiffany looked like she was going to puke.

"Hey kiddo, what's up; you look green?" I asked her.

"I am going to be an aunt."

"That's awesome."

"I guess is your Mama coming today?"

"Already here, what do you need?"

"It can wait till later."

"Ok, enjoy your books."

I walked over to Genevieve who had moved to play cars with Paul and Sadie. I leaned down and whispered in her ear "Sticks and stones may break my bones but whips and chains excite me" It was a saying on a shirt I had picked out for her in hot topic, while she was finding things on Sadie and Tiffany's lists.

She choked turning bright red and had to stop her car to recompose herself.

Sadie gave me a lost look.

I shrugged.

Kyle's family and Kevin's mom had arrived and were talking and watching their boys build.

"Alex," Kyle's step dad pulled me aside "Kyle's father is back in town, we told Dave and Ana but figured we should tell you too. I am sure it goes without saying we don't want him anywhere near Kyle."

"Oh, of course, absolutely" I nodded. I had never met Kyle's biological father, but all Kyle's paper work said that his mother had sole custody and that his father was allowed no contact with him.

Anthony was brought back after lunch; he was wearing a suit and tie that matched Paul's. "Alex, come see me after work" Dave said and left. Around one thirty Greg finally brought me that Advil.

Will came in carrying a rose for Tiny and said hi to me.

"You look like Santa's reindeer kicked your butt" Carter laughed.

"I know she is over there, good luck every one still sucks."

Will laughed "I figured, good luck with Ana's dad."

"I don't need luck with that he said yes I have to talk to her Godfather, but mostly I need the Advil to kick in before Santa gets here."

They left and went to be with Tiny.

Andy came in the same time as my brothers.

"Al where . . ."

". . . is he?" The twins nearly ran over Andy thundering down the hall yelling.

I groaned and hushed them, then pointed to where Anthony was playing dominos with Paul, Sadie, and Tiffany.

"They are most spirited" Andy smiled at me.

"No, Ms. Andy, they are just plain evil. Genevieve will be back soon she is helping Dave, something about the camera."

"Ok, thank you" She took a seat near my uncle.

Mama hugged me "Stressed?"

"No tired and I have a bad headache. Also if you have a moment . . ."

"Alex is this your mom or your mama?" Tiffany interrupted.

"My mama," I sighed, "Mama this is Tiffany she would like to speak to you."

Mama gave me a look that said I need more patients and went to speak to Tiffany.

"I like your sign" Mom laughed, bringing Nick's back pack to him.

"Thanks Mom" I nodded.

Ms. Meyers came around two and was gone by two fifteen. She mostly spoke to the boys about how they were doing and how they liked being with Ana and I, Anthony expressed an opinion on how he couldn't tell her because it was her fault he didn't live with me; after she left I spoke to him about being polite and how it wasn't her fault he was there.

Santa finally arrived around two forty my head ache had not improved as I had spent a large portion of the past twenty minutes convincing Amelia to behave. Dave shot her a look that said if she said one wrong thing Will and Carter would be leaving without her. I was happy Mr. Johnson played Santa here and at the charity breakfast as it would be Paul who would be able to tell the difference.

"Ho-ho-ho" Santa said and Dave had to shoot Amelia another look.

"SANTA!" Paul jumped in to his arms.

"Ho-ho-ho Hi Paul, how about you sit with Anthony and wait your turn. Then I have a very special gift for you."

Paul listened without a fit, thankfully.

I glared at Dave. He shrugged and stuck his tongue out, someone forgot to tell that man he was in his sixties not six. I think that's why the kids loved him.

We had Kevin and Kyle go first so they could leave. Kevin carried out his "big" present. The gift wasn't actually large; Dave had just wrapped a note saying his National Geographic would start in January. He would be very happy when he opened the box. Amelia went next I think Dave just wanted her gone so that she wouldn't make a scene. Carter held his breath; Will was talking to my uncle, not looking phased.

"Amelia smile" Dave said aiming the camera.

I readjusted my position to the back of the room in between Andy and Carter.

"That is how my Genie was before" Andy said sounding more amused than shocked.

"Yeah," I sighed, "The sad part is she is only here until Dave feels she has healed enough from the pneumonia to terrorize her boyfriend."

"Terrorize is an understatement," Carter laughed "She behaves hideously and he loves her any way."

"Someone has too" I gnashed my teeth.

"Day start by fighting with her?" He asked.

"The day started yesterday, with a snow mobile ride and hasn't ended yet."

He laughed "Ana?"

"She likes speed; the faster the better."

He laughed harder "Well I get to carry her stuff, see you later."

After Amelia, Sadie and Tiffany went. I think Sadie's frightening looked scared Santa too. Dave made the twins carry their stuff to their room, Tiffany carried Sadie whom had broke down crying.

"I next dog breath" Genevieve jumped up on my back.

"Of course, as long as you open your gift from me before you leave" I set her down.

"Ok" She smiled.

"What did you get her?" Andy asked.

"A T-shirt that says 'sticks and stones may break my bones but wipes and chains excite me' and some silver eye shadow. It seemed fitting."

"It does fit her; she asked if I had her gifts in the car and could she have the whip early."

I shook my head "She is a good kid Ms. Andy."

"Can I still call you if we need you?"

"Of course you can, do you need the number again."

"Oh no I have it just wanted to make sure it was ok."

"Ok."

"By Dog Breath" Genevieve jumped on my back again "I get to go home this year!"

"Oh really is that so?" I laughed hugging her tight "Ok you take it slow one day at a time, Andy has my number if you need and most important have fun."

"Yeah, yeah, I'll be fine Dog Breath."

"Open your gift yet?"

"Dave said I couldn't because your twin brothers can read."

I laughed "Good point; have a good holiday."

"Thanks, Dog Breath" She giggled dragging Andy down the hall.

"Get in the picture with your boys" Dave growled at me.

"Er I . . ."

"Shut your mouth and get your butt in my picture!" Dave frowned at me.

Sadie and Tiffany were stifling laughs right along with my brothers and uncles. I mumbled several choice phrases under my breath I took my place near my sons and Ana.

"Ooooooo," Paul giggled, "I heard that, Daddy."

I shook my head and stood smiling waiting for the heat in my face to dissipate and to return to my normal ivory tone instead of the Santa suite red I was. Dave took like six or seven pictures, I had to step to the side and blink the spots away.

Santa talked to Paul and Anthony, telling them how good they had both been and how big they had gotten.

Dave said "Let's go take the girls to their room and leave them unattended while you, Ana and I will talk in my office I have a special gift for you. The boys are fine here with your mothers."

Tiffany blushed "I . . . I . . . It was . . . ."

Sadie laughed "He is teasing you, Hunny."

We walked them back to their room and went to Dave's office. "I am letting Anthony go home until the New Year on the condition he is in here on Friday so the other state workers see him like he was here the whole time and on Wednesday for his consoling. It's really important the state doesn't find out."

"What happens when Ms. Meyers comes on to check on Paul?" Ana Asked I was still in shock.

"Jules won't be stopping in this week, like I said it's important no one else from the state finds out or we will all lose our jobs and you will lose your boys."

I nodded.

"Al breathe" Ana laughed "You heard him right."

"Also, Alexander I don't want to see you in here until Wednesday."

"di ringraziamento(Thank-you)" I hugged him.

"Yeah, yeah" Dave hugged me back "Get off me and English. Boy, speak English. Now go home and get some sleep."

"Paul has a new habit of crawling into bed with us and kicking Al in the ribs."

"Well get him home, I have two girls and a Buddy to entertain."

Mama had loaded my brothers into the van and mom was getting the boys in to their snowsuits and their snowmobile gear.

"Paul, are you going to ride with me or . . ."

"I am riding with Mommy, you drive too slow" He said with an air of finality.

Mom and Ana laughed.

Ana picked Paul up "We will meet you out side with the checks so we aren't late to dinner or anything else."

Paul giggled and stuck his tongue out at me.

"Sounds like a good idea, you two maniacs drive too fast anyway" I stuck my tongue out at Paul.

"Daddy what are we riding?" Anthony looked up at me.

"Snowmobiles" I sighed.

"We will meet you at dinner" Mom hugged Anthony and I good bye.

I lifted Anthony "I have to clock me out and sign you out I think . . ."

He giggled "Dave already did that this morning, told Nana you would forget so he signed me out."

I laughed.

I clocked out wishing ever one a happy holiday and went out. Ana and Paul were already on her snowmobile circling the parking lot. Anthony stared wide eyed at my snowmobile as I fastened his helmet and mine on. I sat him on and climbed on myself; he looked up at me and I put his hands on the handle bars placing mine over his. I lifted my feet into place and drove over to Ana. He started to shake so I turned off the snowmobile and turned him around so he was holding on to me until he relaxed.

Ana pulled up to me and pulled her helmet off "What's wrong?"

Paul was leaned forward going broom, broom.

I yanked my helmet up "You and fearless there go on ahead. We are going to go around here slow for a bit until he feels safe, tell Mom we are coming."

"Ok" She put her helmet back on and she took off Ana and I had never needed each other to function, and often already knew what the other wanted to do.

I took Anthony's helmet off "Talk to me what's wrong?"

"I feel like I am going to fall."

"I won't let you fall." I put his helmet back on and turned him back around and drove around the parking lot till he was begging me to go faster.

We got to dinner just as everyone else was being seated I took off Anthony's snowsuit and riding gear, while Ana changed out of her work clothes. Uncle Christian had me put the gear in the van until we needed it again. I brought the boys to the table and excused myself to the men's room to change out of my work scrubs into my jeans and my long sleeve T-shirt that said 'if you have to read my shirt you need a new hobby'. When I came out Paul was in his booster seat coloring on a paper place mat and Anthony was sitting in Ana's arms I sat down so that Anthony's place was in between Ana and I.

"Ok Anthony" I took off his tie shoving it in my pocket.

"Yeah, Ana and I are playing hang man" He smiled.

"How about I introduce you to everyone, since it was too busy at the center?"

He looked up and his eyes widened; he just nodded.

"Ok you know my mothers and my uncles" I gestured toward them.

"Yeah Great Uncle Chris couldn't get my tie right this morning so Nana had to move him and fix it. She said Great Uncle Christian would have done it but he and grandma were getting everyone else."

My brothers, Mom and Ana started laughing; Mama, Uncle Christian and I all stifled our laughter when Uncle Chris turned red.

"He never could tie them, I always did his or Nikki did" Mama laughed.

"Ok" I choked trying not to laugh more "Next to my uncle Christian is my Uncle Donavan."

Uncle Donavan smiled "Sembra intelligente(He looks smart), Alex"

"Grazie (Thanks), he is."

"Every one speaks that other langue" Anthony whispered.

"Italian and yes, but don't worry you will learn it too. Uncle Donavan said you look smart."

"Thank you, Sir" Anthony gulped.

"Mmm already like his father" Uncle Donavan muttered.

"Hush Don" Mama threw a bread stick at him "Don't mind him Anthony he is just a grump."

"From all his boo boos?" Anthony looked at Uncle Donavan's arm.

"I wish" She laughed "But you pay his crankiness no mind."

Anthony nodded.

"Next to my uncle Chris is Ms. Nikki" I told him. "I think they're dating" I whispered in his ear.

"Like I have told your father, your uncles and your brother auntie is fine someday your uncle will marry me" She smiled at Anthony.

Mama and Uncle Christian stifled laughs I raised an eyebrow.

"Colt" Anthony smiled.

"That's Uncle Colt to you" Colt said smugly.

Uncle Christian shot him a warning look "That's one I get to three you're grounded for the holiday."

Ana raised an eye brow "Bad day?"

"He is all bella" Uncle Donavan laughed "And mainly her mouth."

I laughed.

Anthony tugged on my arm "Daddy I think I am seeing things."

I laughed "Yeah. Things fit but there is nothing wrong with your vision. They are my brothers Christopher and Christian."

"Identical twins" Anthony smiled.

"Yes but I prefer to call them beasts."

"Don't teach him . . ."

". . . That we love . . ."

". . . Our nephews."

Anthony stared at them terrified.

"Don't worry you will get use to that, that is how they speak, I have often wondered what would happen if we separate them and make one talk if we would only get only half a thought."

Mom frowned at me "Alexander."

"What it's true."

"Alex"

"Sorry" I blushed "Any way next to them is Nick."

Nick didn't even look up from his book.

"He likes to read, Next to Nick is Kenny and his girlfriend Juliet; don't get to close to her, if she talks you will see why."

"Alex!" Ana frowned.

"What I am right."

"Doesn't mean you say that."

"I am not going to lie to him."

Ana frowned and her and Anthony went back to their Hang man game. I started discussing work with Uncle Christian and Uncle Donavan.

"Where is every one?" Mama said looking around.

"Daddy called me; he and Davie said they would just meet us at the pool hall, and that Uncle Kork was setting up the pool hall" Ana offered.

"Oh not them Sweetie, I already spoke to them, I mean the waiters I am hungry."

Mom laughed "Honey they are coming, they need time to cook it."

"What is dinner?" I asked.

"Pizza and milk shakes, Anthony, do you like chocolate milkshakes?" Mama asked.

"Yeah!" He smiled ear to ear.

"Aweberry Nana" Paul objected.

"Oh yes, Paul, yours and Nick's are strawberry."

Ana was laughing.

"What, what did I miss?" I asked.

"Last Saturday" Ana laughed "Mama offered him a sip of her chocolate shake and he told her he didn't like chocolate shake just chocolate candy. Then drank all her shake and then thanked her for the strawberry shake and told her it tasted good."

I laughed "What topping did you order?"

"Cheese, as your brothers couldn't manage to pick one."

After five slices of pizza and my milkshake I felt better. Anthony looked over my clothes as I redressed him in his snowmobile gear.

"I don't wear scrubs all the time that is just a work uniform."

"I know that, Dad, do you have a change of clothes for me?"

"I will, when I found out you were coming home with me I asked my uncle Mike to pick up a few outfits for you until I could take you shopping myself." I took his suite jacket off and put it in the bag with my scrubs. "Better?"

"Yes, thank you. Dad do I have a bed at your house?"

"Of course you have a bed at home."

Ana looked up in shock as she put Paul in his pajamas in the van near Anthony and his suit in the bag with mine. "Don't worry" She smiled at him, putting on Paul's gear "We have everything you will need and we are going shopping in the morning. You like Christmas lights? We are going to look at the light display."

He nodded, pulling his helmet on.

We pulled in to the pool hall at quarter to eight. There was a sign on the door advertising Mama's band special for the holiday even thought they had said they would not play until Ana's uncle Kyle returned, which would have been a full six months. Mom pulled in after us and we stripped the boys and ourselves of our riding gear. I pulled Anthony up on my shoulders and went in slowly; I had not socially gone to the pool hall even to hear my mother's play in over a year with the exception of the last two weeks. Paul ran over to the bar and pulled himself up on the stool.

"UNCLE KORK I IS HERE!!!!!!!!!!!!!!!!! UNCLE KORK MY SANTA LET ME BRING MY ANTONY HOME!"

Ana's uncle Ken turned from mixing a customer's drink "Really Paul is that so? Then where is he?"

He pointed at me "DADDY HAS HIM ON HIS SHOULDERDS."

Mr. Wittson laughed "Your nana gave you milk shake huh?"

"YEAH! WHERE AUNTIE KISTALINE? SHE NEED TO ME ME ANTONY!"

"Paul" Ana sighed "Don't be rude."

I sat Anthony down on a stool near Paul. "Anthony that is Ana's Uncle Ken or as he told your brother Kork. Mr. Wittson have you seen Uncle Mike he has Pajamas for Anthony?"

"Mi . . . Mi . . . Mik . . . Mik . . . Mike . . . . Mikey . . ."

There were some noises under the counter.

Mr. Wittson laughed "Michael, Michael motor cycle" He kicked something on the floor that groaned and swore. "He is fixing the grill that I asked him five hours ago to fix so we don't have a riot over curly fries and cheese burgers."

I felt a hand on my shoulder steering me toward the back room "Hi Uncle Marc, how are you?

"Good, I know where Anthony's pajamas are."

"Dad!?" Anthony shot into my leg.

"It's ok, I am just getting your pajamas; this is my uncle Marc."

"Can I come Daddy?"

"Of course you can" I took his hand.

"There are too many people in here Alex lift him up" Uncle Marc commanded. "Nice to meet you Anthony; I will see you again tomorrow at your uncle Kork's for dinner. I am here if you need me but right now I must go assist your Grandma, Nana, and Papa set up instruments." He handed me a bag.

I looked around the kitchen K-4 was washing dishes, Aunt Amy and Mrs. Wittson were preparing curly fries. I pulled the pajamas out of the bag they were blue tie dyed footed ones. I showed Anthony he smiled.

"Thank-you Aunt Amy."

"No problem, your uncle wanted to put that baby in tank tops and boxers" She shook her head. "I got him three pairs of jeans, four long sleeve shirts, a pack of boxers and a package of socks. Also a pair of sneakers Ana said he already has snow stuff."

"Thank-you very much; how much do I owe you?"

"Nothing, just get that poor baby out of his suit he looks scared and exhausted."

"He met Uncle Marc" I laughed. "Ok the boy over there is your cousin we call him K-4 or Kenneth and over there is Ana's aunt Crystalline and my aunt Amy."

He nodded "Thank-you, for my clothes."

"Awe what a sweetie you have." Mrs. Wittson smiled.

"Thank—you Ma'am, where can I change him? It's a zoo out there like a good half hour wait on the bathroom."

"Back here is fine, kiddo" Mrs. Wittson said "Ken already set cots up for them."

"Ok, thank-you." I took Anthony back to one of the cots and helped him in to his pajamas.

He put his suit in the bag with my work clothes and Paul's suit. "Does your uncle play music?" He yawned.

"Yes, all my uncles you will meet tonight play music, except my uncle Donavan I am not sure if he can or not."

"They play here?"

"Yep, so do my mothers, Ana's father and uncles."

"Oh, Are we going back out to Paul?"

"We should before he causes a riot over chocolate milk or Ana picks a fight with her cousin Sam."

He just looked at me.

"I know huge family."

Sam slammed in to the kitchen and threw dishes in to the sink. "Al, your mom is looking for you and Ana is dancing with some ugly kid with a stupid Mohawk" Sam slammed back out.

"That's our cue" I lifted Anthony "That was Sam."

"Ana is talking with Mohawk and Spike, Al, Sam is just hating on her because Dad removed Justin from her life permanently" K-4 sighed.

"I wasn't too worried, I am Ana's she loves me and she has her hands too full to be doing too much. Paul is out there giving your dad what for" I laughed.

"It's good for him" K-4 laughed.

"Styling P.J.s, handsome, let's dance" Ana took Anthony off the stool next to Paul and danced him out on to the floor.

I laid my head on the counter watching Paul spin himself dizzy.

"GOOD EVENING POOL HALL!" I heard Uncle Marc yell.

"Jerk" Jr. muttered slamming on to the stool next to Paul.

"Pardon" I raised an eyebrow at him.

"Oh sorry Al, not you or squirt that guy over there won't leave Adam and I alone."

"Adam can take care of himself and if you don't want trouble then don't hustle pool."

He muttered under his breath and flagged down uncle Donavan whom was tending bar. "Two root beer floats please, sir."

Uncle Donavan made the drinks and hand them to Adam. "Quit hustling and you won't be spending your trust funds on sodas" He growled at Jr.

Uncle Donavan growling startled Paul out of his spinning "Jr." He squealed.

"That's sad Jr.; he associates Uncle Donavan growling with you."

After a while Ana came back with Anthony fast asleep on her shoulder, I took him back to the cot and she carried Paul just because it seemed like a good idea to do. Paul sat on the prep table talking to everyone instead of on his cot though. I pushed K-4 into the wall "Anthony makes the slightest whimper come get me!" I growled "Or if Paul needs me. Is that clear?"

"Crystal" He choked cowering away from me.

"Good."

"He worries too much for a little boy" Ana said as we danced.

"I know" I held her close breathing in her perfume and kissing gently along her neck.

"Mmm, I believe you owe me a game of darts"

"It can wait I just want to hold you and dance."

"That sounds good she nuzzled me."

We left the pool hall early as both boys had fallen asleep; we carried them up and tucked them in to their beds. We quickly wrapped and hid Anthony's Christmas presents and went to bed ourselves.

"I love you" I held Ana closer moving hair from her eyes and rubbing her back.

"He still wants a sibling and it *is* Friday" She gave me an evil grin.

I sighed and laughed "So you did hear that, go look in my sock draw and then come help me practice" I kissed her.

CHAPTER 25

THE BIG DINNER

I WOKE WITH ANTHONY IN between us, he had woke crying in the middle of the night and Ana had put her pajamas on to go get him while I was in the bathroom. I softly rubbed his back, I looked at the clock it was Only 7:30. I could hear Kenny moving on the other side of the divider. "Morning" I called over to him.

"You sound extra happy," He laughed, "Mom was looking for you last night."

I blushed, "I will go finder her now." I groaned as I stood up and stretched.

"You sound like your three thousand years old; she is outside with Mama and Paul."

"Thanks, anything I should know?"

"We are out of waffles, egg sandwiches or cereal for breakfast and Uncle Donavan is asleep in his coffee."

"Always, I think Mama wakes him early out of spite" I picked up clothes slowly placing them in the hamper.

"Probably, what is with you? Clothes everywhere, perky in the morning; did you and Ana have a wild night?" He pushed the divider back grinning at me with a crooked smile.

"First of all it doesn't have to be wild to be good and he is the best. Not that it is any of *your* business!" Ana hugged me from behind.

I choked blushing.

Kenny's eyes widened and he went back to his side re-shutting the divider laughing hysterically.

"Shut up you immature goon" Ana called after him laughing. "You know he is the sexiest man on earth."

"I am going down stairs to shower" I shook my head "And maybe you could not discuss my personals as Anthony is now up".

Three bathrooms and only two showers can cause quite the clog in the morning. I shook out my hair tying it back and surrendering the bathroom to Christopher. I went out and sat at my breakfast.

"Are you well? You look like you have seen a spirit" Uncle Donavan asked.

"A ghost? No I am just nervous" I smiled.

He nodded returning to his paper.

Uncle Christian came up the stairs in a fit "Where is Anthony? Where are his clothes?"

"He is on the couch watching cartoons and his clothes or lack thereof, are in his dresser" I looked at Uncle Christian.

"I'll be back I have to get his suit washed and then he needs a bath . . ." Uncle Christian trailed off.

Mom came up carrying a load of dry laundry "Morning Al you and Ana ok you guys left early."

I stood and hugged Mom "Morning Mom, we're fine. Is Uncle Christian ok; he is acting odd?"

"Oh he is fine just stressing on something you know *he has to clean*" She laughed "Anthony come eat breakfast."

"Morning Grandma" He yawned stretching and climbed up on the stool so he could still see cartoons.

"Anthony in this house when a female in the house greets us we stand, hug them and greet them back" Uncle Donavan said "It is a sign of respect."

Anthony ducked shaking like someone was going to swing at him.

Mama had just come in with Paul "Hush fool" She shook her head at uncle Donavan and hugged Anthony "Don't you listen to him Sweetie, you will catch on."

I stood and hugged Mama "Morning Mama other than dinner tonight what are we doing?"

"Well, karate is at nine and it would be nice if you would join us, you haven't been in over a month. The boys have a game at five and somewhere in there is lunch."

"Sounds good?" I ran up stairs to dig out my Ghi and belt.

Ana was in the bathroom and called out "Al is that you?"

"Yeah, I am taking the boys to karate."

"Sounds good wait for me I'll be down in a minute."

I raced down stairs and added Ana's and my gear bag to the pile near the front door. Uncle Christian had bathed and dressed Anthony. He was now wearing black jeans and a long sleeve t-shirt that said daddy's hero.

"Looking sharp little man" I smiled.

"Thank-you, Great Uncle Christian says I have a busy day."

"He is right, but it will be fun."

"What are you wearing; it looks like a funny bath robe?"

"My karate uniform, it's called a ghi you will get yours when we get to the studio."

"Really? What belt will I be?"

"Every one starts at white."

"What belt is Paul?"

"Paul has to wait a year before he can take karate, but he will be a white belt when he starts too."

"Oh what belt are you?"

"Black" I laughed "I have been in karate since I was five."

"Oh, you're old."

"Yep, thanks I think."

Mama and the boys came into the living room. Mama was a fourth level black belt, the beasts were red black belts with two stripes and colt was a green belt.

"Where is Nick?" I asked.

"Upstairs" Colt sighed "He's looking for his belt; I can't believe he already lost his brown belt, he just got it Thursday."

I stifled a laugh "You mean the brown belt tied to his gear bag?"

Colt scowled and yelled up the stairs "NICK IT'S DOWN HEAR!"

Every one plugged their ears.

I handed Anthony his snow suit "Mama Can we ride with you?"

"Of course, your Uncle found an old booster he can use until he has his own."

I rolled my eyes "Thank-you Uncle Christian" I called to him. I grabbed Anthony, Paul and Mom's and my gear bag. "Meet you at the car I need to talk to Mom."

"Ok, she's down at the car."

I looked at my Mama "I, oh never mind you're getting old, see you at the car."

Mama shot me a mind yourself look or a cut me some slack your brothers are fighting look.

"Are we going to sled to karate?" Anthony asked.

I laughed "No, no, in the winter with the all the snow and ice it is just safer to park the cars at the bottom of the hill."

"Oh."

"Hold tight to Paul" I said kicking off.

"Zoom. Zoom. Zoom." Giggled Paul "Antony you huggings too tight."

"Better he hold you tight than you go flying off the sled" I laughed.

We skidded to a stop in front of Ana's Uncle Kyle's house. Paul stood up and took off at a snow suit waddle to the burned down gas station.

"Follow Paul, Grandma is at the car."

"No snow mobile today?"

"No, well at least not for this trip." I hit the return button for the sled and Anthony's eyes widened. "Uncle Mike installed it, it's better than walking it back up the hill. There's also a bell on the other end incase no one is outside and there are grocery's."

He nodded.

"I am glad your Uncle got this big thing" Mom greeted me, belting Paul in. "A fifteen person van comes in handy."

I nodded helping Anthony in to the booster seat. The poor thing looked lost and confused as I buckled him in. "I am so nervous."

"It's ok to be nervous" Mom said.

"Kenny said Nana will be there."

"I know I bribed your mother with chocolate."

"So it's going to be us and . . ."

"Yes Al, the entire family."

"I swallowed hard."

Mom and Mama took their places next to the other black belts and I took Anthony to the office.

"Eric" I bowed "This is my son Anthony"

"Is he to start today?"

"Yes."

He turned opening a small closet behind him "I have red, black, red and black, green, blue and white what color?"

"Like Daddy's please" Anthony mumbled.

I tried not to laugh.

"What size is he, Al?"

"He's a 4/5" I smiled.

Eric handed Anthony black pants and a red top, then handed me the belt.

"Thanks Eric"

"Mmhmm, just nice to see you in class again Al" Eric nodded.

Paul ran in "Ear ic Nana says you has to give me a G, too."

Eric laughed "Ok Paul, you can have a Ghi but you tell your nana you are still too young for classes."

"No I not. I tree, I a big boy. I gets a geen G like Uncle Nick."

I stifled a laugh "Paul don't be rude ask nicely for your Ghi."

Paul scowled at me "Ear ic may I pease have a geen G like Uncle Nick's"

"He is a 2T if you have one that small. I am going to go help Anthony get into his before he is late for his first class."

I took Anthony in to the changing room. Just as I was tying on Anthony's belt Paul came flying in chattering a mile a minute, Uncle Christian right behind him carrying his Ghi.

"Daddy I gots a geen G" Paul beamed.

"I see" I laughed.

"Your mothers" Uncle Christian rolled his eyes "Wish pictures."

"Given" I sighed "But I need to get Anthony out there before he is late for his class."

I took my place at the front of the room near the other black belts, to lead the beginner class. Anthony stared nervously around the room as we did warm up stretches. The four to nine age groups was working belt sheets, so they were split up by belts. I was with the orange belts working their kicks; Eric had Anthony over by himself teaching him blocks.

By the end of the class he only flinched every couple of times someone hit a pad. I took him to the changing room. Paul was playing with Ana; Anthony sat down next to Uncle Christian. I skipped helping with the nine to fourteen class to fill out registration forms and play with Paul. Anthony showed Ana and Uncle Christian everything he learned. It seemed he liked his first class.

At ten forty-five I formed up with the rest of my class. I stood proudly in my front row spot as we bowed in then I lead in warm up exercises, it meant a lot to me that Eric still had respect for me despite my last class being over three months ago and not ending well. We started with sparring I partnered with Ana. I got distracted watching Mama Spar with Uncle Chris and Ana caught me hard in the shoulder with a well placed round house.

"Lost in thought?" She laughed.

"Um yeah" I blushed. "Sorry"

After sparring we worked on belt sheets I worked with the white belts. There were three of them a young lady who looked like she might cry if she broke nail. And two boys who look to be about the beasts' age, one looked like he might cry the other was hitting on the girl. I looked at their belt sheets they all started three weeks ago and all needed their first kata, I went and got a punch and kick pad.

"Take it easy on them Al" Eric laughed as I walked past muttering, he was with the blue belts.

"You owe me one" I grumbled.

"They're community service rats."

"I noticed like I said you owe me one."

I sighed, took a deep centering breath and mentally prepared myself for this. four years ago Eric join a 'support our cities youth' group and to give "juvenile delinquents" a way to "better" themselves and "rejoin" polite society he agreed to let them do community service at the karate studio. Ninety percent of the time they were nothing but a head ache and after their court ordered hours were up they left never making it past white belts.

I walked back to them "Ok I am Alex and . . ."

"I know who you are you're dating Sam's cousin" The one who had been hitting on the girl said.

Justin, I knew he had looked familiar this is the closet I had ever seen him without it being the back of his head. Mr. Wittson spent a lot of time not letting him near Samantha. I looked over at the red belts K-4 and Jeremiah were there but Sam was not. "Yes, well anyways as I was saying we are going to run through blocks, punches, kicks, and then we will start the first kata."

The girl rolled her eyes, Justin looked at the pads in my hand and the other boy nodded.

After karate we dropped Mom, Mama, Uncle Chris and the boys off and went to run errands. When we got to the Wal-Mart plaza Uncle Christian started to grumble about the way I buckled Anthony. "Seven years and seventy pounds" He lifted Anthony "He is thirty-five, forty at best. Are you trying to get yourself arrested?" He shook his head. "Come Anthony we are going to Baby World while your father gets the items from the hardware."

Anthony looked lost and confused "But I'm not a baby."

"I am well aware of your age we need to get you a proper booster seat not a car seat like Paul's with a five point harness but a booster for safety."

"Oh ok, can I have one with rocket ships on it?" Anthony asked.

"The proper phrase is may have not can I have, and yes you may if they have one in stock" Uncle Christian said lifting Anthony on to his shoulders.

I thought Anthony must think Uncle Christian is crazy for continually insisting upon proper grammar of the English language with such a thick Italian accent. I lifted Paul on to my shoulders as we approached the door. I heard Uncle Christian behind me laughing.

Ana raised and eye brow at me.

"Last time Paul and I were here he had a moment of three with no nap in the paint sample chips."

"Oh" She smiled.

I set the paints and the three rolls of tape Mama had asked for on the checkout counter after running into Uncle Marc and a very miserable looking Junior and Adam.

"Your mother called, Al . . ." Aunt Amy started to tell me.

I groaned.

Both Ana and Aunt Amy gave me a look.

"What she always does this?"

Aunt Amy grabbed a roll of painter's tape off the counter and stuck it aside to be re-shelved. "She called to say she only needs two rolls she found one at home"

"Oh".

Aunt Amy shook her head at me "Word of advice Alex, just relax a little."

We met up with Anthony and Uncle Christian back in the parking lot. Anthony was holding a stuffed lion and Uncle Christian was placing the box in a recycling bin.

"Daddy we got one with constellations on it" Anthony beamed.

"Did you say thank you? I'd tell him not to spoil you but both Ana and Uncle Christian would thoroughly embarrass me."

Both my boys giggled.

I sighed "Right well, let's get your books."

Two hundred and sixty dollars later I stood in line shaking like a leaf. Uncle Christian had taken Paul and Ana had Anthony. I was gripping the carriage so tight my knuckles were white.

"Alex, what are you doing out?" Mr. Wittson asked.

"A-Anthony needed things" I choked. I put the books on the counter and handed him the two hundred knowing that Mama and or Ana's discount would cover the sixty.

"Uncle Kork!" Paul squealed "Uncle Kork I gets to keeps my Antony longers."

"That is awesome, little man." Mr. Wittson looked at Anthony "I hear you like astrology?"

"Y-yes sir" Anthony mumbled.

"I will tell Santa him and I have it in you can ask Paul I already told Santa about his fire fighter truck love."

"Oh Uncle Ken" Ana smiled "Uncle Marc says you owe him a chess game" Ana stifled a laugh as Uncle Christian involuntarily shuddered.

"I know I do" He laughed "That old fool thinks he can actually win."

"So", Uncle Christian changed the subject, "Who is coming tonight?"

"Everyone; Ky, Liz and the baby are flying in today we have to pick them up around five. Mom came in yesterday and Dad has been driving me nuts since he got here." Mr. Wittson hesitated "Also Fred and Juliet."

At the mention of my grandparents Uncle Christian seized a breath that looked like he was barely letting any air in our out. "Il Mio Piccolo sapere?"

Mr. Wittson laughed.

"Oh sorry, does my little one know?"

"It is ok after this long I can pick out when you're talking about J.J., but yes or well she will we voted Hen tell her at the football game."

Uncle Christian nodded "Well we better be off we still have to get to Wal-Mart and back in time for the boys game or Mio Piccolo and Bella will have my head."

Wal-Mart was packed Anthony had a death grip on Ana and I had a death grip on the cart. Unlike Paul he didn't want everything green and over alls. He liked black cargo pants and dark solid color long sleeve shirts. I offered him out fits with super heroes and cartoon characters on them but he insisted he didn't want them. He chose boxers over briefs witch excited Paul. I got him an extra suit to go with the one Dave bought him. He made a face at every sneaker I showed him, the pair Aunt Amy had grabbed had been labeled wrong and were way to big.

"I want boots like yours" He explained.

"We can get you both, but you need sneakers too, boots are not allowed at the school you will attend when you leave the program and I am almost positive Dave would prefer you wear sneakers also."

Uncle Christian laughed "They made that rule in June 2003."

I raised an eyebrow at him "Twenty-four years ago?"

"Yep I had to where sneakers my final year."

"Why did they make that rule?"

"Picture the twins with steel cased work boots at school."

An involuntary shutter went through me "I see their point."

Anthony finally picked a pair of light up sneakers while Paul sat in the cart playing with them we got boots and bedding. It took a while to find a space theme. I held my breath as Anthony and Ana ran through the isle a top speed to make Paul squeal.

"Her mother is showing in her" Uncle Christian laughed. "Are you ok?"

I looked at him in disbelief "Um no there is way too many people in here."

"That's not the ok I meant, a blind person can see that you are shaking."

"Grazie (Thanks), Yeah, I am ok with that. Look at her Uncle Christian, how could I not want to be with her for the rest of my life?"

He smiled "I feel the same about my love so much so that I don't even care that I am not the one she is with."

"Are you going to tell me who your love is yet? And don't say my mother I have two mothers."

He laughed "It is of no importance who my love is, just that she is happy and her love takes good care of her."

We headed to school supplies that took forever finding things that weren't pink and a backpack that Anthony liked and Uncle Christian felt had proper back support. They finally agreed on a black and red sling strap model with a built in pencil and laptop case. We went to health and beauty next for his tooth brush; that took nearly twice as long as the backpack as Anthony wanted some sort of sing tooth brush and Uncle Christian insisted finding a singing one that was electronically safe and dentist approved. After fifteen minutes he finally found one; and we head towards toys.

"Care to tell me who iron man is?" Uncle Christian asked Anthony, steering him toward the iron man display."

"He's . . . . IRON MAN!" He stared to run to the display then froze.

"It's ok Anthony" Ana picked him up "You can run to the display" She held him tight. "Let's go over together and pick them."

"I get one?"

"Yes, but don't you need two a good guy and bad guy?"

"I get two?"

"Yes, oOo look at this guy he's ugly he must be a bad guy is he good?"

"He's the best bad guy there is" He grabbed Iron man himself. Ana sat him in the back of the carriage with his cloths and talked with him as they walked.

I smiled watching Ana and Anthony play and talk all the way through the toy isles as he relaxed again. Uncle Christian and I went to pets he was getting a new heating lamp for Kenny's iguana, lizard, whatever reptile he owned and I went to get out of the over crowed toy section.

The foot ball game was the last of the season and at half time we were up by twelve making me wonder how the opposing team had made states. Mom closed her eyes every time someone jumped on the beasts and Mama yelled at the referees. Paul had fallen asleep and Anthony was watching in rapt excitement.

"Daddy, who is winning?" Anthony bounced up and down.

"We are" Nick scowled.

"Don't sound so happy" I frowned at him.

"You're not sitting near queen of the air heads"

I stifled a laugh just barely.

Uncle Donavan and Uncle Christian on the other hand didn't not pretending to laugh at something else.

"Don't let Kenny catch you saying that" I sighed; but I had already lost him, all he knew was his girlfriend was keeping score.

At Ana's uncle Ken's the boys and I changed in to our dress suits, we met Ana back down stairs; my heart skipped a beat at the sight of her in her gown. She also had new earrings and a new necklace that complimented the dress nicely.

"Uncle Kyle gave them to me" She beamed "Oh you have to see baby Kyle he looks just like Auntie Liz."

Anthony looked around and clung to me, Paul looked around and spotted Nana and ran over yelling "Great Grammy" and jumped in her arms.

I took Anthony over to the chess table where Uncle Marc was in the middle of a game, Uncle Christian and Uncle Donavan were watching. Instantly Uncle Christian pulled Anthony into his lap closest to Uncle Marc. I whispered thank-you and took off to find Ana's Uncle Kyle.

My brothers, K-4, Jeremiah, Adam and Jr. were up in K-4's room and they all swore they hadn't seen Dr. Wittson. Ms. Nikki, Ms. Liz, Mrs. Wittson, Auntie Kate, Mom, Mama, Ana, Sam, Kimberly, and Aunt Amy were all in the kitchen cooking.

"About ten or twenty minutes" Mrs. Wittson said pushing me out of the kitchen.

"But . . . but . . ." I tried and gave up. Ana's and my grandparents were in the living room so I checked there.

"Paul is out back with Henry and Davie" Grandma told me.

"Um thanks, I am more than sure Paul is fine he makes his presence known. Have you seen Uncle Chris?"

"Oh those boys," Ana's grandma laughed "Him and Kyle are on the front porch."

"Thank you Ma'am" I rushed outside taking deep heaving breaths of crisp cold air.

"Easy killer you shouldn't have gone shopping today" Uncle Chris caught me.

"I'm alright" I slowed down. "Dr. Wittson, congratulations on your son, he is gorgeous."

"Thank you and congratulations on your boys. My brother won't let me near Anthony until you're in there, but Paul is adorable and so friendly. Also I hear that you are proposing to me niece tonight."

"Yes sir."

"Seeking my blessing?" Dr. Wittsom asked.

"Yes sir"

"As her God Father you have my blessing."

"Thank you sir"

"Alex look at me breathe slowly in through the nose and out through the mouth." He pushed a strand of his white-blonde hair out of his eyes. "Good, good, again that's better."

"Thank you sir." I hated hyperventilating. "Come meet Anthony."

Upon our return to the house Uncle Christian and Uncle Donovan had moved with Anthony to the living room. Anthony was peeking into the port-a-crib.

Ana's uncle knelt down. He was the only person I knew taller than me and that was only by two inches. "Hi Anthony, I am your Great Uncle Kyle, that is my son Kyle Jr. you are looking at."

Anthony looked at him, "He is so tiny."

"He is only three days old."

"Oh, you're Ana's Uncle that was in England."

"Yes I am, I had a job over there and then me girlfriend and I visited me mum for a spell."

Anthony's eyes went wide at the slight switch in accent I know longer noticed in my own uncles. "You sound funny."

Dr. Wittson laughed "I am English. I live here but when I was your age I lived in England half of the year and here the other half."

"Oh, Daddy and Uncle Christian are Italian."

"Your Dad is Italian and English."

"Really?" Anthony looked at me.

"I guess my mothers don't tell me about their childhoods" I shrugged.

Uncle Marc frowned at me "Yes Anthony your Nana is English. And Alex you best not be pushing your mothers about their choice not to tell you everything." He gave me a look that said I better not push him either "Go tell the boys upstairs it is dinner and if my two are smart they will be the first two to the table.

"Yes, Sir" I gulped.

"Marc" Dr. Wittson stood extending his arms for a hug, taking the focus off me "Good to see you."

"Good to have you back home, Dad was worried. Go tell C.J. it is dinner time, before Mum and Juliet have a fit."

"Don't let me mum hear you disrespecting your mum like that."

Paul sat between Uncle Christian and me eating as if he had never seen food a day in his life. Anthony sat between Ana and I shaking like a leaf. I was fiddling with the ring box in my pocket.

"Uncle Kork may I please have more" Anthony mumbled.

"Of course Sweetie eat up; there is plenty" Mrs. Wittson said piling food on his plate.

"Head phones" Ana's Grandmother said "That's what we did for you and your mama Al, worked brilliantly."

"It still does Mum" Mama said.

"Marc Ramond Williams Jr.! I hear that again you are grounded indefinitely" Aunt Kate yelled.

Everyone looked.

"He has too much his father in him."

"Good cleansing fix him" Ana's granddad said.

Every one of my uncles, my mama, Ana's dad, and Ana's uncles all grimaced and shuttered. Uncle Donavan laughed, I just raised an eyebrow.

"Let me tell you, Dad, I am just about there with them" Uncle Marc shook his head.

"Juliet, please pass the potato?" Ana's granddad sighed "Worked for you boys."

I tapped my glass, I couldn't wait any longer or I would self combust. I cleared my throat and stood up "As you all know Ana and I have been d-dating" The room or my head or both started to spin I felt Uncle Christian steady me. "Have been dating for quite a while on and off now and with her father and Godfather's blessing;" I knelt in front of Ana "Ana will you marry me?"

Ana shrieked and passed out, Anthony covered his ears and looked at me. I looked at Uncle Christian confused.

"Way too much Henry in her" Uncle Marc laughed.

"Oi I resemble that, I would like it noted that only Mum and Ana passed out" Ana's dad objected.

"Dad" David sighed "You fainted when Al asked for your blessing."

"Smelling salt" Mr.Wittson offered.

"Er, thank-you, was that a yes?" I looked at Sam who had been sitting on the other side of Ana; but she was still holding her ears.

"I'd say so," Colt laughed, "But wake her up and see if she does it again; it was hilarious to see that look on your face."

"COLT DANIEL WILLIAMS" Growled Mama, "PORCH NOW!"

I ran the smelling salt under Ana's nose; she came around slowly. "Hi beautiful" I smiled at her.

"You . . . you . . . you proposed" She stammered.

"Yeah, and you fainted."

She laughed a little and fainted again.

I looked at Uncle Christian who just shrugged.

Sam finally done holding and rubbing her ears said "The scream was a yes, lord only knows why but she told you yes."

Mr. Wittson shot Sam a "behave yourself look".

"Just put her in the living room, Al, she will come around soon" Her father shook his head.

After dinner we all gathered in the living room; sitting and standing around the Christmas tree to open gifts to and from our Aunts, Uncles, and grandparents. Mama had finally allowed Colt back inside for a moment I thought she was going to make him stand out there all night. We all put our names in a hat to see who would pass out the presents.

Mrs. Wittson pulled the name out "Ken?" She looked at all four Kens.

"Not me Mom, I wrote K-4" K-4 said.

"Tis I" Ana's granddad laughed "My father has passed, I am 67 years old and my son is not smart enough to go by his given name so I felt I could go by just Ken finally."

"Of course Sir" Mrs. Wittson blushed.

"Besides Jessi's boy goes by Kenny."

Mrs. Wittson blushed harder and sat by Auntie Kate.

"To Paul from Grammy and I" He handed Paul a large box.

"Thank-you Grandpa" Paul hugged his leg."

"You're welcome sit and be patient we open once all the presents are passed out. Donavan can you please turn on the tree lights and the over head my eyes are getting old."

"Yes, Sir" Uncle Don obliged.

I watched as the piles grew, Paul never left the large package from Ana's granddad. Anthony sat in between Ana and I shaking. Out of nowhere Uncle Marc plopped head phones on his ears.

"Me mum told you, earlier to put head phones on him" Uncle Marc said.

I looked up and nodded.

"It's just kid songs."

I nodded again and after a few minutes Anthony did start to relax.

Finally all the presents were passed out, it was tradition to start with the youngest and open one gift and go youngest to oldest opening one gift until all the gifts were gone as the youngest two were sleeping in a port-a-crib we started with Paul. Paul chose to open the large gift he had been given by Ana's granddad. He tore at the paper with fierce determination; it was a large hulk play set.

"LOOK, DADDY, LOOK!" He bounced up and down, he started to open another.

I stopped him "Not yet, Anthony will open his from Sir now."

I think Anthony was more impressed with the wrapping paper as he opened it slow trying not to rip the paper then folded it gently before looking at his new telescope scope set.

"Thank-you Sir" Anthony said just above a whisper.

"Sir was my father, I am Grandpa" He hugged Anthony "You are very welcome."

Anthony sat running his fingers over the telescope as he waited to open his next gift. After him it went Colt, Nick, Jr., Jeremiah, K-4, The Beasts, Adam, Kenny, Sam, Ana, me, Kimberly, David, Ms. Liz, Ana's uncle Kyle, Ms. Nikki, Mom, Mama, Uncle Chris, Aunt, Amy, Ana's dad, Uncle Mike, Uncle Christian, Mrs. Wittson, Auntie Kate, Mr. Wittson, Uncle Donavan, Uncle Marc, My grandmother, Ana's grandmother, and ended with Ana's granddad. About half way through I noticed that not only Mom and Uncle Christian's gifts but Dr. Wittson's gifts also said Blessed Yule instead of Merry Christmas.

Paul passed out playing with a wooden fire truck from Uncle Marc and Anthony passed out hugging his telescope. Ana had finally put on her ring and stopped fainting, I was organizing my new books and pile of gift cards; I had apparently become hard to shop for according to Uncle Mike.

At midnight Ana carried Paul and I carried Anthony back home. We laid them both in Paul's bed as Anthony's wasn't redone in his bedding yet. And the stack of bags on the table said so. I left the boys with Ana as I ran back to get the stack of stuff from tonight; Ana had gotten some nice jewelry. When I got back Ana had taken all the tags of Anthony's new clothes and was hanging them in the closet. I took his books and put them on the self and together we sorted the toys and games in to the appropriate places.

By the time we were done it was almost two. Mom and Mama had just come in.

"We will watch the boys for you if you wish to go back" Mama offered.

"I am tired" I shook my head "I can hear my bed calling me."

"Ok well if you change your mind or need us we are in our room" Mom smiled.

"Thank-you" Ana smiled "Uncle Kork gave me the book I had been wanting and Al's arms are my favorite place to read so I am headed to his bed too."

Mama laugh with a knowing look in her eyes "You to sleep well."

CHAPTER 26
CHRISTMAS EVE

I SLEPT SOLIDLY AND WHEN I went down to shower in the morning Uncle Christian, Anthony, and Paul were eating breakfast. Uncle Donavan was passed out in his news paper and Uncle Chris was asleep on the couch. As every other Christmas Eve my brothers were passed out between here and Mr. Wittson's. Colt was a sleep in the middle of the door way his legs hanging down the stairs.

"I'd move him, but Jr. would fall down the stairs" Uncle Christian said.

I raised an eye brow and looked for myself sure enough if we were to move Colt, Jr. would fall and there was no way around Colt to lift Jr. first.

By noon everyone was up dressed and ready today we would visit my grandparents. Mom was not thrilled about going to her mother's house, I didn't ask my Uncle Christian respected Uncle Marc and neither one of them would be happy if I did not respect my mothers' choices and pushed them to talk about things they did not wish to. Paul and Anthony were getting tired of dress clothes and quite frankly so was I. Ana was in another gown just as gorgeous as the day before.

By the time we got to Mom's mom the boys were getting tired and I asked Grandma if I could put Paul somewhere to sleep before dinner. She put him in Uncle Josh's room; Anthony chose to lie next to him.

I waited patiently for Uncle Josh to have a moment to play pool. After dinner the boys watched Uncle Josh and I play. Kenny kept telling Anthony to do the opposite of everything I did.

Once again by the time we got home Paul and Anthony were asleep. I carried in Paul and Uncle Chris carried Anthony in. We laid out the gifts we had bought for everyone and then I laid with Ana until she fell asleep as she had a migraine. I was too wired to sleep. I went to sit on the roof and watch the snow fall. I could hear my brothers sledding and my parents talking on the porch. I looked out at the stars enjoying the peaceful night.

"Penny for your thoughts" Uncle Mike sat down next to me.

I jumped a good two feet.

"Breathe I just saw you up here and figured I would come talk to you."

"Sorry, it's so peaceful up here I get lost in the silence."

He laughed "Your Mama use to say that, she'd sleep up here in the summer."

"Uncle Marc let her" I asked, strongly doubting my over protective high strung uncle would ever allow my mama anywhere but a bubble wrap padded room.

"Oh no" He shook his head laughing "He worked second and third shift, while Kork watched us and worked mother's hours. Back then there was three shifts and minum wages was $7.25 an hour."

"Wow, no one could live on that now. How long were the shifts?"

"Couldn't then either, all of us worked to make ends meet, we weren't born into wealth or even middle class. First shift was from seven am to three pm, second shift was from three pm to eleven pm and third shift was from eleven pm to seven am."

"No wonder you worked so hard you only worked eight hours a day now you work seven to seven. What are mother's hours?"

"They were nine am to three pm Monday through Friday."

"Kind of like what Ana has?"

"No, Ana has more of a nine to five."

"A what?"

"A nine to five job; you worked Monday through Friday from nine am to five pm in an office."

"Oh so how did Mama get up here if no one was letting her?"

He laughed deep and hard "Your Mothers weren't so sweet and innocent angels especially your mama."

"My mama is a nice, polite, sweet, warm, helpful, loving woman" I started to protest.

"Now, now she is all that and more, after twenty-one almost twenty-two years as a mother and fifteen years of marriage. Alex, your mother has grown into an elegant woman, and I never doubted for a minute that she wouldn't but it doesn't mean she started off that way. No one starts life as a well rounded adult and sometimes some people never make the adult part."

"Was she like Uncle Chris and the beasts?"

"To an extent, she was hyper and crazy like C.J., but events of our life made her mean and violent too and she had the fists and boots to back it up."

"Boots?" I raised an eye brow.

"Yes, army grade steel case boots, it is all she wore. She kicked C.J. and Christian so much I wasn't sure they would remain boys. The school had to band boots other than snow boots because her senior year she broke some kids shin. Not that C.J. was angel."

"So she's the reason . . ."

"Yep now it's late and tomorrow is Christmas go get rest and oh Marc says to tell you no digging."

"Thanks tell Uncle Marc it isn't digging if it's offered."

CHAPTER 27

CHRISTMAS

I SLEPT SO POORLY ALL night; I woke before everyone else pacing around the house peeking in my stocking and at the things under the tree.

Around six-thirty Uncle Christian came out and looked at me incredulously "You are going to wake Donavan."

"Sorry" I blushed "I am excited."

"I noticed; would you like some breakfast."

"I'm good; I made you coffee and waffles" I beamed.

He nodded hugging me "Merry Christmas nephew."

"Merry Chris . . . . Blessed Yule."

He laughed "Which ever you wish to tell me. You know I did the same thing your first Christmas. Kork thought I had lost my mind. You were a good baby always happy and I got you a fisher price motor cycle. You smiled and sucked the handle bar you were only ten months old."

I laughed.

"I have a picture of it" He added cream and sugar to his coffee.

"Can I look in my sock now?"

"You get out of that!" He frowned, "You know better"

"I added more to Mom and Mama's stockings"

"I noticed" He threw files on the table.

"Working on Christmas?" Uncle Don joined us.

"Proofing, Bella has a meeting tomorrow morning."

I leaned over and looked at the cover page it was the new one my copy was in my car unmercifully buried doomed until spring by the fresh coat of snow.

"Ooo a white Christmas" Uncle Chris yawned joining us.

"Merry Christmas Uncle Chris" I smiled.

"Merry Christmas Al, Don; Blessed Yule Christian" He made himself cup of coffee to go with his waffles.

"Merry Christmas little man" Uncle Christian hugged Uncle Chris "I am going to see if Bella and Mio Piccolo are awake."

"Daaadddddy" Anthony came running down the hall Paul close behind him.

"Daddy it Christmas" Paul yawned.

I laughed scooping them up "Merry Christmas boys"

"I don't know about anyone else, but I could have sworn I heard sleigh bells last night" Uncle Donavan smiled at them.

"SANTA?" Anthony jumped down and ran to the living room half dragging Paul. He came back at full speed bouncing up and down "Daddy, Daddy Santa came, Santa came."

I smiled "Go wake Ana and Uncle Kenny."

I listened to them run up the stairs yelling "Get up Santa came its morning get up."

"How's it feel *Daddy*?" Mom joined us in the kitchen.

"Blessed Yule, Mom, It feels incredible; so awesome I don't know how to explain it."

She laughed "Sounds about right, Merry Christmas."

"Hey *Daddy* get up, Hey *Daddy* Santa came, Hey *Daddy* shut the alarm clock off" Kenny threw balled up socks at my head.

I laughed "Merry Christmas Kenny."

The twins fell down the stairs yelling Merry Christmas, Nick and Colt behind them and Paul on Christopher's back. Ana came down after with Anthony telling her everything he saw under the tree. Mama was peeking in her stocking.

"Mio Piccolo" Uncle Christian frowned at her laughing.

When everyone was ready we sat and everyone opened their socks my mothers both believed Christmas socks were for toys and within seconds there were nine sticky hands flying around the room. Unwrapping presents took about two hours, Paul kept trying to stop and play with each new toy and so did Anthony. They were cute and Mama got some good photos. Around ten-thirty Ana's father and David came over and Uncle Christian started dinner. Paul rode in circles around the house on his tricycle in his new pirate dress up outfit. Anthony had curled up near Nick reading his comic books; Nick was reading something as well. Colt, Christopher and Christian had gone outside to play with their new paintball guns. Kenny was organizing his gifts in to weird neat little piles at the back of the tree; I never questioned it he always did that, before pulling out a model car or puzzle. I set down my new drum sticks and helped Mama clean up.

Ms. Nikki, Uncle Marc's family, Uncle Mike and Aunt Amy arrived just before dinner. Paul had changed out of the pirate into a fire fighter costume; two points to Nana he loved the dress up set. He ran past me with a new fire truck in one hand and a remote control to the one on the floor in the other. Anthony was playing with his action figures and I was cleaning a sea of plastic wrappings.

After dinner Savannah tried to make friends with Paul but Kimberly shoved her in a port-a-crib for a nap. The rest of Ana's family came, Adam, Jr., K-4, Nick, and Jeremiah joined Colt, Christopher, and Christian outside with their new paint ball guns. Sam and Ana were loudly and competitively playing a video game. I was now cleaning a sea of match box track wrappings.

"Clean later" Uncle Don frowned "This mess will be here when you get to it your son's will not."

"Yes, sir" I nodded; I put the trash down and played chutes and ladders with Anthony. Then helped Paul build a castle with his blocks that his cars could drive through, then went to help Anthony with another hot wheels track and showed him how his Nerf gun worked.

By the time every one left, at nine, Paul had passed out in a police officer outfit one car in one hand and the hand with the police car in the castle tunnel. Anthony had passed out hugging his action figures. I removed the toys from their hands and carried them to their beds. Then I picked up more packaging and toys putting the packaging in the trash and the toys neatly under the tree.

"You look awful," Ana laughed, "What time did you get up?"

"Three," I smiled, "I couldn't wait."

She laughed running her hand down my chest.

"Hi"

"Hi as in hi lets go to the roof and watch the stars" She smiled hopefully.

I laughed when we were in high school that was our code for going up to the roof to make out, because her dad didn't want her dating until she was eighteen. I pulled her into my arms and kissed up her neck and whispered in her ear "Or we could just go up to the room and turn the radio up."

She blushed "Um yeah that would work too."

CHAPTER 28

DECEMBER 26, 2027

I STRETCHED SMILING EAR TO ear and ran a hand through Ana's hair moving it out of her face. At my feet Anthony was playing with his coloring book and crayons. "Hey why didn't you wake me?" I asked him.

"You were sleeping."

"Um yeah but . . . never mind have you had breakfast?"

"No should I have, I can go down and get food."

"What? No . . . I . . . let's go get breakfast."

He nodded.

I lifted him and he lifted his army of toys, I carried him down stairs and set him in the living room. I looked at the food calendar and started the coffee pot making enough waffles for Anthony, me, and whoever was outside chopping wood. I checked on Paul he would defiantly be up soon it was only seven thirty. I made more waffles knowing that my uncles and Paul would want food and coffee the second they were up.

"Breakfast looks delicious, Sweetie," Mom hugged me. She had been the one outside as she was dressed and had her gloves on. "It's warm enough out today to take the boys up to the stables after my meeting."

"Um sounds good but I don't know what Ana has planed" I looked up from my book.

"Understood," She hugged me tighter, "My baby boy all grown up."

"Mom" I blushed.

"Mmm, I smell that" Uncle Chris smiled "This plate mine?" He took a plate and sat down, next to Anthony, Mom sat on Uncle Chris' other side. Anthony was aiming his Nerf gun at his action figures.

"Good morning" Mama joined us in the kitchen. Anthony and I both stood to greet her.

"Breakfast?" I asked.

"No thank-you, Dear, I will get my own." Mama always had Kix sometimes I would see her have bacon or waffle with it but, always Kix. She sat as close to Mom as possible, but didn't look too awake yet.

Around quarter to eight Paul came out. "Uncle Nick I hungry" He yawned.

"Nick is still asleep, Sweetie, what can I get you?" Mama asked him.

Paul looked around and crawled in to his booster seat. "Daddy what's breakfast?"

"Waffles, greet your grandparents; while I get them."

He made a face but did as he was told.

At exactly eight the door bell rang.

"That will be Frederica" Mom rushed to the intercom. "Morning" She said into the intercom.

"Best seller, this one will top the best seller list." Rica's voice came through the speaker.

"Come up and meet my grandsons, we can talk up here instead of in the studio my younger boys are still asleep." Mom usually spoke to her agent down stairs in the studio because the beasts were loud.

Mom's Agent Frederica or as she preferred Rica was a Latina lady with short puffy dark brown curls. She had grown up in Manhattan and it showed, she drank large amounts of espresso, smoked two packs a day, had large fake nails, wore tight in fashion business suits and never stayed still longer than thirty seconds.

"I have my husband with me."

"Bring him up we have coffee."

I cleared the breakfast plates to make a clean spot at the table for Mom and Rica to talk and made more coffee, Uncle Don could drink a pot himself. Anthony had rearranged his action figures but still had them under fire of the Nerf gun. He had started to relax more but still didn't let me or his toys out of his site. Paul on the other hand was unaware that anyone or thing but he and his fire truck existed and ran around the house making fire truck noises.

I sat down near Mama making a "to do list", listening to Mom and Rica speak. Frederica kept saying things like best yet, money maker and best seller. Sometimes I wondered if she new Mom didn't write for fame and money she wrote because it is what she liked. They decided that the book tour would kick off on January twenty-fifth in Wisconsin and end February thirteenth in Boston, Mass. Coinciding with Mama's gay pride event; they also made sure that the seventh of February Mom would be in state for her birthday. Mama said she wouldn't be accompanying her this time as she had deadlines of her own to make, but Uncle Chris volunteered to go with her.

"Hi" Paul said sticking his hand in Frederica's face. "Are you the lady everyone wants to like Grandma's book?"

I blushed "Sorry Mom, Sorry Rica; Paul that was very rude apologize to Grandma and Mrs. Gomez right now."

"Sorry grandma, sorry Mrs. Go . . . Go . . ." He looked at me, "Go . . ."

"Gomez, Pumpkin" Rica smiled at him.

"I am so sorry, Mom" I picked Paul up.

"Alex, take a deep breath, he is fine think about all the things you and your brothers did when they were little from accidents to fighting, what Paul did was minor."

"And he is right I am the person who has to like the book," Rica added "But little man agent is the polite word."

Mom laughed "Rica this is my grandson Paul and over there with the Nerf gun on the floor under the tree is my other Grandson Anthony."

"Daddy where's Ana?" Anthony said after hearing his name.

"Excuse me I 'm going to take these guys up stairs, sorry again." I walked over to Anthony so I could hear him better "Ana is still a sleep come on out and we will go up to her."

He grabbed all his toys again and followed Paul and I up the stairs to Ana. I set Paul down and lifted Anthony.

"MOMMY!" Paul jumped in to Ana's arms.

"Ooff" She groaned "Morning Paul." She laughed "Where is Daddy?"

"I'm right here" I laughed my phone went off I set Anthony on the bed and stepped out of the room to answer it as Kenny was probably still asleep. "Williams"

"MERRY CHRISTMAS DOG BREATH!" Genevieve yelled in my ear.

"Merry Christmas to you too Genevieve."

"We don't celebrate Christmas, we celebrate Yule . . ."

"Ok then Blessed Yule" I laughed I could tell someone had already given her chocolate today.

"Ok bye Dog Breath I have to go I get to go to work with Andy today and you don't" She said hanging up.

I went back in to the room laughing Ana raised an eye brow at me. "Andy and Genevieve say Merry Christmas; Genevieve is defiantly being spoiled."

"Ms. Den O Vieve plays cars good" Paul smiled

"Well, silly, she plays cars well" Ana laughed tickling Paul.

"Ana's not mad, we woke her?" Anthony mumbled.

"Why would I be mad?" She looked at me like I had eight heads "I would never be mad because you and Paul want time with me. I would rather spend time with you two than sleep in." She sat up and shifted Paul so she could see Anthony better. "Oh you brought your friends up what do you want to play?"

"Kooties" Paul yelled.

"You come with me, mister man; you can help me make Ana some breakfast."

He giggled playing with my hair; as we left I saw Anthony crawl in to Ana's arms. He need the bonding time with her.

"Morning Ana" Kenny yelled over the divider.

"Morning Kenny, I am sorry if we woke you" She answered.

"No you didn't, share a room with Al you can sleep through anything. Who do you have with you; Al and Paul are not that quiet."

"I have Anthony, we are coloring."

"Cool, Morning Anthony."

"Morning Uncle Kenny" Anthony mumbled.

"Wow, Al is going to have to let Christian and Christopher teach him how to make some noise" Kenny laughed "I can barely hear him."

"He's just shy" Ana hugged Anthony, "What are you up to today?"

"Julie and I are going to lunch."

"Are you staying at Juliet's for the day?"

"No just lunch because then I have to work, I don't want to but my boss has me doing inventory for the next week."

"I hear you when I go back to work I will probably have fifty stacks of paper work."

By noon Anthony had relaxed again and was setting up the board game Uncle Mike had got him called Beware of the Dog so he and Ana could play with Nick and Colt. Ana despite Paul's many protest of not needing a nap and being a big boy, was definitely putting him down for his nap that he very much did need. I sat down at the kitchen table to sort my thoughts out.

"Care to share them?" Uncle Donavan sat next to me.

"Sir?" I looked at him.

"Your thoughts . . . ."

"Are unmercifully tangled" I sighed cutting him off.

He nodded "I may not be Christian but may I take a stab at helping you"

I nodded.

"You're scared about leaving Anthony tomorrow; don't be he will be fine. You wouldn't isolate any other of the kids you work with you would tell their parents that they need to be treated like everyone else and they have to learn the routine of their house hold if they wish to have any chance of adjusting enough to come home."

I sighed he was right.

"You're afraid that you won't be a good father."

I nodded.

"That's stronzate!" He swore; good thing it was not in English Mama would have yelled at him. "You don't need to worry about that you are already a great father."

I looked at my feet, I didn't think anyone but Uncle Christian could read me so well.

"Also you're worrying about getting everything for a wedding you don't even have a date yet for; don't even pay that mind if it is meant to happen all the pieces of that will fall in to place on their own."

I nodded "Where is Uncle Christian?"

"On the roof" He sighed; digging through the mail he had just brought in. "Enough fan mail to kill again" He muttered.

I ran up to the roof, when Ana came out of Paul's room. Uncle Donavan was right but he wasn't Uncle Christian and I wanted Uncle Christian. I fond Uncle Christian meditating; so I sat down next to him and meditated with him. When he tapped my shoulder three hours latter for dinner other than cold and stiff I felt much better; mostly less anxious over nothing.

"Dinner" He said and went in without another conversation.

I followed, wondering what was bothering him as he was normally not withdrawn when it came to us boys. I hugged my boys who were already at the table. Mama had made barbeque chicken, rice, corn, and biscuits with garlic butter.

Nick had invited his girlfriend, Margret; she looked scared and very small compared to my brothers.

"Hi Al," She squeaked "How's my sister?"

I nearly choked on my milk "Pardon?"

"I know she has a problem, I know she isn't on some special field trip, Mom does too but will wait until Sadie tells her, herself."

I nodded "I just didn't hear you over Christopher and Colt. Sadie is doing well she had a meeting with her doctor and consoling today. I can take you to see her Friday if you would like."

Nick held her hand to reassure her.

"No thank-you, this is not the first time she has done this she prefers we stay 'clueless' until she tells us."

"Ok, you know I don't bite you can relax" I looked at her she was shaking almost as bad as I do in a crowded grocery store.

"No Sadie does."

"I have noticed" I laughed.

"Sorry" She squeaked, she didn't say another thing to me all of dinner.

After dinner Christian and Christopher spent time drawing with Anthony and Paul; then I bathed them and Ana put them to bed. Uncle Christian was back on the roof so I would have to wait to speak to him.

"Work tomorrow" Ana kissed me pulling me out of my thoughts "You're going to be bored with no one . . ."

"Buddy," I cut her off, "Amelia and the level ones."

"Oh and we have that thing for Anthony."

"I know Mama is driving him in for it . . ." My cell phone cut me off "Williams" I answered.

"Al, it's Will I need help. It's Sam, Spike found him beaten on the side of the road they have their meetings at."

"Where are you?"

"Bottom of your drive way, witch house is Dr . . . ."

"Stay there on my way" I hung up and threw shoes on.

"Al, Hunny?" Ana looked at me.

"Will, Sam hurt. At Gas station, I'll be back."

"Ok, I will stay with the boys" She smiled still slightly confused.

When I got down the hill I found Will, Sam, and Spike; Will was holding Sam and I would have put money on a broken leg. I took Sam and guided them to Ana's Uncle's house and nearly pounded the door down.

"Whoa Alex, what's wrong . . ." He stopped at the sight of Sam "Liz clear the couch and get my bag please." Ana once told me that her uncle's doctor bag had been her great-great grandfather's back when it was mostly house calls.

Dr. Wittson was what Uncle Chris called and old fashion physician which is what made him such a good doctor. He was the only doctor I ever new or heard of other than his father that made house calls. He was thorough and preferred old fashion remedies to new drugs but accepted and used some of the newer medicines. He was constantly going back to school to learn more and had been featured in several medical magazines. He also had license to practice medicine in more than one country, but what I liked most of all was he was non judgmental, down to earth and a genuinely nice guy.

I laid Sam on the couch and then let Wilson burry his face in my shoulder; it was odd I could feel every tense move he made and how upset he was but I didn't push him away. Spike was trying to blend in to the wall.

"Spike you can't hide from me, go sit in the kitchen with Liz I am sure she will make you a sandwich" Dr. Wittson said not taking his eyes of what he was doing.

"I didn't do it" Spike squeaked.

"I didn't think you did, go relax, Liz call Kork see if Dad is still there, please"

Ms. Liz handed him the phone, she was feeding the baby. "Come on you two" She said to Will and Spike half dragging Spike.

"No . . . Jason's youngest boy got jumped . . . no . . . no . . . I'd say ribs and defiantly leg I can see bone . . . no . . . He's breathing ragged but not impaired . . . pneumonia, yeah that would." I listened to Dr. Wittson talk on the phone. "My guess it's down here ok . . . Kork . . . yes Sir . . . ok five minutes Don's truck."

Five minutes later we left Spike and Will to calm down; and were standing waiting by Uncle Don's pickup truck. I had called Wilson's wife so she didn't worry and Dr. Wittson had called Sam and Will's mom so she would meet him at the hospital.

"Wrap him gently Kyle" Ana's granddad handed Dr. Wittson a pile of quilts.

Dr. Wittson had me lay Sam gently in the back of the truck. "Ok," he hopped up in the truck bed near Sam "You go on home, I have it, if his mom . . ."

"The center, Dave will" I cut him off.

"I know, Dave use to keep his uncle from starvation and freezing to death" He sighed.

When I got home Ana was in bed and Uncle Christian was still on the roof, I checked the chore chart so I didn't miss anything and sighed debating to go bother my uncle or wait.

"He is sulking" Uncle Donavan said from behind his paper. "Is it something I can help you with?"

"Um no thank-you, just wished to tell him good night."

"Well he's up on that roof, he sulks well when his ego is injured, always has."

"Er, ok"

"Good night"

I nodded "Night."

"They are in their room and C.J. went down to Mike's."

I shivered.

"Stop thinking about my survival instincts and go to bed you need to get some rest" He ordered.

I looked at him and shuttered; then practically ran up the stairs. Kenny was at his desk homework I assumed as his classes had started back up. Ana was reading while she waited for me.

"You're going to be exhausted tomorrow, baby" I smiled, stripping out of my clothes and climbing in to bed.

"So are you" She yawned placing her book on the night stand and her head on my chest.

"Yes, but I never get proper sleep" I held her close and turned out the light.

CHAPTER 29

WHY WOULD
HE THINK THAT?

I LAID FOR HOURS PLAYING absently with Ana's long soft beautiful brown hair. Shortly after I had shut my light out, Kenny had shut his out; and soon after that I heard his slow even breaths indicating he had fallen asleep. I closed my eyes still playing with Ana's hair and listened to my uncle crawl back in the attic window above my room and pace around sounding as if he was squaring off with the punching bag. Soon I was proven right and I let the sound of even Ana's even breathing, Kenny's wheezing and the creaking of my uncle's assault on the punching bag lull me to sleep. Although when the alarm went off I felt like I had barely slept for five minutes.

"You look awful, kiddo" Dave eyed me as I slammed the 'see me note' on his desk at noon.

I had spent the morning with Tiffany, Sam and Amelia; it had caused me to randomly involuntarily cringe. The thing for Anthony had been moved around seven times and was finally set for two-thirty. "I didn't do it, I don't have it, it's not my fault, and no we can't make it later Ana and I promised to help my parents with Anthony's half of his and Paul's room."

Dave laughed "I just would like you to take Spike down to Sam."

"I miss my Sammy" Spike was hiding half behind the door.

I grinded my teeth "Mohawk is asleep, but come on I wanted to speak to you anyway."

"Not a drug deal" He said automatically.

I rolled my eyes; I was way too tired for this. "I am not a lawyer, cop, or doctor" I sighed through my teeth.

Dave shoot me a look and I took what should have been a calming breath.

"I didn't . . ."

"Do it, see it, hear it, expect it, or plan it! I know it's called a hate crime." I growled losing my patients "Now please hush, follow and listen I have a migraine your boyfriend is asleep and I need to get back to the girls before they cause a riot."

He squeaked and followed me out the door.

Dave grabbed my arm "Take it easy Al, he is scared enough."

"Yeah, yeah," I sighed "Your Italians getting better."

"What's he doing here?" Tiny shrieked "This is probably his fault."

"It's not Friday" Tiffany growled.

Spike hid behind me and whispered "I didn't do it I was at work."

"Hush Amelia or you can go to Dave; Spike and I are going to talk you and Tiffany can either go to the family room and be patient or back to your rooms."

"Can I go back to my room Sadie was . . ."

"Yes" I cut Tiffany off "Amelia choose please or I . . ."

"Room" She quickly cutting me off fearing I would send her to Dave or worse to group.

"Good" I locked them each in their room, filled out the insubordinate reports for both of them starting with breakfast to their verbal attack on spike and the last of my patients. Then I took Spike to the family room where Mohawk finally coherent was watching discovery channel.

"I should be at school" He looked up at me.

"Only you, Sam" I sighed "I have all your school work.

Spike automatically curled around Sam carefully "I'm so, so sorry . . ."

"Its ok baby, you needed to work; did you make the meeting?" Sam ran his good hand through spikes hair.

"No are you kidding, I found you in a ditch, I think your brother thinks I'm crazy."

I laughed "Spike, Wilson isn't like that, he's probably going just as crazy he isn't paying me thirty a month for Sam's on and off care here for Sam to get jumped."

"Jumped ha more like pulverized" Sam muttered running his good hand down Spikes shoulder.

"Um Sam you probably shouldn't move too much" Sam had a broken arm, leg and ribs, he hated lying in the bed in his room so I had carried him to the family room, the superficial cuts and bruises stuck out from under his chest bandages and hair witch he was growing back out, his down mohawk was about two inches longer than the rest.

"I'm fine Al, my Spiky needs to see it's ok or he won't sleep"

I looked sky ward as Sam nearly choked Spike with his tongue.

Spike turned bright red "S-sorry Alex."

"He's raping you not me, why are you sorry" I was beyond arguing the PG rule and they weren't doing anything more than kiss and were the only ones in the room at the moment.

Sam clucked his tongue at me "He's over eighteen."

"Mm and you aren't so keep your clothes on. Your brother wants to know who and why so he can press . . ."

"NO!" Sam said "No police."

"More debt?"

"Kind of but not really, dealers . . ." Sam trailed off distracted by the pattern on Spikes shirt.

"They get nervous when you stop and go straight, they fear narcs" Spike gulped.

"Baby nothing about us is straight" Sam laughed.

Spike blushed harder.

"Sam take it easy on him" I laughed "He is going to die of embarrassment."

Spike turned near maroon.

"My sexy man likes cuddling and kissing, Al" Sam laughed laying his head against Spikes chest and yawning.

"Your brother won't like this" I shook my head.

"I know" He started kissing Spikes chest through his shirt "Do I get congical visits in prison warden."

I laughed "No and with your injuries I don't think you should try to . . ."

Spike blushed "I have to leave when Al does, Sam."

"I figured" Sam sighed snuggling him.

"Clothes on" I sighed and pointed to the camera "I have this thing for my son behave."

"Can I at least take off his Sh . . ."

"No Sam, ALL clothes on."

Spike's blush crept down his neck "I will just cuddle him to sleep."

"Mm Sleep not *sleep* you two" I shook my head. "Maybe a cold shower too" I added under my breath.

Ana met me out side Dave's office; Dave was standing there with Mom and Anthony. She had him in a dress suit and was fussing with his cow lick in his hair.

"Daddy!" He jumped in to my arms.

"Hey, kiddo how was your morning?"

Uncle Christian is like all nija all the time and Uncle Chris dropped his hammer on his foot when Miss Nikki kissed him and . . . and . . . and . . ."

"Uncle Chris always does that" I laughed.

"And Uncle Colt played video games with me. Paul only plays with Uncle Christian, your scary brothers weren't home and Uncle Kenny left before I got up and . . ."

"Kenny works and yeah they are scary" I laughed "I tried to convince your nana, when they were born, that they were scary and to sell them."

Mom shook her head at me.

"And Uncle Nick left with that girl that's afraid of you" He kept rattling on.

"I am glad you had fun" I set him down to hug Mom "Where's Uncle Christian and Mama?"

"Your uncle is turning his truck around near your snowmobile and your mother is home with Paul and Colt" Mom hugged me back.

"Thanks for bringing him, Mom. How was he today?"

"He is fine, you worry too much. I put his snowmobile gear in his room for when you leave."

"Thanks Mom."

"Mmhmm, Marc's coming Sunday after they get out of church. Also on the way home please stop and pick up your Mama's red paint your aunt has the right shade waiting."

Anthony, Ana, and I walked down to the counseling thing. I didn't like counseling or therapist or therapy offices, they were too small and confining. I paced like a caged lion in the waiting space while Steve spoke with Anthony alone first. It made my skin crawl, Anthony looked like his skin was crawling too when he came out to get us. By the end of the session I had caught the important things; his biggest fear was us not loving him and or us turning out to be like his biological mom. Ana got all mushy and teary hugging on to him tight. I thought the only thing he needed to be afraid of was being hugged to death every time he said that to Ana. I wasn't worried I knew it would take time for him to adjust. When it was over I took Anthony and bolted.

Ana looked at me and rolled her eyes "Sorry Anthony, your father is afraid of small offices and his emotions."

Anthony laughed "Are we going home?"

"Not quite I have one more thing to do today" I left him with Ana and ran to finish up.

As Spike promised he only cuddled Sam to sleep, I carried him back to his room and let Spike tuck him in.

"What's this?" Spike asked as I put my helmet on him.

"Snowmobile helmet did you enjoy yourself?" I answered.

"Of course he is my world. I love him. I love to hold him and watch him sleep and how much he likes school and learning and how smart he is."

"He is fifteen."

"And I am nineteen which is why I was so scared someone would blame me I would never . . ."

I looked at him "I didn't think you did and neither did Wilson seeing as you are still alive."

He squeaked.

"Yes, he finds his little brother very important to him and someone thought he should be legally allowed weapons. Now climb on"

Ana and Anthony were circling the parking lot and stopped by us "Taking him home, I'll see you after school."

"Are you taking him with you?"

"He's staying with Davie; they won't let me take him" She kissed me.

I blinked several times dazed.

Spike laughed.

"What?"

"You legal to drive like that?" He laughed harder.

"Hush and climb on."

He got on and held my shoulders gently.

"Are you aiming to fly off?"

"Um no."

"Then hold on tight my three year old holds tighter."

"But . . ."

"But nothing I am not worried or scared I don't care if you're gay and I'm not or if someone sees I care that you don't fall off."

"Um ok" He adjusted holding me in a bear hug.

"Better, now let's get you home she left Anthony with her brother."

"Is that bad?"

"No, but it could turn bad for me depending on what she told him and how late I am."

He laughed.

I stood looking down at David he was on his knees helping Anthony build a snowman.

"Alex, go home we are building a snowman, I will bring him home when we are done."

"I'll wait."

"Alex, go home your mama needs her paint cans."

I sighed "Anthony you ok here?"

"Yeah we are making a snowman, Daddy."

"Go home Alex" David practically growled at me.

Admitting defeat I hugged and kissed my son and went home. When I got up to the house the beasts, Nick and Colt had built snow forts and were in the middle of a war and I got pelted with four snow balls trying to get in the house.

"Sorry . . ."

". . . Alex" The beasts yelled.

I just shook off and threw a few back. Inside Mama had Paul playing drums. "Teaching him young?"

"Hey sweetie, just waiting on you, what took so long?"

"Sorry Mama didn't mean to worry you, my cell died at work and I had to take Spike home. Then David decided he is holding Anthony hostage."

I heard a large crash from the storage room and raised an eye brow.

"Tuo Zio (your uncle)" Mama mouthed as Paul started to beat on the drums again.

I cringed Paul had a long way to go before it was any real form of music, but he was having fun and that's what counted. I kissed the top of his head and hugged Mama. Then I cautiously walked toward the noise and peeked into the storage room. Mom was throwing things into a box. Uncle Christian was throwing boxes. I took and empty box and quietly set to work putting old pictures and news clippings into it. There were a lot about Mama's band titles like "M2CJ rocks central park" and "M2CJ does benefit concert for gay pride rally." Some were magazine clippings I looked for Mom and Mama's answers but they weren't there. Then one clipping caught my eye hard "Stand in guitarist and body guard for local band M2CJ dies in gas station fire." I seized a deep breath.

Mom startled "Oh, hi Hunny, how was work?"

I just stared at the article.

"Alex," Uncle Christian said "Alexander, what do you have there?"

"It . . . it's Dad's . . ."

"Read it aloud, Sweetie" Mom encouraged.

"Colt Daniel Jacovitti age 21 was tragically killed January 23rd 2006 in an unexpected fire at the CITGO station only minutes from his current residence 284 Pine Crest Ave. Jacovitti was a stand in Guitarist for band M2CJ. Colt was survived by his parents Mr. and Mrs Donavan Giovanni Jacovitti Sr. of Venice, Italy." The page was tore and missing a name but it gave a New York address I assumed it would have been one of my great grandparents. "Brother Christian Joseph Jacovitti 21 of 284 Pine Crest Ave. Colhampus, Ct. Brother Donavan Giovanni Jacovitti Jr.24 of Manhattan, New York. Girlfriend Bridget Calvinson 20 of Middletown, Ct. Unborn son Alexander Joseph Williams to be born to . . ." I heard Glass shatter and looked up; Mama was standing in the door frame a shattered picture frame at her feet. She looked at me and then left.

"I'll go talk to her" Mom smiled at me shakily "I think that startled her."

"I got the glass, Al, you keep Paul out of it, ok" Uncle Christian grabbed a broom.

I nodded I was still in a bit of shock.

"Alex" He shook me "Go reassure Paul his nana is alright."

I nodded again.

"Al we will talk once I clean this" He set Paul in my lap "Paul, Nana is fine she just dropped a picture frame. You tell daddy about your day."

I hugged Paul tight.

"Who's that? He pointed to the picture next to the obituary.

"That is my daddy; he died before I was born."

"Oh you're my first daddy."

I smiled "I love being your daddy, so what did you do today?"

"I GOT TO FEED LIZZY" He yelled.

"How are the horses, Come sono i cavalli?" I said in both languages.

"They is good. Uncle Christian and I is gonna to build Antony and me race tracks."

"First of all mister it is they are, we are going to, and Anthony and I. Second of all where do you think you are building race tracks silly?"

He crinkled his nose at me, he did not like his grammar corrected "Grandma said we could build it in here that is why we is packing things up to live in the garaged."

"Uh huh, well then, let's help them I sat my father's obituary in the box and Paul near the box "Ok Paul you have an important job you have to hold the box still and let nothing run away."

"Paul and I will finish the papers you go finish your Mothers dolls" Uncle Christian said.

I shifted to packing porcelain dolls very carefully and listening to Paul and Uncle Christian.

"One . . . uno . . . two . . . due, who is that?"

"That is I, Paul, I was your father's age there."

"Oh three . . . tre . . . four . . . quattro . . . . Who is he?"

"That's your grandfather."

"Papa?"

"No Paul Daddy's daddy, his name was Colt."

"Oooooooh. Five . . . cinque . . . six . . . sei . . . seven . . . sette he is ugly!"

"Ha-ha-ha that is your Papa he was eighteen there."

Paul tilted his head "Ewe."

"I know it's that hair."

I laughed "I don't ever remember Mr. Wittson with that hair style."

"He shaved it shortly after Ana was born" Uncle Christian laughed.

We continued packing and cleaning the storage room until Mom called us for dinner. Anthony had been brought home and was already in his seat at the table. Mama was sitting in her seat with headphones on she had stopped crying but still looked rattled; I hugged her. Mom had ordered in Chinese I showed Anthony how to use his chop sticks and Uncle Chris showed Paul. Anthony picked up relatively fast and mainly only had trouble with the rice.

After dinner I bathed them and put them to bed. Anthony had written me a long list of questions while I had been at work so I took them down to my drums to read them.

"Don't look so defeated" Uncle Chris looked down at me from the stairs.

"He thinks I won't love him if the court hearing isn't in my favor" I answered.

"He is six Alex and those first six years left a huge negative impact on him. Earlier he mixed up the grains and thought your mother would smack him." He pulled up the keyboard stool and sat next to me "He needs to be shown you and Ana are different than previous adults in his life."

"He thinks I will put him back up for adoption" I stared into space.

"He is six Al, he also thinks the boogie man lives under his bed and making faces at Don will truly freeze his face."

"I think Uncle Donavan would freeze a face too."

"He can't or your Mama's would have been frozen a long time ago. You need to relax and just keep reassuring him that you love him and you aren't going anywhere and make your actions match your words."

"I try, Uncle Chris I try so hard, but I could never be as great a parent as Mom or Mama."

He laughed "Your mothers have had almost twenty-two years of practice; it truly is a learning experience. I use to put your diapers on back words and your Mama nearly washed your skin off so by the time Nick came around your parents had some practice."

"Were your parents good?"

His eyes flashed anger and deep grief and he half snorted "Marc did his best and Kork helped but two unruly eleven year olds and a twelve year old who just lost their father and wanted nothing to do with their mom, step dad or little half brothers was not an easy feat. But yeah Marc was good to us."

"Uncle Chris?"

"You help me get more of that room over there clear and I will tell you more, Marc can't harass you if you didn't ask to be told."

I nodded and stood to help him.

"Sit we will talk first, I am getting old, your mother and I are forty two now, too old to be moving after eating so much besides Chinese food never really did agree with my stomach. I swear that dinner choice was your Mama's revenge for Christian and I letting you read your dad's obituary aloud and looking at all the old band articles earlier."

I laughed.

He rubbed his stomach "Were my parents good, hmm, that is a tough question. Parent is an earned title in my beliefs and my parents never earned that title from me, Ana's grandparents did. My biological father was a fowl mouthed workaholic drunk who died on my eleventh birthday and your grandmother had "her family". So were my Parents good to me, yes Al, the people whom I felt earned that title and the respect that went with it were very good people and very good parents. Does my real mom love me I guess I have been told by her and everyone else she does" He shrugged "My biological parents were divorced when I was three. Juliet, your grandma, has never acted as if she didn't love us, we just didn't live with her, and from what my younger brothers say she is a good mother."

"Uncle Mike said Mama was mean?"

"Your Mama was mean, not cruel or spiteful just miserable and that made her mean."

"Why?"

"That's digging and I am not going to cross my brother or father, I fear to this day scrubbing an entire house of wood floors with a tooth brush."

I raised an eye brow.

"My granddad or whom I called granddad, you'd call him Ana's great grandfather if he were still alive was a strict man fair but strict he expected the very best from his children and grandchildren. Rude, ungrateful behavior was not tolerated and I was . . . wild. Not mean like your Mama was just wild. Now time to clean."

By eleven we had a decent amount of the storage room clean. Kenny was asleep but Ana was not nor was she in bed or either bathroom or any other part of the house so I climbed up on the roof. "Want to talk about it?" I pulled her in to my arms.

"Unlike you" She laughed "I am just up here enjoying the night sky and waiting for my favorite pillow to be done stressing."

"Oh, yeah" I looked up "That's why Mama won't live in a city says she needs the stars."

She snuggled in to my chest looking at her ring "You spent too much on this"

"No I didn't, I didn't spend anything."

She swatted me "Alexander don't lie to me, your heart skips a beat when you lie."

I blushed "Fine how about you don't need to know how much I spent on it."

She shook her head at me "Let's go to bed" She yawned "Morning comes way to fast."

"That, beautiful, is an understatement" I carried her down to bed, she always just felt right in my arms. By the time I got undressed and into bed with the alarm set and light out Ana was half asleep; I held her close playing with her hair.

"Fourth of July on the beach with orchids and lilies and fireworks . . ."

"What silly?"

"Brides maid dress and . . ." She tailed off but I caught on to what she was thinking about.

"Whatever you want baby doll" I held her closer. I could have cared less if we got married in a dumpster with a rat as the J.P. Large crowds, people staring at me and fussy clothes was not my idea of a good time but I would do anything for Ana and if Ana was there I could do anything.

CHAPTER 30

THURSDAY

"No . . . NO . . . YES . . . SÌ, SÌ I KNOW WHAT the fourth of July is" I sighed arguing with a catering company my uncle Mike had suggested, at lunch. I took a few deep breaths and tried to be calm and polite "Look I don't have time for this it is either yes you can or no you can't caterer my wedding." The guy tried to talk me into other days and things like that "forget it you can't be the only Italian restaurant who caters." I hung up.

"Um . . ." Buddy looked at me.

"Wedding plans Ana finally told me where and when she wants it."

"Oh my Aunt had an Italian caterer at her wedding I bet my mom would know."

"Thanks, I will ask her when she brings Kevin back tomorrow."

"They said Sam is back?"

"Yes, he got jumped. His brother pays for a safe place for him to stay when he needs it."

"He chooses to be here?"

"Some days, other days he puts up a bigger fuss than you, because he might miss school."

Buddy looked at me "Over school? He truly is twisted."

I laughed "He is on scholarship at Crimsons. Are you done eating?"

"Yeah, I tasted better in juvy"

"That good huh?"

"I wish it were that good."

"I will get us some contraband as I am hungry too." I picked my phone back up and hit speed dial. "Yeah Wilson when you come up bring two double cheese burgers." He muttered several rude things then agreed I just laughed and hung up.

"Our double cheese burgers are on their way when Will realizes going to work on his day off won't kill him."

"Thanks" He smiled "Can we go play those new virtual games Dave brought in yesterday?"

"Are you allowed back in the family room yet?"

He made a face "Nope, I am not even allowed outside yet, your son is though."

"My son is six and is not violent."

"He's only six!?!" Buddy stared at me in disbelief.

"Yes, I know, we have a hearing coming up to have him removed from here."

"Why if the adoption went through can't you just take him?"

"The state gets that choice because he entered here as a ward of the state."

"Oh, yeah" Buddy looked lost.

Four-thirty came and I tried to bolt but there was a see me note on my locker so I went to wait for Dave to return to his office while Ana went home to the boys.

"Don't give me that look I am not out to kill you; I found you a good lawyer, I think."

"Ok?"

"Are you ok?"

"I spent the day arguing with caterers and Buddy."

"Did you tell Buddy you appreciated him being the lesser of two evils?" Dave laughed at me.

"Very funny Dave, I am trying to surprise Ana. But I have to go I need to run something out to Middle Haddam for Bruno before I head home thanks for the help." I took the business card and went home.

"What's wrong, Al?" Uncle Marc had Adam and JR. shoveling my poor car out today instead of Sunday, His work truck was the big strong kind and he had put chains on the tires so he could get up and down the drive way if he need and would be able to tow my pathetic car down the hill to sit near the van and other vehicles.

"Tired" I muttered.

"They are up stairs; your Uncle is in the storage room."

"I am hungry and tired and haven't seen my sons all day."

"That's a boy" He smiled as I bolted up the stairs.

I punched go on the microwave and sat down to talk to my boys before they had to go to bed.

"Paul's Italian is better than mine" Anthony objected after they had showed me which flash cards they had got when they did them today.

"He is around it more. It is scientifically proven that it is easier to learn more than one language at his age than it is to learn one language then another at an older age."

Paul blinked at me and Anthony looked at Ana.

"You're doing fine, sweetie. It takes time; I had to learn Italian at your age because your father couldn't speak English very well at all."

"Io ancora non, I still don't" I said in both languages for Anthony to hear the difference in my fluency. I set the preschool and first grade flash cards on the table. Anthony could already add but I was using them for Italian numbers.

Paul pushed a fire truck in to Colt's head. "Colts, Colts play fire tucks with me"

Colt rolled over and grabbed a fire truck he looked like he had been working off his grounding and half crawled half dragged himself up to a half slow crawl "whooo whoo" He crawled after Paul his noise far less than enthusiastic.

Anthony grabbed his action figures and started firing at them with his Nerf gun.

Ana frowned "Don't like guns, any guns."

I laughed "It's just a Nerf even Mama likes a Nerf gun, besides your father gave it to him."

"Don't remind me" She rolled her eyes at me.

I laughed "Ok, ok Anthony, do you want to play a board game with me before bed?"

He looked up "Can you teach me about your mini piano?"

I looked at Ana "Pianoforte Mini? (mini piano)"

She shrugged.

"Oh, my Keyboard" I caught on. "Sure but it's a keyboard, not a piano, pianos have a less electric sound and are much bigger."

I took him down stairs and taught him the scale; he would defiantly need more practice. I read to them and tucked them in I explained to Paul that I would have to take Anthony with me and that he would come to visit us later with Mom and Mama. That caused Paul a moment of three; Anthony wasn't thrilled either but didn't melt.

"All tucked in" Uncle Christian asked as I joined him and Colt in the storage room.

"Yeah, did you hear Paul? Whoever said senior citizens had a moment never met a three year old. That was all because he doesn't have to get up at the butt crack of dawn tomorrow."

"To him it is less time with Daddy" Uncle Christian nodded.

"I know I am trying."

"Tougher than you thought?"

"No" I snapped.

"To lie . . ."

"I know I'm not I am just tired of the state lady, I have a lawyer meeting Saturday morning at nine killing my morning with my sons."

"They have karate."

"Doesn't mean I don't want to be there with them, it was the catering company that was the last straw, won't work even on Fourth of July even on overtime pay."

"Have you told anyone other than me yet?"

"No I haven't had a chance I haven't even eaten, yet."

"Colt, vai a prendere il suo cibo. (Go get his food)" Uncle Christian ordered him.

"Lavoro gratuito? (Free labor?)" I laughed.

"Fino a quando è morto mi ha chiamato un disco slave. (Until he is dead he called me a slave driver)."

I laughed "He is never going to be off grounding"

"Not at this rate, he has gone all mouth just like your Mom."

"Don't suppose you'd tell me about her."

"Not a chance, I do not disrespect Mio Piccolo, Bella, or more importantly your uncle Marc."

Uncle Don laughed "Nor do I, he once told me that no one would miss me if he made me disappear."

"I think he meant it, you weren't his favorite person" Uncle Christian made a face.

"I don't think I ever will be" Uncle Don laughed harder "Oh hey look Al, it's your Mama's old sled." It was sleek wood slats on metal runners. It was painted glossy black with 'Princess' painted in frilly pink writing on the side and a curved wood bar on top that moved side to side.

"Che cosa è? (What is it?)" I tilted my head.

"A sled, boy you know Una slitta per slittino sulla neve (a sled for sledding in the snow)." He held up my sled, it was bright blue fiber glass "A sled."

"Ok" I raised an eyebrow "Is it safe?"

"Of course it is, just as safe as yours is."

"Uh huh"

"Don't give it that look works just like yours too" Uncle Donavan shook his head.

"If you say so that thing is girly."

Uncle Christian laughed "She is a girl, you know."

"I have trouble picturing Mama with anything purplish-pink and princess themed toys."

Uncle Don laughed "That is so not why they called her *princess*."

Uncle Christian shot him a look "Go eat Al, your mother wished to speak to you any way."

I took my plate from Colt, before he gave me the look he gave his brother and went to eat talking to my mothers sounded great. Ana was in the living room with Mom and Nick. The twins were most likely at work and the note on the table said that Mama and Uncle Chris had gone to an LGBT meeting to prep for the Feb. thirteenth rally, but would be home by nine.

All of a sudden Mom was right next to me "How was work?"

"Work was fine, I wish the rest was."

"What rest?" She laughed "You worked all day."

"The lawyer meeting Saturday morning."

"That's important."

"I know just nervous."

"Take Don, he will make the lawyer nervous."

I laughed Uncle Donavan did have that air to him. "I want him to win my case not pee his pants."

Mom chuckled "True, true, so how we doing tomorrow? I am bringing Paul in right?"

"Yes, please" I sighed.

"I am so proud of you."

"Why? Instead of decreasing my hours I increased them and now you and Uncle Christian are raising my sons, and we live under your roof and eat your fo . . . ."

"Sh . . . sh . . . sh . . ." She pulled me in to her arms and rocked me like when I was little. "Is that what has been stressing you so badly. I watch my grandson because I choose to and of course you live here it is your house. We love you, you belong here."

"It is ok Alex" Ana sat near mom and I close enough to play with my hair.

"Uh oh "Uncle Chris came in the back door.

"What's wrong?" Mama came in behind him.

"Oh nothing" Mom answered "He is just stressing."

"I bet he is over tired" Kenny said throwing his plate in the sink and standing behind Mom.

"OK, ok everyone is now to close to Alex, please, back up no offense I love you all but I think Kenny is right I am just over tired."

"Ok dear" Mom said night.

I hugged my parents and went to bed.

CHAPTER 31

NIGHTMARE

I WOKE A GOOD TWENTY minutes before the alarm. Ana was sound asleep I quietly grabbed my uniform and slipped down stairs to shower; an extra twenty minutes in the shower would feel incredible on all the sore muscles and bruises. After my long hot shower I combed my hair and threw it in to a loose pony tail then shaved my long past due for a shave, five o'clock shadow. That would make Ana happy she hated when I let the scruff go for more than two days. When I got out of the bathroom it was only five-thirty. I heard someone outside chopping wood so I turned the coffee pot on; then I looked at the food calendar and pulled out a carton of eggs and made mine, Ana's, and Anthony's eggs and left the frying pan and eggs in case it wasn't Mama outside. The food calendar said that it was chicken cutlet for dinner tonight. I checked the chore chart to make sure someone wasn't out there doing my chores as that was the fastest way to upset my parents, to be irresponsible and to act as if we did not need to help around the house. While Ana showered I woke Anthony telling him to stay in his pajamas, but let him bring his Red sox ball cap from Dr. Wittson and his stuff thing. While Ana and Anthony ate I braided Ana's hair and combed Anthony's or tried to he had a seriously defiant cowlick. He was so tired that Ana carried him from the sled to the car and held him while I switched his booster seat from the van to the car. As Uncle Marc had my pathetic 1998 Buick Century unburied and by the van he had also free of charge put chains on my tires the note on the steering wheel said "Stop digging let your mother come to you. Drive safe I love you-Uncle Marc p.s. Next time listen to us about the snow." Ana laughed and I repressed a happy dance over the safer tires and not having to drive the snow mobile in to work.

By the time we got to work Anthony had passed back out snuggling his stuffed thing so I carried him in and tucked him in to his bed he didn't need breakfast with the others he had eaten at home. Half way back to get my instructions for the day and clock in Dave stopped me I gulped hoping it wasn't for giving Harry a hard time about going through security properly again.

"He a sleep?" Dave asked me.

"Yes," I breathed a sigh of relief "Sound asleep he already had breakfast so I felt he should get rest more than sit there staring at Buddy."

Dave laughed "Does he know he isn't staying?"

"Yes and so does Paul it is going to be next week that kills them."

"Ok I will get him ready and save you a trip; I have already punched you in and you have the girls, Anthony and to wait on those returning."

"Can I skip the state worker visit?"

"Al," He frowned. "Jules isn't that bad. She is one of the best and is just doing her job."

"It's just aggravating and a waste of her time and mine."

"I know and you know this but the state doesn't care they have their own system and if you want your boys you and Ana play the game."

"Lo so, Lo so (I know, I know)."

"English" Dave yelled at me as I ran to find Tiffany, Sadie and Amelia.

"Dad, I want the clothes you bought me" Anthony complained at me.

"I know, but it is just until four, we have your clothes in the car" I sighed.

He made a face strangling his stuffed thing "Do I have to talk to the social worker today?"

"If she speaks to you, you will respond politely for it is rude not to; but other than that no you are not required to unless you wish too."

He made another face and crawled up on the couch next to Sam whom was reading more of my copy of my mother's new book. Tiffany sat drumming her hand on a table playing go fish with Amelia. Carter and Will were only three minutes late but apparently it was too much for Amelia.

"Where are they?" She yelled at me for the sixth time.

"Tiny, it is only three minutes after eight give him some time."

"Last week he promised he would be here waiting at the doors until you kicked him out at night every Friday."

"I don't know what to tell you" I sighed, I felt sorry for that boy she was defiantly a high maintenance girlfriend.

"Maybe he is blowing that guy he is always with" Tiffany said, before I caught her, as if she hadn't said anything inappropriate.

"No, they only do that on Thursday" Amelia smiled as if this was acceptable conversation to be having and like she was proud of him.

"Excuse you Six year old in the room" I turned to see that Sam had covered Anthony's ears and breathed a sigh of relief. "Seriously Amelia" Sam clucked his tongue at her "little kids are in the room."

"Unh" She clucked her tongue back at him looked at me and then back at Sam and said "Oh well Al will live."

"Ugh" Sam rolled his eyes "Don't listen to their fowl mouths Anthony they have no class."

"Uh" Tiny clucked her tongue putting her hand on her hips. "Class, you want class mister you haven't combed your ratty hair in two weeks."

I stifled a laugh and stepped in to the hall for a moment before my mouth and not my brains reacted to the tongue clucking hip holding and head swiveling those two were throwing.

Sadie came pounding down the hall from consoling and into the room around nine-thirty followed closely by Ms. Meyers I swallowed the groan I felt rising in my throat.

"Morning" I said through gritted teeth.

It wasn't that she was a mean annoying person, she was a very nice person and I knew she was just doing her job. I didn't like any social workers they were way to invasive. Mom says I got my extreme privacy from my father. I felt I just didn't have time or patience for someone fine combing my day watching my every move. Anthony tried to hide behind Sam; but it didn't work she headed straight for him asking him about counseling, his week and if he knew about the upcoming hearing. I repressed another groan and a mental eye roll. She was speaking to him as if he were two with an I.Q. of zero. Nor did I really want him having to worry about the hearing; that was my job. Then she came and spoke to me asking a whole bunch of fussy little questions about how Paul was, how the boys did on visitation day and how Anthony did with Ana. Bless my girlfriend as if on cue she walked in right at that moment and Anthony jumped happily right in to her arms. Thankfully it distracted Ms. Meyers and she started talking to Ana and not me.

Will and Carter arrived at eleven-thirty and forty-nine seconds. Tiny chewed him out profusely for his assumed tardiness and he just stood there smiling not saying anything to her until she had finished and even then all he said was "I told you last week that this week I my mom had her lady's doctor appointment and I would have to wait on the car but every other week I would be here before or as close to eight as possible."

I looked over at Carter who was standing against the wall and walked over to him and whispered "Wow I am so happy Ana is not like that."

Carter laughed "He has more patients than I could ever in a million years poses he just says it is because he loves her."

"I love Ana but that . . . that I could not handle."

"Me either, not even anything close."

"You're single huh?"

"Yep all days except Thursday, but I been trying to convince Sam and Spike to fill my Monday and Tuesday slots"

"Nope, no, no, nope not listening I don't want to know" I walked away.

He laughed harder and walked over to Sam to talk to him.

At four thirty-four and four seconds I fell face first on to the mattress in the time out room. Dave knocked and looked in at me.

"Che (what)?" I rolled over and glared.

"That good that you can't even say what in English?"

I opened the door "I wish it were that good."

"I am all ears and you need to decompress" He sat down near me.

"Neither Kevin or Kyle wish to be back, Tiffany wants out side and Amelia is . . . wow just wow. Is she free to leave yet? And how did I miss the memo saying it was my day to rule the world?"

"Kevin and Kyle will get over it and I will speak to Tiffany and Amelia. I heard what happened at lunch."

I groaned Amelia had waited till I was the only staff in the cafeteria then started a huge food fight I could barely stop.

"Sorry" He laughed pulling lettuce from my hair.

"She did it in front of four different social workers one being Ms. Meyers" I grimaced at the memory.

"Actually Jules said you handled things very well."

"She is crazier than I thought."

"Al" He laughed "Jules isn't crazy or evil, I saw that look. She is just a state worker she doesn't expect perfection on controlling a whole room of food fighting kids alone. As it is you never give yourself enough credit."

"Ana and Anthony waiting for me?"

"Yep, out at the car."

I nodded "See you Sunday." I ran out to the car hoping Ana wasn't mad at me. Anthony was already buckled in and in his own clothes. Ana was standing next to the car talking to Wilson.

"Here to get Sam before Dave kicks him out" Wilson was saying.

"Dave won't kick him out, he keeps Amelia in line" I laughed joining them.

Ana looked up at me and stuck her hand out for the keys "Sorry to cut this short Wilson but Al needs his music and I told Dad I would help him and Davie chop more wood. Sam's in the family room waiting he wasn't too put out about you being late."

"It's ok Ana, Al should just like get an IV drip of bad nineties metal. See you guys later."

I climbed in the passenger side and handed her the keys I didn't mind not driving. I pushed my CD in and started to head bang. Anthony plugged his ears laughing at me.

Ana frowned at me "Try head phones much?" She turned my music down and plugged head phones in and put them on my head. "Better Anthony?"

He had unplugged his ears but was still giggling "Daddy listens to funny music."

"Funny huh? I suppose funny fits, it is defiantly loud but it makes him feel better" She looked in the review mirror at him as she spoke to him.

My uncle Mike told me once that when my Mama was little she use to bring home stray people like old ladies bring home stray cats. Unfortunately she passed that weirdness on to Kenny and from time to time I had come home to find people my brother had brought home because there mom and or dad kicked them out or whatever. And normally My Uncles or mothers would find a way to warn me and I would not care; today however my uncle Christian and my uncle Donavan had gone into New York and would not be back until later tonight. So when I walked in the door and saw a guy I didn't know playing with Paul I choke slammed him in to the wall demanding answers.

Kenny thundered down the stairs yelling "No Alex, no! Al that's Juliet's cousin, he lives in Maine, he is headed to Topeka . . . uh . . . uh . . ." My other brothers and Juliet right behind him.

"Kansa, reject" I threw the guy down.

"Right" Kenny mumbled half shaking "Mom said he and Juliet could come for dinner tonight."

"Jeffery" The guy said sticking his hand out.

"Alex" I said "Sorry." I turned on Kenny "Prossima volta che decide di lasciare il mio figlio con un non so; Assicurati che il tuo asino è dispiaciuto tornare giù le scale. O meglio ancora smettere di sesso quando si suppone di essere servizio baby-sitter. (next time you feel the need to leave my son with someone I don't know; Make sure your sorry ass is back down the stairs. Or better yet quite having sex when you're supposed to be babysitting!)"

Kenny gulped.

Nick just looked at me.

"Wow . . ."

"Let's go . . ."

"Boys . . ."

"Daddy and . . ."

"Uncle Kenny need to . . ."

"Talk. Let's make a snowman" The twins said shoving themselves and my sons in to snow gear.

It was five-thirty and almost dark out I stirred the gravy on the stove. I knew the beasts would only keep my boys out until dinner.

"I am sorry" Kenny continued to plead "He wasn't hurting Paul, he was helping him pick up his toys."

"That is not the point, where is Mom?"

"They're over at Uncle Marcs" He gulped.

"She left you in charge?"

"Yeah me Al, but he was safe . . ."

"Non è questo il punto! Lei avrebbe dovuto essere qui non so lui da jack! (That's not the point! You should have been down here I don't know him from jack!)"

"I told you . . ."

"Non mi preoccupo di ciò che mi hai detto, Kenny, che è il mio figlio! Non ho bisogno del mio stato respirazione ogni ulteriore collo (I don't care what you told me, Kenny, that's my son! I don't need the state breathing any further down my neck).

"Whoa enough yelling," Mama came in and stood between us "I heard you over at Kork's. What is going on? Colt, Nikolas, don't gawk set the table."

"Al is way over reacting, he choke slammed Jeffery in to the wall."

"Non sto per reagire! Non conosco questo ragazzo e non si sa bene che lui o lei e lo ha lasciato qui da solo Con mio figlio di andare la tua ragazza a vite (I am not over reacting! I don't know this guy and you don't know him that well either and you left him down here alone with my son to go screw your girlfriend)."

"Al deep breath, and slow down." Mama pushed me further away from Kenny "What happened? I was gone for ten minutes. Crystalline had clothes for Nick."

I spotted and took the heavy bag of uniforms she was holding and setting it down near Juliet whom was explaining to her cousin that I spoke English and Italian.

"I ran up stairs really quick to show Juliet something and next thing I know Al is down here screaming and yelling and choking Jeffery. He is over reacting his son was fine."

"Per reagire il mio asino! Solo perché si desidera ottenere prevista non ti dà il diritto di lasciare il mio figlio con uno sconosciuto (Over reacting my ass! Just because you want to get laid doesn't give you the right to leave my son with a total stranger)."

"Alexander, go take a walk and more importantly watch that mouth, your uncle hears you swearing . . . well you know house rules. Go on your son's are fine they are outside with Christopher and Christian."

I heard Nick mumble "I wouldn't call that fine."

Mama shot him a look "Alex go now, Kenny and I are going to speak in my room while Colt and Nick remember how to be gracious host and not let dinner burn."

"Almost forty-three years with that women and she still sends chills down my spine." Uncle Chris came in the back door. "Al, help me load you drum set in Marc's truck . . . Whoa easy there big guy I laid padding."

"Not you, Kenny. Perché il mio bisogno Mama drum set (Why does Mama need my drum set)?"

"A surprise your Mama will tell you after, come on you need outside any way, new set of drum sticks in it for you."

"Grazie Zio Chris (thanks Uncle Chris)." I went down stairs to load my set in to Uncle Marc's truck bed. On the way out I passed Mom.

"Everything ok" She hugged me "The twins told me Kenny is stupid?"

"Sto bene (I'm fine), Mama is talking to him now."

"He must have set you off bad for the twins to be rattled. You look scattered and lost."

"È andato tutto bene, sto bene (it's alright, I'm fine). Can you please tell Mama I have a lawyer meeting tomorrow and no babysitter."

"Shh it's ok?"

I looked at her lost.

"Hush, cari, un problema alla volta. Tutti voi siete ferita, concentrarsi a mettere la vostra batteria del camion, e poi attendere in studio per la cena (Hush, dear, one problem at a time. You are all wound up, just focus on putting your drums in the truck and then wait in the studio for dinner)."

I finished loading the truck as Ana came up the drive way.

"Where are those going?" She asked.

I shrugged "Mama needs them for something tonight, but look what Uncle Chris got me" I showed her my new sticks they were top of the line, professional quality.

Dinner was good and went smoothly Mom kept Kenny and I separated just in case. Apparently my English was still unsteady and apparently it was a dead giveaway that I wasn't ok. Even though I was calmer and not trying to hang him any longer.

"Al" Mama said once I had finished a large portion of my meal "Did your Uncle tell you he rearranged your lawyer meeting before he left for New York?"

I looked up "No, When is it now?"

"Tonight at the pool hall; he . . . he pulled strings his way" I could tell by that she didn't mean Uncle Christian.

I nodded "I . . ."

"You never perished from sitting in that pool hall every Friday and Saturday and neither will your sons." Mom said firmly. "Kork already has their cots set up in the kitchen and we would like you to play with us from now on."

I swallowed hard "Yes ma'am" I did not think I was good enough to be included in their band. After diner I put my sons in their pajamas. I would bathe them in the morning before karate. I put on a suit and packed my shorts and a band shirt from Uncle Christian's dresser he was meeting us there.

"Daddy, where are we going, no bed" Paul yawned as I put him in his snow suit.

"I think Daddy and Ana have a meeting" Anthony called to Paul from where Ana was helping him with his snow stuff.

"Yes we have a meeting; we are going to the pool hall."

"No bed" Paul smiled.

"Yes bed, but not until later" I said. "I have a meeting when we get there so you boy . . ."

"Are going to be fine with your grandmas and I" Uncle Chris laughed "Your daddy is just a worry wart."

We got to the pool hall around seven-thirty and I helped set up my drums. I spotted the lawyer or as Ana called him a liar right away; he was at the bar talking to Mr. Wittson. Uncle Chris had the boys up on a pool table, I just turned and shook my head there was no point in arguing with him; Ana laughed.

"Don't you act like this place is too good for you little boy, your Mom use to sit you on the cue racks and one day she hung you from the dart board."

I turned to face Dr. Wittson "Sorry Sir, I think you miss judged my actions."

"Or you did, either way my brother says to get to the bar with Ana" Dr. Wittson was unnerving in the pool hall like it made him on edge and defensive.

"Yes, sir I was just . . ."

"I don't care what you were just doing; only that you and Ana move it, and I best not see you with that look on your face again tonight."

"Yes Sir" I head toward the bar Ana was already there, I wondered why her uncle had such a defensive edge over me being nervous but it might have looked bad from someone else's eyes my mother had said more than once I made odd faces. It wasn't that I was embarrassed by our life style just not sure what a lawyer would say about having the boys in here. I sat on the stool near Ana and the lawyer I felt like I was sweating bullets. Mr. Wittson put chocolate milk out for me and I put a five on the counter.

He laughed "Since when have you ever paid for your milk, what are you on tonight?"

"Left over fight with Kenny" Ana laughed.

"Right" He shook his head "Any way Alex, this is Mr. Corbin Smith and he is under the impression that he is your lawyer and here to meet with you tonight or a scary Italian guy will show him why Saturday morning was a bad decision."

I laughed and stuck out my hand "Nice to meet you Mr. Smith don't worry about my uncle my mother never lets him actually do anything, he just lacks manners and tact when it comes to what he cares about."

"Right, well I am not taking chances with him and as I told you're uh . . ." He looked at Ana.

"Fiancé" I offered.

"Yes your fiancé" He shuffled papers in a file folder I am not normally on these types of cases so let's see if I have the right information on the case. This hearing is to determine whether your son is too young to be in a treatment center for self mutilation." He made a face like he had smelt something foul.

I gulped "Correct".

He looked at me it was the same look any one in a crowded place or bar gave me "Are you alright?"

"I am fine thank you for asking"

Mr. Wittson snorted and walked over to a customer.

Mr. Smith gave me a skeptical look "There case worker is Julian Meyers?"

"Yes Sir, is that bad?"

"No, no that's actually good; I have heard she pushes for things like this."

"Now this hearing is the tenth, and to tell you the truth I will completely understand if you find a different lawyer, I will do my best but as I said I don't normally do custody cases and don't know all the little loop holes."

We shook hands and Ana and I told him we would be in contact with him one way or the other.

Uncle marc had been sitting on the other side of Ana whistling every time Auntie Kate walked past him.

I laughed.

"What are you laughing at?" Uncle Mike asked from behind the bar where he was fixing the grill again.

I pointed at Uncle Marc "He um . . ."

"Yeah that isn't anything new but I wouldn't let him catch you laughing at him. What did that lawyer have to say, he looked as bright as my shoelace?"

"Nothing he couldn't have told us over the phone."

"Well grab an apron and work off that mood we aren't on yet."

"Me?"

"Get over it your mom wants time with you, and Kyle already told me about your mood still 'being off color'"

"Off color?"

"I couldn't tell you why he says it like that but even I can see you're in a bad mood."

"Sorry, but I am tired and I am not . . ."

"Hush and move you are not above hard labor it won't kill you and neither will the extra pay check." Uncle Mike threw an apron at me the apron came with a pad and pen not a bussing tray, I sighed in relief I hated bussing.

Table fourteen wanted four cokes, three fries, one onion ring, and the band to start, table fifteen and sixteen wanted nothing they were coats and were probably out on the floor dancing to the radio, playing pool or darts, table seventeen had a bar order and table eighteen wanted a chicken basket and five root beers. It had been a long time since I had waited tables and it was showing. I put all ten drinks on one tray forgetting to separate the cokes and the root beers. The gentleman that ordered the scotch didn't like being carded as it was in his words clear to see he was not some kid with as much gray hair as he had. He also had a lot of questions about my parents' band, I told him I was sorry but I was too busy to answer at the moment. The chicken basket was easiest I even remembered the ketchup. Table fourteen seemed to be my problem table. Finally it was nine and Mama was pulling off my apron and shoving my band clothes at me.

"Mama . . . I . . ." I didn't know what to say or do.

"Don't worry all the music is on stage, just play the notes."

"Mama I can't . . ."

"Sing, yes I know you can't, don't even worry about that your mother, I and C.J. sing."

I looked at the stage "Really me . . ."

"Really, now let's go."

I followed Mama on to the stage and studied the music; there were a lot of darker songs today. "Uncle Marc who picked the songs?"

He laughed "Your Mama and Kyle, they tend to lean on the darker side."

I nodded Dr. Wittson was in a darker corner of the stage he was wearing all black, his guitar was black and double necked. "He . . ."

"On stage, yeah it makes him a bit nervous always, he's unique."

"I was going to say can play a double necked guitar."

"Oh yeah" Uncle Marc laughed and took his place in the middle of the stage. He once had told me he stood in the middle between Uncle Chris and Mama because they would fight and she would throw her drum sticks at his head. Mom stood with Uncle Chris near the front of the stage Mr. Wittson stood to the right of Uncle Marc and Uncle Mike to Uncle Marc's left. Ana's dad stood opposite Dr. wittson; just not as far into the shadows. I looked down at the first song; Mama had never learned to read music but I had and the drum notes weren't complex but the words were chilling.

We started with Mom singing. I kept up just fine; I had played this song before in one of my moments when I took my uncles sheet music or Mama's weirdly color coded tabs. The lead vocals switch, I didn't recognize the voice at first and it gave me chills. I nearly missed a beat when I realized it was Dr. Wittson but I recovered and continued with no trouble.

After three songs, Uncle Marc said something about a request can. And the fourth song said new on the sheet music the drum notes were more complex I looked over at Mama and realized she was no longer at her drums but up at the microphone. I played and listened to her sing.

"I didn't ask for this it wasn't my choice. It just sort of happened it wasn't in my plans . . ."

Mama, mom and Uncle Chris all sang the chorus "I had my dreams, I set my goals, my path was clear, my life right on track, and then out of the blue you derailed me."

"One minute everything was 'fine' and 'I love you' then you lied and I cried you didn't care, you weren't here things fell apart like my heart it took all I had but I pulled it together again." Mama's voice cut sharply through everything the song was not slow or soft it wasn't exactly fast either but it was defiantly more impacting then one would have thought if they only read the words and didn't hear Mama's voice.

"I had my dreams, I set my goals, my path was clear, my life right on track, and then out of the blue you derailed me." Uncle Chris seemed to twitch a little every time the chorus came up it was a small twitch almost as if he was involuntarily shifting his head to the left. I looked again and I realized he was this must have been one of the songs Mama would have thrown her sticks at him in; just because my old hand me down sheet music said new didn't mean it was new to them.

"All of a sudden it was 'baby take me back, I didn't mean it, please forgive me forget I said it give me a second chance.' So I rearranged and changed my life to once again fit around you."

"I had my dreams, I set my goals, my path was clear, my life right on track, and then out of the blue you derailed me."

"It was more lies and more cries and you reveled in my pain; this time. You laughed at every single tear. I had my dreams I set my goals you shattered my heart and bruised my soul used me. Abused me. Push prodded and pulled me like a tug of war rope. Promised me the world to take it all away, like part of some cruel game."

"I had my dreams, I set my goals, my path was clear, my life right on track, and then out of the blue you derailed me."

I took the beat to take a deep breath it looked like the drum rests were set to when Mama's lungs would have needed a break. This song had an edge to it and Mama must have sung from her drum set. I could see Mom flinch over certain lines and wondered if it was the song or like Uncle Chris and it was a fear of a drum stick hitting her in the head.

"You beg and you plead 'love me trust me forgive and forget' but why should I believe you this time. I am tired of crying, tired of trying, tired of hurting and yearning"

"I had my dreams, I set my goals, my path was clear, my life right on track, and then out of the blue you derailed me!"

The crowed showed their appreciation; Uncle Chris bent down and took something out of a can at his feet, read it and started laughing. "I have to read this out loud, 'Who is the cute new drummer?"

Several people laughed.

"Well" Uncle Chris laughed "That is my nephew, Alex."

"AND HE IS ENGAGED!" I heard Ana then yell from near the kitchen door.

We sang several more songs and then helped close down. The boys were both asleep on cots in the back by the time I got off stage. Anthony had a chocolate milk mustache and Paul was hugging a spatula and had ketchup down his shirt. I carried them out to the van and buckled them in to their car seats. On my way back into see if there was more to be done, I found Uncle Marc sitting down at the bar. "Uncle Marc can I ask you something about Uncle Chris?"

"Yes" He sighed, he looked tired.

"On the song 'Derailed' Uncle Chris seems to . . ."

"To twitch or shift his head to the left? Yeah I know. Your Mama never meant that song to be played for an audience and she spent a lot of concerts throwing her sticks his head. I don't think that song strikes the same nerve it uses to; and seeing as you and your brothers exist I'd say your mom got her second chance more like tenth."

"Ooh," I exclaimed "That explains Mom's twitch."

"Nope, she and C.J. share that microphone they twitch for the same reason, aim wasn't always perfect and I wasn't so sure she was hitting who she hit on accident."

"She hit Mom?"

"No she hit your Uncle Christian and your father mainly your Uncle Christian; now no more digging."

I laughed. "Oh ok, thanks."

"Yep, go in that kitchen and pull your cousins out by their ears for me I am getting to old for this to begin with let alone waiting up for them to remember they are grounded and not to be hanging out with Kenneth and Jeremiah."

"Yes Sir," I walked back to the kitchen. I opened the door as the room spun I had a flash back of when I was six; running in here to get Mama because Uncle Jesse had told me that if I didn't leave him alone he was going to put me in the blender. I shook my head and everyone was staring at me "Um Uncle Marc says Adam and Jr. need to hurry up."

K-4 was standing closest to me "You look like you saw a ghost Al"

"Ho fatto. ora sto bene grazie.(Did. Fine now thanks.)" I shook my head again the flash backs were part of cutting when you stopped cutting all the memories good and bad came back and not conveniently or all at once scattered more like when they felt like it. I suppose the technical term for it would be with withdrawal because if I were still cutting that would have been a cue to go cut again so that I didn't have to feel any emotion.

"Ok space case" Adam said pushing past me.

Ana pulled me away from the door "You ok?"

"Yeah, baby doll, it was just a flash back, a good memory from when I was little."

"Ok" She kissed me "I picked a date."

"July 4th?"

"How did you know?"

"You talk to me in your sleep" I laughed kissing her back.

"I suppose you want Italian food?"

I gave her a cheesy grin.

She kissed me again and shook her head "Ok if you go dress shopping with me tomorrow."

"Actually I have a surprise for you" I had spent most of my free time meaning time when I should have been asleep finding her mother's wedding dress.

"Now" She smiled.

"At home beautiful."

The ride home was loud, the twins and Nick fought the whole way. Bless my boys them and Colt slept through it. It was only a fifteen minute drive but it was long enough to give me a migraine. I lifted

Paul in one arm and Anthony in the other and raced up stairs away from my brothers. Ana drove the van back down the hill for Mom in case it snowed and took the sled up. Mama waited almost impatiently for Uncle Chris and Mom to get inside, Uncle Christian had not met us and I felt lost without my set which would now live at the pool hall Friday in to Saturday unless there was practice.

"You ok, Mama?" I asked.

"I am fine; I think I should be asking you that, the way you shot out of the van tonight" She answered.

"Oh that, just a migraine, the boys fought all the way home."

"Al!" Ana jumped on my back giggling "Where is my surprise?"

"Oh boy" Mama laughed "Tina come quick they have picked a date"

Ana waited for mom to come to the kitchen "July fourth" She smiled.

"Ok Mama she can see it."

Mama went to her room and pulled out the dress. Ana squealed jumping up and down. She grabbed the dress spinning around hugging it. I laughed watching her. I felt Uncle Christian's presence a moment before I heard him "Don't jump" He breathed in my ear, "I see you are doing well. Don't speak your mama hasn't noticed me yet, I wish to surprise Mio Piccolo."

He had barley breathed it in my ear but it was enough to nearly make me jump. I nodded enough for him to know I understood. He snuck up back around the other way through the hall and by the stair well to the other side of the living room and snuck up behind her wrapping her tight in his arms.

"Mio Piccolo, did you take good care of Bella?"

"Mia roccia(my rock)."

Uncle Don and Uncle Chris pushed through the door laughing.

"Sweet heart Christian's home."

"I see that Don was on the porch smoking when Chris and I came up."

"That's bad for him" I heard Mama mutter, into Uncle Christians shoulder.

"Ana, my love, bed?" I smiled at her still dancing around the kitchen and hugging the gown. "The stars miss you" I winked.

My uncle shot me a look.

I blushed and shook my head no; and to make sure he knew what I meant I signed "Not that I am not Kenny."

"It's perfect" Ana sighed.

"I am glad you like it, aren't you tired?" I smiled.

I finally got her to stop spinning in circles around two am.

CHAPTER 32

PAUL AND ANTHONY WOKE US around eight; Paul had his Ghi on over his pajamas and Anthony was just in his Ghi, no pajamas. I couldn't do anything but laugh at Paul's fashion sense.

"I already showered" Anthony grinned "Uncle Donavan helped."

The words didn't process for me right away and Anthony started to shake.

"Ok, have you had breakfast" Ana was more with it than I was.

"No, is Daddy mad?" Anthony relaxed a little.

"Huh, no" I yawned "I am just not quite awake."

All of a sudden I was nose to nose with Paul "Hi Daddy me go karate today."

I nodded remembering it was Saturday, I lifted both my boys "Ok let's get my Ghi and let Ana get dressed." I pulled my Ghi from the closet and carried the boys down stairs because I remembered under the blanket wrapped around Ana she was in less than decent clothing as she had over heated in her sleep. I sat my Ghi on the couch and greeted my mothers, told my uncles good morning. I pulled Paul's Ghi and pajamas off bathed him and redressed him. Then I showered and dressed. Thankfully the snow had been kind and decided to not fall last night so I pulled the car all the way up after switching the car seats in to it. By then Ana was up dressed and had fed her and the boys. I downed half a carton of orange juice and Mom swatted the back of my head giving me a "you know better" look.

Paul although too young for karate, was more than happy to sit in his ghi on the practice pads and watch Anthony. Anthony seemed to like it too, and was very focused on earning his first stripe.

After karate the boys and I had tux fittings Ana was always way more prepared than I and wanted everything set for July insisting it would come faster than any one realized. Paul was very against his fitting he didn't want to sit still or be prodded. Anthony didn't like it either; and I can't say I had and enjoyable experience with it myself. After that Mom had given me money a list and dryer fresh dress clothes; she WANTED professional family pictures and had scheduled the appointment because she didn't trust me to sit in front of a camera on my own without sever prodding. I groaned internally Paul was getting very tired with the poke, prod and sit still routine. The pictures did Paul in completely he was done with dress clothes and wanted his over alls and shirt, it was past nap, way past lunch and even further past his patients for running crazy in the car. Mom must have known because she had included lunch money and Anthony pick McDonalds. Anthony was tired of it but not fussing, mostly just read in the car. He had just expressed his boredom by asking if he could go sledding when we got home. After lunch we had to pick up a few things at the grocery store. We got home around three-thirty Paul had fallen asleep in the car and woke up cranky. Anthony ran up stairs and got his sledding gear.

"Glad he is adjusting so well."

I nearly jumped out of my skin "I um thanks" I finally saw Uncle Jesse standing off to the side of the porch.

"What's wrong with him?"

I looked at Paul "Over tired no real nap" I shifted him he had his face in my shoulder whine crying "Paul can you say hi to Uncle Jesse?"

"Nooo" He fussed.

Uncle Jesse laughed "He's cute for warned is fore armed. I suggest you don't cross my sister's path tonight."

"Thanks." I sighed it was his way of telling me that my grandmother was here. "I think I will be ok. Uncle . . ."

"Down stairs all three of them, Donavan is keeping Christian down stairs."

"Oh ok Paul and I will play drums."

"Ok."

Uncle Jesse wasn't kidding I could hear my Mama stomping, and feel the suffocating tension. I would have stayed down stairs except Paul needed the bathroom. Ana had run to her fathers. Mom was in the hall rubbing her temples. I mouthed "Sorry" and then "look" I held out the picture package previews. I heard Mama stomping in the kitchen and winced.

"She is very irritated" Mom mouthed.

"You think" I mouthed.

She gave me a "don't be rude" look.

"TINA!" Mama screeched.

"Yes, dear?" Mom rubbed her temples more.

"Has Alex come in yet?"

I mouthed no, but it didn't help.

"Yep, he just showed me the pictures."

"Traitor" I mouthed, she swatted me. "I am right here Mama; do you need help with something?"

"Can you please, come change the light bulb out here it just blew and your uncles . . ."

"Ok, coming, Mama" I went into the kitchen and greeted my grandmother and Mama. Then I changed the light bulb.

"Where are my great grandsons?" Grandma asked me.

"Paul is in the bathroom and Anthony is outside playing in the snow" I answered.

Paul came out of the bathroom "Daddy I can't get me oder alls"

"Come here, Sweetie, let great grandma fix."

"Noooooooooo Nana do" He ran to Mama.

"Sorry Grandma he missed his nap today."

"She will get over it, lei è venuto qui a urlare a me di cose che non hanno controllo. (She will get over it, she came in here yelling at me about things I have no control over.)"

"Jessica it is rude to speak . . ."

"Mom did you come here to tell me how to run my house or were you truly waiting for C.J."

I nearly crushed the bulb I was holding in my hand.

"Jessi bear" Mom said carefully "I think Don needs your help down stairs."

"Donavan can wait!" Mama snapped.

Mama looked so upset I tried to help Mom "We playing tonight at the pool . . ."

"Yes, and yes you are playing" She answered.

I winced talk about taking one for the team; I stomped back down stairs grabbed Uncle Chris' guitar and went up about four stairs. I had seen Mama and Uncle Marc do this a million times; I held the guitar over the railing "un . . . due . . . (one . . . two . . .)"

I heard Uncle Christian laughing.

"Are you crazy that guitar is signed by Slash, Toby Keith, Kenny Rodgers, and . . ."

It was signed by more than that starting with every member of the original Guns 'n' Roses not just Slash. The original Guns 'n' Rose were Mama and Uncle Chris' favorite band. "Go talk to Grandma, Mama, looks like she is going to cry and I can't even ask why without Uncle Marc breathing down my neck."

Within seconds Uncle Christian was up the stairs.

Uncle Donavan leaned against the base of the stairs "You know there ar . . ."

"Non mi importa che la mia mamma! (I don't care that's my Mama)!"

Uncle Don smiled "Bella hiding?"

"No, she is trying to get Mama to relax."

He nodded at the guitar in my hand "Christian will murder you if you cause his little one displeasure C.J."

"J.J. is fine, that woman desires both of us nuts I swear" Uncle Chris muttered.

A minute later Uncle Christian had returned and was dragging Uncle Chris up the stairs by his ear.

I sighed Mama cranky was never good.

"Don't make that face at me; get your rear in here and help me. Your sons are fine one is outside with his mother and the other is up stairs with your mother."

"Yes Sir."

We worked until dinner; there had to have been about seventy porcelain dolls and twice that in monkeys. There were pictures, drawings and note books by the gross. It was just a mess; by dinner we had taken out seven bags of garbage alone and had put in a queen size bed.

"I like my privacy like your father did and I would rather not hear my little brother snoring through the wall" Uncle Donavan said. "Tell your Mom I am keeping Il più giovane (youngest's) curtains."

"Yes sir" I said raising an eye brow.

"Youngest is what I called your father he called me Oldest"

"Oh . . ."

"I call him little brother he called me big brother now he calls me fool or things you are too young to hear."

"Actually I was just going to say see you at dinner" I smiled.

After dinner we put the boys in their pajamas and in to the car, we took my car because Uncle Mike asked to ride with Mama. Anthony and Paul had taken their seats at the bar and were already working on their chocolate milk mustaches. I was bussing tonight and Ana was order taking. I hated bussing some of the things teenagers did to tables were unimaginable.

"Hey you, come take my order!"

I took a deep breath and rolled my eyes thinking maybe I preferred teenagers' messes.

"HEY YOU, ARE YOU DEAF, I SAID GET ME ANOTHER SCOTCH!"

I sighed and pointed to the sign over the bar that said "Harass the staff and customers you're out on your ass" "Can you read sir, or see sir, I am bussing if you can't wait for a waiter or waitress walk over to the bar but I will mention to a waitperson that you would like a refill."

The gentleman became belligerent and foul mouthed.

I groaned "Sir, I think you have had enough to drink already and maybe it is time you leave."

There were signs all over saying things like "This is not a dive or a pub", "This is a family place let's keep it that way", "My kids under eighteen please keep your language under eighteen", "We reserve the right to cut you off or remove you from our establishment", and my favorite wrote in Mama's hand writing in bright rainbow print "Harass our staff or customers you're out on your ass."

The guy was getting louder, ruder and was now on his feet threatening me; but five foot ten doesn't intimidate you when you are seven feet tall and use to being beat on daily from your day job. Mr. and Dr. Wittson joined me but at seven feet and seven foot two they were not easily intimidated by loud drunks either.

"Excuse me sir, but I believed Alex asked you to leave my building" Mr. Wittson said.

The man started to verbally attack Mr. Wittson; witch personally I found amusing. Mr. Wittson was, like me, seven feet tall; he was built like the side of a house and had long balding white blonde/silver hair; the thought of anyone picking a fight with him made me laugh. Dr. Wittson was seven foot two inches and had the easy muscles of someone born with them. The man tried to shove passed me towards the bar yelling he would just get his own. I laughed and went back to bussing my uncles we not all that small their selves Uncle Christian was six foot eight and Uncle Don was also seven feet. And after a few minutes I heard the man being "helped" out of the bar. I looked at the clock it was going to be a long night the band on stage was ok not as good as Mom's but not as bad as the band that opened for us last night.

"Excuse me" A small boy tugged on my shirt "Can you help me I am looking for someone?"

"One second, just let me set my tray in the kitchen." I had the kid who was between ten and thirteen stand by the door to the kitchen and wait for me; while I set my full tray in the sink.

"Oi splash much?" Uncle Mike growled whipping soap suds from his face."

"Sorry Uncle Mike, busy."

"Yeah, yeah" He sighed as I ran back out.

Getting a better look at the kid he may have been as young as ten but he looked like he belonged down on eighteenth and Simon "Ok, who you looking for?"

"My Aunt" He said, he looked like Colt's evil twin almost "And uncles."

"I need a name, sorry."

"I don't know. Look I just turned twelve, my mom died last night, she told me before she died to come here to this town to this bar."

"Not a bar" I corrected "Pool hall."

"Whatever, she said I would find people who look just like me and the first one I find should be able to help me and from where I am standing you look like me just older."

"Well you look like my little brother, have a little faith and patients in me. Let's start with I'm Alex" I stuck my hand out.

"Lorenzo" he looked at my hand "My mom use to say that."

"What?"

"Faith and patients."

"My uncle Marc says it a lot, but most of my uncles say it."

He looked me over "You shake and your dressed odd."

"Um . . . Thanks I think but I know I shake. Come with me." I looked for Uncle Christian but could only find Uncle Mike.

"Holy evil twins, that kid could be Colt, what's your Mama's name?" Uncle Mike said spotting Lorenzo.

Lorenzo winced and snapped "I ain't got one."

"I lost my mother" I corrected Lorenzo "Uncle Mike this is Lorenzo, he says his Mama's last words to him sent him to us more specifically anyone looking like my father."

"Who's your daddy boy?" Uncle Mike was already irritated and we weren't even on stage yet.

"Never had one" Lorenzo cut his eyes.

"What is your Mama's Name?"

"Olivia Louisa"

"She got a last name kid, I don't have time for this Al and I have to be on stage in five minutes and those dishes don't wash themselves when my nephews take off and leave them."

"Loui . . ."

"Maiden name?" Uncle Mike sighed.

"That's the only name I have known her to have like I told you I ain't got no dad never did."

I flinched "I have never had" I corrected again.

"Whatever, my mom's name was Olivia Louisa."

"Ok, so your last name is Louisa?" Uncle Mike was rubbing the bridge of his nose.

"Yeeah" Lorenzo had a thick New York accent. I'd say queens or Brooklyn.

"Fine I have to be on stage now, labor laws say I can't make you work but your mouth and features say your family so feel free to do the dishes."

"I ain't no chick, I don't do dishes."

I lost it "The proper grammar is I am not a; and in this establishment . . ."

"Breath Al, get on stage tell your mothers I am coming, Lorenzo needs some manners."

"Yes, Sir."

"Me too . . ." Paul crawled into my arms at my drum set.

"You too" I laughed "Where is Anthony?"

"Mommy and him is playing with tables."

I hugged him "It is are playing not is. Who were you with that you took off on?"

"Uncle Marc."

"Ok."

I listened to Uncle Marc give his opening speech as I adjusted Paul and my music. My kit sat near Mama's she was looking at Mom. I looked at todays play list all the songs were aggressive tonight. The first song was "Who said your thought counted". As Uncle Mike counted off I put my sound blocking head phones on Paul and started to play, I had gotten very good at playing with Paul on my lap, but he slid off and started dancing in between Mama and I. As the song ended Anthony crawled on stage with Ana's help and stood near Uncle Marc.

The next song was "How"; Uncle Marc had put His Ear plugs on Anthony. The drum part of the song was not hard but to me the bass solo looked hard Uncle Christian, Uncle Marc, and Mr. Wittson had said with practice it was easy. People were putting suggestions in the can left and right; but they did that on nights they, I should say we as it seemed I was permanently part of the band now, didn't play "Cool Kid" or "Heartbreaker" in the first set.

"When did it come to this? When did it get this bad? Why didn't you speak up, Speak out, yell, scream and shout? We would have heard, we have ears, we would have been there, we do care. How can you leave me like this?" Uncle Chris Sang the last chorus.

We had one more song before Uncle Marc would pull from the can. Mom and Mama sang this one, it was called "Experiment" it was wrote during one of Mom and Mama's fights Uncle Christian said they use to fight well. I listened to my mother's sing as I played.

"You told me you liked me! You told me it was ok! You helped me come out! Then how come I'm the experiment? You have my heart wrapped around your finger, you pull I come hither at your beckon call! You push away I sit and watch as you love real men. You told me you liked me! You told me it was ok! You helped me come out! Then how come I'm the experiment? I let the pain seep in, suck it up swallow it down, door mat style all the way. Love you no matter what it does to me. Until the very end I will always be your fill in! You told me you liked me! You told me it was ok for a girl to love a girl! You helped me come out! So how come I am only just your experiment!"

When the song ended Uncle Marc picked the can up. "Let's see three for "Heart Breaker", four "Fallen Angle" and ooo a question. 'How long have you worked and played here?' Um" He looked at us.

"Well work we have worked here since Mum and Dad opened it in 1999, family owned family run. Alex has just joined the band but he has worked here since he turned thirteen" Mr. Wittson said.

"As for playing as a band" Uncle Marc closed his eyes in thought "I'd say between 2000 and 2002 somewhere in there depending on the individuals due to our ages and hobbies."

After that we sang "Fallen Angel" and "Heart breaker". Uncle Chris hated "Heart Breaker"; Ms. Nikki said it was because the song was about him.

After the first set I went back to bussing Uncle Mike took Uncle Christian to meet Lorenzo.

"How's the floor coming?" Uncle Mike asked Lorenzo.

Lorenzo just glared. His mouth was duct taped oddly with cotton over his lips so when removed it wouldn't hurt him too much. He was tied to the counter at his waist with a tooth brush taped in his hand.

"MIKE!" Uncle Christian yelled untying and taking the tape off Lorenzo "You can't do this to a kid; well the duct tape and tying anyway." Uncle Christian added after getting a good look at Lorenzo.

"He is fine" Uncle Mike said "Just way to mouthy."

"Owe" Lorenzo winced as Uncle Christian pulled him to his feet.

"Toughen up" Uncle Christian looked closer at him "And keep that thought to yourself."

Lorenzo made a face at him instead; not a particularly a smart move.

"Don't give me that look either. Go back to scrubbing that floor and tell me how my sister died."

Lorenzo's eyes widened in anger "You're my Uncle!"

"Yes now answer me I have no patience, I just lost my little sister and I am busy."

"Cancer."

Uncle Christian nodded "Would have been nice if she had told Don and I she was ill."

"Where's my aunt I have a note?" Lorenzo snapped.

"I am not married nor with anyone" Uncle Christian read the note.

"How come I never knew about . . ."

"Not now after work. Alexander!"

"Si" I stuck my head around the door smiling ear to ear.

"Aren't you chipper" Uncle Mike laughed.

"I um . . . well . . ."

"Hush" Uncle Christian frowned "Take your cousin and teach him how to bus tables and every time he shoots his mouth off stick this in his mouth, worked for your mother."

I caught the soap "Mom or Mama?"

"Don't even try that go" Uncle Christian shook his head.

I grabbed an apron and a bussing tray and put it on him he was definitely not use to hard work and wined a lot.

"It's too heavy" He whined over a half full tray.

"Toughen up and hold it like I showed you" I sighed.

"It's too hard."

"Life's hard."

"Man, why you . . ." I stuck the soap in his mouth.

"Are you trying to kill your nephew" Mama watched me trying to be patient with Lorenzo and failing.

"My *nephews* are fine they need to bond and I am seeing if Alex is truly close to cutting, but I need to speak to you Mio Piccolo."

"Has it come time for you to leave us Mio Roccia?" Deep worry almost to panic creased Mama's face.

"I could never ever leave you and Bella, but I must ask too much of you once more and add another to our family. My sister has passed."

She hugged him tight "I suppose that the young man you are punishing Al with is her son then; he has grown since the picture she sent."

"Si Mio Piccolo (yes little one), he is twelve now."

"And must have quite the mouth and attitude to be walking around with Tina's soap in his mouth" Mama laughed.

"Si, she sent him here" He showed Mama the note.

"Have you spoken to C.J. and Tina?"

"Si Mio Piccolo, they didn't see a problem either."

"Nor do I but until Don is out of Danny's room where will we put him?"

"On the roof, no sorry the couch will suffice he needs some humbling."

Mama frowned "You best mean Donavan that child needs love and stability now his Mama just died."

"Either"

"Mio Roccia" She frowned again at him "Does he have a name?"

"Mud he ever speaks to me like that again or if his mouth doesn't clear up that's the seventh time Al has shoved soap in his mouth; but my sister named him Lorenzo Donavan Louisa, he thinks that's her maiden name."

"Isn't that . . ."

"Yeah, his dad is Gabby's brother."

"He doesn't know his father?"

"Never did"; Uncle Christian signed "Gang fight" and "Dead".

"Let's hear it for gangs" Mama rolled her eyes.

At closing I was ready to kill Lorenzo, my boys were asleep on their cots and Ana was nearly strangling Sam.

"Why do I have to vacuum, that's woman's work" He whined for the millionth time. "Ow" He whined more when Uncle Donavan smacked the back of his head.

"Boy your Mama needed to teach you manners not how to be your father, I hear that disrespectful tone and phrase again your Aunt Tina is going to have the cleanest house I have ever seen and that whining it best go immediately" Uncle Donavan growled.

"Don" Mama frowned "Let the boy be, you can terrorize him tomorrow."

"Boy's been spoiled long enough" Uncle Don grumbled.

At home I carried the boys to their room. My brothers went to their rooms I was sure Kenny was actually at his new laptop he got for Christmas. Mama went to the shower, Uncle Chris and Mom Brought Ms. Nikki home, Uncle Donavan went to bed and Lorenzo fought with Uncle Christian.

"Why do I have to sleep on a couch?" Lorenzo whined.

"The phrase is thank you sir for allowing me in your house, and to answer you because your Aunt said I couldn't tie you to the roof."

Lorenzo made a face.

"I strongly suggest you don't make that face at me again. We will talk more and you will meet more of your cousins than Kenny and Alex tomorrow. I also strongly suggest you sleep well tomorrow might actually kill you" Uncle Christian tucked Lorenzo in and went to bed himself."

CHAPTER 33
NEW YEARS EVE

"Ooff" I hit the floor when the alarm went off.

"Have a good work day, dear" Ana said.

"Uuuuunnnn . . . ."

Ana laughed "Your fine, go to work, you don't wish to be here when they realign Lorenzo."

"I'm going just sore."

"Go to work whinny" She laughed more.

"You look like road kill" Dave laughed at me.

"I think I need to shift my days off."

Dave laughed "Go home, Al I will see you Tuesday instead and your Mama wants you to pick up the party pa . . ."

"I know, I know"

"Hush and don't forget your son tomorrow."

"Uuuuuunnnnnnn."

"That's nice you knew."

"But he has adjusted . . . kinda."

"Alexander, don't make me call your parents."

I sighed "I know"

"See you tomorrow, Alex."

The store was a mad house and I was shaking so bad I had to sit in the car for ten minutes before I could drive home.

At home my boys and brothers were gathered around the T.V. Lorenzo was at the table eating breakfast.

He looked at me "It's Sunday doesn't anyone here go to church?"

"Um sometimes Nick goes with Davie and Ana's dad but, Chruch is our choice. Besides it is kind of hard to get up when you work until one-thirty am or later."

"I am feeling that, that little one over there woke me at seven" He evil eyed Paul.

"Paul" I corrected "It's um nine now if you get dressed and ready in fifteen minutes I am sure Uncle Christian would let you go with Mr. Wittson."

Uncle Donavan snored into his newspaper.

Lorenzo raised an eyebrow at him.

"I know, that's every morning" I tried not to laugh.

"Don" Uncle Chris shook him "Got back to bed fool."

"Huh, nah, C.J. I am good" Uncle Donavan yawned.

"Right, nutter" Uncle Chris muttered on his way back to the living room.

"Am not, I heard that little boy" Uncle Don yelled after him. "Oh, morning Alex, don't you work Sundays?"

"Dave changed my hours I work Monday through Friday now" I laughed.

"Well about time that old coot saw things my way" Mama said coming out of the shower.

"Morning Mama" I bent down and hugged her.

"Morning Al, thank you for getting these for me" She took the bag from my hand and handed me the twenty. "Mangia, Lorenzo, your cereal is getting soggy."

"Get up and greet your aunt, boy" Uncle Donavan growled at Lorenzo.

Lorenzo looked lost "I told her good morning when she gave me my cereal."

"Hush, Don, let him be." Mama bent down and hugged him. "Good morning Lorenzo"

He looked even more lost.

I just shook my head my uncles were going to eat him alive.

"Mommy" Paul flew in to Ana's arms.

"Morning Ana" Anthony joined Paul in her arms.

"Morning my loves" She held them close.

"Mommy, Mommy Daddy's home" Paul squealed spotting me over Ana's shoulder.

"Dad" Anthony yelled running into my arms.

"Ooff" I laughed "Miss me much? I was only gone two hours."

"You don't work today?" He looked up at me.

"Dave switched my hours, I now work Tuesdays and have the whole weekend off."

Ana made her way through the living room stepping over my brothers to me for a hug and kiss "That man spoils you rotten." She laughed, sat Paul down and headed to the Apple Jax Uncle Christian was taunting her with.

"Where's Mom?" I asked after noticing she was not around.

"Sleeping stupid" Colt chucked a pillow at me "Now shut up this is the good part."

I threw the pillow back at him. "Anthony, Paul do you two want to go sledding?"

"Can we play ooties?" Paul yawned.

"Sure, Anthony you want to play too?"

"Daddy who is he?" Anthony pointed at Lorenzo.

"That is our cousin" I looked at Uncle Christian for accuracy "And we don't point it's rude."

"Why is he here?"

"No of you business" Lorenzo snapped.

Uncle Donavan smacked the back of his head and Uncle Christian shoved a bar of soap in his mouth.

"Wow, you learn slow that's the sixth time in an hour" Kenny shook his head bringing out his juice cup to the sink.

"Anthony, Lorenzo is your cousin, he is my sister's son and she recently died so he will be staying here for a while" Uncle Christian explained.

"Oh ok" Anthony smiled "Dad can I play cooties too?"

"I just . . . I . . . never mind of course you can" I sighed.

"Have fun *Daddy*" My uncle laughed at me.

I played with my son's all day it was nice. Ana did laundry; I looked at the chore chart I had dinner dishes. I only had chores two days a week other than my own laundry and own messes or getting in trouble we all only had chores two times a week. Mainly because Uncle Christian fussed and did all the house work and would take over our chores if my mothers would let him, but my parents believed chores were good for us kept us from being lazy, ungrateful or spoiled. Uncle Marc swore Uncle Christian had an affair with the vacuum.

At seven thirty I put the boys to bed.

"Why can't I sit up?" Anthony whined.

"You are six and we have to be up early tomorrow" I hugged him.

"So" He yawned.

"Little boys, who start their day early, need to go to bed early so they get plenty of rest."

"Why do I have to be up so early?"

"You have to go back tomorrow."

"No" He started to cry "But I was a good boy! I didn't cut, don't you love me? Don't you want to be my Daddy?"

My heart broke, I handed Ana Paul's books and lifted Anthony. "You are a very good boy and we love you and Paul very much and I am your Daddy, but this one I don't get say in. The tenth we go to see about you getting to come home permanently with just out patient consoling." I walked up and down the hall rocking and soothing him until he fell asleep.

Mama shook me at eleven fifty-nine shoving a glass of sparkling apple cider in my hand. My brain registered a mixture of counting in multiple languages. At midnight I managed a slurred Happy New Year to everyone and crawled up to bed not even bothering to change out of my clothes.

"That boy" Uncle Christian sighed "Is running himself into the ground."

Ana laid down next to me and held me tight. She buried her face in to my chest and whispered "It will be alright Al."

CHAPTER 34

BUT DADDY

"NOOOOOOOOOOOOOOOOOO!" Anthony wailed "I want to live with you."

It took both Ana and I to get Anthony dressed and down the stairs. He would not eat and threw his cereal all over the floor. While he was in time out I managed to do my hair and Ana's. He did not like time out and screamed and cried, kicking and yelling and throwing one large fit. The fit woke Lorenzo but I wasn't overly concerned about his ability to fall back to sleep seeing as I sent him to Anthony's bed after soaping his mouth. I was starting to think that Lorenzo liked the taste of soap. Getting Anthony down stairs and out the doors was a bit interesting; we had to carry him like a long rolled up rug because he kept grapping the railing and door frames.

"My goodness Anthony!" Ana sighed as she flopped into the passenger seat of the car.

By the time I got him into the car and belted in he had cried himself to sleep. I drove to work in shocked silence I had never seen Anthony behave like that.

"Well at least we know he loves us" Ana smiled at me as I carried him through security.

"Yeah" I sighed. "See you at the end of the day"

She went forward to her desk and I went to the left through the locker room to hang our coats and empty my pockets and pick up my work list, and then further left down to Anthony's room.

"Good morning" Dave caught me outside Anthony's room.

"Morning" I groaned.

"Smile, it's the new year"

I just looked at him.

"Ok, how about we go with lay your son down to sleep and meet me in my office the girls are with Sue for the morning and Buddy is already in time out."

I laid him in his bed and went to talk to Dave.

Dave slapped a steak on my eye "Who did you pick a fight with?"

"My son agrees with me. He melted last night and threw one colossal tantrum this morning about coming back here."

"Did he cut or try to cut?"

"No he shook and screamed, but in my family . . ."

"He is a little kid they throw tantrums, and hell I have spoiled you so rotten little boy you are my biggest tantrum of all. What did you do?"

"I put him in time out, he whipped his cereal at the floor and I just let him scream and yell and kick what else was I suppose to do, it was the loudest six minutes of my life."

Dave laughed "Nothing, you did just fine, now clean the steak blood off your face and come help me in the family room, redo the bins before the kids come back."

Every year after Christmas we cleaned out the toy bins in the family room. There was a bin with special cases like Amelia and each child in the B and D hall's name on it and then there were bins for shared toys. We cleaned out the broken toys and garbage and put in the new items from Christmas. Only pajamas witch I had already put in Anthony's room and a special approved stuffed animal were allowed in their rooms. Only permanent residence like Buddy or Curtis or higher levels like Genevieve could have personal belongings in their room; such as books, approved toys and non center clothing. The center clothing given to ever one else was a navy blue t-shirt that said C.H.T.D.C. and a pair of black or gray sweat pants.

Dave had put a baby monitor in Anthony's room while we redid the family room or as it's door said family room B. We had to work quickly as at noon we had three new teens to speak to and, then at three o'clock everyone would be returning. We cleaned about thirty or more broken crayons out and thirty different half card decks out of Kevin's bin. I put in the box of ninety-six Crayola crayons and a full deck of cards. I spent two hours counting board game pieces, coloring book pages, match box wheels, Lego things, and action figure body parts.

Anthony woke around nine "DADDY" He yelled into the baby monitor.

I nearly jumped out of my skin.

"DAVE . . . DADDY"

Dave laughed at me and picked up the monitor "Morning sleepy head, let Buddy out of time out and have him walk you down to the family room."

"My doors unlocked? Ok" He sounded cute.

"You taught him that?" I sighed when Dave put the monitor down.

"Yep, also taught Buddy to put himself in time out and in to the 'restraint vest' so I didn't look like your eye all the time" Dave laughed.

I just shook my head.

Dave sat Anthony on the couch and gave Buddy the option of his room or the time out room; Buddy went back to his room. Dave wasn't giving him second chances today Dave didn't take being hit as gently as I did. Anthony played with his action figures until eleven when he had counseling and I had lunch or well I ate my lunch while I paced and waited for Anthony to be done. At noon I took Anthony to lunch and went to the orientation room. There were four girls in there between fifteen or seventeen and a boy about thirteen. I sighed and hoped he wasn't cutting and was maybe a food disorder as they combined the D-hall and the B-hall for everything, and it just undid me to see them that young cutting or whatever else they did to hurt themselves. Dave said we were getting three. The boy looked lost and confused and the girls all had the same miserable looks that most new comers had; that said they would rather be anywhere but here. Dave made his speech and then the reprehensive from the B-hall made hers taking two of the girls back to the B-hall with her, leaving me the boy and the meaner looking two of the four girls. I was more than thankful that today I was not bleeding and my eye wasn't two bad thanks to the cold steak Dave had put on it.

Dave introduced me and I took a deep breath "Hi I am Alex."

"So what" The brunette said.

I sighed and tried again "I said hi I am Alex, how are you today? Today I am over tired."

"Hi I am Jupiter" The boy spoke up "And today I am scared."

I looked at him and only years of my mothers' gay pride rallies and my uncle teaching us not to show our true thoughts of the truly unique sounding or looking things in life kept me from laughing or questioning his name as the file on the podium said it was his given name. "Nice to meet you Jupiter" I made a mental note to thank my Mama for naming me Alexander and not Saturn or something equally out there. "Why are you scared today? I am overtired because I don't sleep well."

The girls were whispering and giggling totally ignoring me, so I ignored them and stayed focus on Jupiter so he would follow my lead in regards to the girls as well as the conversation.

"I am scared because I am here alone after I scared myself by cutting two deep; I don't want to die, I'm only fifteen." He moved his sleeve and showed me a long jagged cut with crude self made stitches. "I can sew my dad taught me" he shrugged.

"I see I can too, my uncle taught me to sew; I didn't sew what he taught to me either." I lifted my sleeve and showed him my scar. "I have been there it is called rock bottom."

"Can this really work?"

"The program?"

"Stopping, can you really stop?"

"Yes, it is possible to stop. Like you I hit rock bottom and then I stopped I made the choice to stop, to change my life. I have stopped I have not cut in almost five years."

"Is it hard?"

"Very hard, it takes effort and a strong will to change, you have to truly want to stop not for a girlfriend, boyfriend, parent, friend or cause the court says so but for you." I turned on the girls laughing and mocking us thoroughly irritated by their lack of manners. "And if you treat the program as nothing more than a joke because you are here because you are court ordered or your mother made you; you will have a very long and unpleasant stay here."

Dave sat in the back laughing to himself he got some weird thrill out of them trying to push my buttons and normally only Amelia could.

"Why should we listen to you you're a hypocrite you just said you cut but you're telling us not to."

"I told you I don't cut anymore, I never have and never will say not to, and that's just poor grammar. I will tell you I strongly suggest you make a better choice but I will not tell you don't cut. I will tell you if you choose to cut I will have to follow the consequences in the center's rule book but by the look of your arms you prefer to burn yourself I never did that and I can tell you don't burn yourself."

"Hypocrite" The brunette said.

I sighed noticing the bracelet on the blonde's wrist was bi pride I tried a new root you couldn't go to the local L.B.G.T. center without knowing who my parents were. They had helped build it and run it for twenty years. "I am Alexander Williams and if I were truly a hypocrite my mother would have ended my life before you got a chance to meet me." My Mama was very big on not lying or being a hypocrite.

Dave was laughing again.

The blonde's eyes widened and she looked at me with new respect.

The brunette didn't catch on she rolled her eyes at me "Whatever."

I ignored her I got called hypocrite at least once a month it stopped bothering me a while ago, but rude grated my nerves "Now are there any questions?"

"Can you shut up?" The brunette asked.

"That's two one more and you are in the time out room. I try very hard to be patient, but rude I cannot and will not tolerate. I will not be rude or disrespectful to you in return I ask the same courtesy and seeing as on a good day my three year old can follow that so can you."

"How tall are you?" The blonde asked.

I laughed "I am seven feet tall, my dark brown hair is to my waist my eyes are brown and I love my crazy possessive fiancé."

"Get the question a lot?" She smiled.

"Almost daily" I smiled.

"Daddy" Anthony jumped on me.

I lifted him "How . . ."

"Crazy possessive huh?" Ana laughed at me "That is an understatement."

I laughed.

"I just have a message for Dave and then Anthony and I are head to play Lego's." She kissed me.

I turned at least ten shades of red.

"That's your son?" Jupiter asked mostly to himself "but he's wearing . . ."

"Yes he is wearing center clothes; I adopted him therefore the state says when I can take him home."

The blonde looked at Anthony "How old is he, he is small."

"He is six."

"Isn't he too young for this problem?"

"No, see that's just it, there is no definite criteria, I can't say oh you're a brunette or a blonde so you're going to cut. Like all illness and addiction it's a great equalizer it can happen to anyone."

"Isn't he mad at you for making him stay here?"

I pointed at my eye "I could be wrong but I'd say he is downright angry with me."

The blonde nodded.

Jupiter laughed.

The brunette looked at me "You let him hit you?"

"Let, no I did not let him kick me. He enjoyed his time out as much as I enjoyed being kicked in the face."

"How long did it take to stop?" Jupiter asked.

"It isn't that simple it's not like a cold you're not going to wake up after a week and go oh look I am all better. It is a day to day effort I have been clean for four years now."

"Why did you cut?"

"Anxiety control, Anxiety is my biggest trigger."

"Do you get withdrawals" Jupiter was smart, you could see he wanted to clean up.

"Me or in general?"

"Both?"

"Me, oh yeah I do. In general that depends on each individual."

"What happens with your withdrawals?"

He was putting me through my paces "Shaking, cold sweats, night mares, flash blacks, and to me my scars stick out and are all I can see."

"And he is paranoid, crabby and has lots of nervous energy" Ana added grabbing Anthony on her way out.

I blushed.

"Are there other side effects besides withdrawals" Jupiter asked.

"It's not some stupid O.T.C. drug, moron" The brunette sneered.

"Three young lady," I sighed "As soon as I answer that question someone will escort you to the time out room."

"Yeah me" She rolled her eye.

I ignored her "I wouldn't call them side effects, Jupiter, but yes you have to learn a different way to think, cope and react to and with everyday life. I got anxious"

"Get" Dave laughed.

"Fine I still get a bit anxious, triggers became over whelming and the memories of things you "cut away" Come back."

The blonde looked at me "For how long?"

"My guess is till they all come back I am still getting them."

The brunette snorted "Whatever this is lame."

"Brittany, Jared will escort you out now" Dave said sounding like he was no longer amused with her attempt to push my buttons.

At three I met Jared and Quentin in the family room to collect the returning kids. Kevin looked miserable and Kyle was chewing something. Andy was crying in the hall and had asked to speak with me and Genevieve was on top of the book case crying.

Kevin told Dave he never wanted to go home again. And Kyle's stepfather said he gave Kyle dental wax to chew because it was better than crayons Kyle chewed when he was nervous. But neither had cut or in Kevin's case slammed their body parts under rocks.

"I am proud of you Kevin, and you too Kyle" I hugged them.

"Are we with you?" Kevin asked.

"Nope, sorry you two are with Dave, I have Genevieve."

"Go away Dog Breath" She yelled at me.

"Ok Genevieve, I have to go speak to Andy when I come back we will talk about those tears."

Jared took the boys to Dave and Quentin brought all the other kids where they belonged. I left Genevieve to cry she didn't need or like an audience.

"Ms. Andy you had wished a word with me?" I offered her tissue.

"Oh Alex" She dabbed at her eyes "Thank-you so much for making time for me."

"It's my job" I nodded.

"She is so hard on herself."

I nodded.

"She hasn't cut. Wanted to, came close, and tried to. We fought horrible this morning about her coming back here" Andy began to cry harder and dabbed more at her eyes.

"So did Anthony and I" I pointed to my eye. "Genevieve is doing fine, she is going to withdrawal. She might even slip up and go backwards or sideways for a bit. Don't get angry but defiantly reassure even though you are there for her you don't approve."

She surprised me by hugging me "Take care of my Genie in a Bottle for me."

"I always do Ms. Andy."

She laughed "You are always so tense and so formal. Oh and thank you for getting her that whip, her and I had a blast."

I turned bright red "Um you're—you're welcome."

"Hey now that's my father's job" Ana laughed.

"He blushes so easy" Andy smiled.

"Oh I know it's so cute I love to make him blush" To prove her point she hugged and kissed me "Oh and thank you again for the gift Andy."

"Gift?" I said trying insanely to go from fire engine red to a normal skin tone.

"You will see later go back to work Andy and I are going to set family counseling days for her and Genevieve."

"Right because our session worked so well" I muttered under my breath headed back into Genevieve.

"Only works if you want it to" Ana sighed; "That boy he hates therapist" Ana laughed. "Too much like his Mom."

"Will he like the gift" Andy laughed "Or even know what it's for?"

"Yeah" Ana laughed he knows what it is, what it's for and will like it. It's a matter of slowing him down to enjoy it."

"Hmm I thought they would slow him down some and help him relax. The aroma therapy candles are lavender and chamomile Genie said he has allergies but couldn't remember to what."

"Yes, but that is not one of them, thank you again it was very generous of you."

"Ok Genevieve, talk to me"

"You first."

"Fine, I will play the game."

"Your eye?"

"Anthony, he expressed his loving feelings towards returning today. Your tears?"

"I don't want to be back here either. You look like you saw a ghost?"

"Close enough to one your girlfriend and mine were playing the 'who can make Alex blush the hardest' game. If it pleases you, Andy won glad you like your whip. The face you have almost permanent red streaks?"

She blushed slightly when I mentioned her whip "It feels like all I do is cry now over every little thing, my eyes have started to burn from it, and I feel so weak. What did Ana say?"

"It is not weak it is a healthy way to relieve stress. Ana said yes and now what did I miss because now we are now both digging?"

"Nothing visible, I am worried I am a level four and I am now in transition soon I will be a level five without patient only, Dog Breath.

"Those are good things, go ahead it's ok to be nervous, but don't dwell on it."

"What did you . . ."

"DADDY!" Anthony shot into my leg Sue entered shortly behind him.

"Ok you got him" She wheezed "He is fast Dave says to tell you, you three have fun."

"Thanks" I smiled at her. "Anthony can you go play for a moment; I was speaking with Genevieve."

"Genevieve?" He looked up and then hugged tight to me "Genevieve can you play with me?"

"In a minute" She sniffled and whipped her eyes.

"Ok" He pouted and went to the Lego table.

"Genevieve?" I prompted.

"Oh yeah sorry, what did you have for breakfast?"

"Wow you are definitely digging, ok I had apple jax I think it was some sort of cereal I grabbed the bowl and box and poured my body remembered how to do the rest. What's scaring you?"

"What if I screw up. What color is your room?"

"You screw up you start over, you move on accept you and you alone caused the mistake and make the changes so it doesn't keep happening. My side is black, dark gray, and blood red, Kenny's is blue. Wouldn't it just be easier to tell me what's wrong?"

"No, what shade of blue?"

I sighed I was too tired for this today "Blue, like too bright for my eyes blue no shade of it just primary color blue. What do you really want to say to me?"

"I am scared to be outpatient only. What color is his room?" She gestured to Anthony.

"His is side is outer space and Paul's side is a fire house. Why are you scared to be out patient?"

"What if I can't reach you? What if you are too busy for me just because I am outpatient? What are you doing tomorrow?"

"You will be able to reach me I am not like that and you should know that by now. Andy has my number and if that don't work come here or the pool hall. You know my daily routine. You know me I have always been just a call away. I work tomorrow I now have Saturdays and Sundays off. Why would you ever think I wouldn't make time for you or another person on this planet who wished my help or my time and attention, I even stop to speak to Quentin if he wishes a word from me.

"I don't know nerves I guess, I just know I can't do this without you, I feel safe knowing you are there if I need you even if I never do need you."

"Thank-you, I will always be here for you. Are we good now?"

She nodded wiping more tears.

"Daddy, daddy, daddy can I interrupt yet?" Anthony was almost ready to explode.

"Yes" I smiled.

"Daddy I am level three now, Dave said so!" He bounced up and down on my feet.

"Congrats" Genevieve hugged him starting to cry again.

"Good job, what exactly did Dave say?"

"That I did a good job and I earned a level three spot because I was doing things most kids don't do until level four."

I nodded, he was but I was still going to talk to Dave later.

"Genevieve why are you crying?" Anthony asked.

"I don't know" She wiped at her tears "It's stupid and needs to stop."

"Crying isn't stupid! If your crying you need to cry and your suppose to let all the tears out until there are no more, my Uncle Marc said so." He hugged on to her to try and comfort her; it was cute.

I neglected to tell him that in my entire life I had never seen or heard Uncle Marc cry, but Uncle Marc was constantly telling us that. They played and watched TV. all afternoon; at five I took them to dinner, clocked out and laid down in the time out room.

"Mad at me" Dave stared down at me.

"Nope" I sighed "Wondering if he's ready, but . . ."

"If he weren't ready I wouldn't have done it and you know that. Are you waiting on Ana?"

"Yes."

"Ok she is almost done I will let you . . ."

"Sleep, Dave I was trying to sleep."

He laughed "Ok we will go with sleep, sweet dreams."

I nodded back out until five thirty when Ana woke me. We said our good-byes to Anthony and headed home.

There were two plates of smothered chicken in the microwave and Paul was running around in his pajamas.

"Daddy where is Antony?" Paul demanded.

"Anthony has to stay there for the week, he will be home on weekends" I sighed fearing a meltdown "But he loves and misses you."

Paul got contemplative then smiled and said "Ok snack time."

I laughed and picked him up "Tell me about your day while Ana and I eat."

Paul told me about sledding, drawing, his hot coco, Nick, Colt and the twins. He told me about cleaning the spare room down stairs, and Lorenzo; and how Lorenzo ate a lot of soap because of his potty mouth. How Lorenzo touched the instruments even though he was told no. Mostly told me about how Uncle Christian and Uncle Donavan reacted to Lorenzo and he giggled and giggled about it. I put him to bed and told my parents, uncles, brothers and cousin good night I was completely exhausted.

Ana was sitting on our bed playing with a basket of prettily designed bottles of bath beads and massage oils. Lying next to her on the bed were four candles, they were all my favorite sent.

"Ours from Andy and Genevieve?" I said grabbing a candle.

"Uh huh" She said lost in the bath bead bottle.

"We will get her a thank-you card." I said lighting the candle and placing it on my night stand; I left a note for Kenny to blow it out. Then got in to bed, I looked at the massage oil in Ana's hand "Oh sorry, babe I work tomorrow."

"I know" She laughed "I was reading the ingredients, but I was thinking Friday it has been a while since you gave me a good back massage."

"Sounds great you have fun I need sleep, now." It was the first time I was asleep before ten pm without being sick in a long time. But I regretted it when I woke at three to someone death griping my arm and shaking me. "Ana?"

"No" Lorenzo whispered "Uncle Christian said to wake you."

I nodded feeling the cold "Wood stove."

"Um yeah"

I tucked Ana in good and followed Lorenzo down to the wood stove.

"Um when does . . ."

"Friday, I don't talk at three am."

"Um ok"

Uncle Christian had already started to load the wood stove. "Forget something" He greeted me.

"Check the chore chart" I groaned and took over loading the wood stove.

"Uncle Christian?"

"Go back to bed Lorenzo" Uncle Christian said.

"Uncle Christian, Auntie's calling you" He argued

"Yes I know she is; tell her I am coming."

"W . . ."

"The only thing that better be is yes sir!"

"Yes, sir" He muttered Italian curses all the way up the stairs.

"Sir . . ." I went to speak.

"Let him mutter."

"No I . . ."

"Finish the logs we will speak tomorrow."

"Yes sir" I said finishing as swiftly as I could.

CHAPTER 35

GIRLS, GIRLS, GIRLS

"MORNING" UNCLE CHRISTIAN GREETED ME.

"Morning sir, thank-you" I took the waffles slightly confused.

"Situare (sit down)"

I sat down.

"He is my little sister's son; she disowned us when she married his father whom died in a gang fight. He is a year older than Colt. My mother told my brothers and I; she also sent us a picture of him at three. I didn't know she was sick or I would have been there but you know that. They lived in Queens, I didn't realize that she would even remember where I lived she never returned my calls. She worked Lorenzo ran wild, her name was Olivia and she felt that was better than coming home to us. He never met his father, Don made sure of that it was the last things he did before she disowned us."

I nodded, to stunned to speak.

"Anything else you need to know?"

"Nope, you covered it."

"Good, have a good work day see you at . . ."

"Four thirty, Paul's preschool screening, I promise I will be there."

Uncle Christian had gotten Paul an appointment to be screened at Crimson based on his speech.

———— ❖ ————

"Penny for your thoughts" Ana said after I nearly missed our turn.

"That state lady is still insisting that Paul be in day care for socialization."

"Oh he will love preschool"

I sighed.

"DAVE!"

"What? For crying out loud little boy don't yell."

"Tiffany, Sadie, Genevieve, Tiny and the two new girls!"

Dave laughed "Oh hush they are all in class except Amelia she is in the time out room."

"But . . ."

"Oh hush, here sit and read the charts on Brittany and Lynn."

I took the charts and sat down to read them, Brittany was here on a court order the cutting was the least of her issues. Lynn was not court ordered but doctor suggested for the burning; the doctor stated that it was the twentieth time he had found self inflicted third degree burns on her. I looked at Dave "He dropped the ball."

"Who?"

"Lynn's doctor twenty times before trying to do anything?"

Dave shrugged "*Not everyone can be Doctor Kyle Wittson*; that takes a truly unique person."

Bell rang at noon, I went to collect them.

"You suck" Tiny yelled jumping on my back.

"I agree with her" Brittany clucked her tongue.

"Brittany I strongly suggest you reconsider" Tiffany had her pinned to the wall.

"Tiffany! Release her right now!" I gasped.

"She has been insulting you all day" Tiffany objected.

I blinked at her "*Because you would never do that.* Now please put her down we have to go get Sadie and Genevieve."

"Or we can get you, Dog Breath" Genevieve laughed smiling ear to ear "I am level four I can walk Sadie and I to you."

"Right" I sighed "Sadie could you . . ."

Sadie laughed "Tiff put her down. Come walk me to lunch."

I looked at Lynn "keep up and make noise." I sighed "And Brittany, Amelia is not telling me I suck as in she is displeased with me but she is merrily referring to my ability to suck things such as lolly pops."

"Show her, show her" Tiny jumped off my back."

"Oh, no even you were not supposed to see that, I thought you were asleep" I laughed and walked them to lunch.

"Dog Breath?"

"Huh"

"Are you with us?"

"Sort of what did I say?"

"Lasagna" Tiffany looked at me. "And that was just to Brittany, you told Sadie blue and silver."

"Dog Breath" Genevieve laughed "I realize you're the girl in you and Ana's relationship but you have been drooling all day, what would Dave say."

I blushed hard "Sorry guys."

"I'm a girl" Brittany clucked her tongue in objection.

I rolled my eyes "*Sorry ladies*" I exaggerated. "What was I asked?"

"I asked" Brittany rolled her eyes "If you had ever read the <u>Scarlett Letter</u>? It's our English book."

I stared blankly at the four sophomores and two seniors until it clicked that they were talking about books "Oh yeah in middle school I think."

"Wow, were you like super dweeb or something?"

"He's not a Dweeb, he's a nerd" Amelia pushed Brittany playfully.

"Oh good grief Charlie Brown" Greg laughed at me "I came to give Amelia her medicine but I can wait until you three are done."

"It's not funny Bevis, it is immature and infuriating" Genevieve scowled.

I was on the floor trying to keep the girls apart, to no avail. "Greg instead of picking on Genevieve and laughing at me get the broken spoon from Brittany."

"Sorry" He laughed, reaching for the spoon as Brittany swung at Amelia's face and throat. I also reached for the broken spoon blocking it from hitting Tiny at the same time. The sharpest part of the broken spoon bit in to my forearm and sliced a long jagged cut down it as I lost balance and slammed my head on the floor.

"Uh—Ooh" I gasped staring at the blood on my arm.

"Alex?" Greg looked at me.

No one knew how truly deep a properly yielded plastic spoon could cut in to the skin or they would stop giving them to these kids. There was a lot of blood to try and hide from a room full of kids and I was starting to get flash backs but mostly I was light headed and dizzy. Greg got hold of Brittany and kept her from swing at Tiny. I tried to stand and got even dizzier and nearly fell "OW" I winced.

"Al" Genevieve said again.

I didn't answer I was watching flash backs and the room spin.

"Al" Genevieve gave up and grabbed my walkie-talkie. "Dave, Greg and Jared have Brittany headed to time out, but you and Ana need to come get Al he hit his head pretty hard and doing something odd to his arm where Brittany sliced him."

"We are on our way I just spoke to Jared. Where's Quentin?"

"He is ignoring Tiffany and Sadie and Amelia is trying to keep Al with us and the other new girl is trying to keep Anthony calm."

"I'm coming."

"Hey dave . . ."

"Yes Genevieve?"

"There is a lot of blood, I need Nate."

"Go, you did great I am proud of you."

"Thanks Dave I am giving the phone to Ana she is here" Genevieve bolted to her consoler.

Ana moved Tiny and looked at me "Al, talk to us what happened."

I managed a few cures words in Italian before passing out.

I could hear them calling my name I had come to kind of I could feel the searing pain in my arm trying to convert to good feeling like a self inflicted wound for a half second I stopped fighting it. What was it Uncle Christian always said to do when we couldn't make a choice? Pro and con list and then follow our heart, yeah that was right. Ok so um pros . . . I wouldn't feel all the stress none of it, would they blame me? Could they blame me? I mean I was drowning in it no sleep, work, the media ugh they were awful how my mothers handled it I will never know. Just this morning the local paper plastered my hearing info on the front page. It was suffocating and so, so, so hard and draining to constantly fight the withdrawals and try and be the perfect father for the kids and a perfect fiancé for Ana and the perfect son for my parents and a perfect brother, but if I started again if I even just gave into this pain from the cut I didn't make I would lose everything. I wouldn't have to worry about that stupid hearing, because I wouldn't have kids, or a fiancé, would they understand couldn't I have both. I'd defiantly lose my job. Ok list now where did my heart lie?